THE WELL
PETER LABROW

Thanks

For Ruth, Dave and Mike

This book simply would not be what it is without the enormous support I received from friends and family.

The biggest thanks go to Ruth, Dave and Mike who had to put up with me while I was writing this. But next in line has to be Claire Mooney, who gave me a much-needed initial kick up the arse. For Emma Clarke I reserve special thanks: her endless help, advice and encouragement helped to support this project from beginning to end.

Of course there's also Claire Andrews, for providing the writer's essential safety net and an excellent editing service.

Sven Carter, a police officer who became a family friend after the untimely death of Ruth's brother, provided the essential insights into how a police search operates and how families respond to the stress of a loved one going missing.

I am also extremely grateful to those who read the early drafts and provided me with insightful and valuable feedback: Djamila Swindells, Emma Clarke, Gay Freeman, Jaycee Jewett, Kathy Lawton, Lizzy Russell, Rob Clarke – and, of course, Ruth. I can't express enough thanks for how these readers helped to refine and shape this book.

Cover
Composition and illustration: *Daryl Joyce, www.daryljoyce.co.uk*
Original cottage photograph: *Martin R Mackenzie*
Original well photograph: *Hanna Apaja, kivutar.deviantart.com*

The Well
Copyright © 2010 Peter Labrow
All rights reserved

ISBN: 978-1-4467-6438-1

Keep updated: www.peterlabrow.com

FRIDAY

1

Becca took a deep breath, cupped her hands around her mouth and screamed as loudly as she could, "Help!"

Her cry echoed around the inside of the well, but she doubted that it could be heard even just a dozen yards from the well's mouth, around twenty feet above her.

She craned her neck back as far as she could and looked up, tottering slightly, pain shooting upwards from her ankle. The early evening sky was a bright disc at the end of a black vertical tunnel. Above her, she could see what remained of the metal grating, dangling at the top of the well.

She shouted again and her balance wavered. She instinctively reached out, steadying herself against the well wall, muddy water sloshing around her knees as she almost stumbled.

Beside her, Matt groaned. His breathing was an unnatural wet rasping sound. She knelt to face him, the cold water rising to her waist.

She tried as hard as she could to see how badly he was hurt, but her eyes hadn't adjusted to the dark. Everything was reduced to being a series of vague shapes.

She shook him, carefully. "Matt!"

Matt's head lolled against his shoulder and he let out a low, throaty moan. Trying to discover where he was hurt, Becca's hands fumbled quickly over Matt's body beneath the water. Her hands found metal; she caught her breath and her heart missed a beat. Part of the grille that had once covered the well's mouth was protruding from Matt's midriff. She felt around his body and was horrified to find that the metal had gone completely through him and was jutting out of his back.

Her own injuries seemed trivial. Although her right forearm hurt badly and the top of her head was throbbing like hell, she thought that they were probably just scuffed. Her side ached sharply where she had fallen onto the metal grating. Her knees, left shin and ankle also hurt, causing her to wince and falter as she stood again, looking upwards. Her shin was probably scraped; her ankle possibly sprained.

Becca yelled again and again, with a voice so loud and desperate it was as though she was trying to reach the whole world. No one was listening and she knew it. On a planet of over six billion people – and possibly just a few hundred yards from the nearest of them – Becca and Matt might as well have been on the moon. No one could hear. No one knew they were there.

Becca worked to fight back her growing panic. She inhaled deeply, trying but failing to bring her runaway breathing under control – before repeatedly slapping the well wall, half gasping, half sobbing in rhythm to her increasingly desperate smacks, "Shit, shit, shit, shit, shit!"

Somewhere above, a bird cawed.

2

"Fifty feet at least. Probably more."

Becca shifted her weight, her bottom uncomfortable on the uneven stonework. What had survived of the old well wall varied in height between two or three stones – fewer in places – though the tens of stones that were strewn, half-hidden, around the overgrown grass suggested that it had once been at least half a dozen rows higher. She leaned her upper body tentatively over the edge – careful to keep a grip on the stones and balance her weight with her hips. She peered into the dark, straining her eyes. No matter how hard she tried, she couldn't quite see the bottom: the inside wall of the well gradually became a dark, empty space about fifteen feet below her. The ancient, half-broken and somewhat battered metal grating that capped the well's mouth didn't seem to offer much in the way of protection. Deeply unnerved, she drew back and shook her head.

"No way," she said, "It's never fifty feet. Maybe not even thirty."

Matt smiled – a knowing, superior smile – and dropped the stone that he had been holding at arm's length. It fell neatly between the gnarled, rusty bars and instantly disappeared into the dark. Becca counted, in her head. Somewhere between "one" and "two" she heard a distant plop!

"See," he said, "easily fifty feet."

Becca shook her head, convinced that he was teasing her. "Nowhere near. I still think it's way less than thirty feet. And you can't prove it either way." Despite herself, she couldn't suppress the spoilt, childish tone in her voice. At fourteen (almost fifteen, as Becca would correct people when they mentioned her age), she considered herself to be more of a woman than a child – and self-consciously chided herself when her behaviour betrayed her youth. Especially when it was to Matt.

Becca eased herself down off the stones and sat beside her schoolbag on the warm, dry grass, her lower back resting against the ruined wall of the well. Matt dropped his backpack to the ground and sat next to her, his hip lightly in contact with hers. She considered shifting her weight towards him, ever so slightly, to make the contact more definite – but she didn't want him to know that she either appreciated or encouraged his tentative overture.

He can wait, she thought. She glanced at her watch – it was almost four-thirty.

She was pretty sure that Mum and Jim would have left by now. But she wanted to be certain, so she and Matt had come to the well to pass an hour or so. (Becca knew that if she'd been at home to wave goodbye to her mother, she'd feel too weird to close the door and, well, *do it* with Matt – especially since it would be her first time. It'd be as if her Mum was still there. They'd have the house to themselves for the whole weekend. She'd been putting Matt off for weeks; he could wait another hour.)

Matt took his cigarettes and lighter from his backpack and lit one without offering one to her. Smoking wasn't the only thing Matt did that Becca didn't like, but it was probably the worst. He drew deeply on the cigarette and exhaled. Becca pulled her knees up against her body and tried not to let her disapproval show.

It's not that Becca didn't *want* to smoke – after all, plenty of other kids did, though few of her closest friends – it's just that she wanted her lungs to stay just the way they were, thank you very much. Becca didn't excel at much, but she easily led the school swimming team – which somehow made up for the Cs and Bs she otherwise struggled to get. Petite, with a light build that seemed made for cutting through water, she could, by quite a margin, swim further and faster than anyone in the school – including old Stubbs, the sports teacher. Despite her size, she was strong and could be very determined – able to keep pushing herself when her body was aching to stop. She amazed people by swimming under water for minutes at a time, looking serene on the outside – but on the inside forcing herself on. (Her record was just under four minutes, which had taken *a lot* of practice.) Being the school's best swimmer made her *Becca the fish*: not exactly great, but better and cooler than being *Bony Becca* or *stick-insect*, which is what she'd been called until year five.

"I don't like this place," she said, shivering slightly despite the warm breeze. "It's creepy."

Matt looked into her eyes. "You only think it's creepy because you've been told it's creepy." He took another long pull on the cigarette. "I like it."

The breeze blew Becca's fine dark hair across her face and she absently brushed it away. "Why?"

He smiled. "No one comes here. Where else do we get to be properly alone?"

Becca felt herself flush and hoped it didn't show. "Someone might come."

Matt sighed and put his arm around her, pulling her close.

"It's OK," he said, "you know no one comes here."

He tilted his head and their hair gently touched, though their heads barely connected. Becca wanted to kiss him but really wished he hadn't lit the cigarette. Yet, to her, the moment still felt almost electric.

Matt didn't quite feel the same way. Sure, he was turned on to an extent he couldn't believe – and having to work very hard not to screw things up. After all, he'd invested a lot of time in Becca. For starters, he'd lied – he wasn't a virgin. What's more, the one girl he'd had sex with, Natalie White, had been drunk at the time and didn't exactly qualify as willing. The (very brief) sex hadn't been great – but Becca was just about to give it all up, non-stop for a whole weekend, and all he'd had to do was be nice to her and tell a few small lies. Of course, being nice was easier now that he lived over forty miles from his mates (something about which his father was *very* pleased). No, he didn't want to push things and end up blowing his chances with Becca, although he did have a packet of condoms in his pocket just in case she wanted to start early; he knew *he* did.

Just turned sixteen, Matt was a boy at a turning point in his life – "difficult" was how he'd been described by his English teacher, who was being both diplomatic and charitable. If he worked at it, Matt could probably change, but the decisions he made almost always pointed in the same direction: bad. For instance, he had considered that having sex with a clearly underage Becca might be wrong (wrong enough to keep his desires to himself: even if he did score with Becca he doubted that he'd brag about it). Becca might be almost fifteen, but her build was that of someone almost two years younger. But he easily dismissed these feelings – if no one knew about it, then what's the problem? He also knew that he would be *pissing on his own doorstep*, as the saying went. If things went bad, his life could become very unpleasant. *So*, he thought, *things won't have to go bad.* Matt guessed that he could keep Becca warm for months, maybe until he left home – which he planned to do as soon as he could. He doubted she'd ever tell anyone, just because of what her friends and mother would think of her.

Becca didn't know anything about Natalie White, but she was aware that Matt used to have some pretty unpleasant friends and had a reputation for solving problems with his fists. But Becca believed that was the old Matt; that he'd changed once he and his Dad had moved in with her and Mum. When her Mum and Jim had first been dating, Matt had been pretty cool towards her, but he seemed to have warmed once they all lived under one roof. Matt had been interested in her; attentive even. And so, talking had turned to friendship; friendship to flirting; flirting to kissing; kissing to petting. Becca didn't know if it was *the real thing*, but it did seem like *a good thing* – and she absolutely enjoyed her first experience of male attention. No one else had noticed their relationship develop – after all, they were almost brother and sister.

Matt knew damn well it *wasn't* the real thing, but he too thought it was a good thing; in his mind, compensation for having to move to a shitty backwater town. Becca and her mother, Sarah, were, in his book, just a bit *too nice*. Matt, being far from stupid, knew it was pointless to hold back the inevitable. His Dad and Sarah were going to get married and that was that.

But when he saw Becca swim for the first time, he decided that his new family unit might have some bonuses. *That body*: not model-nice, she was even skinny perhaps – but very graceful, lithe and firm. If he *played nice* with her, he thought he could get her to play nice with him. *Very nice.* And it hadn't taken *that* long – just a few months of being sweet and patient. The problem was, Matt wasn't patient by nature: he was generally quick to anger and slow to cool down. Every day of the last few months he'd felt himself tighten just that little bit more and had to work progressively harder to present a calm exterior. Every time they kissed, or when Becca let him slip his hand inside her blouse, he'd edged closer to losing control. He felt like he'd really earned the coming weekend.

Matt glanced at Becca and smiled. He tried his best to push down the desire inside him – and drew long and hard on the cigarette, sucking almost two centimetres of it out of existence with a single inhalation.

Becca felt uncomfortably warm and acutely aware of herself; the breeze gently stroked her arms and legs, raising goose bumps. She seemed to feel the fibres of her clothes as they brushed against her skin and, where the grass swayed against her thighs, she felt exposed. She pulled her knees a little tighter to her chest and self-consciously wrapped her skirt underneath her. She realised – too late – that although this made her *feel* less vulnerable, it actually exposed more of her thighs. Somewhere close, a bird cawed: a loud, harsh cry that made her start.

She glanced around, to the ruined cottage, just thirty or forty yards from the well. The cottage had never been large: just a handful of rooms in a single-storey building, now half-hidden in an overgrown jumble of thorny brambles and dense bushes, themselves blending into the edge of woods. In some places, the gaps in the ruined walls came almost to the ground. Through a vaguely oblong hole in one wall – all that remained of a window – she could see that the inside of the cottage was as overgrown as the outside.

The bird cawed again, and she saw it, perched on what remained of the cottage's chimney. Large and black, perhaps almost two foot from head to tail, it was a crow, raven or rook – she didn't know the difference between them, if indeed there was a difference. The bird regarded her, its head cocked to one side, eyes occasionally blinking. She shivered, unexpectedly chilled.

Matt followed her gaze. "It's just a bird," he said – more mocking than comforting.

"It's creepy and you know it," she said, defending her reaction. "This place – it's like something from a crap horror film. A ruined cottage in the woods. Two kids, alone." She laughed, nervously. The cottage couldn't be more typecast if it tried. Still, its reputation, though it may be based on clichés, had persisted for years – a local myth. Matt, being new to the area, neither respected nor believed the stories that surrounded the place – but Becca was fighting against the sheer weight of tales that passed between local children, handed down from one generation to the next in the school playground. It didn't help that these stories were later confirmed in local history lessons – at least to some degree.

Matt squeezed her hand and stood up. He picked a rock about the size of an apple up from the ground – and threw it hard at the bird. His aim was good, striking the crumbling wall within just a few feet of the bird. Amid an explosion of rock shards and dust, the bird briefly fluttered its wings, cawed again, but otherwise didn't flinch.

"Bold bastard," muttered Matt. He threw another rock, this time landing closer. Again, the bird didn't move. It cawed loudly, either ignorant of them or teasing them. Matt stooped for another rock – but when he stood, rock in hand, the bird opened its not inconsiderable wings and took flight. It disappeared into the trees at the edge of the wood. Matt threw the rock anyway. With a brief rustle of leaves, it too vanished into the trees, followed by a distant thud as it hit the ground.

Matt sat back down next to Becca, took a last draw on the cigarette and stubbed it out against the wall before tossing the smoking butt into the well. He sensed that the moment of warmth was passing and his best strategy might be to get Becca home. He asked, "How much longer?" Becca looked again at her watch. "Mum should have called or texted by now," she said. "Maybe Jim got held up at work." She wasn't anywhere near ready to start calling Jim *Dad*. Not that she had any affection for her own father, come to that.

Matt put his arm back around Becca's slim shoulders and gently pulled her close; she didn't resist. Their heads turned to meet and they kissed – a kiss that was tainted by the taste of tobacco, but a warm close kiss nonetheless.

Becca jumped involuntarily as her mobile phone chimed with the arrival of a text message. Matt leaned away slightly and allowed his arm to drop to Becca's waist. Although startled, Becca was relieved that her Mum had sent a text instead of calling: it would be far easier to lie when replying. She pulled her phone from her schoolbag and read the text: JUST ARRIVED. LONG DRIVE SET OFF EARLY. POSH PLACE, LOOKS GOOD. HOPE YOU ARE BOTH OK. WILL CALL LATER. LOVE MUM XXX. Becca sighed, and said to Matt, "We could've gone straight home. They set off ages ago." She hit the reply key. JUST LEAVING BASKETBALL. MATT WAITED SO I DIDN'T HAVE TO WALK HOME ON MY OWN. HOME SOON. NO NEED 2 CALL LATER. GOING 2 WATCH FILM. GOT LOTS OF HOMEWORK 4 WKEND. HAVE A GREAT TIME – YOU DON'T HAVE TO KEEP CALLING OR TXTING JUST HAVE FUN XXX BECKS.

The lie was so easy – and her mother would never know. After all, she did occasionally stay for basketball, but tonight wasn't a basketball night. She pressed send and stood up, putting her phone into her bag and her bag over her shoulder. Matt did the same. He was almost a head taller than her, so when they kissed she had to go tippy toed – making her feel more like a child than ever, yet somehow more feminine at the same time.

"Let's go home," she said.

And they almost did, but Matt playfully pulled her close for another kiss, smiling. She smiled back and kissed him, neck stretching. The weekend was going to be so good.

She hopped lightly onto the well wall, to give her the same height advantage that Matt normally had over her – but the loose stones shifted under her weight. Unbalanced by the weight of her schoolbag, she toppled backwards, shrieking, instinctively twisting and extending her right arm to take the impact. She hit the metal grating hard, her forearm first; her body instantly afterwards, kicking the breath from her. The top of her head banged against the inside of the well's far wall.

The grating, rotten and old, offered little resistance against Becca's weight, slight though she was. It buckled under the impact, almost folding itself in two. The grating had been held in place by six metal wall-ties, bolted to the grating and cemented (securely, long ago) into the wall. As Becca struggled to get herself upright, three of the ties ripped away from the wall and the grating fell open like a hatch. She tumbled, following the arc of the grating as it swung downwards, her hands frantically trying to grasp something, anything. As the grating twisted down, another tie came free.

In a manoeuvre she could neither have rehearsed nor repeated, she grabbed hold of the grating with her right hand just as her body crashed forwards into the inside of the wall – the impact jolting her backwards and almost forcing her to let go. Wrenched hard, her right hand screamed in pain.

Somehow she managed to not only hang on, but after two attempts (hampered by her loosely swinging schoolbag) she got a firm hold of the grating with both hands.

She hung there for less than a second before one of the three remaining wall-ties gave way, jolting her downwards by almost a foot. Knowing with absolute certainty that she would fall, she screamed, a desperate terror-filled yell, "Matt!"

The whole thing had happened so quickly that Matt hadn't been able to take it in. Becca had fallen backwards, rolling and crashing into the grating in one blurry second. He wasn't standing idly by – there had barely been time to blink, let alone to help her.

He knelt quickly at the edge of the well and leaned over, straining to reach her. She was too far away, by just a few inches, even before the grating had jolted downwards. He reached around himself, took off his shoulder bag and dangled it down, wrapping the strap tightly around his wrist so he wouldn't lose hold. "Grab this," he shouted.

Becca grabbed the bag with one hand, not wanting to let go of the grating.

It was not one of the remaining, ancient wall-ties that failed, but the grating itself. Ancient, corroded and stressed, the grating unfolded where it had just been creased – and all but one of the metal latticework strips snapped apart. Becca felt herself jolted again, and the last jolt was enough to split what remained of the metal in two. Half of the grating fell into the well and Becca fell with it. She let go of the grating but somehow managed to hold on to the bag. Matt, who had been on one knee and leaning over as far as he could, was at the edge of his balance. He was yanked downwards into the well.

As Becca, who mostly paid attention at school, would have remembered from science (and Matt, who mostly didn't pay attention, and so would not), any two objects which fall at the same time will land at the same time. In this case, the broken half of the grating had slightly slowed its descent by bouncing against the stone walls of the well. Becca landed feet first, splashing into the cold dirty water. Her feet hit years of sediment, a deep cushion of mud. A lightning bolt of pain shot up from her left ankle as she hit the hard stone beneath the mud. She twisted and rolled, falling backwards and sideways against the well wall, her head briefly going under the water. She came to rest on her backside, almost up to her neck in water, spluttering. The grating had already crashed loudly at her side, twisted and broken, rolling slightly, sharp metal pointing upwards.

Matt, who was falling more or less headfirst, arrived a second later. He landed directly on the grating, his body doubling over it as it impaled his abdomen.

In the darkness, Becca couldn't see what had happened, but the sound of Matt's scream being cut short as he hit the grating was deeply chilling. The impact was a sickening mixture of crunching bone and squelching flesh.

Metal scraped against brick as Matt's weight took him backwards into something close to a sitting position, bringing the grating – from which he couldn't now be separated – with him. He came to rest with his back against the wall.

Becca screamed.

3

Sarah Ann Richards lay on her side, naked, on the untidy sheets that were strewn across the four-poster bed. She was holding her phone, scrolling through her daughter's text message. "Do you think I should call her?"

Jim Bradshaw snuggled up behind her and kissed her neck, his arm encircling her stomach. "Call her tomorrow," he said. "She's fine. Let her enjoy some time without us."

Sarah hesitated. As much as she wanted to call Becca, she knew that Jim was right. After all, they'd only seen her this morning. She also knew that this weekend was supposed to be about her and Jim, not the kids – Jim had even left his golf clubs at home, as he'd promised. She switched her phone to silent, put it on the bedside table and turned to face him. "How long before dinner?"

He kissed her and pulled her closer. "Plenty of time."

4

Two hours earlier Becca had been sitting on the low school wall, legs swinging, listening to her iPod, waiting for Matt and looking forward to the weekend.

In a daily end-of-school ritual, Becca removed her scrunchie – freeing her long, dark hair from its tight ponytail.

As she did, she noticed – *felt* – the eye of the school's crossing warden on her. It was only a glance but Becca shuddered as an uncomfortable chill passed over her.

Children and parents alike called Tom by his first name; he was well-liked, affable and friendly. Indeed, Tom Randle was almost as much a part of the school as its windows and roof. An ex-pupil, Tom might only be paid to tend the crossing three times a day, but he volunteered to help out at almost every school event, including sports days and open evenings. He took photographs for the school website and newsletter, gave prints to the parents – and even had some of his pictures printed in the local newspaper. Although bearded, grey and elderly looking, Randle was only just over sixty; he walked with a slight limp gained in Belfast during the 1970s. He had lost a kneecap when a car bomb exploded ("It gives me trouble for my trouble in the Troubles," he'd often quip, seemingly without bitterness).

Randle caught himself staring at Becca and sensed her discomfort. He smiled, a broad friendly smile. She smiled back. Randle limped into the road and stopped the traffic, ushering a group of smaller children across before returning to the side of the road, unconsciously adjusting his glasses.

One by one, and in groups, the children left – some on their own; some collected by parents. Absently twiddling with her scrunchie, caught in the music, Becca didn't notice two of her friends approaching until she felt a hard prod.

"Becca, you walking home?"

Becca pulled out her earbuds. "Sorry?"

Nisha asked again, "You walking home?"

Becca shook her head. "I'm waiting for Matt," she said.

Of the two girls, Becca knew Nisha Hirani (Neats to her friends) the least. Enough to speak to, walk home with, pass time in the playground with – but not enough to do planned things with, like watching a film. The other girl, Hannah Davis, had until recently been very much one of Becca's best friends (if not her *best* friend). But the more time Becca had spent with Matt, the less she had for previous close girlfriends. Becca was not especially gregarious, so her change of behaviour had gone mostly unnoticed, except by Hannah and perhaps Susie Campbell and Kate Williams.

Recently, Hannah and Nisha had become closer and were now often to be seen together.

"He's probably already gone," said Hannah.

"I think he's been held back again," said Becca. Hannah shrugged, *no surprise there.* Becca ignored it as sour grapes, which it mostly was.

"Hi Hannah." A couple of boys walked past, both from her class. Hannah gave a half-hearted reply and turned her attention back to Becca.

"I think he likes you," teased Becca.

Hannah looked cross. "Who, Simon? Nahh."

"You know he does."

"Well, OK, but he's the biggest geek in the school."

"Does that matter, if he likes you?" asked Nisha.

"As a matter of fact, it does," said Hannah, stealing a quick look at Simon. "I have standards."

While her friends talked, Becca glanced at Randle, who was helping another stream of children across the road. Something in her expression caused Hannah to look around too. "What's up?"

Becca shrugged. "I dunno. He was staring at me. He creeps me out a bit."

"Old Tom? Nahh," said Hannah. "He's alright. He's been here since before my Mum was at school."

Hannah sat down beside Becca and asked, "Come on, girl. What are you doing this weekend? Fancy going shopping on Saturday? Pizza? Or a film?"

Hannah's questions weren't intended to make Becca feel guilty, but they did. She loved spending time with Matt – well, she loved what they did when they spent time together (not *quite* the same thing) but she missed Hannah.

"I can't. I'm grounded this weekend," Becca lied.

"You, grounded?" Hannah's disbelief was good-natured and sincere. "No way! What did you do?"

Becca had already rehearsed her excuses, so that she wouldn't hesitate or blush. "I broke one of lover Jim's golf clubs," she lied. "Cost him nearly £300, he said. So I'm in all weekend. No friends, no phone, no Internet."

"That sucks," said Hannah, swallowing the deception. She knew that Becca thought Jim was pretty much an arsehole and that Becca's Mum didn't punish her daughter often. In fact, Hannah couldn't recall Becca being grounded before and guessed that Jim would have made her do it. The way Becca described Jim, he was laid-back to the point of being dull, but maybe he flipped every now and then. But that sounded pretty good to Hannah, whose father could be very hotheaded, especially after a drink or two.

Hannah slipped down off the wall. "Big brother's coming," she said, nodding towards Matt, who was just coming out of the school entrance. "Maybe next weekend?"

It was a genuine overture: Becca smiled – in fact, she almost glowed. "Great," she said.

Nisha, who was visibly frowning, tugged at Hannah.

"Come on," said Nisha. "I need to get home."

By the time Matt had walked over, the two girls were already crossing the road.

Matt didn't apologise for being late. "Let's hang back a bit," he said. Neither he nor Becca wanted any of their friends to see them heading off in the opposite direction to home.

So they sat on the wall and chatted for a couple of minutes until Hannah and Nisha were out of sight. Once they had gone, Becca and Matt didn't cross the road as they normally would, but headed up the main road towards the lane at the edge of the school grounds.

They were almost brother and sister, going for a walk. Not touching. No obvious body language. No one would read anything into it. But Tom Randle did. He could *sense it.*

He walked over to where Becca had been sitting and spotted something on the ground. Her scrunchie. He looked around and, seeing no one looking, scooped it up and put it in his pocket. He felt it between his fingers, imagining it was still warm.

A blue VW Beetle pulled out of the school driveway. Louise Sanderson, the geography teacher, wound her window down. "Night, Tom," she said, smiling with genuine affection at probably the most trusted man in school.

"Night, Louise," he said.

As her car disappeared down the road, Randle's fingers stroked the scrunchie in his pocket. He went and stood in his normal spot, thinking of Becca.

5

Becca and Matt wandered along the lane. It was bordered to their right by a high hedge and to their left by the school fence; beyond the fence the sports field was empty. Their chat was mostly small talk: things that had happened at school.

Matt would have been happy to go straight home, but Becca was insistent. She wanted her Mum and his Dad gone when they got home. Matt didn't really understand that, but he didn't need to: he just needed to pretend to. *That* he understood.

The school faded behind them, the hedge now bordering both sides of the lane.

The afternoon May air was unseasonably warm for Lancashire, almost like July or perhaps even August. Both Becca and Matt had removed their blue school jumpers; Becca's was tied around her waist while Matt's was stuffed into his shoulder bag. A cabbage white butterfly flitted around the hedge and somewhere a bird chirped repeatedly.

Few cars came down Harper's Lane, as there was really nowhere to go. It skirted the border of Bankside in a way that was so inefficient, with a surface that was so uneven, that no one bothered to use it – other than the people who lived at the farm about halfway along it, or that photographer guy who lived at Heddon Farm, on the hill.

After another five minutes, where the dusty lane took a sharp left, they left it for the field to their right, climbing over the old stile which cut a gap in the hedge. They walked up the grassy hill, towards the old quarry.

The field was empty, although sometimes people came here to walk their dogs; in the summer holidays plenty of kids hung out around the quarry pool, and even swam in it, though they were not supposed to.

They skirted the edge of the quarry pool. If the pool had been on anyone's route home from school, it might not have been so quiet. Later in the day, once the town's children had been home, changed and eaten, it might perhaps have a few visitors, but at this time it was deserted.

At about sixty yards across, the pool was large enough and deep enough to swim in. Its steep sides offered plenty of places for the brave to dive in, despite the warning signs. Even at the edges, the pool quickly became deep – you couldn't paddle more than a few steps before the bottom fell away. It had once been fenced off, but now the rotten fencing was mostly broken or gone.

They climbed the side of the steep hill that curved around the left side of the pool, where the stone had been cut away long ago. To their right, around fifteen feet up from the pool's surface and roughly in the centre of the rough-hewn wall, water trickled from a manhole-sized culvert, dribbling lazily into the otherwise still water. After stormy weather, the water was pushed out from the quarry's wall in a forceful arc, but today it couldn't even be called a rivulet.

Panting hard, they reached the top of the hill and paused for breath, taking in the view. Becca could see beyond the school, even to the housing estate where she – *they* – lived. Manchester was a grey smudge in the distance. Some miles away, hidden over the hill behind them was Hawksleigh, the next village. Between Bankside and Hawksleigh, thankfully hidden, was the grey eyesore that was the medical research company Ederon, the largest employer in the area.

While some people might climb the hill for the excellent view of Bankside, few people ventured further – as they would do today.

About ten yards beyond the top of the quarry pool they reached the old stone wall which bordered the deserted Whitaker estate. At least three feet taller than Matt, the once ostentatious wall was now overgrown, crumbling and, in many places, largely obscured by bushes and trees. The combination of the wall and local legends was enough to keep most people out of the Whitaker estate – especially at this side of the estate, where the old cottage lay in ruins.

Becca and Matt worked their way into the undergrowth to a hidden spot where the wall had been partly breached by a tree, forcing its way through over time.

They still had to climb to get in, but it wasn't too hard to scale the broken stones.

Matt went first. As they descended the other side of the wall, Matt held Becca's hand as she carefully worked her way down the gap in the wall. It was the first time they'd touched since leaving school, but now it was OK: no one could see them. Becca stepped onto the long, unkempt grass and they finally kissed, long and slow. Then they walked, hand in hand, the last few yards towards the old well – to kill some time.

6

With the back of her hand, Becca wiped at the tears that were streaming down her face. Her strong inner voice, the one that pushed her on when she was swimming, was telling her to get a grip – yet she was shaking uncontrollably.

Beside her, Matt coughed harshly. His breathing was a grotesque liquid-filled rasping sound. Becca forced herself under control, pushing back her own distress with some shame.

She took her schoolbag from over her shoulder, dropped it into the water and squatted down next to Matt, the cold water rising above her waist. She felt her feet shift and sink a little further in the deep mud. Matt was a dark shape, almost lost in the gloomy well. She strained to see him properly.

"Matt," she said. He coughed again, but gave no indication of having heard her. She stroked the hair from his forehead. "Matt, can you hear me?"

He nodded. It wasn't much of a nod, but it was there. Her tears came again and she tried her best to hold them back. She forced herself to feel Matt's body under the water, more carefully this time. Around two feet of grating protruded from his abdomen and perhaps four or five inches of it jutted out of his back. He was more or less pinned into a sitting position, the grating pressing against the curved side of the well wall. Although she couldn't see it, Becca knew that he would be bleeding heavily into the water.

"We're gonna get out, Matt," she said, knowing that for Matt, whether they got out or not probably wouldn't make any difference.

Matt coughed again and spat liquid – a lot of liquid. Becca wiped his mouth with her hand. Although she couldn't see what was on her palm she felt sure it would be blood.

Becca knew that she couldn't (and in any case probably shouldn't) extract the metal from inside Matt, but she thought that she may be able to make it less painful if she unpinned him from the wall. If she could bring Matt closer to the centre of the well, there was more space. She felt along the grating to the point where it touched the wall, her fingers groping around. The grating seemed to have cut a gouge in the stone. It wasn't especially deep, but deep enough to hold it firmly in place.

She went back to Matt, put her arm around him and kissed him on the cheek. He stirred and coughed again.

"Matt, I'm going to try to move you. It might hurt a bit," she said, realising how stupid her words were. Matt was almost certainly living in a whole world of pain right now. "Is that OK?"

Matt's head moved a little, but she couldn't tell if it was a nod. She tried again. "It could hurt, maybe a lot, but after it should hurt less," she said. "Can you hear me?"

Under the water, she felt something fumble against her thigh: his hand. She reached into the water and held it. "Can you hear me?" she asked again. She felt his hand tighten slightly in hers and he croaked out a wet, "Yeah."

She squeezed his hand and let go, feeling her way along the grating. Gripping it tightly, she pulled as gently as she could to test how firmly it was stuck. Matt groaned as it shifted a little. *Good*, she thought, *it probably wasn't held totally fast.* "Get ready," she said, "I'm gonna pull hard now." She squatted and braced herself with her feet as much as she could. "One, two, three –"

On *three*, Becca pulled hard. With a scraping sound, the grating came free from the wall. She fell backwards into the water, her hands grasping beside her for purchase in the deep mud. Matt screamed; it was the most horrific sound Becca had ever heard. It echoed loudly around the well.

She went back to Matt's side, crying freely. "I'm sorry, I'm sorry," she said through her sobs. "I'm really sorry." Matt was closer to the centre of the well, and the front of the grating was now free, but the back of it was still pressing against the wall behind him. She knew she had to move him again, to lean his shoulder against the wall; while the grating was leaning against the wall, his weight would press his body into the metal.

"Matt," she said, softly, into his ear. "I need to move you again, so it's not pressing into you." This time, Matt's head did move: it shook from side to side, slowly. "Fuck, no," he said.

"I *have* to," she said. "Just one more move. It will help, I promise." She found his hand again and squeezed it. He didn't respond.

She got on her knees, as close to him as she could, hoping it would help her keep her balance. In the mud, her bare knees were scraping against something hard – stones perhaps – but she ignored the discomfort. She put her arms around Matt's shoulder. "I'll do it as gently as I can," she promised, earnestly.

Becca carefully pulled Matt slightly forwards, taking him away from the well wall. She twisted him gently, pulling him sideways at the same time. He groaned. *Christ, he's heavy*, she thought. She didn't need to move him far; within a minute she'd managed to rest his shoulder against the stone wall.

She knelt next to him, water sloshing around them both. "All done," she said, kissing him again. Her vision was getting accustomed to the dark – she saw his eyes flicker open and look at her. "Thanks," he rasped, before coughing again and closing his eyes.

That one word filled her with relief. She stroked his head for a short while. His breathing became a little less laboured.

Becca stood, instinctively wiping the grit and small stones from her knees. She sat down, facing Matt, her back against the wall, water lapping around her. *I need to think*, she realised, bringing her tears under control. *I need to calm down, get my breath back and think.*

No one knows we're here, she realised. *There's no one nearby. The nearest anybody comes is to the quarry. The quarry isn't that far. Probably less than a hundred yards.* Poor at judging distances, she had to think hard. *It was probably quite a bit less than that*, she decided. *Would anyone there hear if I shouted? Probably not – they'd have to be pretty close to the top of the well to hear.*

Mum might phone –

Becca jumped to her feet. *Phone, stupid!*

She pulled her bag from the water and rummaged through its sodden contents, her hand seeking her phone in the dark. She pulled it out and flipped it open, discarding her bag. It lit up: a brief flash of light momentarily illuminating the bottom of the well before going dark again.

"No!" she screamed; Matt stirred slightly and moaned. She felt for the power-on button and pressed it. Again, the phone lit up – and again it died. *The water*, she thought. *It's soaked.* She tried again. This time it didn't even light up. She felt like throwing it against the well wall, but knew that was stupid. *It just needs to dry out.*

Matt's phone.

She pushed her bag to one side and pulled Matt's out of the water, hunting desperately through its equally soaked contents. *There's a chance*, she thought. *There's got to be a chance.* But she couldn't find his phone. She pushed the contents of his bag around wildly but it wasn't there: exercise books, what seemed to be his sports kit (in a plastic carrier bag), a drinks can, cigarette packet, lighter – but no phone.

Where the –?

For a moment, she thought that he'd dropped it when falling into the well but then realised where it would be.

She squatted next to Matt and felt gently for his trouser pocket. Inside, her fingers touched something – a soaked cardboard packet. She pulled it out but in the darkness couldn't read the package. Opening it up, she felt three plastic wrappers, each containing something firm and circular. She had no idea what they were. She dropped both them and the packet into the water before reaching her hand around to Matt's far pocket. Since this was at the side of Matt that was leaning against the wall, it wasn't easy to get her fingers inside. She stretched and her fingertips touched hard plastic: the phone. She pulled it from his pocket and pressed the call button. Nothing. No light, nothing. It was as dead as hers. She stood, a phone in each hand, wondering what to do.

I need to dry them out. Where? If I could bloody see –

Again, her mind made a connection: *Matt's lighter.* It would be wet, but it should work. Transferring both phones into her left hand, she squatted down and rummaged through Matt's floating backpack.

She found the lighter and flicked it: nothing. Again: nothing. She realised that she was gritting her teeth and tried to steady herself.

The lighter was wet, but there was nothing to dry it with – all of her clothes were soaked. She flicked it four more times before it finally lit. The inside of the well sprang into view, flickering and eerie.

Banishing the dark helped to calm her a little. She raised the lighter a little and looked around, taking in her surroundings.

The well was wide: in the centre, she could probably just about touch both sides with her arms outstretched. The stonework was ancient, covered with moss that grew up to perhaps ten feet above the waterline. She placed the two phones into her shirt pocket, then reached out and touched the wall – the stones were slick where they had been splashed, but even above that, the moss was still slippery. The well was built from stones that were large and uneven in size and shape, although most were perhaps ten inches by four (or five – it was hard to tell). There were slight gaps between some of the stones, where there had once perhaps been some form of mortar. Becca explored the gaps with her fingers but they didn't feel as though they would provide enough of a hold with which to climb.

Something moved to her right and she spun around. A spider scuttled out of the light. She shuddered. She didn't have a fear of spiders, but she didn't like them much either.

The water was around her knees. If it had been much higher, Matt, in his sitting position, would be completely submerged. She held the lighter towards Matt and felt herself wanting to retch. Much of the water was a deep, oily red. Floating on the water were their schoolbags; two exercise books floated along with them. There was also the packet that she'd found in Matt's pocket, along with its contents. *Condoms,* she realised. Their weekend plans seemed an impossible age away. She felt her heart flutter and her stomach sank with the loss.

Matt looked terrible. His face was incredibly pale and his eyes were black and sunken, as if he were wearing Halloween zombie make-up. His head hung loosely on his chest.

She raised the lighter higher and slowly rotated herself so that she could see all of the wall. A few stones – not many, perhaps half a dozen – protruded proud of the wall. They stood out enough to use as footholds and handholds, but there were not enough to guarantee passage out of the well. In a couple of places, stones were missing, creating dark empty gaps in the wall. *Or shelves*, she thought.

She took the phones from her pocket, reached up and put them into one of the gaps, where they could hopefully dry out. Her hand was hot and growing tired, so she flipped the lighter off. The darkness snapped back into place. The well seemed blacker than ever and she realised that, before using the lighter, she'd started to become accustomed to the dark.

She flipped the lighter on again and looked around.

She could try to climb out; it seemed as though it might be possible, though difficult. *Very difficult.* And, if she fell, she could really hurt herself.

It occurred to Becca that if she wasn't able to climb out, it could be days before they were found. *It could be a day or more before they even start looking. It's the weekend. Mum and Jim are away. Everyone thinks I'm grounded. It could be Sunday before anyone knows we're missing.* She doubted that Matt would last anything like that long. God knows what damage the grating had done and, to make matters worse, his submerged wounds were bleeding into dirty water. Not that infection was her main worry – sitting in the water, Matt was going to carry on bleeding until he was drained of blood. Becca recalled how, on television dramas, most suicides seemed to involve people slashing their wrists in the bath so that their blood wouldn't clot. There was no way of getting Matt out of the water – he couldn't stand for even a moment, even if she had been able to help him to his feet.

That thought made up her mind. She *had* to climb. There was no choice, no other way out.

Becca squatted beside Matt and strained her eyes. His eyes were closed but his face was twitching with pain. Every now and then he groaned or mumbled. "Matt," she said, shaking him gently. His head lolled around, but he didn't look at her. She shook him again, a little more urgently. "Matt!" His head turned to her, then his eyelids fluttered and half opened. He looked toward her through glassy, watery eyes, his focus vague. She spoke his name again and their eyes met properly.

"I'm going to climb out and get help," Becca said, slowly, to make sure Matt could understand. Matt didn't seem to grasp what Becca had said. He wearily spat out a mouthful of blood and croaked, "Out?" Becca nodded. "Out of the well. We fell in. Don't you remember?"

Matt didn't, in fact he wasn't really aware of anything except the pain that now consumed all of his senses. He closed his eyes and thought hard. He remembered a kiss in the afternoon sunlight, a sweet moment during which the cynical Matt gave way briefly to someone who actually liked Becca; possibly *more than liked her.* She had stood on the well wall to kiss him, smiling. The thought slipped away. Matt had no memory of falling, only of pain: incredible pain which drove away everything else.

He was barely aware of the dark or even the water in which he was sitting. Everything was pain. He shook his head, as much to try to clear his thoughts as to show that he couldn't remember.

With her free hand, Becca stroked his cheek. "We fell in the well. You tried to save me but I pulled you in." Guilty tears ran down Becca's face. "No one knows we're here; I have to climb out." She paused. "You're hurt. Very badly. I need to get help. You fell on the grating."

Matt grimaced as he shifted his weight a little. With one hand, he felt around his abdomen for the source of the horrendous pain. His fingers touched where he and the grating had become one being, fused with wet, broken flesh. With the discovery came realisation of the true extent of his situation. He inhaled. Tears formed in his eyes.

Becca pushed back her own tears. "I have to go. I have to go *now*." Matt shook his head and whispered, "Don't leave me." His face was full of fear. She knew what he was thinking and he was probably right. It would take her *at least* a couple of hours – probably more – to climb out, walk to town, get help and then come back. She wasn't sure that Matt had two hours left in him.

She leaned forward and kissed his cheek: not a brief peck, but a lingering kiss, as if she were kissing his lips. "I have to go. You need help. I'll be as quick as I can."

The sheer effort of talking seemed to have drained Matt. He was fading back into semi-consciousness. Becca decided to wait for a few minutes until he had drifted off. She stayed beside him, squatting in the water, her calves and knees aching, until he was quieter. His breathing shallowed, but still sounded as if he was dragging air through thick liquid. She kissed him once more, gently this time. She was terrified, but she knew what she had to do.

Becca looked up, studying the well wall. The well wasn't that deep, but it would be a tough climb. If the well had been narrower, she could scale it in the way she'd seen climbers on television, bracing their backs and feet against opposite sides. But there was no way: the well was simply too wide.

Although the stones were rough and uneven, there weren't anything like enough handholds – and those that there were didn't seem very large. The few gaps and protruding stones she'd already seen could perhaps get her started, although it was hard to see if there were more further up. And of course there was the damp, slimy moss covering the bottom ten feet or so of the well. Not exactly ideal climbing conditions.

She decided to test a few of the first handholds – and then realised that there was another significant obstacle: the light, or lack of it. To see the handholds, she needed the lighter. If she used the lighter, she would only have one hand free and couldn't possibly climb.

Climbing with the lighter was impossible, she decided, *whereas climbing without it would be just nearly impossible.* She flipped the lighter off, and put it into her shirt pocket. At the bottom of the well, the darkness was almost complete. As she looked up, her eyes blinked against the early evening sunlight. Annoyingly, she'd need to get accustomed enough to the darkness to see the handholds – and then try to not look up as she climbed, otherwise she'd be blinded by the sunlight above. It was impossible – she needed to look up to find the next handholds. Becca gritted her teeth and exhaled, swearing under her breath. She didn't need to read Joseph Heller's Catch-22 to know what the now common catchphrase meant. *Screwed if you do, screwed if you don't,* she thought.

She felt around the wall and found that with a little patience, she could build up a mental image of the handholds.

Not as good as being able to see, but good enough?

She felt fear and determination in equal measure but decided to give it a try. *Just a few feet at first. Enough to see how hard it will be.*

With her left hand, she reached up and found the first sizeable gap in the wall and then found one not quite so high for her right hand. Carefully, she moved her right foot, seeking somewhere to place it. She found a slight crack, just enough, and pushed herself slowly upwards. Grasping the wall with straining fingers (and only a foot from the muddy bottom) she felt around with her right hand for a way to advance. She found a tiny crack: *not enough.* Then, something larger. She took hold and prepared to shift her weight. Tentatively, she moved her left foot around the wall, hunting for somewhere to place it that would push her a little further up. When she found something, it was near the edge of her reach, so she couldn't get a strong enough foothold. She withdrew her foot, trying to locate something nearer. At first she thought that there was nothing, but she found that one of the stones near to her knees jutted out enough to provide a toehold, though nothing more.

She shifted her weight, pulled herself up and took stock, realising just how hard the task was. She was already sweating profusely, her fingers and toes aching, her feet and hands trembling. It was very hard to hold on to the wall, very hard indeed. The full climb, at this speed, could easily take half an hour, or perhaps an hour, and each foot of progress would make just one slip all the more dangerous. If she came to a place without handholds, what then? Climbing back down would probably be even harder than going up. She felt that it might be possible to use the lighter between each short climb, just to find the next handhold. *Possible, but not easy.* If there was one positive thing, it was that Becca's eyes were adjusting again and she could make out a few of the shapes of the stones.

She closed her eyes and took a deep breath. She knew that her success at swimming wasn't because she was especially gifted: she just pushed herself on where most others would quit. She knew that she had to do the same here.

She opened her eyes, a little calmer. Her eyes and hands hunted around.

What looked like a good handhold directly above her turned out to be not much more than a tiny crack. Then she found a gap between the stones just a little to the right; as she secured her fingers something crawled across her hand and she almost lost her grip, fighting the instinct to brush it away. She felt around with her feet until she found another gap, secured her toes and pushed herself upwards, pulling with her hand at the same time. Her muscles strained; it was a far greater effort than she could have imagined. This was different from climbing in the gym, where handholds were easy to find. She had to keep her fingers and toes tense all of the time, to stop herself sliding off the mossy wall.

Slowly, she climbed up the wall, sometimes having to waste time by moving sideways because there were no handholds above. She lost track of time, engrossed and focused on her task. Her fingers and toes hurt enormously. The muscles in her arms, legs, shoulders and neck protested.

Then Becca stopped. As much as she searched, she couldn't find another handhold – not above, nor to the left or right. Hanging on the wall was agony and she allowed herself to relax, just a little. She gathered her strength and looked again: nothing. She felt a combination of failure and of having been cheated. *There has to be something, somewhere*, she thought. No matter how much she looked and felt, there was nothing. Carefully, she looked down, holding on tightly in case she lost her balance. She'd not climbed as far as she thought: perhaps just ten feet.

It was high enough to feel exposed. *A fall from this height could do some real damage*, she thought. *I could easily break a leg. Christ I was lucky*, she realised. *I fell much further without getting more than a few scrapes.* Becca's fear came back, stronger than ever. This was the end of the line; there was no way to climb higher. No way at all. Worse still, she couldn't simply drop back down. She'd have to climb – and that was going to be even harder than the climb up.

Becca looked up, blinking at the sunlight. She took a deep breath and screamed as loud as she could, "Help! Help! Help me!"

She waited, but couldn't hear any reply from above. In her heart, she knew that even if she screamed for several minutes, the response would be the same.

Becca felt crushed and considered jumping down. It was risky, but it would be quick. She dismissed the thought. "Shit," she said, through clenched teeth. Her determination grew again. *I won't fall*, she thought. She started to climb backwards and immediately slipped, but managed to just hang on. She took a few moments to compose herself, panting, her heart pounding. Then she began to climb down.

As she had thought, going down was even harder than climbing up. It took ages to find any handholds – and she couldn't reach as far downwards as she could upwards, so progress was much slower. But she took her time and tried not to panic. She'd been climbing down for perhaps fifteen minutes when she realised that her body was about to give in. Her hands were shaking and she was having real difficulty hanging on to the wall. She looked down. She was perhaps five feet from the water. *It will have to be enough,* she thought. She pushed herself from the wall, trying to clear where Matt was sitting, and braced herself for a rough touchdown.

She landed on her feet, pain again shooting up from her ankle, and fell backwards into the well wall. She hit the stones hard with both her spine and the back of her head, struggling briefly to avoid falling over.

"Shit!" she said. *God that was hard,* she thought. *And I was only a few feet off the ground.*

Becca wasn't a quitter, but she felt for certain that climbing out wasn't an option. Again, she considered just how damned lucky she'd been when she fell in. *Not like Matt.* With that thought, she checked on Matt again, squatting beside him. He was breathing noisily, each inhalation shallow, laboured and almost a gargle.

"Shit!" she said again, this time between her teeth.

She sat down in the water next to him, wheezing for breath. Where she wasn't hurting from the fall, she was aching from the climb. As she brought her breathing under control, she briefly contemplated waking Matt and telling him what had happened. She decided against it. Best he rested.

After about half an hour, she stood, and considered her injuries.

She knew that she had been hurt in the first fall, but she'd been too concerned about Matt to pay much attention to her own injuries. She pulled the lighter from her pocket and snapped it on, then ran it over herself to see how badly she was hurt.

First, she noticed her fingers holding the lighter. They were grimy, filthy, Dickensian fingers that didn't even look as if they belonged to her. She shook her head and continued to look herself over. Her left arm seemed fine. She transferred the lighter to her left hand to get a better look at her right arm, which really hurt. Her right forearm sported a long scrape – deeper than just the top layer of skin, but not too deep. Although it was covered with blood, it didn't seem to be bleeding now. Her skin on her knees had been rasped away and they looked raw, but they didn't hurt as badly as they looked. Her left shin had a six-inch-long scrape on it, but the skin was mostly unbroken – although it looked as if it were turning a nasty dark colour. *Probably bruising.*

She leaned against the wall and bent her left leg up while reaching down. She felt inside her sock. Her ankle was very tender to her touch. She moved it gently. It hurt enormously, though perhaps a little less than it had.

She stood again and twisted around to see the injury on her side, but couldn't quite. She felt around with her hand and winced: it was very sore, but again the skin didn't seem broken. She didn't have any way of seeing the top of her head, but it was very sore under the gentle touch of her fingers. It felt wet – it could be blood, but then she was soaked from head to toe. She looked at her fingers in the light: it was blood. *At least it's out of the water where it should heal,* she thought.

Dry. Nothing's any good if it's wet, she realised, and started to scoop up their belongings. It was hard working with one hand, while using the other to hold the lighter.

Her bag contained her swimsuit, towel and swimming goggles; like Matt's they were within a supermarket carrier bag, but wet nonetheless. The bag also contained her exercise books (English, science and history), a copy of Jane Eyre, a calculator, pencil case (filled with pencils and pens), a small half-empty bottle of water, an apple and a bag of crisps (which she had saved for the walk home), her plastic sandwich box (empty apart from some crumbs), her iPod and its headphones. She pressed the iPod. Bizarrely, it still worked.

She placed the iPod, headphones, water bottle, apple and crisps into the largest of the gaps in the wall. She hung her towel and her jumper on one of the protruding stones where perhaps they could dry. The rest she returned to her bag, which she then hung from another of the stones; not likely to dry, but out of the way.

Matt's bag offered up his sports kit and towel, exercise books (English and French), his art sketchbook, a can of fizzy orange and a chocolate bar. She placed the can and the chocolate in the gap. The sports kit, condoms and school books she returned to the bag, though she spent a moment looking through the sketchbook. As she already knew, Matt's drawings were pretty good. Art was one of the few subjects at which he did well, but he kept his work mostly to himself, as if embarrassed by his ability. She hadn't seen most of these drawings and paused at one which seemed to be of her, sitting in a window, reading a book. She ran her fingers slowly along the wet paper. *He probably drew it when I thought he was watching television.*

She felt tears roll down her cheeks again. She pushed the sketchbook into the bag, which she then hung alongside hers.

Reluctantly, she flipped off the lighter to save fuel. The well became a black void again. She felt around for the recess and placed the lighter with the rest of her things.

Then she sat down next to Matt. She felt for his hand and closed hers around it. He mumbled slightly, but otherwise didn't respond. Her eyes could see only dark, but the smells in the well were rank. Now that she'd stopped moving, the water seemed very cold; the walls very close. Something moved quickly across the top of her head. She brushed it away and shivered.

She pulled herself as close as she could to Matt, sharing the little warmth and time they had, sobbing to herself, not wanting to disturb him.

Thomas Randle closed the door gently behind him and dropped the security chain into place. He reached to both the top and bottom of the door, drawing the two bolts home. Randle believed that in a world where nearly everyone says one thing while thinking another, you couldn't be too careful – and there were few things, or people, in which Randle trusted.

He stowed his plastic high-visibility jacket, cap and road sign in the tiny cupboard, pressing the reluctant door closed against the bulging mass of coats. Shuffling into the living room, he flicked on the light. The low-wattage bulb's dull yellow glow only just illuminated the grubby flat. Randle's flat was tiny: a living room, bedroom, kitchen and bathroom, each room smaller than the last. It was all he could afford. He'd completed two tours of Northern Ireland before being sent home, useless and almost lame, with a military pension that only just kept him going. Although his leg had improved to the point where it was a bearable disability, moving at anything other than a steady walking pace was forever beyond him. Before the bomb, he had a life and career; every year thereafter it seemed he had progressively less. His cramped flat was just one more thing to resent at the end of three decades of disappointment, dissatisfaction and rejection.

In films and on television, life alone was often characterised by an untidy coffee table covered with takeaway boxes; Randle had no space for a coffee table and could only occasionally spare the money for a pizza. It had taken him almost four years of scrimping and saving to muster enough money for one of the cheapest computers money could buy – and still he could only connect to the Internet courtesy of his neighbour's unsecured wireless router. Of course, people find money to fund the things that are dearest to them. Randle was no gourmet: to him food was fuel, not pleasure – so he'd eat the cheapest beans and spend years saving pennies if it bought him closer to the things he wanted the most. Randle had found that technology provided salvation from social exclusion. With his computer, he could roam the world as an anonymous voyeur, indulging himself without the sanctimonious judgement of others. His camera had provided further gratification: although his photographs were innocent in composition, they were of girls he saw every day, real flesh you could almost touch – and that somehow made them more powerful than stateside pornography. He was a good enough photographer to make himself indispensable at school events: trusted by teachers, children and parents – some of whom even paid for his work.

Sure, his acquisitions had taken sacrifice – but what didn't? Life was a haul. A long haul. Some people had things handed to them. Some people had to take what they could. Randle had been given little and took even less – but his days as an onlooker were drawing to a close, and he knew that he was getting ready to take.

Randle rubbed Becca's scrunchie between thumb and forefinger, feeling its texture. He held it up to look at it, adjusting his glasses to see it more clearly. The fine, dark hairs caught within its elastic were even more precious than the item itself. They were hairs that had been on *her* head, *part of her: alive. Something she might have brushed out. Something her mother might have stroked. Something that could have been spread out on a pillow, around her head, that a lover could look down on.* The thought made him hard.

Randle had a box of keepsakes. He'd had it for years. It contained things that had been dropped, discarded – or, in some cases, stolen. Not many things. A hair slide. A school tie. Exercise books. A well-thumbed copy of *The Hobbit*. A purse: with money, photographs and a front door key. A swimsuit and towel that had, until today, been the best of his collection. Many nights he'd held the towel and imagined it rubbing a young girl dry; stroked the swimsuit knowing it had been against a naked body. But he didn't know to whom they had belonged – they'd just been left in a plastic bag – and knowing the owner would have made touching them so much better. The apparently far more innocent scrunchie, with its prized hairs, belonged to someone he knew; someone he could name; someone he had photographed. Many times.

Becca had been easy to photograph. She was at every swimming event or competition and frequently won. He took the pictures: of her preparing to dive in the pool, diving in, swimming, receiving an award and, his personal favourite, her wet body as she climbed out of the pool. Until today, she was just one of many girls he photographed, but the physical link provided by the scrunchie made her special.

His girls were filed away, by name where he knew them. He even had separate albums for several of the girls (including older albums for girls who were now grown and married). As top performer within the school, Becca had a larger album than most. Building a collection of photographs of her hadn't been difficult. Becca's slight unease when he'd photographed her had made her more special: their connection was more real because she *almost* saw the real him.

This gave Randle a problem. Should he keep the scrunchie with his other physical artefacts, or store it with his pictures of Becca?

No contest, he decided. The scrunchie belonged with the photographs. It wasn't just a piece of random junk, it was a real, physical link between two people. It was the first time he'd combined photographs and possessions.

Even with storage space at a premium, half of his wardrobe was given over to his girls. He shuffled boxes around to clear an entire shelf – a first for any one person.

He reached for a flat-pack cardboard box and popped it into shape. He placed Becca's two photo albums and newspaper scrapbook inside it, along with her scrunchie. It felt good; very good; very *right*. He located a black marker pen and wrote on the side of the box: **REBECCA RICHARDS.** Then he slid the box into place on the empty shelf, just for the pleasure of seeing where it belonged in his thirty-year collection. It was the culmination of years of desire; decades of watching and waiting.

The scrunchie was someone he could actually touch. Randle felt, for the first time, that it was right to move from merely looking. He wanted it, *needed it* and he knew that she was ready for it. More than ready.

It had been months since he had been this turned on. He took one of the photo albums and the scrunchie – and retired to bed.

8

Jim drew the zip up the back of Sarah's black dress, which was snug but not tight. She looked, in Jim's opinion, knockout – and he said so. Sarah flushed slightly. She knew that her figure was pretty good for a woman in her early forties, but she also knew that Jim didn't really see her as she herself did (a bit mumsy, carrying a few extra pounds and just starting to lose the fight against gravity). *Still*, she reflected, *his selective vision is no bad thing. It's good to feel younger and sexier.*

They wouldn't ordinarily dress for dinner, but the hotel was a cut above the usual for them – and they both wanted every second of the weekend to be special.

She straightened Jim's tie and instinctively put her mobile phone into her black evening bag. Jim wagged his finger in a good-natured way. "No phones," he said. "Not tonight."

Sarah conceded that, if she had her phone with her, she'd want to text or call Becca. She'd never been without her daughter for this long and not an hour had gone past without her at least briefly considering sending another text. But in truth, she was starting to enjoy time away from the household. *It feels good*, she thought, *to feel like a real woman again: a sexy woman, not just a mum.*

She put the phone back on the bedside table.

They went downstairs to dinner, Jim appreciatively watching Sarah's hips sway as she walked ahead of him down the stairs. Soon, they were eating and drinking – it was a great meal accompanied by two bottles of wine, lots of laughter and not a little flirting. Sarah basked in the feeling of being wanted, enjoying Jim's attentive and tactile nature. It was as though they were dining in a bubble, where they could only see and hear each other, their only interruptions from a waiter or waitress.

It was late when they got back to the room, drunk, and made love for the third (and, in Sarah's view, easily the best) time that day.

And although she would never have believed it, Sarah didn't think of Becca once the whole evening – and wouldn't until she woke, late, the next morning.

9

Hannah lay in bed, fuming. For sure, it had been a dull Friday night with nothing to do, but that wasn't why she was annoyed. No: she'd decided to try to smooth things over with Becca and, during the course of the evening, had sent her three text messages. Becca hadn't responded to any of them.

No friends, no phone, no Internet, Becca had said, but the more Hannah thought about it, the less she believed it. Sarah just wasn't that harsh.

Becca had definitely behaved awkwardly outside school, but at least she had spoken to her. But ignoring her was unreasonable, infuriating and without justification. Hannah had no idea what she'd done wrong. She reckoned she knew Becca better than anyone, but this increasing distance from everyone (*and,* she thought, *especially me*) was baffling.

Earlier tonight Hannah had decided that the whys and wherefores didn't matter, so she'd sent Becca one text after another, over the course of a couple of hours, wanting to chat things through. *And the bloody cow hadn't even replied.*

Hannah checked her phone once again, even though she would have heard a text message arriving. Nothing. She put the phone on the shelf above her head and then switched off the bedside lamp.

"Screw you, Rebecca Richards," muttered Hannah to herself, turning over onto her side. She had been toying with the idea of calling over to see Becca during the weekend and was pretty sure she could sweet-talk her Mum into letting her in, even if Becca was grounded. Now she could forget it.

Hannah was surprised to find that she had to brush away a tear, and this made her even more annoyed. *Cow,* she thought. *Well sod you.*

10

Despite the relative warmth of the night air, Becca and Matt were shivering almost uncontrollably. There was no getting away from the cold water; Becca had found that it was better to sit in it (just) than to stand dripping out of it. She thought that if she could only get herself dry, it might be different – although her feet would remain wet – yet if she were standing, she wouldn't be able to comfort Matt.

Matt had been conscious for perhaps half an hour just before twilight. Becca didn't know if it was better for him to be awake or not. When he drifted from consciousness, she was scared that he'd not wake; when he was awake, his pain was all-consuming. Either way, there was little she could do other than keep as close to him as she could, holding his hand and stroking his matted hair.

There was a short while where Matt was both awake and lucid, though Becca could see that he was clearly in agony.

"It's only a matter of time before we're found," Matt stammered.

Becca didn't share his confidence. "It's Friday," she said. "Mum and Jim aren't back until Sunday."

"No," groaned Matt. "Your Mum won't last all night without calling you. When she can't get you, she'll know something's up."

"I guess," said Becca, not really believing it.

"Go on then," said Matt. "Who won?"

"What? Who won what?"

"How deep is it? The well?"

Becca squeezed Matt's hand, appreciating his brave humour. "Nowhere near as deep as you thought," she said.

"Can you climb out?" asked Matt.

"I've tried," said Becca. "The walls are too slimy and there's nothing to hold on to. Don't you remember me trying?"

Becca could see the dark shape of Matt shaking his head.

"It was really hard. I tried as best I could but I just couldn't do it." Becca felt a twinge of guilt, wondering if she was exaggerating and really hadn't tried hard enough. If Matt thought that might be the case, he didn't say. Not that he said much: he talked between gritted teeth, his words interspersed with groans; his voice unsteady because of the continual trembling of his body.

Becca tried to give him a little of the water, but found that he couldn't swallow it without coughing violently – which in turn increased his agony. Although thirsty, she decided that she would hold off drinking as long as she could: there was very little water and no telling how long it would need to last. One thing was obvious: the water in the well wasn't drinkable.

Gradually Matt became silent, apart from his breathing. When Becca was sure that Matt was either asleep or unconscious (there was no way of knowing which) she checked the mobile phones again. They were both still dead.

In the darkness of the night, the black inside the well became almost absolute. Earlier in the evening, her eyes had grown accustomed to the dark, but being able to see more clearly didn't bring her any comfort. Even unconscious, Matt's features were twisted in deep-felt pain. The well itself was dirty; the walls covered with a thick moss over which insects continually ran. Now, in the black, the well seemed to close in tightly around them. The cold became something that reached deep inside her. She doubted that she was passing any warmth at all to Matt. Her hand, grasping his, felt cold and numb.

Worse, she desperately needed to pee. The feeling had been growing most of the day, but now, in the pitch-black, it became a shouting, urgent need. The thought of going in the same water in which she was sitting repulsed her, but she couldn't see an alternative. (True, she could pee into the plastic lunchbox, but that would be a fair old feat to achieve – and then what would she do with it?)

While she was considering her options – or lack of them – she heard what seemed to be a sound from above. She sat, silent, her ears straining to hear anything in the silence. The noise came again. It was impossible to tell what it was – something or someone moving around? An animal rummaging around in the dirt? She carefully untangled herself from around Matt and stood, cold and shivering.

"Hey," she shouted, as loudly as she could, looking up. The moonlight in the night sky seemed bright against the dark of the well, although she couldn't see the moon itself. "Anybody there?" There was no answer other than silence. Matt stirred, but didn't wake. "Help! If there's someone there, help! We're in the well! In the well – look in the well!"

A shape moved at the edge of the well. It was hard to see what it was until it hopped a few paces and fluttered its wings. It cawed loudly and Becca jumped with fright. The sound echoing around the inside of the well chilled her more than the cold water. She could only see the bird's silhouette against the night sky, but she felt sure that it was looking directly at her. It cawed again, three times in succession, before flapping its wings and disappearing. Becca realised that she was now shaking with fear, not cold. She stood still for ten long minutes, but the bird didn't reappear – although she did hear its call again, once, some distance away.

She sat back in the water and drew herself close to Matt, again finding his hand under the water. Like hers, it felt cold and rubbery from being submerged for so long. Her trembling had almost become outright shaking. She forced herself to calm down. *It was just a bird*, she thought. *Just a bird? Any bird? Or the bird?* She couldn't tell one crow from another, but something in her heart told her that it was the same bird. Somehow, in the isolation and dark of the well, it seemed more than just a bird. It seemed to be something knowing; something evil. She gritted her teeth against the cold and the fear.

It's just a bird, she told herself.

The silence grew around her and seemed more awful than the noise of the bird. She was tense, fearful and on edge. And, now that the distraction of the bird had gone, the need to pee grew more powerful. "Fuck," she said to herself and relaxed the muscles that she had been holding so tightly. She felt shameful and feral. The water around her grew pleasantly, if briefly, warm and Becca wondered just how many more indignities she would have to suffer before they were finally found. *If we're found*, she corrected herself. As the warmth from her urine faded, she grew colder than ever.

Her mind alive with fear, her body unable to relax against the cold, she pressed herself even more tightly against Matt. Minutes seemed to take hours to pass and, as the night dragged on, Matt would periodically mutter and shudder. At some point in the early hours of the cold morning, Becca's exhausted body gave in and she finally drifted off into a fitful, troubled sleep.

While she slept, Matt's bubbling breaths became increasingly shallow until, just before dawn, they ceased forever.

SATURDAY

1

Sammy screamed: a scream of heartfelt terror that came from somewhere deep within her. In the dead of night it echoed around the flat.

Abby, already awake, came running into Sammy's bedroom in her night shorts and vest. Panicked by Sammy's screaming, Abby hadn't paused for even a second to pull on her dressing gown, but halted in her tracks when she saw her daughter, momentarily not quite sure what to do.

In the dim yellow glow of the nightlight, Sammy stood on her bed, frantically clawing at the wall as if trying to climb up it. Her nightie flapped loosely around her legs as she scrambled for purchase. All over the bed were scraps of the boyband and film posters that had once been stuck proudly to the wall.

Abby rushed to Sammy and wrapped her arms around her. "Sam! Sammy!"

For a moment, it was as if she hadn't been heard. Sammy's slight eight-year-old body wriggled, fighting her mother's embrace; she continued to scream.

"Sammy!"

Sammy looked at her mother, her eyes wide, thoroughly terrified. Then she relaxed and pulled herself to Abby, sobbing "Mummy, Mummy, Mummy," over and over again.

Abby lifted her daughter to a sitting position and pulled her close. She was hot and drenched with sweat. "Hush," whispered Abby, with a calmness she certainly didn't feel. "It's OK. It's all OK. Just a bad dream." At the mention of the word *dream* Sammy struggled again, though not as hard.

"I was stuck in a dark place," she sobbed. "I couldn't get out."

"It's alright," said Abby, pushing her daughter's blonde, damp hair from her eyes. "It's not real. You're safe. Look. You're in your bedroom. See?" It was chilling for Abby to see her daughter look around intently for confirmation. The disbelief in her eyes was clear.

"I was in a dark place," she said, quietly. "A bad place."

"You're at home. *I promise.* It was a nightmare." Abby kept the tone of her voice as soothing as possible, despite her racing heart. "Do you want to tell me about it?"

Sammy shook her head, but said softly, "It was a bad place. I couldn't get out." Sammy's distress grew. "I couldn't get out!"

"Shhhhhh," whispered Abby. "You don't have to talk about it. It's alright."

Abby glanced at the bedside clock. It read 2:11am. Although still trembling,

Sammy was starting to relax. She sniffed and Abby pulled a tissue from the bedside table and passed it to her and she blew her nose into it, hard. Abby knew that Sammy wasn't going to settle back down right away. "Do you want to get a drink?" she asked. Sammy nodded. "And biscuits?" asked Abby. Sammy nodded again and there was the faint suggestion of a smile. Abby reached for another tissue and wiped the tears (and snot) from Sammy's face. Abby stood and, with some effort, picked Sammy up.

Sammy wrapped her arms around her mother's neck and her legs around her waist. Abby carried Sammy across the landing of their first-floor flat, turning the lights on as she went, making the physical world more solid; pushing Sammy's nightmare further away.

"Do you want to help me make a hot chocolate, Sam?" asked Abby.

Sammy shook her head. "Can I have some milk, Mummy? And biscuits?"

Abby sat Sammy on the kitchen table while she poured them both a glass of milk. She grabbed a packet of biscuits from the cupboard. "Come on, Sam," she said, "let's go and snuggle up on the sofa."

They sat for a while in silence, drinking milk and munching biscuits. After a while, Abby asked, "Are you alright now?"

A darkness flashed across Sammy's face, but she nodded and smiled. "Can we stay up a bit longer, please?" Abby kissed Sammy's nose. "Sure. Why not? You still a bit scared?"

Sammy nodded. "I know it's not real, but it *felt* real," she offered. There was a pause and Abby let her daughter continue.

"I was stuck in a dark place. It was cold and wet. And small." Sammy was struggling to remember now, her forehead furrowed. "I was me and I was someone else, both at the same time. Like I could see this other girl, but she was me. Sorry, Mummy, I know it sounds silly."

"It's a dream," said Abby. "Silly things happen in dreams, but they seem real at the time." Sammy nodded but didn't look convinced.

"I was scared," she continued. "I tried to climb out but I couldn't. And there was someone else there. But I couldn't see him. But I knew it was a boy because –"

Sammy halted, partly because she didn't quite understand how she knew it was a boy, but partly because she felt that her – *the other her* – and the boy had wanted to do *something dirty*. Something she didn't want to tell her mother about. She flushed and Abby let it pass.

"It was a horrible place." Abby felt Sammy shudder. She gave her a comforting squeeze. "But I knew it was going to get badder – really bad, I mean. I think there was *someone else* there, not just the boy. Someone *very bad*. I don't think the other me knew about it, but me, the me-me, I did. It scared me too. A lot." Sammy burst into tears again and Abby pulled her closer, gently rocking her back and forth.

It disturbed Abby that Sammy, who could normally communicate with a maturity way beyond her years, was talking just like any other eight-year-old.

"It's OK darling," said Abby, "It's OK." Even as she said it, Abby knew that she was lying and wondered if Sammy could tell. She'd woken, terrified, from exactly the same awful dream, just seconds before Sammy had cried out. But unlike Sammy, Abby knew what the dream meant – and that scared her more than the dream itself.

She cradled Sammy for almost half an hour, until her sobbing ceased and she had drifted off to sleep. Then she carefully picked her up.

She passed Sammy's bedroom and took her into her own, placing her gently between the sheets of the double bed. She watched for a few moments as Sammy settled down. She was sleeping deeply: a child's gift for self-preservation that so often eluded adults.

Abby quietly went back to Sammy's room and grabbed her favourite stuffed doll, Lady Mango (named by Sammy, who insisted that was all the doll ever ate – and that she *was* a *real* lady).

Once she was sure that Sammy wasn't going to wake, she took her mobile phone from the bedside cabinet and left the room, pulling the door almost, but not quite, closed. She went downstairs and through to the tiny sitting room behind her shop. Sitting on the small couch, she took a deep breath and pressed the first number on her speed-dial list.

A groggy voice answered. "Hello?"

"Helen, it's Ab."

"Abby? It's three-thirty. Please tell me you're not just feeling randy. Is everything alright?"

Abby hesitated; she didn't know how to answer.

"Ab, you OK?"

"No, I'm not. Can you come over? I really need to talk. Me and Sam, we – we both just had the same dream." Abby burst into tears. "My God, Helen, I think – I think it's happening."

2

It had been light for less than an hour when Becca woke, with only a vague recollection of having slept. In the depths of the well, the air seemed colder than the day before. She was chilled to the core; even in her sleep she'd been restless and shivery.

Her eyes were much more accustomed to the darkness in the well. Her bottom felt numb and her legs stiff. She shifted her weight a little.

Beside her, Matt was quiet and still. Their hands were still together, though hers were so numb that she couldn't feel anything properly. She moved her fingers.

They felt stiff, bloated and unfeeling; Matt's hands were cold and unyielding.

She turned to look at him, a warning sounding inside her. His head hung down, unmoving, but he looked peaceful. Even though her vision was improved, his face was still little more than a series of shadows. She looked more carefully, reaching over with her other hand to brush the hair from his eyes. Then she realised what was missing: the gross watery dragging sound of his laboured breathing.

She squeezed his hand, fear rising within her. "Matt?" Nothing: although her own fingers were almost without sensation, she could sense that the way his flesh yielded against her squeeze somehow wasn't right.

In one quick movement she squatted beside him and, with difficulty, untangled her fingers from his. They were uncooperative in a way that was somehow different from the response of a sleeping hand. She shook him. "Matt!" His head flopped to one side. She put a hand to his cheek, but her own skin was so cold it was hard to discern whether his face was warm or cold.

The panic within her was like a physical pain that took away her breath. Tears were flowing from her eyes. Instinctively, she brushed them away, but her hands, dirty and soaked, made her face wetter than ever.

Her voice was desperate, somewhere between a scream and a gasp. "Matt!" She shook him again, hard. It was like shaking a doll. His reluctant, wobbly movements were just the offbeat echoes of her own frantic shaking.

Her screams descended into broken sobs, repeating his name over and over. An overwhelming mixture of emotions hit her. Loss, grief, love and especially guilt: guilt for being asleep when he died; guilt for pulling him down into the well; guilt for stepping up onto the well wall for a kiss. Just a kiss: that was all she'd intended.

Becca curled up next to Matt and cried as she had never cried before.

3

Outside, the tiny town of Bankside stirred into life. It was still early, but the noise of the occasional passing car reminded Abby that, before long, she'd need to open her shop. Saturday was usually busier than a weekday and it was trade that Abby couldn't afford to miss.

The sunlight, streaming in between the protective steel bars of the shop's back room window, promised a warm day ahead. She'd had the bars installed after a break-in six years ago. Nothing had been taken; why would it be? Abby's shop, *No Stone Unturned*, sold only homeopathic medicines, natural remedies and new-age stuff such as rocks, crystals and folklore books. Whoever broke in was probably expecting to find some kind of drugs, but they'd have been better off burgling the chemist down the road. They'd left the place a mess, yet hadn't woken Abby, who had been sleeping upstairs with Sammy. Just two at the time, Sammy had still been sharing Abby's bed. Crime was almost unheard of in the small town, and it shook up Abby enough to have the bars and an alarm installed. Hers was still probably one of the few businesses to have done so.

"More coffee?" asked Helen.

Abby nodded. "Yeah, please."

They'd be more comfortable in the flat upstairs, but they didn't want to wake Sammy. Hopefully, when Sammy woke, her dream would have faded. But Abby doubted it.

Abby had slowly retold the dream, visibly shaking, while Helen listened intently. Then she'd described how Sammy had woken, petrified, from the same dream.

Helen was a good listener; it was one of the things that Abby loved about her. She had held Abby's hand gently, her rich, black skin starkly contrasted against Abby's pale hand. Helen let Abby speak without interruption and only occasionally questioned her.

The kettle boiled and Helen poured the hot water into two cups. It was their third cup of the night.

The silence between them was as comforting as any hug. They'd been friends for five years; lovers for not much less. Only their equally independent natures (and, of course, the small minds of a small town) stopped them from living together. Abby had slept with only one man – and that was for the sole purpose of having a child. It had been her foretold destiny; something she'd never questioned. Until they'd met, Helen had only ever had relationships with men – and had not once been attracted to women. Both believed that their meeting and subsequent love was, if not fate, then not chance either; they enjoyed an intense closeness to which few relationships could even aspire.

Helen taught history at the local school, but since she taught the older children, her relationship with Abby shouldn't be an issue for Sammy until she moved up to year seven. (Not that the school could officially say anything: Abby was more worried about the inevitable teasing of other children. Helen wasn't even worried about that – and had once joked that more people would raise their eyebrows because Abby's partner was black than because she was a woman.)

Helen sat down beside Abby and offered her a steaming mug. "You OK, Ab?"

Abby nodded. "I think so. But knowing about something, expecting something, it's different. Different from when it happens. You can only prepare so much. I don't know how strong I can be."

Helen pushed Abby's blonde hair back behind her ears and kissed her. "Strong enough," she said. Her voice was confident and knowing.

Abby smiled. "Easy for you to say," she said, without malice.

"All we can do is wait," said Helen. "We might find out today who's missing, though we might not. But we will on Monday, once I'm in school. Until then, we'll just have to listen out. Other than that, what can we do? Carry on as normal."

Abby nodded.

"It won't be easy. But I'm here for you," said Helen. "I should move in for a bit." It wasn't a question and Abby didn't offer any resistance. It made sense.

"This will be hard for Sammy," said Abby. "She won't understand; she's not ready to understand. The dreams will probably get worse." Abby held back a tear.

"Hey, we don't know that." Helen put down her coffee on the table and wrapped her arm around Abby. "And we don't know how long this will last. It could be over tomorrow."

"It might, but I don't think so," said Abby, shaking her head. "That's not what it – what it – *felt* like. It's going to be agony working in the shop today, just waiting."

"Look Ab," said Helen firmly. "This is your moment. You have to be strong. You know what depends on it. And you have to pull through, for Sammy. You can't change any of those things – but you can change what could happen. You. Only you. But I'll help as much as I can."

Abby was grateful for Helen's strength and clear thinking; she drew upon it and calmed herself. "We need to be sure," she said. "I'm going up there."

"Oh, no." Helen smiled. "Think about it. It's Saturday. Summer. Odds are there will be people at the quarry pool. You'd be seen – and that won't look great later, will it?"

Abby nodded. "Fair enough. I'll go tonight. Late."

"Engage brain, Ab. You need to be here tonight. You have to be here for Sammy. *I'll go.*"

Abby started to object, but Helen silenced her. "I know what you're going to say, but this is something I *can* do. Just a quick look, that's all we need. I'll go well after midnight. I'll take my phone. I'll call you once I'm done and then come straight back here." She squeezed Abby's shoulders.

Abby felt both unnerved and unhappy. "I think I might be safe there, Helen. But I'm sure you're not."

"I'm not sure anyone's safe there, but I'll be safe enough." Helen's voice was, as always, calm and confident but in truth, Helen was worried. Something that had been told to her as a story, as little more than a folk tale, was now coming true. *I accepted it as a story*, thought Helen. *Because I never thought it would come true. But if it is true...* She shuddered. Parts of the story deeply unnerved her, however unruffled she might be on the outside.

"I don't know –" started Abby.

"The fact is, you need to be here. You know it. Let me do this. I can do this." Helen paused. "You *need* to be with Sammy and you know it." Her words were direct, but contained no ill feeling. Abby and Helen had only once come close to arguing; they resolved differences with honest discussion.

They held each other's gaze for almost a minute and, not for the first time, Abby thought that Helen's deep brown eyes were (with the exception of Sammy, of course) the most beautiful thing she'd ever seen.

Finally, Abby smiled. It was a warm, grateful smile, radiating something she felt deep within her. "I love you," she said.

Helen smiled back and kissed her. "I know it."

The door creaked. Standing there, Lady Mango in hand, was Sammy. Her eyes were bleary and unfocused.

Abby and Helen drew apart, but not because they'd been caught out. They didn't hide their relationship from Sammy. Indeed, they only kept one secret from her – although that was a biggie. It was something they had hoped to keep secret for a few more years, but the next few days would determine that.

"Hey Sams," said Abby, opening her arms wide.

Sammy wandered over to her mother and sat on her knee. "Hi Mummy," said Sammy. "Hi Helen."

"Hi baby," said Helen, ruffling Sammy's already tousled hair. "How are you feeling?"

"Fine," she said. "What's for breakfast?"

4

"Come on, sleepyhead."

Jim screwed up his eyes against the late morning sun and groaned. "What time is it?"

"It's after ten. Come on, let's get this day on the road. We've missed breakfast, we'll have to get some out."

Jim sat up, yawning and rubbing his eyes. He was surprised to find that he didn't have a hangover. He didn't feel terribly bright, though.

Already showered and dressed, Sarah was partway through putting on her make-up.

"How long have you been up?" he asked.

"Not long. Less than an hour," said Sarah, concentrating on applying her mascara. "I don't want to sleep the weekend away and – well, I was thinking about the kids."

Jim sighed to himself. He'd never really had much of a problem leaving Matt alone. Matt and he didn't exactly spend much time together anyway. Before they moved to Bankside, Matt would either be out with his mates or in his bedroom; since they moved, he'd not really made many new friends so he stayed mostly in his bedroom, talking to his old mates on the Internet – although he had started to spend more time with Becca. Jim wouldn't have seen much more of Matt if he'd been in the same house all weekend. If either he or Sarah should be worried about one of their kids, it should be him – which was why Jim couldn't understand quite how much Sarah fretted about Becca. Matt didn't really care what his father thought, but Becca wouldn't knowingly do anything to upset Sarah.

When Sarah's protective nature first collided with Jim's more easy-going temperament, it had created some conflict in their relationship. Given Matt's bumpy past and often-abrasive nature, Sarah couldn't understand why Jim didn't mind leaving him on his own. Before they moved in together, Jim would mostly stay at Sarah's house rather than she at his. It made some sense: Matt was the older child; theoretically old enough to be left alone. (Sure, Jim would come home to an untidy house, but what do you expect from a teenage boy?) Yet when Sarah came to stay at Jim's house she always brought Becca; Sarah never left her at home or with friends. For months, they *never* had any time alone. And, the first time the two of them had gone away alone, it had been a disaster. Becca had arranged that two of her friends stay with her, but Sarah had either called her or sent a text every hour or so. Over the course of a couple of days, Jim had grown more annoyed – after all, if she couldn't forget Becca for thirty minutes, then they weren't *really* alone. *The children are important*, he had thought, *but so is our relationship.* They'd had a massive row, after which Sarah *had* accepted that perhaps she needed to give Becca a bit more space. That said, she had stood firm about one thing: she was a worrier by nature. OK, maybe she needed to cut loose a bit, but if Jim didn't like her nature, then tough. At forty-three, she wasn't going to change that much. Jim accepted that: one or two calls a day was fine, although he personally would still only call Matt once a day (or even every couple of days) at the most.

This was their first weekend away alone since then. Jim knew that Sarah would be missing Becca, even though it was less than a day since they'd spoken.

Jim got out of bed and kissed her on the forehead. "Why don't you give Becca a quick call?"

Sarah seemed relieved. "Should I?"

"Why not? You know you'll be thinking about it until you do."

Sarah looked at Jim, to see if he was annoyed. If he was, he wasn't showing it. She gave him a kiss back. "OK. And you," she said, picking up a towel and throwing it at him, "go get a shower."

While Jim showered, Sarah called Becca's mobile – which went straight through to her voicemail. It was good to hear her daughter's chirpy voice. "Hi, it's Becca. Not here – so leave a message!"

"Hi Becca," said Sarah, "it's Mum. Just calling to see if you're OK. I'll call again later. Love you." She glanced at her watch; it was ten-forty.

Sarah carried on getting ready until Jim came out of the shower, rubbing himself dry. *Forty-six and in darned good shape*, thought Sarah. "Did you speak to Becca?" he asked.

"No. I just got her answer phone."

Jim glanced at the clock. "Well, it's ten to eleven, Becca's probably still in bed or, if she's up, she'll have gone swimming – and Matt *will* be in bed until way after twelve. We can call them later."

Sarah knew Jim was right.

"OK. Now get dressed and let's get out – let's see if you can show a lady a good time when you're *out* of bed."

<h1 style="text-align:center">5</h1>

Hannah finished brushing her short blonde hair. She placed her hairbrush back on the dressing table, which was a jumble of make-up and cheap jewellery.

Although her phone had been silent for the last hour, she checked it again. There was still nothing from Becca.

Hannah was still cross, but considerably calmer than she'd been last night. The more she thought about it, the more Becca's silence nagged at her. While it was true that she'd seen progressively less of Becca for the last few months, Becca had never totally ignored her before.

When she'd woken up, it had crossed Hannah's mind that perhaps Becca's phone was simply switched off or was charging, but as the morning had crawled by, she'd begun to doubt the idea. As with all teenagers, Becca and her phone were seldom separated. On top of that, she'd not been on the Internet last night or this morning.

Ordinarily, Becca might have been out: she often went swimming on Saturday morning. But not this weekend, since she was grounded. (Now and again, Hannah had gone swimming with Becca – and while she enjoyed it, she wasn't obsessed like her friend.)

Until Jim and Matt moved in, Hannah and Becca had been good friends, in fact, in Hannah's view, BFF – best friends forever. Hanging out with Nisha, Susie, Kate, Jessi and Elle was OK, but Hannah really missed Becca.

Hannah's phone chimed as a text message came in. She picked up her phone quickly, hoping that the message was from Becca. She sighed, disappointed. It was from Nisha.

GOIN 2 TOWN 2DAY? BORED.

Hannah tapped in a quick reply. **CAN DO. WHEN?**

Almost instantly, Nisha came back with: **HALF AN HOUR. KATE + ELLE COMIN. CALL FOR U IN 20?**

Hannah almost replied with a yes, then changed her mind.

GOT SOMETHIN 2 DO FIRST. C U L8R. TEXT U IN AN HOUR.

She quickly pulled on her trainers, ran downstairs and popped her head around the kitchen door. "Mum," she said. "I'm just going round to see Becca."

6

Although Becca had ceased crying, she felt more desperate than ever.

She'd wept for over an hour, her sobs and wails interspersed with angry screams. Several times she'd thought she was cried out; that she'd run dry and it wasn't possible to cry any more – but then she'd simply start crying again. The anguish was like a physical pain, as if a multi-bladed knife was twisting inside her. It was so all-enveloping that it even blotted out the cold, thirst, hunger and discomfort.

But eventually, she *had* stopped crying – or at least, she had stopped crying continually. Every now and then she broke down again. It seemed that almost any thought was enough to set her off.

As the morning wore on, she started to regain something of her composure. The reality of her situation became clearer.

Her recurring thought was that it was entirely possible that she wouldn't get out of the well alive. Each time this unwanted idea surfaced, she worked as hard as possible to push it away – but there was no denying that things looked very grim.

There was only one way out: up. Yet she'd tried that and only got around halfway – and it was one of the hardest things she'd ever done.

She had very little to eat or drink. She had no way of signalling for help. The water in the well was rank and cold. As a keen swimmer, she knew something of the danger of staying in cold water for a long time; although the water was far from freezing, it was cold enough to keep her body temperature well below normal.

But all of those physical things, the practicalities, she felt she could cope with. What was harder – *much* harder – was the way in which being in the well was messing with her head. She'd been down the well for less than a day and was already struggling to keep track of time. With nothing to do except think, minutes dragged terribly. The reality of her situation was a tedium that gave her little to do but wrestle with her growing fears. The well seemed to get smaller by the hour. The isolation was awful. Few sounds came from above, no matter how quiet she was or how hard she listened – and yet, for all she knew, there could be people playing in the quarry pool just a hundred yards or so away.

Strangely, she was now even starting to fear being rescued – because she'd have to explain what had happened, why they fell in and when Matt had died. She'd have to give accounts, probably over and over, of things she didn't even want to think about.

Becca couldn't comprehend that Matt was dead. Just a few hours ago he had held her, kissed her. All that warmth was now gone. Three times she'd gone back to *his body*; touched him; shaken him. She'd never seen a dead body and it seemed curious to her that in death, Matt was little different from in life. He didn't look peaceful or at rest, but he didn't look *dead* either. Becca fluctuated between desperately wanting to hold him and not wanting to touch him at all.

Get a grip, Becca thought, *or you'll go bonkers.*

Deal with the practicalities. She decided to again take stock of her meagre belongings. She pulled out the lighter and flipped it on, her eyes squinting in the sudden light. Becca made an effort not to look at Matt, but found it impossible. She determined that Matt's body was just another practicality that she'd have to deal with. She knelt beside him and kissed him kindly on the forehead. His skin was stone cold against her lips, but the act was surprisingly rewarding. "I'm sorry," she said. It was a genuine apology, not an expression of self-pity. Her tears flowed again, but she stopped herself from losing control.

She stood up and raised the lighter, locating the mobile phones. She found hers and pressed the on button, holding her breath. The screen lit briefly and then died. After that, no matter how many times she pressed it, the phone remained dark. Matt's phone was as dead as ever. She thought about this. *They should dry out.*

With some difficulty, holding the lighter in one hand, she managed to pop the battery out of Matt's phone. She placed both Matt's phone and its battery back in the gap in the wall and did the same with her phone. *It will help them to dry out*, she hoped. Her towel and jumper were still damp; truth be told, more than damp. She couldn't use those to dry the phones. *It's damp down here*, she realised. *It's going to take things much longer to dry.*

The iPod still worked and listening to music would pass some time – but sitting next to Matt, listening to *Foo Fighters*, didn't seem right.

Although it had been gnawing at her all morning, she hadn't admitted to herself that she was either hungry or thirsty, but once her eyes rested on the water, her stomach groaned. She ran her tongue over her lips: they were rough and parched. *Crisps, chocolate, an apple, fizzy orange and water. Things could be far worse*, she decided. Normally, they'd have come home with everything eaten. She glanced at Matt and realised that she couldn't yet bring herself to eat – but she *needed* a drink. She pulled down the water bottle and found that she couldn't open it with one hand, so she flipped the lighter off and put it back into her shirt pocket. It felt hot against her skin. She opened the water bottle and took a careful mouthful, swilling it around her mouth before swallowing it. It tasted cold and delicious. She shook the bottle. There wasn't much in it. Becca had no idea how much water someone had to drink each day to stay alive, but she was sure it was more than a mouthful. She took another drink, but was careful to take less this time.

That'll have to do, she thought. She replaced the cap and fumbled around to locate the gap from where she had taken the bottle, but couldn't find it. Frustrated, she flipped the lighter on again.

From above came a sudden, loud, fluttering sound. Startled, Becca dropped the bottle into the water, her heart pounding. *Shit! If the cap had been off* –

She fished the bottle out of the water and looked up. The bird was back, silhouetted against the blue sky. It cawed, forcefully.

"Go away!" she screamed. The bird didn't even flinch.

She placed the bottle back into the gap and flipped the lighter off. She was somehow certain that the crow, rook – or whatever the hell it was – was the same bird. The bird hopped around the wall, doing almost a full circuit of the well. It cawed again, louder than ever.

Becca's instinct was to shout at it, swear at it or throw something at it. All equally pointless, she decided.

It's less than thirty feet above me, she thought, bitterly, *yet it's free and I'm trapped.* Becca clenched her teeth together and closed her eyes. The bird cawed again. *Just fuck off,* she thought – but it didn't. The bird stayed, hopping around, occasionally fluttering its wings and squawking regularly.

All the while, Becca grew more and more disconcerted.

After perhaps half an hour (or an hour – Becca honestly couldn't tell) the bird left, with a boisterous flutter of wings.

The silence that followed was an empty void that left Becca alone, to continually relive the previous day and brood on her darkest fears.

7

Unable to push the image of Becca's youthful body from his thoughts, Tom Randle had barely slept. The combination of photographs and the recently acquired scrunchie had been a powerful one. His orgasm had been both rapid and intense; yet it left him wanting. Afterwards he lay alone, gloriously spent but restless and brooding.

Eventually, he gave up the idea of sleep. He sat alone, nursing a cup of hot tea, flicking through the albums of Becca's photos. Like his other favourites, Becca had originally just been one of many girls he'd photographed indiscriminately – but once she'd caught his eye he'd enjoyed watching her develop. In another year she'd mature beyond his tastes, but right now she was perfect.

He stroked a recent photograph, taken at the inter-school swimming competition. It had been reproduced in the Bankside Reporter and was one of many he'd had published. Via the newspaper, Becca's mother had asked for a print – which he'd gladly supplied. Another connection: no matter how tenuous the link, it always excited him. Becca had been in the newspaper several times. (It was how he first found out her name: Rebecca Beverley Richards. Eventually, after months of eavesdropping, he discovered that people only ever called her Becca.)

He only took pictures; he was *just looking*. But he'd watched so many girls grow and slip beyond his reach. *Enough was enough,* he thought. He lifted the scrunchie to his nose and inhaled. It could be his imagination, but it seemed he could smell *her*. He desperately wanted to touch her; wanted to get to her before *the boy* did.

It wouldn't be too difficult, he decided. He knew where she lived, because he'd followed her home several times. From the field behind her house, he'd watched her study or play in her bedroom.

Randle knew he may not get away with it, but the fear of capture made it all the more arousing. *And I've got fuck all to lose,* he thought. *It's a toss-up between perhaps another decade of frustrated contemplation, or, for once, perhaps only once, the unbelievable sensation of touching such youthful skin.* Of course, hers wouldn't be a willing body – not in the way it would if he were *the boy*. Yet that might somehow make it all the easier: a pleading, distressed vessel on which to vent his years of longing, hatred and resentment.

I'll have to move quickly, he realised, *to beat the boy.*

With a great deal of reluctance, Randle put away his photographs and the scrunchie and got on with the day. A shower, breakfast and then shopping – his normal Saturday.

He stopped around the supermarket to chat with parents who he saw every day at the school; smiled at their children; sometimes fondly ruffled their hair. The only real deviation from his usual routine was to add some washing line, duct tape, heavy-duty bin bags and an especially sharp kitchen knife to his shopping.

On his way home, he stopped into Arthur's flat.

Randle didn't know Arthur's last name: he was just someone he'd met at the gym. They'd talked for two reasons: first, because they were the only two people in their sixties who frequented the gym and second, because they lived on the same estate. Randle didn't especially like Arthur, but he didn't dislike him either. Arthur was just someone he saw, talked to and forgot about for the next few days until he saw him again. Arthur had gone to stay with his son, who lived in Devon, for a few weeks and he'd asked Randle to look in on his flat every now and again. It was no trouble – there were no plants to water or pets to feed. All he had to do was clear the post and newspapers from the doormat, then take a quick look around to make sure that everything was secure.

After lunch, Randle took a stroll over to Becca's house, conscious as ever of his slightly stiff, limping gait. He took his camera. People around the town were used to seeing him with it, and the telephoto lens could be as useful – and less suspicious – than binoculars.

He walked all the way past the house, studying it carefully from the corner of his eye. There was only one car on the drive, which Randle recognised as the mother's. Becca mostly walked to and from school; when she didn't it was usually, though not always, her mother who brought her. Two bottles of milk were on the doorstep, despite being early afternoon. The curtains were open. *It's all about the detail*, his sergeant used to tell him. *Take in the detail; assess the situation.* The uncollected milk bottles told him that no one was in – and possibly hadn't been all night. The lone car told him that the family were probably all out together.

At the end of Lincoln Street, he turned right onto the main road and followed it for a few hundred yards until he reached the path that cut behind the housing estate.

In the field, a few children were playing and a couple were walking their dog. He waved to the children and they waved back. He walked slowly, as close to the back of the house as he could. Again, the curtains were open. The house looked empty.

Randle walked around the field, enjoying the sun, contemplating taking a closer look at the house. When he was sure no one was looking, he raised his camera to his eye and focused. The lens hunted from room to room, but he couldn't see any movement. He watched for around ten minutes before putting the lens cap back on and continuing around the field.

It might be difficult to get Becca alone, he realised. She hung around with *that boy* a lot or she was with her mother. He needed to know more about her routine. *It would mean taking a few risks*, he realised, deciding to approach the house. If challenged, he'd already prepared a response: he'd brought Becca's scrunchie. He'd seen her drop it, but because of his leg he hadn't been quick enough to follow her with it. He happened to be walking this way anyway, so it had been no trouble to drop it off. As an excuse it was far too lame to bear scrutiny, he knew, but might be just about good enough coming from an old fart like good old fucking Tom. *And,* he thought, *it was better than nothing. Just.*

Randle made his way back to the main road and then turned left, back into Lincoln Street. As it had been before, the street was virtually empty, just the odd car passing now and then. He slowed his pace slightly before casually walking up the short tarmac driveway. He half-paused, touching the bonnet of the small car: cold. His heart was racing, but outside he was calm. He reached the front door, adjusting his glasses while he gathered his thoughts. He pushed the bell and heard it ring around the house.

He waited for an agonising ten seconds, counting each one off in his head to make sure he didn't rush. There wasn't a sound in the house. *No dog, good.* He rang the bell again, and again there was no response. *No one home.*

Randle looked around. He couldn't see anyone on the street or looking from the windows of the houses close by. He walked down the side of the house, into the back garden, knowing that he was now crossing a line where his story wouldn't hold up.

He wasn't looking for something specific, just anything that would tell him a little more about Becca – especially how, when, he might get her alone.

The French windows were a godsend. He could see clearly into the open-plan house. The lounge and kitchen were spotlessly tidy. The television was off. His eyes scanned, looked for anything useful. Amidst the clump of paper held to the fridge with novelty fridge magnets was an especially large and prominent note. He strained to read it in the dim interior of the house, but couldn't, even after cleaning his glasses. He looked around to the field behind him; the children were still playing and didn't seem to have noticed him. He took the lens cap off the camera and raised it up, focusing on the note. It still wasn't easy to read.

Becca/Matt – there's some money on the fireplace. Don't get takeaways for every meal! Call me if you need anything. Have a nice weekend. See you Sunday. Mum/Sarah xx

He lowered the camera, taking in the information.

The one car meant that the parents were away. The unmoved milk, and the unanswered doorbell, meant that the kids had stayed out – at a party or with friends probably. Still, it created opportunities. *See you Sunday*, the note had read.

Maybe another twenty-four hours.

A ginger cat jumped down from the garden fence and walked up to Randle, purring. The children in the field behind him screamed wildly. Randle felt suddenly exposed. He gave the cat a gentle swipe with his boot. His instinct had been to kick it hard, but he didn't want it to make a noise. The cat padded to the other side of the garden and settled down in the longer grass. Randle walked back to the front of the house, checking the street carefully before walking up the drive.

Halfway up the drive, he almost froze. Turning the corner into the street was one of Becca's friends – the one with the short blonde hair. He briefly considered retreating into the back garden but dismissed the idea as stupid: he'd clearly look suspicious. Instead he carried on – ignoring the approaching girl and, once he'd reached the end of the drive, walking in the opposite direction. As he turned to walk away, he stole a brief glance in her direction. She was texting on her mobile phone and didn't seem to have noticed him. He smiled.

Once he was out of sight, he backtracked behind the bushes in a neighbour's garden and took a few photographs of Hannah as she approached the house, rang the bell and waited – his telephoto lens enabling her lovely young face to fill the frame.

It would only be later that he realised that Hannah had presented him with exactly what he wanted: a lone girl. That was an opportunity, he decided, that he wouldn't miss again.

8

It all happened in a moment.

Distracted by Nisha's incoming text, Hannah half-stumbled as she rounded the corner into Lincoln Street. As she regained her balance, she noticed Randle emerging from Becca's driveway. Out of context and uniform, she didn't immediately recognise him – until she noticed his limp.

He creeps me out a bit, Becca's voice echoed in her head. If it hadn't been for that remark, Hannah probably wouldn't have thought anything of seeing the friendly old man that she and the other kids called Old Tom.

Instinctively, she lowered her head as if reading the text from her phone, carefully glancing out of the top of her eyes.

He looked over to her, ever so briefly, but then continued on his way – thankfully in the opposite direction. Hannah wasn't sure she could have even said *hello* without blushing.

Then, like a drop in the breeze, the moment passed and was gone from Hannah's mind.

Hannah gathered as much courage as she could and walked up the drive. It was bad enough having to try to sort things out with Becca, without having to worry about facing her Mum – or Jim – during a weekend where she was grounded. If either of them opened the door, she hoped she could smile sweetly enough. With a bit of luck, Becca would answer.

But, even after ringing the bell four times, no one answered.

Hannah felt deflated and puzzled. Jim's car wasn't in, so they were clearly all out. She noticed the milk bottles on the doorstep – they'd either been out all night, or had left really early. It didn't tally with what Becca had said yesterday, *but hey*, she thought, *people changed their minds all the time*.

Hannah's phone chimed as a text arrived; from Becca, Hannah hoped.

It was from Nisha.

U R TAKING AGES. WHEN U HERE? NEATS X

Hannah sighed and tapped in a quick reply. **ON MY WAY.**

She turned and left. *I'll call again later*, she thought. As she walked to the bus stop, she wondered what Becca was doing.

9

The day was perfect. Hot sun, blue skies and just enough breeze to keep the heat in check. Sarah and Jim strolled unhurriedly, hand in hand, through Bamburgh Castle and its estate. In truth, wandering around stately homes wasn't exactly Sarah's thing, but it was a passion of Jim's and pleasant enough on a day like today.

It wasn't until early afternoon, when they were sitting on the grass in the castle's grounds, eating ice cream, that Sarah called Becca. Again, her call cut straight through to the answer phone. "Hi, it's Becca. Not here – so leave a message!"

Sarah frowned, worry growing inside her. "Becca, it's Mum," she said, trying to sound concerned but not annoyed. "I've been trying to get you since yesterday. Can you call me, please? Just to let me know you're OK?"

Sarah snapped her phone closed. "No reply again. Do you think they're OK?"

"I'm sure they are," comforted Jim, leaning back to pull his mobile phone out of his trouser pocket. "I'll call Matt."

Jim tapped the speed dial and lifted the phone to his ear, listening. His brow furrowed. "Matt, it's Dad. Sarah's been trying to get hold of Becca. Is she with you? Call me back. Cheers." He pushed the red button, closing the call, pausing before dialling their home phone. After four rings, Sarah's voice answered, "Hiya. You've reached Sarah and Becca. Please leave a message if you want a call back." *We really must update that message,* thought Jim, reminded briefly that he and Matt had been resident at Sarah's home for just a few months. "Matt, Becca, it's me. We've been calling you on your mobiles but not getting through. Can you give one of us a call? Thanks."

Jim pocketed his phone and thoughtfully licked his ice cream. "Can you call any of Becca's friends, like Hannah or Kate?"

Sarah shook her head. "I don't have their numbers on my mobile," she said. "They're on the pad at home." She thought for a moment and then dialled as she spoke. "I'll call Jan," she said, "and ask her to pop around."

Janet lived next door but one to Sarah. Although not the closest of friends, they were a touch more than merely acquaintances. As neighbours, one of them would, of course, often keep an eye on the other's house at holiday times (Sarah usually fed Janet's cat if she was away). But they were also close enough to share the odd night out – or in, with a film, wine and pizza.

"Hi Jan, it's Sarah," she said, with a cheeriness she didn't feel. Two hundred miles away, Janet was more than a little surprised. "Hi Sarah. You OK?"

Sarah was relieved to be able to skip the inevitable small talk.

"Jan, would you do me a favour?" asked Sarah. "I've been trying to get hold of either Becca or Matt – and can't get a reply from either their mobiles or the house phone. Have you seen them?"

Jan suppressed a groan. Sarah had confided in her about her arguments with Jim following the first time they'd gone away together. Of course, she'd sided with Sarah, but inside she thought that Jim did have a point. Jan and her husband, Ron, didn't have children; Jan would be the first person to admit that she wasn't especially maternal, but did think that Sarah could do herself and Becca a favour if she cut loose a bit.

"Nope, not seen them," she replied. "But I think they're in – I'm sure I saw one of Becca's friends leaving the house not long ago."

"Hannah?" asked Sarah.

"I don't know her name," replied Jan, "the one with the shortish blonde hair."

"Yep, Hannah," said Sarah, feeling some relief. She'd not seen Hannah for weeks – maybe more – and had thought that she and Becca had perhaps fallen out. "Jan, would you mind popping round and just checking if they are OK? I know I'm fussing, but I'm just a bit worried because they're not answering their phones."

"No problem," said Jan. "I'll look now and give you a call straight back, OK?"

"That's great – thanks Jan."

"OK, bye."

Leaving her front door open, Jan walked down to Sarah's house.

The milk was still on the doorstep. She rang the doorbell. There was no answer, even after ringing four times and banging hard on the door. She moved to the front window and peered in. Everything was tidy. The house looked empty. She made her way around the back. Her cat, Marmalade, was sunning himself in the long grass at the bottom of the garden. "Hey Marmy," she said, "You seen anyone?" Marmalade afforded her a glance before getting back to the business of the day: sleeping.

Shielding her eyes against the sun, she pressed her face up to the French windows. There was definitely no one in.

She made her way back home, picking up the warm milk on the way. *Better to take it in than let people know no one's home*, she thought.

She put the milk into the fridge and then called Sarah, who picked up on the first ring.

"Hi Jan," said Sarah, without waiting for Jan to greet her. "Any luck?"

"Not really. There's no one home. I rang and knocked but no one answered. The house is tidy – I looked through the windows." She knew Sarah well enough to realise that she would start to panic. "I'm sure they've just gone out, Sarah."

Sarah was at a loss what to say. She didn't want to overreact, but she couldn't disguise her concern. She cursed herself for not leaving a key with Jan. "You're probably right," she said, knowing she'd failed to hide the uncertainty in her voice.

Jan decided that it wouldn't help to tell Sarah about the milk, *it would only make her more worried*. "Look Sarah," said Jan warmly. "I'll keep an eye out. When they get back – *which they will* – I'll give you a ring. If I don't see them, I'll call you later anyway, to let you know. But don't panic. They'll be fine. They'll be at one of their friend's or in town for the day. Or at the cinema, somewhere they won't have their phones on."

"OK Jan," said Sarah, unsure, but a little happier. "Call me later."

"I will. And Sarah –?"

"Yes?"

"Relax. Enjoy yourself. *They'll be fine*. OK?"

"OK. Bye."

Sarah slowly closed her phone. Jim put his arm around her shoulders and pulled her close.

"No joy?" he asked.

Sarah shook her head. She recounted what Jan had told her. "I'm sorry, I know I shouldn't be worried, but I am."

"It's OK," said Jim. "Nothing to be sorry about. They should have called or at least have their phones on. Look – they're OK. They'll have stayed over at a party, or gone to a friend's or any one of a hundred other things. They know we're away and they'll be making the most of it."

"You're right. You know I can't stop worrying. I won't relax until I hear from Becca."

"*And I said it's fine*. Look, I know we had a blow-up about this, but you don't have to pretend not to be worried. How does this sound? We'll call again later. If there's still no reply, we'll set off back tomorrow, first thing. Or earlier."

"You're sure you don't mind?"

Jim shook his head. The truth was, he was starting to get a little worried himself, but didn't want to show it. "No. Of course not." He squeezed her hand. "But trust me, they're fine."

10

The day dragged on. As each minute dragged past, Becca felt not only colder but also more miserable. The desperation penetrated her body deeper than the inescapable cold.

Becca had explored her surroundings as thoroughly as possible, but there wasn't much to discover. She worked her way round the well wall, feeling carefully with her grubby fingers and looking as closely as she could in the near-dark. She explored from the waterline up to as far as she could reach, but it told her little that she didn't already know. The well was more roughly built than she'd first thought, but not so uneven that it offered enough handholds for her to climb out. In a couple of places there were sizeable gaps between the stones, behind which she could feel packed earth.

She'd tried climbing out again. Despite her determination – and moving in slow, careful steps – she didn't even manage to get as far as she had the first time.

Handholds seemed harder to find. Her fingers trembled terribly, unable to hold her weight. Her toes kept sliding, seldom gaining a firm enough toehold on the gaps in the stones. She was much more fatigued today, she realised.

In the end, she reluctantly conceded defeat. She sat back down in the water, crushed, opposite from Matt. She wished she were braver and could continue to sit with him, but it was getting harder to think of him as a person. Whatever gave a body its life had gone – he was now just an inert carcass, too unnaturally cold and rigid to gain comfort from.

Becca's thoughts flitted like a butterfly from one regret to the next; dwelling on one for a while before moving on to another. Naturally enough, given her circumstance, this thought pattern had begun with Matt. He was dead because of her. That last kiss had intended to be light-hearted, fun, loving, but actually she'd just been plain foolish. There were bigger regrets too: for the time together they would never share; the sex that had been so close. *Matt died a virgin*, she thought, *and I probably will too.* More guilt, because she'd kept him at arm's length for so long – especially when she had wanted him as much as he had wanted her. It had been a game, a tease. She wanted him, but enjoyed keeping him waiting. Now, probably more than anything else, she wished that she'd slept with him. She guessed that plenty of girls her age had slept with their boyfriends, despite their protestations. And now – well, what would it have mattered?

From Matt, she moved her regrets to Jim. Essentially a decent (if slightly dull) bloke, he'd made her Mum happy for the first time in years. Yet she'd been standoffish, perhaps not actually rude (well, not all of the time), but holding back from accepting him. *Why? Was it just jealousy,* she thought, *because I didn't have Mum to myself any more?*

From there, the next leap was to her Mum. Not accepting Jim had made it harder for her Mum, *probably much harder.* Like the first time they'd gone away, when she'd behaved like a spoilt brat, playing on her mother's insecurities until she'd convinced her to come home. Becca hadn't planned to (or even really meant to) – it was just something she had done on autopilot, driven by a feeling from deep within her, the pain of no longer being her mother's sole love.

Finally, her thoughts settled on her father. Normally, Becca seldom thought about him. But now, bizarrely, she was regretting not seeing him for so long. That had been her choice; she remembered it clearly. *Because of what he'd done.* She'd only been nine at the time – before she had insisted on being called Becca (with two Cs, not two Ks or a C and a K) and *not* Rebecca or Becky.

Her Dad, Will, had been driving home from a night away on business when another car broadsided his, putting him in hospital. He'd been hurt – at the time, Becca didn't really know how badly, but it had been bad enough for him to be kept in intensive care for a couple of weeks.

William Richards would take months to recover, but his laptop (sadly for him) was almost undamaged, sitting as it was, in a padded case in the boot of his car. While Will was suffering his fifth day of intensive care, his ever-practical wife fired up his laptop because Stewart, Will's boss (who was deeply apologetic and offered to do it himself) needed some spreadsheets for the monthly board meeting. *No problem*, said Sarah, who quickly found the spreadsheets and launched the e-mail program to send them to Stewart. Within the last few days' unopened e-mails was one with the unambiguous subject line *Let's make it the whole weekend next time*. She wasn't prying – at least at first – but that subject line was hard to ignore. It turned out that Will hadn't been on a business trip, after all. He'd been engaged in some extra-marital recreation with someone called Maria Kennedy.

Fuming, Sarah dug deeper into his e-mails and found that Will had been seeing not one other woman, but two. They didn't appear to know about each other – and he saw one (Maria) more than the other (Olivia). Sarah hadn't had even the slightest suspicion that her husband had been cheating on her.

She immediately stopped visiting Will in hospital; in fact the only time Sarah saw her husband again was a couple of weeks later. She'd had a call to say that Will was now able to sit up on his own. She had decided that it was time to pay him what he must have thought was a strangely belated visit. It was a visit that didn't last long and turned very nasty indeed. Sarah had printed off dozens of the e-mails between Will, Maria and Olivia. She slammed them down on Will's bed and demanded, through gritted teeth, that he explain them all to a distraught Becca – who was unused to seeing her mother so angry. Will couldn't, so Sarah read a few out loud. Becca was young but not stupid: she soon realised what was going on. The whole visit lasted probably less than five minutes, but it felt like hours to Becca. She didn't know what was worse – what her Dad had done, or how her mother had dealt with it. (When she was twelve, Becca had plucked up the courage to ask why her mother had done this in front of her. Sarah had replied, *Because you needed to see the man he really was.*) Sarah had led her sobbing daughter away and, not long after, she and Becca moved to the village where Sarah had been brought up.

It was almost two years before they heard from Will. Her father wanted to see Becca and, despite what he'd done, her mother agreed. *It would be wrong*, she'd said, *for her to stop him.* Becca felt otherwise. The incident with her father had changed both Becca and her mother. Her mother became less trusting and more protective. Becca had become harder, someone who could find (and stick to) a firm resolve – even when she was clearly wrong. (*Determined*, as she would often be described in school reports. *Bloody-minded*, her mother sometimes said; something she later acknowledged as a weakness and not always a strength.) No matter how much her mother had tried, she couldn't persuade Becca to see her father. Finally, it was agreed that she'd see him 'when she was ready'. So, Becca hadn't seen him since that day in the hospital.

Now she realised how much she wanted to see him. *Not that it let him off the hook*, she thought. He was a shit. He'd not had to live with her mother afterwards: it had taken her years to get herself together properly. But, nonetheless, Becca missed him. Now, realising that she'd probably never see him again, the loss was awful to her. All, all, all her fault.

But at least I could see Dad if I wanted, she thought. Matt's mother, Christine, had died of leukaemia when Matt was twelve or thirteen. Like her own father, she was seldom referred to, so Becca hadn't built up a clear picture of her. *She's gone*, thought Becca. *Totally gone. Like Matt.* Becca realised that her own sense of loss was trivial compared to what Jim's was going to be.

Miserable, Becca got up to stretch her cramped legs. She could now see reasonably well within the dark; in fact, looking up at the sunlight hurt her eyes.

Her stomach groaned. Her lips were cracked and dry. Becca had been putting off eating and drinking to conserve what little food and drink she had. She decided that she needed something. She pulled out the lighter and found the apple and the can of orange. She knew that the water would be better, but resolved to keep it for later. She opened the can and sipped a little of the orange. It tasted delicious, but seemed to run off her numb, parched lips. She carefully ate half of the apple. With each mouthful, her stomach groaned even more – somehow making her thirst and hunger worse. She drank perhaps a quarter of the orange (it was hard to tell) and then placed the can, with the apple, back on the shelf.

She looked at her hands in the flickering light. They were grimy, but also puffy, wrinkled and prune-like, as if she'd been in the bath, but much worse.

She turned the lighter off and shook it to her ear. There seemed to be plenty of lighter fluid left, but it was hard to tell.

She waited until her eyes adjusted to the dark again, wondering what she could do – if not to get out, then at least to pass the time – with only Matt to look at. She shuddered and suppressed another tear. *For fuck's sake*, she thought, *don't they ever run dry?* She again considered listening to music on her iPod, but that still seemed way too weird a thing to do under the circumstances.

Becca tried to dismiss another uncomfortable growing feeling. She really wanted to go to the toilet again, but this time not to pee. She was holding back but knew that this was something she was going to have to do at some point soon. And there was only one place to do it. Becca couldn't think of anything more degrading – and the image that this created in her mind was enough to help her put off the inevitable. For now, at least.

The small amount of food and drink helped to restore her resolve. She wasn't, she decided, going to sit here and die. She was going to get out, whatever it took.

She relit the lighter and took Matt's bag down from the wall. She pulled out his football shirt and carefully placed it over his face. She knew that kind of thing was supposed to be respectful, but that wasn't why she'd done it. She needed to be strong and it didn't help seeing Matt's dead face all the time. She replaced the bag and turned off the lighter, dropping it back into her pocket.

One reason she'd struggled to climb out, she decided, was because of the moss covering the well walls. She felt around under the water and quickly found a flattish stone that was just a bit bigger than a pocket calculator. It fitted snugly in her hand. Slowly and with great determination, she methodically set about scraping the moss from the stones. It was hard work – the moss was difficult to remove and it was hard to see when a stone was clear; Becca had to work mostly by feeling her progress. It was going to take a long time, Becca knew, but she didn't have anything better to do.

The sure knowledge that she wouldn't be finished today didn't sit well with Becca. More than anything, she was dreading the coming night.

11

By the time Jan called Sarah, she regretted not having told her right away about the milk bottles. Although she was *fairly* sure the children were *probably* fine, it was worrying that she'd not seen any sign of them all day. Now it was night and they'd still not come home. The house was in darkness. Jan was torn – she didn't want Sarah to worry when it was likely that everything was alright, but she was getting a little anxious herself.

If I panic her, thought Jan, *she'll be down here like a shot. And chances are that by the time she gets home the kids will be back from whatever party or sleepover they couldn't be bothered to tell their parents about.*

"No, they're not home," said Jan, as casually as she could – holding back about the milk bottles – partly to keep Sarah's fear in check, but mainly because it would make her look bad.

"No signs at all?" asked Sarah.

"No," said Jan. "But honestly, I wouldn't worry. You know what's happened. You and Jim are away and they'll be up to something with their mates. The worst thing that's going to happen is their red faces when they're busted."

Sarah finished the call with Jan and rang the house again, once more getting the answer phone. She called Becca's mobile, and then Matt's, without leaving any message when their recorded voices answered.

"Jim, I'm worried," she said, firmly.

"Me too. Me too." He put his arm around her, but she didn't pull herself into him.

"I want to go home." Sarah's voice was small, that of a little girl pleading.

"I know," said Jim, reflecting. "And I know this is worrying, but I'm sure they're OK."

Sarah didn't look in any way reassured.

"I know you think I'm not being sympathetic enough," said Jim, "but you know as well as I do that we're likely to be fretting over nothing. We'll go high-tailing it back home and they'll be sat there watching a film."

Sarah folded her arms. "Well, if they're home, watching a film, I'll be happy. Right now I'm not."

Jim glanced at his watch. "Look, it's late. I'll go down to reception and check out now, and we'll leave as early as we can in the morning. How does that sound?"

To Sarah, it sounded like a cop-out, but at the same time not entirely unreasonable. But that was her logical mind speaking; her heart said that she wanted to go home, *now*, and no amount of Jim or Jan telling her that everything was alright would change that. But Jim was right about one thing: it was late. They were both tired and it was a long drive home.

Jim went downstairs. Sarah called Becca again. Once Becca's voicemail message had finished, she said, "Becks, I'm really worried. Please call me. I just need to hear from you. Love you."

She hung up and set the alarm on the phone for 7:00am. She thought again and changed it to 6:00am – and then to 5:45am. She prepared herself for bed and, when Jim came back, she was already on her side, facing away from him, pretending to be asleep. He cuddled up to her, but she didn't move. It was a long time before she slept.

12

Becca awoke from her shallow sleep with a scream, scrabbling to sit upright, her hands splashing around in the cold water.

Exhausted and aching from clearing the moss from the stones, it had been light when she had sat down to rest. *Just for a few minutes*, she had thought at the time. Despite being extremely uncomfortable in the cold water, she must have nodded off.

Becca had no idea what time it was, but it was now pitch black. She guessed that it was very late – or very early. Tired and hungry, she had to think for a few moments to work out which day it was. *Saturday*, she thought. *Only Saturday?* It felt as though she had been in the well for a week.

Every part of her body seemed to be protesting. Her fingers and arms ached from her exertions. Her stomach felt so empty it was almost as if someone had punched her. Her buttocks hurt from sitting on the stony well floor. She ran her tongue over her lips: they were rough and dry. The inescapable cold cut deep into her. Worse than any of these things, she desperately needed to move her bowels.

She looked up. Part of the moon was clearly visible, high in the clear sky.

It cast a dim but eerie light inside the well. She glanced over at Matt, a dark shape in the black.

If it's now Sunday, she thought, *I could have something to eat and drink.* Becca had been holding off eating the second half of the apple until the next day, but as she had worked, she couldn't get the image of it out of her mind. *Apple, with fizzy orange*, she mused, *although the orange would probably be flat by now.* She pushed the yearning away. *I'll wait until it's light at least.*

From above came vague noises. It was difficult to tell what they were. Trees in the breeze, birds or bats – she had no idea. Then, something truly awful: something seemed to stroke against her leg, right at the hemline of her skirt. Terrified, she jumped up, shrieking and kicking the water in panic and fear.

After thirty frenzied seconds, she realised that her feet were connecting with nothing more than empty water. Weeping, she worked to calm herself, her mind trying – without much success – to put her runaway emotions into check. *You imagined it*, she thought, without really believing it. *It could have been anything*, she reasoned, but couldn't actually think of anything that might live at the bottom of a well. She moved her feet around tentatively, testing the water. Apart from the water itself, the only things she felt were the mud and stones that lay on the floor of the well.

Just as she'd started to relax, Becca felt certain that she heard a sound from above; something more distinct – a branch snapping. She looked up again, holding her breath. Long moments passed. Becca remained tense, listening. Her chest almost hurt as her heart pounded within it. The remnants of her tears felt icy on her cheeks. The noise came again, closer, and with it, something surprising – a moving light. *A torch?*

"Hey!" Becca screamed as loud as she could. "Help! Down here, in the well!"

Her voice echoed around the well, piercingly loud.

The instant she shouted, the light vanished. She held her breath again, listening hard. A minute dragged by; it felt like an age. She strained her eyes, staring into the night sky, which seemed almost light against the dark of the well. Briefly, a dark shape appeared. Her first thought was that it was the bird, but it was too big. It was a person, Becca felt sure.

"Help me! Please, help me. I'm stuck!"

There was a brief pause; Becca didn't move and nor did the shadow above. Then came a sound that was both appalling and familiar: a rasping, loud caw. The figure above vanished and Becca felt sure she briefly heard the sound of running feet.

"Hey!" she shouted. "Don't leave me. Please!"

The bird landed on the edge of the well and cawed again, wings flapping. Worse, Becca could hear that the bird was now not alone; somewhere she could hear other birds shrieking loudly. It was deafening, but hard to tell whether there were a handful of birds, dozens – or more.

"No, no, no, no!" Becca screamed, directing her anguish upwards to the opening of the well.

The bird at the top of the well was joined by several more, landing one after the other on the circular wall.

Becca backed herself down into a sitting position, crying openly. "No," she sobbed to herself. "No. Please."

Above her, the birds cawed in an unholy chorus.

Tears streaming down her face, Becca pulled her knees tightly to her chest, cold dirty water lapping around her shaking body.

13

Scrambling up the steep bank of the quarry pool was perilous in the dark. Helen needed to see, but not be seen; so she'd covered her torch with a dark stocking to dull its glare.

She reached the top, panting hard, and was relieved to move away from the edge: it was one hell of a drop into the pool. She worked her way around the wall to where she knew there was a gap.

She climbed the wall, displacing loose stones as she went. In the quiet, her movements sounded abnormally loud. Her heart pounded, as much from fear as exertion.

As she got closer to the well, she turned off the torch and waited for her eyes to acclimatise to the dark. The moonlight was bright, casting enough of a glow to allow her to negotiate the stony ground – if she was cautious. She crept forwards carefully, but tripped and landed on her knees, arms outstretched.

Helen stayed on all fours for a minute, regaining her composure and gathering her breath. She didn't want to remain still for long – in truth, she was terrified and wanted to do what she needed to and get away as quickly as possible.

She stood again and moved towards the well. After a couple of paces, she felt something break beneath her right foot. It was too late to pull back; the sound of her foot breaking the branch dominated the night air. She stood, motionless, waiting. All she could hear was the breeze through the trees.

Helen decided she was near enough and flipped the torch on. Even covered with the stocking, it seemed to illuminate everything from yards around.

Somewhere ahead of her, a muffled voice cried, "Hey! Help! Down here, in the well!"

Panicking, Helen turned off the torch. *Shit, this is hard,* she thought. Although part of her was relieved to confirm that Abby and Sammy's dreams were indeed echoes of reality, the reality of the situation was deeply unsettling: a distressed young girl, trapped, alone in the night. Helen remained still, trying to calm herself. Behind her, the trees rustled.

Come on, she thought. *Do what you have to and go.*

Helen moved forwards to the well, knelt down and peered into the dark. It was a featureless void.

The girl's voice came again, clearer this time. The terror in her voice was desperately cutting. "Help me! Please, help me. I'm stuck!"

Helen had heard enough. "I'm so sorry," she whispered to herself.

This is so hard, she thought. *That's a real, live person down there. Not someone in a story – a young girl who's going to die if we leave her there. A child. It's killing a child. How the hell did Abby live with this? How can she have this on her conscience?*

She considered turning on the torch to look more clearly down the well, but before she could, a terrifyingly loud sound came from close behind her: the caw of a bird.

Helen scrambled to her feet, almost losing her balance. She had to go, she knew: and go now. She ran hard in the direction of the wall. Behind her, she could hear the girl shouting something, but she didn't hear what.

A multitude of birds flapped around her, squawking loudly. The tips of their wings fluttered in her hair and she instinctively covered her face with her arms. It was all she could do to not scream. They were driving her away, channelling her towards the estate wall.

She stumbled as she climbed over the breach in the wall and fell to the ground, losing her torch. She felt a sharp pain as one of the birds tried to peck her face – but instead bit deep into her arm, which was raised to protect her eyes.

"I'm going!" she cried, hunting around for her torch in the dark. Her fingers closed on it and she flipped it on. The sight of dozens of huge black shapes swooping around her was monstrous. The dull light from the torch wasn't enough, so she pulled the stocking from it, bathing the ground around her in a bright yellow light.

She was gripped with panic but knew that to give into it now would mean almost certain death – a fall into the quarry pool. *If they wanted to really hurt me, they would have,* she realised. The thought helped to calm her a little. She tried her best to disregard the birds and carefully – but quickly – made her way back down the steep, treacherous path. Once at the bottom of the hill, she realised that she'd left the birds behind her.

At the field beyond the quarry pool she let herself fall to the ground, sweating, gasping for breath and shaking with fear. *I've been tested*, she thought, *and I've failed.* It was the truth – and deeply unsettling when she considered the challenge of the days ahead.

Once she'd steadied her breathing, she pulled out her mobile phone and called

Abby, who answered instantly. "Helen?"

"Ab!" Helen shrieked.

"Helen?" There was fear in Abby's voice.

Helen halted herself. Abby would panic and feel compelled to come out here – and that would solve nothing. She took a deep breath, quietly, and tried again. "Ab, it's me."

"Are you OK?"

"I'm fine. A bit shook up. I'll tell you later."

"And –"

The word hung in the air.

"You were right. There's a girl there. She's still alive. I heard her shout. I didn't see the boy, it was too dark. But I guess he's there too."

A moment's silence. "Shit."

"Shit indeed," said Helen. *And it's our shit*, she thought. "Ab – how's Sammy?"

"I gave her something to sleep. She's been restless, but she's sleeping." Abby paused. "Helen, come on home."

"I will. I just need to get myself together. Give me a minute. Don't hang up."

The two women remained connected, though silent, for the best part of two minutes. "I'm OK now," said Helen. "I'm coming back. I love you."

"I know it," said Abby.

SUNDAY

1

The moment that the first glimmer of sunlight fell across Sarah's face, she was awake. She glanced at her watch: 4:51am. She'd slept, which surprised her, but she felt completely unrefreshed.

She reached for her phone. No texts, no missed calls and no answer phone messages. *Shit.* She swung her feet out of bed, dialling her home number. It rang four times before she heard her own recorded voice, then hung up without leaving a message. She wanted to call Jan again, but it was far too early.

Enough, she thought.

She shook Jim, probably harder than she needed to. "Jim: wake up. We're going home."

2

It was mid-morning before Becca woke, aching and tired. She'd slept only fitfully, spending the night drifting in and out of a half-sleep. She shivered; she had almost completely forgotten what it felt like to be warm.

She looked up at the sky. Clear blue: another warm day up there.

Sunday, she thought, not completely certain. *Sunday. Mum's coming home tonight. She'll call the police. She'll start looking.*

Becca's hope was half-hearted. *If she looked, it wouldn't be here. No one would look here for days.*

She stood up, stretching, her body sore, her legs tight and cramped. Water fell from her and she trembled all over, colder than ever. She rubbed her hands together but it was hard to feel them, they were so cold and numb. *And*, she thought, *swollen.* She looked at them in the dim light. They seemed puffy. She blew into them and rubbed them together, hard, until the feeling started to come back.

Hunger gnawed at her: far more than just pangs, this was a hunger which gripped her insides like a claw, twisting. Every so often, her stomach made obscene noises, like faulty plumbing. Her lips were as dry as ever.

She greedily ate the remainder of the apple, as she'd promised herself, washing it down with orange juice. Normally, she'd leave the core, but she ate it all without thinking, pips included. She drank more of the orange than she'd intended, but left perhaps a quarter of the can, replacing it on the shelf. When she'd finished, she felt no less hungry or thirsty.

She moved around as much as she could in the well, avoiding Matt's body. Her feet sloshed about and it felt as if she had small stones in her shoes. *Grit from the bottom of the well,* she thought. She leaned against the side of the well, and lifted one leg up, slipping her shoe off with some effort. Her socks were totally drenched. She swished the shoe around in the water, then did the same with her foot, rubbing the pebbles off her sock. When she replaced her shoe, she noticed that it was much harder to put back on. *My feet are swollen too,* she thought as she did the same with her other foot.

Although it made her feel a little more comfortable, it also seemed pointless. Becca didn't need a mirror to know how rough she looked. Apart from her shoulders and above, she was drenched, filthy and thoroughly cold. Her clothes clung uncomfortably to her skin. She rubbed her hands through her matted, straggly hair.

A distant, droning noise came from above. She looked up, squinting at the bright sky. A small plane came briefly into view, high in the sky. Within moments it was gone; the sound of its engines faded a minute or so later.

The world keeps going, she thought. *Everything's normal out there, carrying on, just a few feet away. No one knows I'm here.*

The certainty that she would slowly die here enveloped her like a constricting snake that was now starting to tighten its death grip.

With some effort, she pushed the dark thoughts of her inevitable fate to one side.

She flipped the cigarette lighter on and examined the results of her efforts. *Not bad,* she thought. She looked for where she'd left off, grabbed the stone from where she'd left it and set to work again.

Above her, a huge black bird fluttered loudly, landing at the top of the well. It cawed, twice.

"Screw you," she muttered underneath her breath, scraping hard.

3

Abby let Helen sleep late. She'd returned exhausted and frightened. Abby had cleaned and bandaged her arm; then they'd gone to bed and talked. It was light before Helen felt that she had unwound enough to relax and sleep. She dozed off in Abby's arms and shortly after, Abby had fallen asleep too.

Sammy had slept through the night – no surprise, since Abby had laced her bedtime drink with a mild sedative. If she could protect Sammy from the nightmares she would – but her daughter had not slept peacefully. Each time Abby had checked on Sammy, she was hot, sweating and restless, sometimes murmuring to herself.

Abby slept for just a few hours and awoke glad that it was Sunday, so she wouldn't have to open the shop. She lay next to Helen for several minutes, holding her, before quietly getting up and putting on her robe. She crept past Sammy's room; she was now soundly asleep.

She made herself some coffee and sat in the kitchen of the upstairs flat. She'd long known that something like this could happen, and knew her expected part in it. Not exactly these events, of course. Now that it was here, she felt as though she'd climbed on a roller coaster – there was no going back, no time for bad decisions. Everything from here on in counted. But what was the right thing to do? How would she know? What should Sammy be told, if anything?

I'll have to follow my heart, she decided. *I'll know at the time. And if I don't know what to do, please let me know what* NOT *to do.* Like now: she didn't know what to do, but she did know *what not to:* she shouldn't tell anyone about the girl or in any way help her. That was certainly right.

It had all seemed so easy, she thought, *when it wasn't real. Yet all I have to do is – well, nothing. Just wait. Let someone die. Someone I don't even know. Shit, can I really, really do that?*

For a fleeting moment, she thought that she could perhaps bring the end faster for the girl, as you would for a sick animal, but Abby truly didn't know if that could be the way of it. *No,* she thought. *I have to let things play out. People will start looking soon. And let's face it,* she thought, *you don't really have the stomach for that, do you?* Abby shuddered at the thought. It wouldn't be hard and no one would know: just drop a few large stones into the well, onto her, and it would be over. She shuddered again.

I can't believe I'm even considering that, she thought, disgusted with herself. *In any event, it's not my right to do it. Not unless there's absolutely no other choice.*

Outside, a car drove past. *People going about their business,* reflected Abby. *We all have our business. Sometimes we choose it and sometimes it chooses you. You just have to get on with it.* Although she had Helen and Sammy, the chances were that this business would be hers to face alone.

She let another hour pass until, feeling isolated and in need of comfort, she finished her now cold coffee and made two more mug-fulls. She took them to her bedroom, passing the still-sleeping Sammy. She put the mugs down, removed her robe and slipped in next to Helen, immediately feeling better. Helen stirred and Abby woke her with a long slow kiss.

"Hey you," Abby said, brushing Helen's hair back. "How are you feeling?"

"Better. More human. That coffee?" They sat up and Helen took the mug from Abby. She drank almost half of it in one go. "Oh, I needed that."

Helen regarded Abby and realised that something was amiss. "You OK?"

Abby shook her head. "Not really. I'm scared."

"You'll cope, I promise," said Helen. She held her hand. "I'm here for you." For a moment, Helen considered keeping her reservations to herself and then decided against it. It wasn't how their relationship worked. "I'm struggling with this, Abs," she said.

Abby looked at Helen, who lowered her eyes. "Me too, Helen. Do I look like I'm finding it easy?"

There was a pause. "I guess, yes. Easier than – well, than I would like of you. This is serious stuff, Abby."

"Don't I know it. Well, I'm not finding it easy, trust me. If it looks like I am, well, it's just because I've lived it for longer."

Helen squeezed Abby's hand.

The bedroom door opened and a sleepy Sammy half-stumbled in.

"Hey, Sams," said Abby. "Come on in."

"Hi Mummy. Hi Helen," she said.

"I had another bad dream," said Sammy, slipping between the sheets. "And you were in it, Helen. You hurt your arm. A bad bird hurt your arm." She pointed to Helen's bandage, not in the least surprised to see it covering her arm.

"See," said Sammy, "just there."

4

By the time it was nine o'clock, Sarah and Jim were over halfway home. It had taken them longer to get ready and leave than she had expected, which Sarah had found frustrating. (In truth, they were in the car and moving in under half an hour, but it seemed almost twice that to her.)

Sarah was conflicted: her thoughts flipping between her deep-rooted instinct that something was seriously wrong and the very real probability that their fears would turn out to be ungrounded. The most likely scenario was that the day would end in a series of flaming rows, between them and the kids and probably between her and Jim. *Damned if I'm right, and damned if I'm wrong*, she thought.

Jim hadn't protested about going home early and she was grateful for that. She knew he was worried too, but in her current state of mind she was finding it hard to talk to him. They'd exchanged only a few words and the atmosphere in the car was pensive, to say the least. That alone upset Sarah, because she knew it was her doing. There was no reason for this to cause antagonism between them, but Sarah couldn't help it. She was scared and annoyed and found it hard to have a conversation without snapping.

Their relationship might be relatively new, but Jim understood Sarah pretty well, and he knew that right now his best strategy was to keep quiet and stay calm. Inside, he was now almost as worried as Sarah. Try as he might, he couldn't come up with any sensible explanation of the children's silence. Possibly they'd stayed over at a friend's and both of their phone batteries had died – he mulled that one over, but couldn't make it stick. But part of him suspected (and hoped) that they'd be at home, or turn up later (after all, he and Sarah were not expected home until the evening) unaware of their parents' panic. Jim drove as quickly as he could, but – being Jim – not irresponsibly. Even on a Sunday morning, that could turn the day into a genuine disaster.

"How long before we get home?" Sarah asked, trying her best not to be curt and not entirely succeeding.

"Less than a couple of hours now, if we don't stop," replied Jim, evenly. He felt sure that neither of them had any intention of stopping.

Sarah glanced at her watch. "Do you think it's too early to call Jan?"

Jim shrugged. "I don't know. Maybe. It is a Sunday. But she probably won't mind." He wanted to add that it would be a touch more sociable to leave it until after ten, but thought better of it. He knew that Sarah would be thinking the same thing. *There's no point in waking Jan*, he thought. *We can't get home any faster, whatever she says.* He decided to keep this opinion to himself.

As she had done several times already during the journey, Sarah dialled the house and then both of the mobiles. Still no reply. She huffed, loudly; Jim let it pass. *This isn't another "I'm sure it will be all right" moment*, he thought. Any reply he could think of would almost certainly spark an argument, except the one he decided to give, "Ring Jan."

Sarah looked at him and then at her watch. "It's still too early," she said, wanting to call Jan but not wanting to take all of the responsibility.

"She'll get over it. It's important. And how many times do you look after her cat when she's away?"

That was all the confirmation Sarah needed. She dialled and waited.

Sarah needn't have worried: Janet was already awake and up. She'd not slept well, worrying about Becca and Matt. Once in the night, and once early in the morning, she'd walked around to the house but it was still empty. Janet was expecting Sarah's call and had been dreading telling her about the milk. At the time, she had thought that she was protecting Sarah – but now it seemed a stupid omission.

"I've been around twice," said Jan, aware that Sarah would be just a step or two away from total panic. "No signs of the children either time."

Jan could hear Sarah catch her breath. "Do you want me to go around again?" she asked.

"Please," replied Sarah, numbly.

"I'll call you back in a couple of minutes," said Jan. She rang off and walked around to the house, her heart heavy.

As before, the house was silent. Indeed, the whole street was quiet. She did see one person, carrying a camera. He seemed to be hanging around at the bottom of Lincoln Street. When she saw him, he smiled and adjusted his glasses, walking away in the direction of the fields behind the houses. *Probably out to photograph the birds or something*, she thought. Not having children of her own, Janet didn't recognise Tom Randle – although he did briefly strike her as being a little odd, for no reason she could quite put her finger on.

Despondent, she returned home and called Sarah. "Still nobody there," she said.

"OK, thanks for looking," said Sarah, "and sorry for calling so early on a Sunday."

"It's no problem." Janet paused. "Sarah –"

"Yes?"

"When I went around last night, I noticed that the milk was still on the doorstep." *It was only a small lie*, she decided. *No harm, no foul.*

There was only silence on the phone.

"Sarah?"

Sarah's heart had skipped a beat when Jan had mentioned the milk, but it didn't really tell them anything new. They'd already guessed that the children hadn't been home, so this shouldn't really be a surprise. But somehow, it made everything more real; more worrying.

"Thanks Jan. It looks like they've not been home – but I just wish I knew where they were."

Jan felt enormously relieved – and not a little bit guilty. "When are you back?"

"Within a couple of hours. We'll see you then."

"OK. See you then."

Sarah rang off. She told Jim about the milk; he frowned. "I just don't get it," he said. *Stuff it*, he thought, and pressed his foot harder on the accelerator, taking the car ten miles per hour over the legal limit. *Hopefully that's not enough to draw the attention of the traffic police*, he thought.

Sarah felt the car accelerate. She put her hand on Jim's and squeezed it gently.

Just thirty miles later, a traffic queue brought them to a standstill. Jim opened the car door and stood on the motorway, peering ahead.

"What is it?" asked Sarah.

"Looks like a crash up ahead," replied Jim, grimly, just about able to see blue flashing lights in the distance, ahead of the cars tailing back all the way from the accident.

"Bloody shit," said Sarah, punching the dashboard. "Can't you drive on the hard shoulder?"

"I think the accident's on there too," said Jim. "In any event, it's needed for emergency vehicles."

As if on cue, an ambulance and police car sped past them on the hard shoulder, sirens blaring.

"Just great," said Sarah, her frustration bordering on rage. "We could be here for hours."

5

By early afternoon, Becca felt exhausted – but very satisfied with her progress. As high as she could reach, and for around a third of the well's circumference, she'd cleared most of the moss from the well wall.

The work had been hard, as she had been fatigued before she began. The longer she worked, the more her arms and hands protested. Her injuries joined in to create a concert of pain that seemed to affect most of her body. Her right forearm especially hurt like hell. Her left shin and ankle grew more painful by the hour, and her head had started to throb again – a pulsating pain from which there seemed no relief.

She flipped the lighter on and examined her work briefly before flipping it off again. She was getting through the lighter fuel at one heck of a rate and was starting to worry about it running out.

She decided to rest a while and prepare herself for the climb. She pulled the water bottle down from its home and drank deeply. *Probably too much*, she thought, but she was desperately thirsty. *And, if I don't make it out of the well this time, it probably won't make any difference.*

Becca mentally flipped a coin to choose between the packet of crisps and the chocolate bar – and then decided that this wasn't something to leave to chance. She'd eat the chocolate bar, which would give her the biggest (if briefest) energy rush. *But*, she thought, *I'll wait until just before I climb.*

That left one more thing – and try as she might, she couldn't leave it any longer. She had hoped that she would have been able to wait until she'd climbed out of the well, but her lower abdomen was cramping badly. The thought of defecating into the well sickened her. It was bad enough having to sit in water in which she had peed several times – but having her own faeces floating around beside her was just too degrading to imagine. Of course, she was hoping to make it out of the well on the next climb, but if she didn't – Becca shuddered.

"Oh bollocks," she said to herself. She squatted in the water and slid her knickers down to her ankles, hating herself. Just before she let go, inspiration hit. She pulled her knickers back up (thinking, as she did so, *for whose benefit?*) and retrieved one of the supermarket carrier bags. With difficulty, she managed to empty her bowels into that. The relief was immense. When she'd finished, she washed herself with the well water and then wiped herself with one of the towels. *A regular fucking bidet*, she thought, loathing what she had done. She tied up the top of the carrier bag tightly, before putting it into Matt's bag. She almost hung the towel back where it was, but decided there was too much chance of her mixing up the clean and soiled towel, so, with some reluctance, placed it on Matt's shoulder, next to the football shirt covering his head. "Sorry, Matt," she whispered. *That*, she thought, *was not nice.*

She sat back in the water, disgusted that it was where she'd just cleaned her dirty bottom. *It's probably no worse than what was already in here*, she thought, trying to console herself.

She tried to rest and gather her strength but found it impossible to relax. She wondered what her mother and Jim were doing. They weren't due back until the evening, probably late on, so right now they would almost certainly be out enjoying themselves. The thought that they would soon be back encouraged her, though. *At least they'll start searching before long*, she thought, *even if they're not likely to look here for ages.*

The thought of seeing her mother brought her to tears again. A couple of days ago she'd considered herself a woman, but right now the one thing she wanted more than anything was to be hugged by her Mum as if she were a little girl.

She glanced over at Matt again. *If I ever get out of this*, she thought, *the first thing I'm going to do is hug Mum and tell her how much I love her. The second thing is to shag someone.* For the first time in a couple of days, she smiled to herself and wiped her eyes, spreading tears and dirt around her face.

She stood, retrieved the chocolate bar and ate it hungrily. It tasted incredibly good but was gone far too soon. Nonetheless, it gave her body the kick it needed; she quickly felt more alert and ready for the climb. She took one more swig of the water and noted that there was very little left. *I have to get out this time*, she thought. *If I don't, I won't have the energy to try again and there's not enough food and drink for me to last long here.* The thought galvanised her.

Becca stretched her hands and arms, then touched her toes to stretch her body. *Well*, she thought. *This is it.* She imagined herself coming down the steep hill at the side of the quarry pool, a filthy bedraggled urchin, while other children, playing there, looked up in astonishment. The thought actually made her hesitate; she played the scenario out in her mind. She'd only imagined being back in her mother's arms – but the reality would be a lot less pleasant: *police cars, ambulances, retrieving Matt's body, perhaps news reporters, bloody therapists, the whispered stories and teasing around school* – all of this (and probably more) would make escape as much an ordeal as imprisonment.

She almost felt reluctant to leave, but then checked herself. *At least I'd be alive*, she thought, finding her first foothold.

The work that she'd done clearing the moss did help, but not anywhere near as much as she'd hoped. The walls still didn't provide a reliable grip. The only way to hold on was to keep her fingers and toes as tense as possible, which she knew would be difficult to maintain for long.

She worked herself up the wall a little faster than before, more from desperation than confidence. Her strategy, she'd decided, was to move quickly but take brief rests when she needed.

It was tough going. Her fingers, numb from the cold, were lacking feeling, so she found it very hard to rely on what her senses were telling her. She had to press hard to feel anything, so she was probably gripping tighter than she needed.

Once fully out of the water, she also became much colder – and felt hindered by the soaked, icy clothes clinging to her shivering body.

When she had climbed about eight feet, she took her first rest, clutching the wall and avoiding looking directly up, where the sunlight would blind her. It was an enormous feat to simply remain motionless, so the value of the rest was negligible. After a couple of minutes she worked her way upwards again, her hands and feet seeking any kind of purchase on the ancient stonework.

When Becca reached roughly halfway, her fear started to overtake her resolve. Much higher, and she could really hurt herself if she slipped. Her fingers had moved on from simply trembling to almost shaking – a combination of fatigue, cold and sheer panic. She paused and chanced a glance upwards. It still seemed so far to climb. *You can do it*, Becca thought, as she often had during swimming competitions. *You have to do it. Put your head down and push on.*

But Becca was finding it virtually impossible to move much further. She was almost totally exhausted and every single part of her screamed in pain. Her unfeeling, shaking hands refused to respond to her commands. *Come on. You can do this. Slowly, just one row of stones at a time.*

She inched her way upwards, each bit of painful, hard-won progress feeling more like a defeat than a victory. She closed her eyes and gritted her teeth, trying desperately hard to muster enough strength to finish the climb.

Then she heard it. Loud and clear, from beneath her – *not above* – a woman's voice, "No you don't, *girl.*" The last word was spat out with real hate and Becca could swear that she felt long, cold fingers wrap themselves around her ankle – and pull.

Becca screamed and fell.

6

Despite the house being obviously empty, Sarah and Jim checked every room. It was exactly as they'd left it on Friday. Sarah, who had ironed on Thursday night, checked both Becca and Matt's bedroom drawers. None of the newly ironed clothes had been worn.

Sarah flipped through the household address book, found Hannah's mobile telephone number and dialled. Hannah answered almost straight away, "Becks?"

"No, it's Sarah. Have you seen Becca this weekend?"

Hannah diverted her attention away from her computer. "No. Not since school on Friday. I've called her loads of times, but got no answer. And I went to yours yesterday; there was no one there. Is everything alright?"

Sarah frowned. "I don't know. We've come back early because neither Becca nor Matt have been answering their phones. There's no one here." Sarah paused a moment and then asked, "Was there a party or anything on at the weekend? Anything Becca wouldn't have wanted to tell me about?"

Hannah sounded genuinely puzzled. *Come back early? What did that mean?* "Well, no. I thought she'd be in all weekend, with her being grounded and all."

"Grounded?"

Hannah felt herself flush. "That's what she told me on Friday. She said she'd been grounded. Wasn't she?"

"I don't think I've ever grounded Becca," said Sarah, realising too late that she was chiding Hannah. More warmly, she said, "I certainly hadn't this weekend, what with me and Jim being away, that would be pointless."

Jim looked on, baffled, only hearing Sarah's half of the conversation.

The penny had dropped for Hannah, but she kept her thoughts to herself. *No wonder she didn't want anyone around.* Part of her was annoyed that Becca hadn't confided in her. After all, when she'd snogged Gary Radcliffe and let him briefly feel her breasts in the back bedroom at Katy's party, she'd told Becca the next day. *But where is she?* wondered Hannah. *If they've got the house to themselves, why go somewhere else?* Reluctantly, Hannah offered, "Erm – she didn't say you were going away. She just said she was grounded."

Sarah was stumped. She had no reason to doubt Hannah, but what she said made no sense. "Look, Hannah – I have to go. If you hear from Becca or Matt, will you tell them to call me, right away? I'm really worried."

"Sure."

Sarah rang off, without saying goodbye. She told Jim what Hannah had said and then called another three of Becca's friends. None of them had seen her since school. Each call took her panic up a notch.

By the time she made her fifth call, to the police, she was sobbing.

7

Abby and Helen walked along the beach, linking arms, with Sammy running ahead of them. The couple drew the occasional glance, though fewer than if they'd walked hand in hand – and far fewer than had they both been men. Sometimes this might make them feel self-conscious but today neither of them either noticed or cared.

They'd decided that if they hung around Bankside, the flat or the shop, then the day would drag. Since the weather was good, and they were all in need of distraction, Abby had announced that a drive to the seaside was in order. Yet, as pleasant as the day was, neither she nor Helen could shake the feeling of dread inside them.

"This seems wrong," said Helen. "Killing time while – that poor girl's stuck. What on Earth must she be going through?"

"I don't see what else we can do," said Abby.

"Don't you?"

Abby knew what Helen meant, but shook her head. "*That* is not the answer."

"Ab, I hate the idea, too. But it would save a lot of suffering. Not to mention uncertainty. She could still get out, or be found."

Abby shrugged. "If that's what happens, then that's what happens. I don't want to *directly* become a murderer unless I have to – unless *I really have to*. And think it through. How would you do it? Drop a few stones down? And then what happens if she's found? It becomes murder – the whole place will be investigated. Your footprints are already up there. We'd probably leave DNA. Helen – it's a last resort. And even then…"

Something in Helen's eyes made Abby pause. "Hang on," said Abby. "You're not really suggesting this, are you? You're testing me – to see if I'd be prepared to do it. Oh, Helen – for heaven's sake."

"Sorry, Abby – it's just – well, as I said, I'm struggling with this. We've been together for five years. I thought I knew your values. This…"

"Helen," said Abby softly. "You *do* know me. I'm no different today than I was last week. You have to trust in that; in us."

Helen stayed silent, though she squeezed Abby's arm to show she'd not meant to offend. Abby gently took hold of Helen's hand and returned the squeeze.

"I know it's not easy," said Abby, "but the best thing we can do is just wait. And tire Sammy out. If the girl continues to survive, her dreams are probably going to get more frightening."

"They're worse for her, aren't they?"

"Much."

"Because she's younger?"

Abby hesitated. "Maybe. Or partly. But mostly just because she's *better*. To be honest, I'm an amateur. She's gifted. I don't – can't – catch a fraction of what she does."

Sammy came running back to them. "Mummy! Can I have an ice cream?"

Abby lifted her up, which wasn't anything like as easy as it had once been. "Sure, Sams. And fish and chips for lunch. How's that?"

"Yeah!" shouted a jubilant Sammy, jumping back down from her mother so that she could run ahead to the ice cream van.

They sat together on the beach, eating their ice creams, watching the seagulls fly and the children play. Sammy winced and rubbed her shoulder, as if she'd hurt it. "Ouch," she said, her discomfort evident. For a fleeting second, Abby felt a whisper of pain in her own shoulder and instinctively knew it to be a shadow of what Sammy was feeling.

"What's the matter, baby, did you fall?"

Sammy shook her head. "Not me, Mummy. The girl."

Abby and Helen looked at each other.

Helen asked, "When did she fall, Sammy? Last night?"

"No," said Sammy simply. "Just now."

8

Randle found Sunday enormously difficult. He was becoming impatient – which, he knew, could be dangerous.

He wasn't a fool: no young girl would ever surrender herself to him. And he knew that once he'd taken, he'd probably get caught. But he'd decided that it would be worth it: *better that*, he thought, *than this monotonous, celibate, sorry hamster-wheel of an existence.* But if he was going to get caught, it had better be good.

He'd lain awake much of the night, his mind skipping between fantasies. With each hour, he found himself grow more willing to be reckless. *That won't do*, he thought. Rushing meant mistakes.

Once the day got going, he welcomed falling into his Sunday routine. His two hours at the gym were especially good. *Once a soldier, always a soldier*, he thought. For his age, he was strong and could be agile – just his knee let him down. He couldn't afford to go to the more expensive health clubs in town, but the community gym was more than good enough for him. Like him, the equipment was ageing and bent out of shape, but it did the job. He kept himself to himself, working his way around the upper-body equipment and weights. Despite his lack of sleep, he worked himself much longer and harder than he would normally.

The exertion helped to calm the hunger inside of him; to balance him out. *I need to plan*, he thought, as he drove his fists into the old leather punchbag. *But I need to not let opportunities pass me by, either.*

"Whoa, granddad, easy up!"

Randle slowed his punches and looked to where the voice came from. A younger man, waiting for the bag, was smiling at him. "Leave some life in it for me!"

Randle smiled back and gave as good a thumbs up as he could in his boxing gloves. "Five minutes and I'm done," he shouted back.

He was glad that he'd kept in shape. Teenagers could be quick – and if there was one thing he couldn't do, it was to outrun someone. He'd have to move in hard and strong – and not give her the chance to run. He'd need every ounce of his strength.

9

Becca knew that she had been extremely lucky. She'd again landed on her feet and, although it had been incredibly painful, she didn't think that she had broken anything. When she had landed, she had fallen to one side, banging both her left shoulder and the side of her head sharply. Both throbbed horribly, but at least she didn't seem to be bleeding.

Becca's ankle felt cold and sore, as if icy fingers had left an impression where they'd grasped her.

She looked frantically around the well, panicking. Although she could now see more clearly, it was still a place of darkness and shadows. Sobbing, she flipped on the lighter, casting the well in a ghostly, dancing light.

Becca was sure, one hundred per cent sure, that she hadn't imagined either the voice or the hand's grip. But it was impossible. *I'm going mad*, she thought. *There's no one here, other than Matt.* Reluctantly, she went over to Matt and felt under the water for his hand. It was as cold as stone and almost as solid.

I know what I heard; I know what I felt, she thought, shaking with fear.

"Hello?" she said tentatively, her voice shaking. There was no response.

I can't have imagined it, thought Becca. *But – what's worse? Imagining it, or it really happening?* She tried to inhale deeply, to slow her runaway breathing, but couldn't quell the panic deep within her. *Get a grip*, she told herself, without success. *Deal with what's real.*

After a few minutes examining the empty well, Becca reluctantly flipped off the lighter and sat back down. *If I'm here for some time*, she thought, *I'm going to have to conserve what I have.* But in her heart, she knew the precious little she had would be unlikely to last more than another day or so. She brooded, worried that she'd imagined the voice (after all, she was tired and hungry) or, worse still, that she hadn't. She really didn't like to think about the local stories of the cottage and its well. A wave of deep dread, almost like a wind, ran over her. She shuddered, then shook her head. *Get a grip, girl,* she thought again, more firmly, the first faint sparkle of Becca's usual defiance creeping back.

Sitting in the water, head in her hands, Becca cried for the best part of fifteen minutes, unable to shake the feeling of utter failure.

She reviewed her situation. She was exhausted, cold, hungry and almost every part of her was severely sore. She had very little left to eat or drink. It could be days – at the least – before she might be found. It became all too much for her. Her tears turned to anger and she shrieked loudly, slapping the water continually with the palms of her hands. *It's not fair,* she thought.

She stood up, dripping wet, furious. *I am not going to die here,* she screamed to herself. As loud as she could, she shouted, again and again, "Help!!" With each shout, she invested more energy until, after half an hour, she was almost totally drained.

Although feeling drained and ready to sleep she pushed herself upright, deciding to check the mobile phones again – pointless though it seemed. She fumbled around and found Matt's first. She replaced its batteries and switched it on, but it remained stubbornly dead. She sighed, replaced it and then picked hers up. Astonishingly, at the first press, it lit up. She held her breath, waiting for it to die. As the seconds passed, her heart soared. *It's working,* she thought. *Holy Christ, it's working.* Tears streamed down her face; she couldn't remember ever, ever feeling so overjoyed. "Thank you, thank you," she said, to no one in particular.

NO SIGNAL, said the phone, in bright text. She waited. NO SIGNAL.

"No!" she shouted, stamping her foot like a child. "No, no, bloody hell no!"

The phone remained unchanged: NO SIGNAL. She held it as high as she could. Still, there was NO SIGNAL. She wondered if she were able to climb up the wall a little, if that might change. She doubted it. *Aren't telephone signals line-of-sight? If they are,* she thought, *I'd have to be almost at the top of the well.*

She sighed, and then wondered: *OK, if I can't climb that high, can I throw it out?*

Becca looked up to the top of the well. It was pretty high, she was very tired and she'd only have one shot – but she thought she could do it. She smiled to herself, heartened again.

She hit the button to compose a new text message. *What the hell am I going to say?* She imagined her mother, hundreds of miles away, suddenly getting the text. She'd think it was a joke. *Well, maybe at first. But when she tries to call* – Becca knew her mother well. It would probably be enough to panic her, if bloody Jim doesn't convince her otherwise. *How much should I tell her? Should I tell her about Matt?*

She decided that Jim hearing about his son's death via a text message wasn't a good idea and began tapping in the message. *Probably,* she reflected, *this is the most important message I'll ever send.*

MUM. AM REALLY SORRY. ME+MATT HAVE FALLEN IN THE WITCHS WELL NR THE QUARRY. HURT. STUCK SINCE FRI. NEED HELP. AM SERIOUS. PLSE BELIEVE ME. HELP.

Becca read it through twice. The message read like a joke, but she couldn't think of any better way of wording it.

Well, she thought, *here goes.*

Becca looked up, calculating where to throw it. *One chance.* She was only just better than average at ball games, having put most of her effort into swimming, but she could generally throw a good enough ball at rounders.

She pressed send, and threw the phone upwards, underarm, as hard as she could, desperately trying to achieve an angle shallow enough for it to exit the well but deep enough for it not to simply fall back.

The phone disappeared from sight and she heard a gentle *thud* as it hit the ground.

"Yes, yes, yes, YES!" Becca punched the air in triumph. She knew that the phone would get enough of a signal to send the message at the top of the well; it may not find the signal right away, but the text would keep trying to resend until it did.

What Becca hadn't seen was that the phone had landed hard, on its side, popping the battery out as it hit the ground. Its tiny screen went from NO SIGNAL to totally dark.

10

It took almost an hour for the police to arrive.

While they waited, Sarah and Jim telephoned more of Becca's friends, each call with the same result. As far as Jim knew, Matt hadn't really made any firm friends since they had moved to Bankside, so he had no one to call.

Then they searched the house for any kind of clues as to the children's whereabouts. There was nothing unusual, although Jim found four packets of condoms in Matt's room, tucked away at the back of the top shelf of his wardrobe in a paper bag. He wasn't shocked (although he was a little surprised that Matt could actually be so responsible) but he wasn't aware that his son had a girlfriend. Not for the first time, he felt downhearted when he compared the close nature of Sarah and Becca's relationship to his and Matt's. He wondered how it was possible that Matt had a girlfriend and he didn't know. *Because he doesn't want me to know,* thought Jim. He dismissed the condoms as irrelevant and didn't even consider telling Sarah.

When the police arrived, their measured and professional nature went a long way towards calming Sarah. They introduced themselves more informally than Jim would have expected, as Stephen Carter and Jenny Greenwood.

Jim made everyone a cup of tea, while Sarah started to answer their questions.

"And how old are the children?" Jim heard Stephen Carter ask.

"Rebecca's fourteen, fifteen in just under two months," replied Sarah. "Matt was sixteen last month." There was an almost imperceptible pause; Jim, out of eyeshot, didn't see the police officers exchange a glance. Sarah did. Her nerves already frayed, she asked tersely, "Is that a problem?"

Stephen cleared his throat. "No, of course not," he said, thinking that the children might have been a little young to be left alone. "Was anyone looking in on them?"

Sarah's hackles rose. "What exactly are you saying?" Jim was about to come in from the kitchen to help calm Sarah down, when Jenny Greenwood interjected.

"Mrs Richards," she said. "I'm sorry. We don't mean to be either insensitive or rude. We just have to ask questions. We don't know what will be relevant."

Jim brought the tea in, passed the cups around and then sat down. "I think Officer Greenwood is right, Sarah," he said. "It won't help if we can't keep calm."

Sarah took a deep breath and Jim reached over to take her hand. "The most important thing," said Jim, "is to find the kids, right?"

Sarah nodded.

"If it helps to find them, we'll do anything," added Jim.

Sarah nodded again and visibly relaxed a little.

Stephen Carter asked most of the questions and Sarah supplied most of the answers, losing her composure now and again, stammering out the answers tearfully. They went through everything that Sarah and Jim knew, little though it was – and then through most of the details again.

Stephen Carter scratched his head. "Can you think of any reason why Rebecca might lie about being grounded?"

Sarah shook her head and looked at Jim. He did the same, adding, "All I can think is that they were invited to a party or something that they didn't want some of their friends to know about. But I can't imagine why they'd do that."

Stephen smiled. "I know it doesn't seem to make any sense right now," he said, "but you'd be amazed how these kinds of mysteries have a reasonable explanation."

Sarah didn't look convinced, but nodded.

"We'd like to talk to some of Rebecca and Matt's friends," said Stephen, "if that's OK? Do you have their names and addresses?"

"Some," said Sarah. "I think Hannah and Nisha were the last to talk to her, as I said."

"Do you have their full names?"

"Some of them. Hannah's her best friend, Hannah Davis."

A look of recognition passed over Stephen's face. "I know Hannah," he said. "Her

Dad's on the force. Works with me. He's been a policeman in Bankside all his life, you must have seen him around?"

Sarah nodded, "Yes, dropping Hannah off at school, but I didn't know he was a policeman. I don't really know him."

Sarah listed Becca's other friends, although she couldn't remember how to spell Nisha's surname.

"What about Matt's friends?" asked Stephen.

"As far as I know," said Jim, "Matt's not made any real friends since we moved here." He saw Stephen's eyebrows furrow and realised that they'd missed out a key part of the story. "Matt and I only moved in with Sarah and Bec-*Rebecca* a few months ago," he said.

"Everyone calls her Becca," interjected Sarah.

"I used to live on the other side of Manchester. When Sarah and I decided to live together, this seemed a nicer place to live."

Jim looked uncomfortable and Sarah shot him a glance: *go on*.

"Er – and we thought it would be better for Matt to get away from some of his friends. He'd fallen in with a bit of a bad crowd and had started getting into trouble. Nothing serious. He's been so much better since we moved here."

"I'm sorry to have to ask," said Stephen, "but what kind of things?"

Jim flushed. "Bullying at school. Smoking. That kind of thing. He'd had a warning from school."

"You'd be amazed how many upstanding people have a bumpy start in life," said Stephen. "As you said, nothing serious, or relevant."

Stephen paused. "What about Becca's father? Are you separated?"

Sarah nodded. "Yes. Why?"

"Have you told him that Becca's missing?"

"I doubt that he'd care," said Sarah, knowing it not to be true. She softened a little. "I guess I'd better call him."

"Is there any chance that Becca would have gone to him?"

Sarah shook her head emphatically. "Not in the slightest, trust me. Neither of us have seen him for years and that's the way we both like it."

"All the same –"

Sarah sighed. "I'll call him."

The doorbell rang. Sarah ran to answer it and was dismayed to find that it wasn't Becca – and concerned to see two more policemen at the door.

Jenny Greenwood went to Sarah and led her back to the sofa and sat down beside her. "I know this is frightening," she said. "But most missing children honestly turn up pretty quickly once we start looking – especially when there's more than one missing."

"Why's that?" asked Sarah.

"Well, it's fairly rare that more than one child is abducted at the same time, especially if one of them is an older boy. From what you'd said, it sounds like Matt can handle himself. We can't rule it out, but it makes abduction less probable. Very likely we'll find them before long." Jenny paused and looked Sarah directly in the eye. "But we take this *very* seriously. That means a lot of police are going to be involved very quickly. That in itself can be frightening, but we're just doing what you'd want us to do."

Sarah nodded. Jim noted that they'd singled Sarah out as the one most in need of support.

"You'll be assigned a liaison officer," said Jenny. "Just so you're only having to talk to one person. That person will tell you whatever we find out, whenever it happens."

"Will it be you?"

"I don't know, but it's likely to be me or Officer Carter – Stephen."

"So what's the first step?" asked Jim.

Stephen, who had been talking to the other two policemen, stepped in again.

"We'll start by talking to her friends. As soon as we can organise it, we'll search along their normal route home. We'll need you to show us where you think that is. Then we'll start checking CCTV footage along the route: shops, petrol forecourts, banks, pubs – you name it. You'd be amazed how many cameras there are even in a small town like this. We'll also be requesting help from neighbouring forces – what you see here is nearly half of Bankside's finest."

Stephen saw the panic on Sarah's face.

"Don't worry, Mrs Richards. We have procedures for events like this. We may not have the manpower out in the sticks, but we can soon draft it in. That includes CID as well as bobbies. We'll set up an incident room – probably at the school or the community centre, since our station isn't big enough. And someone will be put in charge – what we call a SOCO, a scene of crime officer."

"Oh God," said Sarah, breaking down, feeling that she was now at the centre of something unstoppable and massive. Jim went to comfort her, but he was now feeling tearful himself.

"I know it sounds scary," said Jenny.

Sarah nodded, tears streaming down her face.

"What if they turn up in half an hour?" asked Jim.

"No one will be more pleased than us," said Jenny. "Honestly. But we can't assume that will happen. So we have to get moving and apply as much effort and resources as we can."

"Don't worry," said Stephen. "I'm sure we'll find them."

11

Becca sat in the chilly water, watching the daylight fading slowly above her.

She was truly worn out; every single part of her body was aching and tired. She'd also started to cough, her body shaking against the cold.

For the last few hours, she'd forced herself to stay awake, hoping to hear the mobile phone chime with an incoming text or, better still, ring. Even though she couldn't possibly answer it, it would be comforting to know that people were starting to look for them. But she'd heard nothing and now the idea was growing inside her that somehow, for some reason, her call had failed. Her elation had slowly turned to despondency, like a weight that dragged her heart down.

Now, tired beyond measure, her eyes closed and she fell into a deep and much-needed sleep, beyond caring about the possible terrors of the night ahead.

12

"Hannah?"

There was a gentle knock on the door.

"Hannah? You awake? It's Dad."

Edward Davis slowly pushed the door open, as Hannah struggled to sit up, rubbing her eyes.

"What time is it?" asked Hannah.

"Half past late," said Ed. "Sorry to wake you, Han, I thought you might still be up."

"What's up?"

Ed sat on the edge of Hannah's bed. She noticed that her Mum was standing just inside the door. Her father's breath smelt of beer, as it often did. She hoped that he wasn't in a bad mood. Although she wasn't sure if her father had hit anyone when he was drunk (since he had never hit her), he and Hannah's mother did have some epic arguments. All the same, when he had been drinking, she tried to keep out of his way.

"What's up?" she asked again, her voice now alert and worried. "Is it Grandma?"

"No, Han," said Ed. "It's Becca." He paused. "She's missing. So's Matt."

"Shi – sorry, Dad."

"It's OK. I think when your best friend goes missing it's OK to say shit."

Hannah tried not to blush. "Did Becca's Mum call?"

"Well, no," said Ed. "Sarah's called the police. Steve was on duty. He said you were one of the last people to see her."

Hannah nodded.

"Well, look. We'll need to interview you properly, tomorrow. You understand?"

Hannah nodded again. "Yes, Dad."

"But when someone goes missing, it's important to move quickly. Do you mind me asking you some questions?"

Hannah shook her head. "No." She didn't sound convinced.

"Look," reassured Ed. "I know it could be a bit embarrassing. I'm your Dad, and normally I wouldn't interview you. But I want to speed things up. It's important. And there's nothing – *nothing* – you can tell me that will make me angry. Becca and Matt are missing and we have to find them. OK, Han?"

Hannah pulled her quilt to herself, glanced down and then looked her father in the eye. "It's fine, Dad, honestly."

"Good girl. Now, when did you last see Becca?"

Hannah reiterated what she'd said to Sarah – but more thoroughly. Her father quizzed her on every sentence, gently teasing out all of the detail.

"Why do you think Becca lied to you?" asked Ed, his eyes watching her carefully.

She dropped her gaze. "Dad –"

"It's OK, Han. I don't care what it is. We just need to find them. Anything could help."

Hannah swallowed. She'd turned bright red. *Shit*, she thought, *this is not a conversation you want to have with your Dad.* Her mother came into the room and sat down beside Ed. She reached for Hannah's hand; Hannah grasped hers and held it tightly.

"Julia –" Ed began. Julia shot him a glance and he gritted his teeth. After fifteen years on the force, he was a good interrogator, but when it came to Hannah he knew (but resented) that Julia would probably get answers more readily than he.

"It's OK, Hannah," said Julia. "I know this is hard. I know you don't want to tell on your best friend. But anything you know could help. Please."

"Mum, *please.*" Hannah took a deep breath. "I think that Becca and Matt were – you know – *doing it.*"

Ed and Julia looked at each other.

"I know it sounds icky," said Hannah. "But they're not proper brother and sister."

"Hannah," said Ed, more sternly than he'd intended. "Becca's only fourteen."

"*Daadd!*"

Julia quickly tried to smooth things over. "What makes you think that Becca and Matt have been sleeping together, Han?"

Hannah explained as best she could, but the more she explained, the less likely it seemed. *It's just a random collection of little things*, she thought. But her mother and father didn't seem to doubt her.

"Hannah," said Ed, "do you think they would run away together?"

Hannah shrugged. "I dunno. It doesn't seem like Becca." She hesitated.

"And not like Matt."

Julia stroked her daughter's hand. "Don't you like Matt?"

"He's OK. Well, not really. He keeps himself to himself. I don't really know him."

"Did you notice anything different about him on Friday?" asked Ed.

"I didn't talk to him," said Hannah. "Becca was waiting for him and we left when he turned up."

"And did Becca seem normal?"

"Yes. Well, I've not seen her much since Matt moved in, like I said. But she seemed – better. She was in a good mood." Hannah hesitated. *It's not important.*

"Is there something else?" asked Ed.

"Not really. It's just that Becca was a bit freaked out by the crossing guy. She said he kept looking at her."

"Is that what she said? Her exact words?"

Hannah furrowed her brow. "I think she said he *creeped her out.* Not freaked her out: creeped her out."

"Does he creep you out?"

"Nah. He's nice. Friendly."

Ed thought that he recalled the crossing attendant from when he'd dropped Hannah at school, but wanted her to confirm it. "What does he look like?"

"Oldish. Older than you, not as old as Granddad. He's pretty big though, not fat-big, but like a fighter. He has a beard. He wears glasses and walks with a –"

As she said it, the memory came back to Hannah.

"Hannah?" asked Julia.

"A limp. He walks with a limp."

Ed nodded, remembering Randle. "Is there something else? What made you hesitate?"

"Yes. I'd forgot. Oh God. When I went round to Becca's, I think he was there."

"What was he doing, Han?"

"I don't know. Hanging around the house. I think maybe he was coming out of their drive. Maybe."

Ed was silent for a moment. "OK, Hannah, I think that's enough for tonight. You'll probably have to answer some more questions tomorrow, I'm afraid." He leaned forwards, kissed her forehead and stood up.

"Dad – will Becca be OK?"

"I hope so, Han. We're already looking for her."

Julia kissed her daughter. "If you can't sleep, come and get me," she said.

"OK, Mum."

Julia followed Ed from the room and pulled the door closed.

"This is serious, isn't it?" she asked.

"Hopefully not. Give me a few minutes, I need to call Steve."

"Ed –"

"Yep?"

"You shouldn't really have done this, should you? Talked to Hannah?"

"Not really. But it won't be a problem. I couldn't really have left it, could I?"

She hesitated. "No, I guess not. But don't do anything rash."

Ed scowled, but he knew as well as Julia that he often acted first and thought second. "I won't. But I think we should keep Hannah off school tomorrow. Maybe for a couple of days."

"Because of that man?"

"Partly. But also so she can help out without everyone knowing about it."

"Wouldn't it look more odd if she's off?"

"That's true," said Ed, reflecting. "But we won't let her walk in."

Hannah lay in her bed, listening to her parents talking, but she couldn't quite make out what they were saying. She lay awake, restless, for what seemed ages, thinking about Becca and Matt – but her principal recurring and terribly uncomfortable thought was of Randle, glancing over towards her.

13

It was late, but not yet midnight, when Becca was wrenched back from her deep sleep by the sound of a bird cawing. She shifted her position, her buttocks aching. She rubbed her stiff legs with numb hands and her shoulder protested under the effort. She looked up. Sitting on the top of the well was the big black bird.

She coughed loudly, then stretched her legs under the water and wriggled her toes to try to get her circulation going.

The bird cawed again. "Oh shut up," said Becca. "Go and bother someone else."

"He's not here to bother you," said a woman's voice in the dark. "He's here to guard you. To keep others away."

Becca leapt to her feet in absolute terror, screaming. The bird joined in with her cries, shrieking loudly. She pressed herself back against the wall of the well. Becca desperately didn't want to look in the direction of the voice, but she was drawn to it. At the other side of the well, she could see the dark shape that was Matt. Next to it was the vague shape of another person.

"Can't see me?" said the voice. "I can see you, *girl.*"

"No!" screamed Becca, shaking uncontrollably from both cold and fright. "You're not real." *It's in my mind*, thought Becca. *A dream, a nightmare – or because of lack of food and water. I'm going mad.*

"Real enough," said the woman, standing. The dark shape moved and Becca felt an iron grip encircle her throat. She tried hard to pull the hand away, but couldn't. Even to her numb fingers, the hand around her neck felt icy cold. It squeezed, slowly but firmly. Becca couldn't breathe. Then, without warning, the hand relaxed – and was gone.

Becca doubled over, coughing and wheezing. A hand grasped her shoulder and pushed her upright, back against the wall. She struggled, but the one hand easily held her tight. Becca screamed again. Another hand came to her mouth to silence her and the shape moved closer until its dark face was just inches from Becca. *Oh my God*, thought Becca, *her breath is freezing.*

"Shhhhhhhhuuusshhh," said the voice. Becca tried to bring her breathing under control but couldn't stop shaking. Hyperventilating, she became distantly aware that a warm stream of urine was running down her leg.

"Shhhhhhhhuuusshhh," said the woman, stepping back and releasing her grip. "Now's not your time to die. You just need to know how close you are. When I want you, I will take you."

The woman's voice was soft, clear and oddly accented. It was like a jumble of French, German, Spanish, Russian and even Italian – yet it had a distinctive tone of its own. For long moments, they stood facing each other in the dark. All Becca could see was a fuzzy shape. Becca rubbed her neck; it was sore and tender.

"Go on," said the voice.

Becca had no idea what to do. The fear inside her rose.

"Go on. You want to look at me." The woman prodded Becca's pocket, where the lighter was, rocking her backwards slightly.

"No, I don't," stammered Becca. In a way, it was true. She didn't want to look at the woman, in the way you instinctively didn't want to watch open-heart surgery on the television. But, in the same way, she was drawn to look.

"In truth, you do. I show you."

The hand took the lighter from Becca's pocket and flipped it on. Becca backed away, her imagination tricking her senses. The light danced wildly – and what had at first seemed to be an old woman flickered into something else.

Becca was facing a woman who she guessed was in her early twenties, perhaps a little younger. Long, dark, curly hair fell around her shoulders. She was slim and attractive – *stunning even* – although the dress she wore was dirty and raggedy. She regarded Becca with large, dark eyes.

She smiled at Becca, her lips full and sensual. "Not so bad?" The light flipped off and Becca felt the warmth of the lighter as it was replaced in her pocket. A hand patted the pocket.

Becca shuddered. "What do you want?"

"Just to show you the truth, *girl*. The truth looks good, but it isn't. It's bad. Worse than you can imagine. Here's another truth. Your – *boyfriend*." The woman lingered on the word. "He no love you. He barely liked you. He just wanted to *fuck* you." She spat out the last words.

"No," sobbed Becca, "it's not true."

"And the real truth is," said the cold voice, "you didn't really love him either. You just wanted the same thing."

"Enough!" shouted Becca, rushing at the shape, banging its chest with her forearms. It was like hitting a statue.

Cold hands gripped her arms and forced her back against the wall. She felt the frozen breath of the woman on her face.

"All true. *You know it.* Also true – your time is nearly here. The boy is already mine. You will be mine."

The woman's cold, flat, extended hand rested on Becca's breast. "Feel it. In your heart. You *know* it."

Far above, the bird cawed.

The woman released her grip. Becca massaged her arms roughly to take away the pain.

"And," said the woman, "so you don't forget –"

Becca felt a solid hand hit her face hard – as if it were the flat edge of a cricket bat. She fell backwards, both into the water and against the wall, screaming. Becca broke down completely. The pain was crippling. She felt dizzy and sick. The previously solid walls of the well seemed to spin around. When she did manage to look up, a few minutes later, she was alone again.

14

Sleeping between Abby and Helen, Sammy was extraordinarily restless. She'd fallen asleep in the car once they had started back from the seaside and, back home, Abby had slipped another sedative into her bedtime drink. Sammy had slept soundly until around midnight, when she started to toss and turn in her sleep, mumbling loudly in a distressed voice.

Abby stroked her daughter's fevered forehead, whispering "Shhhhhhuussshh," every so often. Helen switched on the bedside light, looking on anxiously.

Abby gazed at Sammy intently, trying to feel with her mind what was going on in her daughter's head, to understand the connection between her and the trapped girl. She caught some of it, like loud music in the distance. *Sammy feels exactly what she feels*, realised Abby, without fully feeling it herself.

After a few minutes, Sammy became almost tormented, writhing around in the bed, shouting, without fully waking. She started to calm, and then screamed, sitting bolt upright in the bed. Abby pulled Sammy to her, and held her close while she sobbed. Yet, all the while, Abby was convinced that her daughter was still asleep.

Eventually, Sammy settled. Abby lay her back down on the bed, where she curled up, sucking her thumb for the first time in four years.

"Ab, look," said Helen, gently pulling back the neck of Sammy's nightie.

Abby drew a sharp breath.

Around Sammy's neck were red, raw marks – just as if someone had tried to strangle her.

MONDAY

1

Although Becca had sat awake in the dark for over two hours, restless, terrified and in agony, sleep finally claimed her weary body.

When she woke – coughing violently – it was, she guessed, maybe mid-morning. It was hard to tell. The previous days' sunshine had vanished and the once-blue sky was now grey, cloudy and overcast. Deep inside the well, it seemed colder than ever.

Becca felt truly awful. Not only was she freezing from the inescapable cold, sore and hurt from her injuries, but she was now also sweating and coughing profusely. She hawked phlegm from her rasping chest into her mouth and spat it out. Her shivering body felt alternately hot and cold – and she struggled to think clearly. *Just great*, she thought, bitterly. *It just gets better.*

She tried not to think about the previous night, but the impression of the woman seemed to be burned into her mind, like the afterimage left dancing on the inside of the eyelids after staring at a bright object. *If she walked down the street*, thought Becca, *she'd really turn men's heads. But if they looked into her eyes, she'd freeze their hearts. Very poetic*, she thought, coughing again. Becca felt sure that the woman could easily tear someone's heart right out.

It was easier when I thought I might be going mad, thought Becca, sure that everything she remembered had in fact happened.

She stood, her feet shaky, trying to gather her thoughts. *Even if this is just a cold*, she thought, *down here it's serious.* But, after being sat in rank water for days, she also knew it might be more than a cold – although there was little she could do about it.

Food and drink first, she thought. *If I'm getting sick, it's what I need the most.* She ate the crisps as slowly as she could, while moving around within the confined space of the well. When she'd finished, she turned the empty bag inside out and licked it clean, savouring every last speck. The salt had worsened her thirst – she drank the last of the orange and even some of the water.

Becca coughed again. She considered finishing off the water – not that there was much left – but determined to leave the last few mouthfuls until later. She could almost hear Doctor Armstrong telling her to "drink plenty of fluids". *There was plenty of water alright*, she thought, *I just can't drink any of it.* Even as the thought crossed her mind she realised that, by tomorrow, she would have no clean water whatsoever. She would almost certainly drink the rank water from the well if that's what she needed to do to stay alive. She began to regret scraping the moss from the wall into the water.

The thought of yet another day, stretching out before her with nothing to amuse her but her own thoughts, filled her with dread. But it was infinitely better than the thought of the night that would follow.

Becca coughed again, her chest tearing painfully. *Hang on*, she thought. She felt the clean towel; the one that she hadn't wiped her bottom with. Incredibly, it still wasn't dry, but it was far drier than she was. She took the lighter from her shirt pocket and placed it on one of the shelves. Then she stripped off her shirt, peeling the clinging wet cotton away from her body. She took down the towel and placed the shirt where the towel had been. Next, she took off her skirt and then, self-consciously, she removed her bra. It was hard to undo the clasp: her fingers were numb, fat and rubbery. She put her bra and skirt with her shirt. Coughing continually, she began to rub herself as vigorously as her injured, aching limbs could bear. After some hesitation, she removed her knickers. She placed them with her other clothes and then dried herself as thoroughly as she could. She was still cold, but did feel better.

She grabbed her jumper, which was cold and still a little damp, but much drier than her other clothes. She pulled it on, feeling the material take the edge off the cold. It only came down to her waist and she felt both ridiculous and exposed. *Hang on*, she thought again. She fished Matt's football shorts out of his bag and put them on. They weren't exactly clean, but they were almost dry. Then she had another thought. *That's not going to be easy. But I need all the heat I can get.* Slowly, Becca took the football shirt from Matt's face, trying not to look at him. Even in the half-light, his face looked grey and lifeless. She covered his face with the faeces-soiled towel that had been on his shoulder, perhaps the ultimate indignity for this lifeless form. "I'm sorry, Matt," she whispered between coughs.

She pulled the football shirt on over her jumper. It felt better than she could have hoped. It was wonderful to have dry cloth next to her skin; clothes that didn't cling uncomfortably to her. She knew the sensation would be short-lived – she couldn't stand out of the water all day and all night – but it provided a welcome respite. She wrapped the clean towel around her shoulders.

It was hard to stand when the thing she most desperately wanted was to lie down and curl up. Becca tried to keep moving but every so often her cough would halt her; sometimes it would almost double her up.

God the day's going to drag again, she thought. *Stuff it –*

She fumbled around for the iPod and clipped it to her shirt, switching it on. The glow from the display half-illuminated the bottom of the well. It had almost a full charge. *I'll ration it*, she thought. *Half an hour at the most.* Then she thought *what the hell* and decided on an hour. Worried that she'd miss hearing anyone above, she only placed one of the earbuds in. Then she picked up her shirt, wafting it around to try to dry it, vaguely in time to the music.

Becca almost smiled, aware that if someone were to find her now she'd look pretty ridiculous. *The thing is,* she thought, *it might look funny, but it really isn't.*

2

Officers Carter and Greenwood – Stephen and Jenny – left at around two in the morning. Although tired and bleary-eyed, neither Jim nor Sarah even tried to sleep. They talked pointlessly (and tearfully) around the same topics all night long: wondering where the children were, why they'd left, if someone had taken them and – of course – if they were alright.

Sarah had desperately wanted to phone Rachel, her sister, but Jim had thought it best to leave it until morning. At first, reluctantly, Sarah had agreed – but then she thought *screw it* and called Rachel anyway. She knew Jim was being practical but now, more than ever, she needed a family closeness that she didn't feel she could get from Jim. She knew she was being unfair to Jim but couldn't help it. Even under pressure, Jim was able to think straight – which should have been comforting, but just seemed irritating.

Sarah had made an uncomfortable call to Will, who'd confirmed that Becca wasn't with him – but had pressed Sarah hard to let him come round.

"Will, that's not a good idea," Sarah had said, firmly.

"Whatever happened between us," said Will, "I'm still Becca's father."

"A father who she doesn't want to see."

"This isn't about what Becca wants, Sarah," Will had retorted.

Sarah swallowed hard. The last thing she wanted was Will, *in her house,* but she couldn't see a way of keeping him away. Finally she said, "Look, Will – the fact is I *really* don't want you here. This is hard enough as it is. You come through that door and – well, you'll make things harder for everyone."

"Except me."

Sarah could tell Will was fuming.

"Granted. But there's nothing, *nothing,* you can do to help. I promise, I'll call you any time we hear anything. Right away. But I don't want you here. It might not be fair, but –" Sarah stifled a sob.

"Sarah?"

"I can't handle this as it is, Will. Having you here... *please. For me.* I don't want it. I can't handle it. I promise I'll call you the second we hear anything."

"Sarah, I –"

"Will, this situation is so crap that I'm having difficulty keeping it together with the man that I love. I don't want to have to cope with having the man that I *fucking hate* around here." Sarah drew a deep breath, silently, hoping she'd sounded stronger than she felt. *"Please,"* she said, finally.

Will had reluctantly agreed and Sarah was relieved when the call was over.

Despite the adrenalin, anxiety and endless coffee, Sarah and Jim had both fallen asleep on the sofa at some time around five – Sarah huddled under Jim's arm. Sarah drifted away first, and Jim waited until he was sure she was asleep before closing his eyes. He understood that Sarah was frustrated with him but he didn't know how to be anything other than what he was – besides, someone needed to keep calm. Inside, he was as annoyed, frightened and upset as Sarah, but he knew that it wouldn't help if they both lost it.

Just before seven, they were awoken by the doorbell. Sarah, instantly awake, pushed Jim to one side and rushed to the door. It was another policeman and, although he hadn't been at the house the night before, he seemed familiar.

"Hello Mrs Richards," he said, extending his hand with greater informality than she would have expected of a police officer. "I'm Ed Davis." Sarah obviously looked puzzled, because he then offered, "Hannah's Dad?"

Of course, thought Sarah. "I'm sorry," she said, "I didn't recognise you in uniform." She hesitated. "Is there some news?"

Ed shook his head. "I'm sorry, no, I'm just on my way in and wanted to ask you a few more questions. I'm sorry for calling so early."

Sarah felt a veil of despondency descend and, with some effort, pushed it to one side. She invited Ed in. Jim was already automatically making more coffee. Although her mouth tasted foul from too many cups the night before, she accepted another, making a mental note to shower and clean her teeth as soon as she could. *I must look like crap,* she thought, not really caring.

Once they were seated, Ed explained that he'd spoken to Hannah the previous night. He then asked carefully, "Do you think that there might be a physical relationship between Becca and Matt?" There was a stunned silence.

Sarah's eyes widened, as much with anger as astonishment. "What?" She'd started to rise from her seat, but Jim placed his hand on hers. "What?" she repeated, slightly more calmly. "Is that what Hannah said?"

Ed nodded. "I have to stress that she doesn't know for sure. Becca hasn't confided in her. It's just – well, I'd say a guess, but Hannah knows Becca pretty well."

"Better than me?" The words came out cold, almost through gritted teeth. At her side, Jim began to speak. "Sarah –" Sarah silenced him with a glare.

Ed kept quiet while he let the information sink in. If there's one thing he'd learned from situations like this it's that the parents always have to blame someone – sometimes themselves, sometimes the children and sometimes other people.

Jim started to speak but thought better of it. Instead, he got up, went upstairs and returned with the bag of condoms, passing them to Sarah. "I found these in Matt's wardrobe," he said.

Sarah opened the bag. Coloured, ribbed and flavoured. *Just bloody great,* she thought. "She's just a kid," said Sarah. "And *this* doesn't *prove* anything. It's not like they were in *her* room." Jim put his arm around her; she was shaking.

"Like you said," said Jim, "this doesn't prove anything. But we have to accept that it might – that they might..." Jim ran out of words.

"She's only fourteen, for Christ's sake," she said, softly.

"I know," said Jim.

"No you don't know!" Sarah's voice rose. "Matt's sixteen. She's just a baby." She threw the bag of condoms against the wall. The bag hit the floor and the boxes spilled out. One of the boxes opened, scattering wrapped condoms.

Sarah brushed Jim away and stood up. She walked to the window, arms wrapped around herself, trying to regain some calm. Outside, in contrast to the previous week's weather, the morning was overcast and cloudy.

Ed knew when it was time to interject. He'd found out the first thing he wanted to know: neither of the parents knew that their kids were having sex. "Mrs Richards," he said, evenly. "I do honestly know how you feel. Hannah's the same age. But right now, we have to put those feelings to one side and focus on finding the children."

There was a long silence. Sarah nodded. She sniffed and brushed away a tear. Inside, she was mad as hell. Sarah's first time had been awkward, brief and unloving, in the woods close to the school, when she was fifteen. She'd wanted better for Becca. *And Matt* – she was furious with him. *I could kill him,* she thought. *And Jim won't do anything. That's why Matt's like he is. When it boils down to it,* she thought, *men are all the same.* She sat down next to Jim, but not so close that they were touching. Jim put his hand lightly on her knee. *He always knows the right thing to do,* she thought, but found it even more annoying.

Jim felt Sarah's leg stiffen against his touch. He didn't know what to say. Somehow, not only was Matt at fault, he felt that he was too. He was tempted to withdraw his hand, but kept it in place and squeezed her leg gently. Sarah didn't respond.

"Can I talk to Hannah?" asked Sarah.

"It would be best if you didn't," said Ed. "She's pretty embarrassed about this and thinks she's let Becca down by telling me. And, although you know her, it's best if you let us do our job."

Sarah nodded.

"This may change how we approach things," said Ed. "Today, we're starting to search locally, following their possible routes home from school. But we're now going to look at CCTV on national rail, bus and coach networks too. Given that they're both missing, it's possible that they've run away rather than having been taken."

Ed could see that both Sarah and Jim accepted what he was saying, so he pressed home his point. "If we were to ignore a relationship between Becca and Matt as a possibility, we could be searching in the wrong place." Both Sarah and Jim nodded, glancing at each other. "We have to work together. Any piece of information, no matter how unlikely, or unpleasant, may be important."

"We understand," said Sarah.

Ed stood up. "Thanks for your time. And the coffee. Sorry to have upset you, Mrs Richards."

Sarah flushed. "No, I'm sorry. I shouldn't have got angry. And please – call me Sarah."

Ed shook her hand. "Oh, there is one more question," he asked, as casually as he could. "Did either Matt or Becca mention anything about someone following them or watching them?"

"Why?" said Sarah. "Is that something Hannah said?"

Ed didn't like lying to Sarah and Jim, but when a child goes missing, everyone – including the parents – are suspects. Information is something that is given out at a speed that benefits the investigation. He sidestepped the question and hoped that neither Jim nor Sarah noticed. "We have to consider everything," he said. "Something that one of them may have mentioned in passing could be important now."

Sarah shrugged. "Nothing springs to mind." She looked at Jim. He shook his head. "Nope," he said.

"Well, if you think of anything, let us know. Your liaison officer will be assigned today. He or she will probably ask you again. Have a think. And they'll be wanting recent photos of Becca and Matt. Have you got some?"

"We have loads of Becca," said Sarah. "Good ones – she's on the school swimming team, so the Bankside Reporter takes pictures. We've got some of Matt, too." She looked at Jim for confirmation. He nodded. "Not as recent," he said, "but recent enough."

"That's good," said Ed. "If you can fish them out, it will save time later."

Ed said his goodbyes and left. As she closed the door, Sarah felt the silence of the house surround her, oppressive and close. She stood with her back to the door and let the tears flow down her face. Jim came to her, carefully, and put his arms around her. She let him embrace her, but didn't respond. She hated herself for that – she knew that Jim hadn't done anything, but couldn't help herself.

After a moment, she wiped her face and brushed past Jim. "I'm going for a shower," she said.

3

Abby lay in bed, watching Helen dress; it was something she never tired of. Beside her, Sammy slept soundly.

Helen caught her gaze and smiled; Abby smiled back.

"I like it when you're here," said Abby.

"I stay half the week," said Helen.

"You should be here the other half, too. Why don't you move in?"

It was asked as a casual question and was something they'd discussed before. There were several reasons why the two women lived apart, but in the end, Helen reflected, they were all just excuses. The truth was that both women, much as they loved each other, also prized their independence. But, after the last couple of days, things felt different to Helen. Their relationship hadn't previously suffered any kind of crisis and had always felt indestructible. Right now, although she wasn't showing it, Helen was worried: worried about Sammy, about Abby and about the days to come. But most of all she was worried about what would happen *after* the days to come; about what would be left of them and their relationship.

"OK," said Helen, "why not?"

The answer was clearly unexpected to Abby. "What? You mean it?"

"Abigail Henshall, I do believe I've managed to surprise you. Yes, of course I mean it." She leaned over and gave Abby a long kiss.

"Oh Helen, that's fantastic. What changed your mind?"

Helen shrugged. "What changed yours? You're the one who asked."

"The time felt right. That seems daft, doesn't it? Once I realised that I didn't want to go through this without you, I realised that I didn't want to go through *anything* without you."

Helen nodded. "Me too." Although she didn't say so, she was more than uncomfortable with the morality of the situation and felt that now wasn't the time to be living apart.

She gently ruffled Abby's hair and stood up. She reached for her skirt and put it on. "You keeping Sammy off school today?"

Abby nodded. "Probably all week, maybe a bit more. I need to be with her – and it wouldn't be great if someone saw her neck, would it? I'll call the school and say she's sick: a cold or something."

Helen pulled her jumper over her head. "I'll call you later." Helen didn't want to go into work, but it made sense – it's where she'd find out the most about the missing girl. *She might even be someone I teach*, thought Helen. In the dark, she'd only been able to tell that it was a teenage girl – she hadn't recognised her voice.

"Helen?"

"Yep?"

"Can I tell Sammy you're moving in? She'll be really pleased."

"Of course you can," replied Helen with a knowing smile, "if she doesn't know already."

Sammy had always liked Helen, right from the first time she'd seen her.

4

"Hi, Helen!"

It was the very first time that Helen Goodwin had stepped inside Abby's small shop – which was a busy, cluttered place, with shelves full of rocks, crystals, books, candles and a seemingly random collection of homeopathic remedies. The air smelled faintly of incense. Behind the counter, a woman with long blonde hair looked up and smiled, but it wasn't she who had spoken. At the side of the counter, playing on the floor with a doll, was a young child. She was three, perhaps four. The child was smiling directly at her.

"Well, hi yourself," said Helen. "What's your name?"

"I'm Sammy," proclaimed the little girl, as if Helen should have known. *Cute kid,* thought Helen, puzzled.

"She's a darling," said Helen to the blonde woman.

"Thanks."

"How old is she?"

Sammy interrupted. "I'm a big three," she said, proudly. "Do you like my dolly? I just got her."

"I do, I do. What's her name?"

"I don't know yet, 'cause she's new. But I think she's special. Like a princess. Or a lady."

Helen smiled warmly. "You could be right."

"Can I help you?" asked the blonde woman.

"Yes, I hope so. I – I'm wondering how your daughter knew my name."

The blonde woman shrugged, smiling. "I guess she must have seen you around. She's got a great memory and she's nosy as hell."

Helen nodded. "I guess. I've only just moved into town. I've just got a job as a supply teacher at the school. Big kids, though." Helen realised that she was rambling. "I'm looking for local history books. My name's Helen, by the way."

"I know," said the woman, nodding toward Sammy. She held out her hand. "Welcome to town. I'm Abby. We've got some books – pretty much all you can see is what we have. Trying to find out more about your new home?"

Helen flicked through the books. "Partly. I'm a bit of a local history nerd, I'm afraid. This place is new to me, so I thought I'd find out what I could, even if I'm only here for a few months."

"Not staying?"

"Don't know yet. It's a six-month contract. I'll see how it goes." Helen picked out three of the books. "I'll take these."

Abby bagged the books, then took Helen's credit card and rang up the payment. "Well," she said, handing Helen the books, "I hope you like it here."

Helen smiled. "Me too. Thanks very much. Bye." She turned to Sammy. "Bye Sammy."

"Bye Helen." Helen found Sammy's familiarity both slightly unnerving and strangely endearing. She'd not been sure about Bankside when she arrived, but there was something welcoming about this little shop.

As Helen left the shop, Abby noticed that she looked back – and their eyes met. Helen's eyes were a deep, warm dark brown that seemed to naturally express joy. Abby found it impossible not to smile and Helen smiled back.

They met again just over a week later, in The Tea Tree, one of Bankside's small cafés. Helen was reading one of the books she'd bought, sipping tea. Sammy saw her first, and went straight to her, clambering onto the seat beside her without asking. "Hi Helen," she said. Helen smiled. "Well hello –" Helen briefly searched her memory. "Sammy, isn't it?" Sammy nodded.

"I'm sorry," said Abby. "Sammy's stopping you reading. Come on Sam, let's find another table."

"Awwww," said Sammy, pulling a cartoon glum face.

"No it's OK," said Helen, closing her book. "I'm glad of the company. I still don't know anyone around here."

So they sat together, chatting for around an hour. The conversation was easy. Every now and then Sammy chipped in with a comment or question and Abby couldn't help noticing how well Sammy and Helen got on.

Helen, Abby noted, was one of those rare naturally upbeat people who are a pleasure to be around. She was petite and pretty, her long black hair pulled tightly back and held in place by a butterfly hair comb. She made Abby feel ungainly, angular and ever so slightly unkempt.

"She's great," said Helen. "You must be really proud."

"I am," said Abby.

"I hope you don't mind me asking," said Helen, "but I noticed you're not wearing a ring?"

"I'm not married," said Abby.

"Divorced? Separated?"

Abby looked a little uncomfortable and subconsciously pulled at her lower lip with her fingers. She lowered her voice a little, checking if Sammy was listening. "Her Dad died. Before she was born."

"Oh, I'm really sorry," said Helen. She meant it, Abby could tell.

There was an awkward silence, the first since Abby sat down. She considered whether it was time to leave, but Helen ordered some more tea and then deftly changed the subject, asking about the shop, what she sold and how good business was. Abby couldn't help but like her and sensed the beginning of a genuine friendship.

"Do you like the books?" asked Abby, indicating the book on the table, which Helen had bought from her shop. "We don't sell that many of those, to be honest."

"I do," replied Helen. "Although I've been reading up a bit at the library on some more colourful local legends. And my landlord likes to tell me stuff too."

"Ah," said Abby, smiling. "You mean the stories about our local witch."

Helen nodded. "I didn't see any books about that in your shop."

"A waste of shelf space, to be honest," said Abby. "Populist crap, most of it. I used to carry the odd title, but I don't now."

Abby sipped her tea and decided to change the subject. "How's the job?"

"It's good. Great, actually. I'm seriously thinking of staying on if they offer me a permanent job."

They chatted for another half an hour or so before Helen glanced at her watch and realised the time. "I'm sorry, Abby," she said. "I need to get going. I've got to prep for school next week." Despite Abby's protestations, Helen paid the bill before gathering up her things, saying her goodbyes and leaving.

Abby sat with Sammy, reflecting on the meeting. Despite living in Bankside most of her life, she didn't really have many close friends. Just as she drained the last of her tea, Helen came back in.

"Forget something?"

Helen looked a little awkward. "No. I just wondered, since I don't know anyone, if you'd fancy going for a drink sometime?"

Abby smiled. "Yes," she said. "That would be great."

They went out several times, getting on better and better each time. Before long, they were meeting regularly. It wasn't easy for Abby, who didn't have a family, to find a babysitter she trusted. On top of that, the shop only just about made money, so she didn't have much spare cash for either a babysitter or an active social life. When she raised this with her new friend, Helen was deeply embarrassed. "I didn't think," Helen said. "I'm sorry."

Abby felt embarrassed too. "I didn't mean to make you feel bad."

"Look. We don't have to go out. I'll just grab a bottle of wine and come around to yours. That way, we solve both problems *and* I get to see Sammy."

So it was that they had dinner for the first time at the flat. Helen had come around early enough to play with Sammy, while Abby prepared the meal. Once Sammy was asleep, they ate, drank and chatted. After they cleared the dishes, they sat on the sofa.

When Helen reached to stroke her arm, Abby honestly hadn't expected it – but it didn't feel unnatural either. Her tummy fluttered and she hoped that she didn't look nervous.

Abby took a sip of wine and said carefully, "Helen. I'm really sorry. I haven't meant to lead you on or send the wrong signals. But I'm not gay."

There was a moment's silence. "That's OK," said Helen. "I don't think I am either. At least, I've only ever had boyfriends. But you haven't stopped me stroking your arm."

There was a pause. Abby smiled. "That's because it feels nice."

Helen beamed, taking the tension from the room; then she took a deep breath. "Abby, I'm not thinking about being straight or gay. I'm thinking about how I feel. I know you feel like I do." She leaned forwards to kiss Abby, but she had lowered her head.

"I don't know," whispered Abby. "I mean – I do feel like that. I know we're more than friends and probably more than soul mates – but I don't want to spoil what we have."

"I don't think we'll spoil it," said Helen. "That's not what my heart tells me."

Helen gently lifted Abby's chin. Their eyes met. "What does your heart tell you?" she asked.

Without waiting for a reply, Helen leaned towards Abby and kissed her lightly on the lips.

Abby hesitantly, almost fearfully, allowed Helen's lips to kiss hers. With that first touch, all of her apprehension melted. The kiss was so – right. So perfect. It was a place she wanted to be, a place she belonged. She hadn't expected it, but Abby found it easy and natural to respond to Helen's kiss.

It was that easy; that fast; that natural. That night, they made love for the first time. It was the closest that Abby had ever felt to anyone; a closeness that was deeper than she could have imagined. Their lovemaking was warm and soft, as if love were a blanket in which you could wrap yourself. Although Abby had previously only slept with one person (and would herself admit that she was hardly experienced), for the first time she truly appreciated the difference between having sex and making love.

Afterwards they lay together – Helen lay on her back, with Abby on her side, her leg wrapped around Helen's middle. Abby ran her hand up Helen's forearm, then slowly, the palms of their hands were together, their fingers entwined, Abby entranced by the rich, dark coffee colour of Helen's skin.

Helen said, "I think you're a bit more gay than you thought."

"I'm not the only one," said Abby. "Do you still claim it's your first time?"

"I'm afraid so. But I'm sure I'll improve."

"*That* I can't imagine. But it will be fun trying."

Their relationship quickly grew deeper. Over the next few months, Helen would stay over once or twice a week, sometimes more. They spent more and more time together, and with Sammy.

One night, they were lying in bed, Helen curled up under Abby's arm, her free hand lazily stroking Abby's chest.

"You were late tonight," said Abby. "Busy at school?"

"No, I was reading up on a really fascinating local legend. You know me. I got distracted and lost track of time."

"Not the witch?"

"Got it in one."

Abby sighed, and Helen, whose head was resting against Abby's chest, could feel that her heart rate had jumped. "Go on," said Abby. "Tell me all."

"There's not that much to tell," said Helen. "It's not like one of those rich stories – like Old Demdike, the Lancashire witch, where there's lots of detail. But basically, there used to be an old woman who lived in the woods at the edge of the old estate."

"The Whitaker estate," interjected Abby.

"Right. She was poor, this woman, so she created herbal medicine to barter. Unfortunately, this took trade away from the apothecary in the village. The apothecary's wife accused the woman of witchcraft and of stealing children – since more than one had gone missing around that time. The villagers strung her up over the well near her cottage and hanged her. But not before she cursed the surrounding land. That's the short version. It's not that different from a lot of witch legends – more likely a scorned woman getting revenge than anything supernatural."

As Helen got to the end of the short tale, she realised that Abby had tensed up. Now, as she finished, Abby disentangled herself from Helen and sat up, pulling the quilt over her breasts. Helen sat up next to her. "Abby?"

Abby said, in a low voice, "You know who I am, don't you?"

There was an uncomfortable silence. Helen almost felt the room chill. "No," she said, carefully.

"Please don't lie to me." If Abby was angry, she hid it well. Her voice remained even, if cool. "What are you, some kind of witchcraft groupie? Doesn't our relationship mean *anything* to you?" Abby pulled the quilt closer to herself.

Helen could see that tears were forming in Abby's eyes and she desperately wished she could have turned time back ten minutes.

"Abby, I'm not lying. Well, OK – it seems a bit odd that you sell local history books but don't sell books about the local witch, especially when you have an obvious Wiccan bent." Abby's eyebrows raised. "Come on, Abby. Your homeopathic remedies are mainly pagan – but I just assumed you had, well, a bit of an interest in witchcraft and maybe didn't like the people of a small town tittle-tattling about it, nothing else."

Abby was silent.

"Abby, it's the truth. I promise." Abby looked down, then wiped a tear away. Helen took Abby's hands and waited until they had both made eye contact. There was no anger in Abby's eyes, only sadness.

"Abby. Listen. I was drawn to you because of *you*. Nothing else. Abby: I would never want to hurt you. Abby, I love you."

Abby exclaimed, "You *love* me?" She looked into Helen's eyes and Helen squeezed her hands.

"Don't you know it?" Helen asked.

There was a brief pause. Abby nodded. "I know it," she said, pulling Helen back to her.

They held each other for long minutes, Helen not daring to speak but not understanding Abby's emotional response to a story she must have heard so many times.

Eventually, Abby said, quietly, "The real story's not quite like that. Very few people know it."

Helen waited.

"The witch was no hag or crone," continued Abby. She spoke slowly and carefully. "In fact, she was said to be young – perhaps 16 or 17, maybe less – and very beautiful. She came from what I suppose is now Eastern Europe. I don't know where. Romania, Hungary, maybe the Ukraine. Europe was different then – and I don't know exactly when *then* was. There wasn't really a proper town here, just a few close villages. She came with a bunch of travellers. They'd picked up both her and her mother some time before and they'd travelled with them. The mother made medicine, it's said that the girl sold her body. They camped on the edge of one of the villages. The local landowner slept with the girl many times and when the time came for the travellers to leave, he asked her to stay on, professing his love – which must have been a bit annoying for his wife. But it wasn't just about love, if at all. The girl was pregnant and the landowner's only children were girls. He wanted an heir, even an illegitimate one. Anyhow, the girl stayed, along with her mother. They lived in a cottage at the edge of the estate – it's still there, just about. It's a ruin. Anyway, the child would have been a boy, but the girl lost it in childbirth."

Abby paused, as if thinking. After several seconds, she carried on.

"The two women stayed for years. It's said that they never aged. Stories grew up around them. It didn't help that, every so often, a child from one of the villages would go missing. They weren't trusted, but the mother's medicine was good, possibly as good as her daughter's skills in bed. Or whatever passed for a bed back then."

Abby hesitated.

Helen squeezed her hand, wondering where the story was going but captivated. "You OK?"

Abby nodded. "Rivalry grew up between the local apothecary's family and the two women and – not without good cause. The old woman was taking trade from the apothecary, but it was deeper than that. Remember, these were dark times and people kept any differences hidden. But the apothecary and the old woman had a sure knowledge of the other's – erm – skill, I suppose. The apothecary knew for certain that the potions made by the old woman were beyond normal craft. But the old woman knew that the apothecary's wife had a gift of vision; of *knowing*. Don't ask me how. Maybe she could just tell. Anyway, the apothecary's wife dreamt that the old woman was torturing a local boy, one who'd gone missing. She knew that her dream would be the truth, but couldn't tell anyone for fear of being exposed as a witch. So, the next night, she crept to the cottage. Inside, the old woman had a naked child tied to stakes on the floor. She was reciting spells around him, drawing blood, while her daughter looked on. The apothecary's wife went home and told her husband. She claimed that she was jealous that her husband was losing custom and had gone to the cottage during curfew, perhaps hoping to steal some secrets. Her husband told the parish constable, who called a hue and cry. He and the men of the village made their way to the cottage, where they found the boy – dead."

Helen caught her breath.

"Oh, that's not the worst of it," said Abby. "There wasn't really much of a process for a fair trial in those days, not that it would have helped. The old woman was tied to her chair and the mob burned the house, with her in it. Then, they took turns to rape the young woman before they hung her above the well. There were perhaps fifteen or twenty men in the mob."

"Wow," whistled Helen, "they certainly took any hint of witchcraft seriously in those days."

"Well, it's not as if they were lacking evidence. But, before she died, she cursed the family that had betrayed her and the village itself. She said that, from that day, the apothecary's family would only ever consist of women who bore women – and that any man who sired a child for them would die before the child was born. The curse of the village was that it would continue to lose children to her even after she died – and when she claimed a child, the village had to let her have it – if they didn't, she would take tenfold."

Abby paused. "My mother taught me the curse – one of the more unusual nursery rhymes of my childhood. It goes: *The baby you carry will never be male; the life of the man who sired it will fail. The lives that I take must never grow old; or from you and yours I take back tenfold.*"

There was a long silence while Abby let Helen absorb the story.

"Oh God," said Helen. "You and Sammy. You're descended from the apothecary, aren't you?"

Abby nodded. "You believe me?"

"Of course I do. I'm so, so sorry, Abby."

"Don't be. It just is what it is."

"And Sammy's Dad?"

"You ever read *The World According to Garp*?" asked Abby. Helen shook her head.
"Garp's mother, Jenny, wants a child but not a husband. She's a nurse. She decides to – erm – *take* a soldier who was mentally a vegetable. I guess you could say it was a type of rape. She just wanted his sperm. Well, I kind of did the same thing. To have a child, I have to kill – you have to admit it's one hell of a curse, truly testing a woman's greatest desire. Anyhow, I got an evening job as a hospice volunteer, visiting the terminally ill at home, and chose someone who was already dying. I'd say he was pretty grateful, actually. He got a great send-off and didn't have to suffer his expected prolonged death."

Helen genuinely didn't know what to say.

"Oh don't worry, he didn't die on the job. He died a few days later, when I guess I'd conceived. He was a good man. His name was John. Youngish, late forties I think. His wife had left him; taken his son. He was trying to deal with the cancer on his own. I liked him. A lot. And it wasn't as sordid as it sounds. I made it nice – better than nice. He was being cared for at home. I went around one night, washed him. Lit lots of candles, ate dinner with him. Then we made love. *And it was making love*, not screwing. Well, I thought it was making love – until I met you."

Helen smiled, appreciatively.

Abby continued. "He wasn't physically very able, so I did most of the work. Slowly, sweetly – I made it last, *for him*. I stayed all night; we made love three times. I wanted it to be as fair an exchange as I could. I still put flowers on his grave. I've never slept with anyone else."

"Christ," said Helen.

"Well, what's the alternative? Meet someone in a pub and have a one-night stand?"

"That would be pretty awful," agreed Helen.

"Too true. That's what my mother did."

Helen looked at her, to see if she was joking. She clearly wasn't.

"We have to keep the line alive. And the story. No one else knows the full story, or the curse. If *she* takes a child, it's our job to make sure she can keep him. Her taking the child is bad, but the town getting the child back is worse. Ten times worse." Abby turned on her side and propped her head up with her elbow, her blonde hair falling around the pillow. "Now," she asked, "do you still love me?"

"Every inch," said Helen.

"I come with a fair bit of baggage."

"Don't you just. You're a witch groupie's goldmine."

Abby smiled. "You sure you believe me?"

"Of course I do. Why would I not? It's no weirder than similar folk tales."

"Except this one's true, even if it sounds like a crazy story. I've never told anyone," said Abby. "Ever. And I never for a moment thought that I would. Helen?"

"Yes."

"I never said. I love you too."

Helen smiled and kissed Abby warmly. "You didn't have to. I already know it."

Helen thought for a moment. "So that's why Sammy often knows things without being told?"

Abby nodded. "I have the same gift, but I'm nowhere near as good as Sammy. Even at her age, she's way better than me. In fact, I'm pretty rubbish at it. It's not a reliable thing for me, just something that happens every so often."

"Does she know?"

"Know what? That she sees things in her mind that happen somewhere else? No, I don't think so. She's too young. But before long I'm going to have to start telling her to be careful. She probably won't get burned as a witch, but she could easily get into a lot of trouble."

"When will you tell her what you've told me?"

"When she's older. I don't know when. When she's ready. I was fourteen when my Mum told me."

"And your Mum?" asked Helen.

"Committed suicide when Sammy was six months old."

There was a moment of silence.

"I'm sorry," said Helen.

Abby dismissed Helen's apology with a casual wave. "It was her choice. I guess she couldn't face things any more. It's not an easy thing to live with. I think it weighed heavily on her – more even than it does on me."

"Is that the end of the story?"

"As far as it goes. The cottage and the well are still there, ruined, but few people go there. In the absence of knowing the real story, lots of false legends have sprung up. In any event, people generally stay away."

"Have you ever been there?"

Abby shook her head. "Nope. But one day, I may have to. I'll go if and when I need to. The Whitaker estate has been abandoned for years. Most of it is overgrown. In one room of the cottage, where the old woman died, people say that nothing grows. They never found all of the bodies of the children, though they found some, in a grave, close by. You must have heard what the locals call the old woman?"

"Awful Anna, or something like that. It doesn't sound too scary."

"No it doesn't. She used to be known as *Ufel Anna* and some local historians still know that name. Do you know what ufel means?"

Helen shook her head. "Latin?"

"Nope. Middle English. Ufel means *Evil.*"

"And –" Helen hesitated before asking the question. "Do children still go missing?"

"Now and again," said Abby, sadly. "Not in my lifetime though."

"If you're descended from the apothecary, what about the witch? Does she have descendants?"

"No," said Abby, fixing Helen with a stare. "The witch doesn't need descendants, because she doesn't ever really die."

5

In over twenty years of teaching, and seven as headmistress, this was the first time that Audrey Chadwick had one child missing from the school, let alone two. She took a sip of her now tepid tea, her hands shaking slightly.

Stephen Carter waited patiently while Audrey composed herself. He was no stranger to the school, but this was new territory for him too. His previous visits had been trivial by comparison: petty theft and bullying, the normal staple of police-school interrelation alongside occasional presentations and liaison work. He sat alone with the headmistress, but outside four more officers waited: two male, two female. Jenny Greenwood had been assigned as liaison officer to the family, so she was on her way over to the house. Already the school was abuzz with gossip and rumours – none of which was correct (and most of which was almost as extraordinary as the truth).

Stephen had met Audrey Chadwick before, several times. Although she was likeable, he considered her to be ineffectual – a view shared by most of her staff and a trait often taken advantage of by the sharper pupils.

There was a knock at the door.

"Just a moment," said Audrey. She replaced the teacup, rubbed her eyes and composed herself, breathing in deeply. "Enter," she said, with a greater firmness than Stephen would have expected of her. Brian Garland, the deputy head, stepped tentatively into the room.

"You wanted to see me, Audrey?" he asked, eyeing Stephen.

"Brian – this is Officer Carter. Officer Carter, Brian Garland, the school's deputy head." Stephen liked that: *the school's deputy head, not my deputy head.* They shook hands.

"Brian. Something – something terrible has happened." She paused, and for a moment Stephen thought that she would dither through the whole conversation, but then she pressed on.

"Two children are missing. Rebecca Richards and Matthew Bradshaw. You know them?"

Clearly shocked, Brian nodded. "Oh good grief – er, yes, I teach them both. Matt's new. His father moved in with Becca's Mum, I understand."

Audrey looked over to Stephen, which he took as a cue to take over the conversation. "They've been missing since Saturday, quite possibly Friday, Mr Garland. We don't yet know exactly when."

Garland seemed lost for words. "I – they – where were they last seen?"

"As far as we can tell," continued Stephen, "at school on Friday. Their parents were away over the weekend, so only found out they were missing yesterday. We really need to speak to everyone who came into contact with Rebecca or Matthew on Friday – as a matter of urgency. Teachers *and* children. And parents, too."

"Of course," said Garland. "What do you want us to do?"

"We're going to call a full assembly," said Audrey. "It's the fastest way for Officer Carter to address the school. Just before that, he will brief the heads of years. After the assembly, the children can go to their tutor groups. We'll keep lessons running as normally as we can, but the priority is to enable the police to interview the teachers and children who were with Rebecca and Matthew on Friday."

Garland nodded.

"We may need to speak to *everyone*," said Stephen. "At the moment, there are five police officers here – three from Bankside's force and two we've drafted in. We're expecting more today – a lot more. That will make the job much faster."

"Whatever you need," said Garland. "Just ask."

"The police want to set up an incident room in the school," said Audrey. "I suggested the library annex."

"That's fine," said Garland. "I'll get some of the prefects to move the desks together."

"Don't worry," said Stephen. "We can do that. It's best that the children only speak to us when they're being questioned." Brian looked puzzled. "Partly because it's easy for anything that's overheard to be taken out of context. But also because we don't want to influence what people say."

Audrey glanced at her watch. "If you don't mind, Brian, we need to get moving."

Brian nodded. "Of course. The main hall, fifteen minutes?"

"That would be excellent," said Stephen. Brian left, and Stephen made ready to follow him.

"Anything you need, Mr Carter, just ask."

"Thank you – I will. Can I ask you: how well do you know the children?"

Audrey considered. "Not terribly. I'm as hands-on as I can be, but that's not very much these days. Rebecca's a bit of a shining light in the school: a genuinely talented swimmer. She's won more competitions than any pupil in the history of the school, twice over. We have lots of photographs of her – you'll see them in the awards cabinets. She does OK in school. Not exceptional academically, but certainly by no means dim. Quite strong-minded, but a bit on the quiet side. I don't really know Matthew. He's not been here long." She hesitated. "He's not been in any trouble, but a couple of the teachers have flagged that he can be – well, hard work. He's not really made friends – which can be a concern in itself – and some of the children seem to steer clear of him. But he seems to get on very well with Rebecca."

Stephen remained impassive. "Thanks," he said. "We can speak in more detail later." He went outside to brief the small team, wondering when more bobbies, the CID and his sergeant were going to arrive. *And then,* he thought, *God help us. The social workers will be here next.*

6

Jenny Greenwood ran her finger along the map. "This is the most direct route from school, at the northern edge of town, to here – running through the town centre. So, this is the route that we're currently searching."

Sarah and Jim looked carefully over the map. "God," said Sarah. "It's such a small town – but there are so many different ways for them to get home."

"Do you know what their normal route home would be?"

Sarah shook her head; the question made her feel inadequate. "No. I know I should but –" She stopped, unable to finish the sentence.

"It's OK," said Jenny. "We don't expect any parent to know their child's exact movements. But anything you can tell us, *anything,* could help. For example, do they usually buy sweets from a particular shop? Do they hang around anywhere with friends before coming home?"

"I don't know," said Sarah, running her hands through her hair in exasperation. She and Jim had slept very little in the last thirty hours and she was having trouble thinking straight.

Jenny turned to Jim. "Mr Bradshaw?"

Jim pondered the map, thinking hard. "They didn't always get home at the same time."

"They didn't usually come home together?"

"Sorry, no, I didn't mean that," said Jim. "Sometimes they would be home before five, sometimes a bit after, sometimes it could be almost five-thirty. Does that mean they didn't have one set route?"

"It might," said Jenny, "or it might just mean that sometimes they stopped to chat. Are you sure they never got the bus?"

"Not that I know of, though they may have if it's been raining," said Sarah. "Mostly they'd walk, sometimes one of us would pick them up, but not that often. We tend to run them in more than we pick them up." She studied the map. "God," she said, "they could have gone down any of these roads."

"And we will search them all, Mrs Richards, I promise." Jenny held eye contact with Sarah until she could see that Sarah believed her. "Every single one. But we can't search every route at once. We have to start with the most likely and work outwards. At the moment, we've only managed to draft in a couple of dozen extra hands. But by this afternoon, we'll have twice that."

"What about us," said Jim. "Can't we help?"

It was a difficult but expected question. "Not directly with the main search," she said, avoiding the word *hunt* that the police used between themselves. "We need to be very methodical and not get in the way of the main team." While this was the truth, Jenny knew it wasn't the whole truth: when children go missing, everyone is a suspect, including the parents. The parents need to be involved, but not allowed to compromise the investigation or contaminate any evidence. Jenny was there to not only provide support, but to observe Sarah and Jim too.

Jim nodded, but Sarah wasn't to be put off. "I want to do *something*. I can't just sit here. I *won't*."

"Of course. That's why I said *not directly*," said Jenny. "It would help if we drive around the various routes, to see if anything jogs your memory: shops, houses, parks – anything. Could you do that?"

Sarah nodded, glad to have some kind of purpose.

"I should stay here," said Jim.

Sarah shot him an angry look. "Jim –!"

"In case they call," he said, obviously hurt.

Sarah could see the sense in that, but didn't seem entirely placated. "I'll get my coat," she said.

"Sarah –" Jim began. But she'd already left the room.

"We can't go straight away," said Jenny. "I'll call for someone to stay with you."

"There's no need," said Jim. "I'll be fine."

"Mr Bradshaw," said Jenny, "we don't know what's happened to Rebecca and Matthew. For all we know you might get a phone call from a kidnapper. What would you do then?"

"Oh God," said Jim, sitting down. "Do you really think so?"

"No, not really. But it's one possibility I can think of and there might be dozens I can't. Better to have someone here, just in case." Since Jenny knew that – however unlikely it seemed – one or both of the parents might actually be responsible, neither was best left alone.

Jenny went into the kitchen to call the police station, glancing out of the window as she did. *Looks like it's going to rain*, she thought. *That's not going to help.*

Abby had been anxiously awaiting Helen's call, so, when her mobile phone rang, she answered on the first ring.

"Helen?" Despite being late morning, she tried to keep her voice down. After Helen had left, she'd gone to wake Sammy and found her hot and fevered. She'd helped her weary daughter eat some toast, then given her some paracetamol to try to get her temperature down. Although she'd drifted off to sleep again, she was restless.

Helen quickly outlined what was happening at the school.

"So they're looking in the wrong place?"

"Yes," said Helen. "From what I understand, even after drafting in more police – lots more police – the search could still take days." A group of children went past, huddled in whispered conversation. Helen lowered her voice further. "It could be two, three or four days before they start looking anywhere other than likely routes home."

"Well," said Abby, "that's good."

Helen hesitated. "How is it good? This is a little girl we're talking about."

"Helen, I don't like it any more than you do – I'm probably just more used to the idea. I've been dreading it for so long that it's – well, almost a relief now. But you're right, it's not good. It's just less bad."

Helen was silent.

"What's up?" asked Abby.

"Well," said Helen uncomfortably, "this isn't just some folk tale any more. This is a real girl we're talking about."

"I do know that, Helen," said Abby, more sharply than she intended.

"Do you? Really? When I said a real girl, that's what I meant. Someone with a family. A father. A *mother*." Although she was emphatic, there was no anger in Helen's voice; the questions were asked honestly, openly. "What if this girl were Sammy?"

Abby swallowed, took a breath and answered as evenly as she could. "Well, I'd have to deal with it. Like I'm having to deal with it now."

There was a brief uncomfortable silence. "I'm sorry, Abs," said Helen.

"Do you know the girl?" asked Abby, after a pause.

"Not directly. I don't teach her – but I've seen her around and at sports days. Nice girl." Helen couldn't keep the sadness from her voice. "I've taught the boy, though, a couple of times when I was standing in for Marshall. I didn't like him, to be honest, but I couldn't tell you why."

"Helen?"

"Yes?"

"I am sorry, you know. Really."

"I know," said Helen. "I just don't know how you've lived with this. It's awful."

"I just have," said Abby. "I'd no choice."

Helen switched the subject. "How's Sammy?"

"Not good," replied Abby. "She's running a temperature – around a hundred. I'd normally call Doc Armstrong. But I don't actually think it's Sammy who's sick. I think it's the girl."

"The girl?"

"Whatever's happening between Sammy and the girl, it's way stronger than what she normally feels from others. It's like some kind of bond. I'm scared. I told you I'm not that gifted – but I can normally *feel* Sammy, at least a bit. It's like this thing with the girl is blocking me out. When the girl – when this all ends, what happens to Sam?"

Helen had no answer for Abby. The break in their conversation was ended by the loud ringing of the school bell. "I have to go," said Helen. "Break time's over. I'll call later if I hear anything new. And Abby –"

"Yes?"

"You have to be strong."

"I know, thanks."

Abby hung up the phone. As she replaced it on the arm of the sofa, she noticed Sammy at the door. She looked a mess – sweaty, hot and bedraggled. Abby went to her.

"Oh baby, I didn't see you there. Are you OK?"

Sammy shook her heed. "I feel really bad." Sammy coughed, a liquid, congested cough.

Abby led her to the sofa and put her on her knee, hugging her. Sammy felt unnaturally hot. "Well, you don't look great. But we'll get you better. Want some orange juice?"

Sammy nodded. "I'm very thirsty. And hungry." Abby wondered how much of what Sammy was feeling was because of the girl. She carried Sammy to the kitchen to get the juice. "How long were you listening, Sam?"

"Not long, Mummy," lied Sammy. Abby knew the lie for what it was but understood her daughter's fear.

"I was talking to Helen, Sammy," said Abby.

"I know," said Sammy. "About the girl. She's real, isn't she?"

Abby handed Sammy the glass of orange. "Yes, baby, she is." It was pointless lying. *She probably knows more about her than we do,* thought Abby.

"Then why aren't we helping her? She's stuck. And upset. And frightened. Very frightened."

Abby didn't know what to say. "It's complicated, Sammy," she began.

Sammy coughed again, this time bringing up dark green phlegm into her hand. Abby got a tissue and wiped it away. She gave her daughter another tissue. "Here,

Sammy, cough into this." Sammy did so, filling the tissue.

Gross, thought Abby.

"I know it is," said Sammy, "I'm sorry, Mummy." Abby still found it unnerving that her daughter so often knew what she was thinking.

"Can you always tell what I'm thinking?" asked Abby.

Sammy shook her head. "Not always. But often."

"And other people?"

Sammy seemed uncomfortable.

"Sam, it's OK to talk about this, to me and Helen, anyway."

Sammy nodded. "Some other people. Not everyone. Some people a lot. Some just a bit."

"Is it annoying?" Abby tried to imagine the voices of dozens of people in her head, all the time.

Sammy shrugged. "Not really – well, sometimes. I don't always understand it, though. Some people think bad things. I try not to listen."

"What about the girl?"

"She's scared. It's a small dark place. There's someone else there –" the sudden fear in Sammy's eyes was terrible. Tears were forming in her eyes. "A pretty woman. Well, pretty to look at, but bad inside. She's *very bad*. And there's a man. A bad man. He wants her too."

Abby was surprised. "A bad man? In the – with the girl?"

"No. He's somewhere else. I don't know where. I don't like the things he thinks. He's – he's full of bad thoughts, but he pretends to be nice and no one knows. He –" Sammy started crying, her sobs punctuated with deep hacking coughs.

"Shhhh," said Abby. "Let's not talk about this now."

"And her Mummy misses her, she's scared too. And her friends. Her best friend is really upset."

"Sammy," said Abby, softly, "let's leave it. Hush now."

Sammy nodded, sniffing.

"Let's get you back to bed," said Abby. "You need some more sleep."

Abby picked Sammy up. *I won't be able to do this for much longer*, she thought, *she's heavier each time I lift her.*

She carried Sammy to her bedroom and put her into bed, stroking her hair while she calmed herself. Eventually, her sobbing ceased and she closed her eyes. Abby waited a while, then left her to sleep. *It's late*, she thought, *I need to open up the shop.*

As Abby left, Sammy half-opened her eyes. *I don't care what Mummy says*, she thought. *I want to help the girl.*

8

Once Becca's hour of music was up (and, truth be told, she had stretched it to another ten minutes) tedium returned. Her chest ached as if it were torn inside. Every so often she'd break into an uncontrollable coughing fit. She was desperate to drink the water, if only to ease her throat, but was mindful that there was very little left. Her next drink would be her last. After that, with no food or water and getting sicker by the hour, she didn't think she'd last long. She shivered, her body hot and cold at the same time. Every so often, the well seemed to spin around her and she had to hold on to the wall to steady herself, determined not to sit down, but to remain dry as long as she could.

The day grew darker and colder. She had no idea what time it was. Her body clock couldn't help her: her stomach was now always aching for food. The now forbidding, steel-grey sky gave away nothing. It could be lunchtime, mid-afternoon or later.

The smell inside the well had become inescapable, somehow making the air thicker. The last time she used the lighter, just after hanging her school clothes where she could around the well, she'd caught sight of Matt's body. It was as if he wasn't human any more, just a hunk of meat.

What day is it? She thought. She couldn't be sure. She worked her way back through the number of nights, but still couldn't quite decide if it was Monday or Tuesday.

But Becca's permanent, overriding feeling wasn't hunger, thirst, cold or fever – it was fear. She'd never been so scared for so long. It wasn't like the fear of a roller coaster ride, a fear safe in the knowledge that any illusory danger would soon be over. It cut far deeper: a fear that came from the near certainty that her life was now numbered in days – and those days would be increasingly torturous.

She bent double, coughing hard, spitting phlegm into the water. This time, the cough wouldn't go away. Her chest kept hacking in a spasm she couldn't stop as she agonisingly, but uncontrollably, brought viscous mucus from the depths of her lungs. Desperate, she reached for the last of the water and gratefully felt it roll down her ragged throat. For a moment, she had some relief – but there was instantly worse to follow, as she retched and vomited into the water. Whatever little she'd eaten in the last day was now floating, with the moss, on the top of the water – adding to the foul stench in the well. She heaved again and again, emptying herself until she was dry-retching, crying, sweating and panting. Her mouth tasted vile and dizziness threatened to overwhelm her.

Gradually, Becca steadied herself and, after perhaps twenty minutes, even felt a little better. It was as though her body had ejected something poisonous.

There was a familiar flutter of substantial wings above her. She looked up to see the large bird settle itself on the top of the well. It cawed, as if it had come to gloat. Then another bird joined it – and another, then another, until after two or three minutes, the well was encircled by birds. Their chorus was deafening and deeply disturbing.

"Go away!" she screamed. Her voice didn't even dent the din above; there was no way she could rise above it. She reached around in the water for some stones. Finding some, she tried to throw them at the birds but she was far too weak. The stones bounced off the wall back into the well, Becca having to sidestep them to avoid being hit.

Then, all together, as if they had been disturbed, the birds left in a cacophony of frantically beating wings. Silence followed. Becca strained her ears, but heard nothing. *Was there someone above?*

She looked up and could see only gloomy clouds.

Then, on her forehead, a fat splat of water landed. She squinted as it ran down into her eyes. She rubbed it away but the raindrop was followed by another. Within seconds, the raindrops were coming thick and fast. *Just fucking great,* she thought, knowing that not only would she get soaked again, but there was no way of keeping her school clothes dry. *Unless* – she quickly scooped up her clothes, not yet dry but at least not drenched as they had been, and bundled them into the remaining plastic carrier bag, with her iPod, which she then put into her schoolbag.

By the time Becca had rescued her clothes, the rain was coming down hard. Thunder growled above and the sky darkened further. The noise of the rain within the well was deafening. Even beneath the jumper and the football shirt her body was starting to feel wet. She cursed again – and then smiled as she realised that nature had delivered a great gift.

Becca whooped, elated. She cupped her hands together and let the water collect there, before drinking it deeply. It tasted cold, clean and good. She drank another handful, but her stomach twisted in protest. She didn't want to bring it back up, so stopped.

The rain was now pounding down. *I need this*, she thought. *I can't let it go.* She fumbled around for the lunchbox, removed its lid and held it level. Despite the now torrential rain, it seemed to take an age to fill. She emptied the rain into the water bottle, then did the same again, filling the bottle in a couple of attempts. Brushing away her drenched, tangled hair, she then filled the orange can. Finally, she let the sandwich box fill up and snapped the lid into place, satisfied.

Thunder rumbled above and there was a bright flash of lightning. The rain came down even harder.

Becca cupped her hands again and allowed herself another drink. Her stomach fluttered, but she held on to the water. She was again soaked to the skin, but no worse than she'd been for the last few days.

Weary, she sat down in the water, listening to the rainstorm. She smiled. The rain was her first bit of good fortune in days. It renewed her determination.

9

Ed Davis ran across the road, through the pounding rain, to where Tom Randle was gathering a small group of children, ready to cross the road. Ed was amazed that any of the children had braved leaving the school during such stormy weather, but such was the pull of the local chip shop compared to the school's own dinners.

Lunchtime was almost over and the drenched children were huddled together, desperate to get under cover.

Randle had been expecting this moment most of the morning. When he'd arrived, there were already several police officers waiting – not that they paid much attention to him. He was just another old fart doing a dead-end job. *They'd get around to me later, once they'd spoken to the teachers*, thought Randle. *And probably the cleaners.*

Like everyone else, he didn't initially know what was going on – other than it was clearly serious. Even when the school had experienced rare but acute bullying problems, there had only been a couple of policemen.

The day had started with two police cars at the school gates with perhaps a handful of police officers. By lunchtime, that number had more than doubled. Randle didn't usually stay around between his three shifts (when the school opened, at lunchtime and when it closed) but today he made an exception; like everyone else, he wanted to know what was going on.

When he found out, he realised he had something of a problem. He knew he was one of the last people to see Becca and Matt on Friday; he also knew that they'd not been home on Saturday. The fact that he knew these things wasn't in itself a problem. What was most definitely a problem was the way that police worked: one question begets another. Friday at school he could probably get away with. He couldn't recall anything that might raise suspicion, other than Becca's almost hostile eye contact with him and her friend's guarded glance over in his direction while they were both talking. Saturday was considerably more difficult. His alibi of a photographic hobby was paper thin when placed at the home of someone who'd just gone missing. Randle decided that the best strategy was silence. *In a school of around four hundred pupils*, he'd say, *they were just another couple of faces at the crossing*. Offering anything more could encourage a line of questioning that could quickly become very uncomfortable.

"Thomas Randle?" shouted Ed above the noise of the rain.

Randle nodded, a pantomime nod, to make sure the policeman understood him. *Stupid fuck*, thought Randle. *How many other Thomas Randles would be working the crossing at the school?*

"Can we talk?" Ed indicated towards the school with his thumb. "When you've finished?"

Randle nodded. "Sure," he shouted. "Five minutes." He held his hand up, fingers outstretched, to make sure the policeman understood: *five*.

Randle hoped he looked calm and casual, but decided that there probably wasn't a right way to look in situations such as these. Two children had gone missing: calm and casual was almost certainly as incriminating as packing your bags and booking a flight to South America.

He herded the remaining children across the road and waited for the faint ringing of the school bell. Despite what he'd said, he was contracted to hang around for another ten minutes. The police would have to wait; anything else would look suspicious.

When Randle made it across the road into the school, he was drenched, despite his plastic rainwear.

"You had lunch?" asked Ed.

Randle propped his crossing sign against the wall, then took off his jacket and shook it outside the door. "Nope. I'll grab some in a bit. Got to be back here before three."

"Can you spare fifteen minutes? We could do with talking to you about the missing children."

"Sure," said Randle, wiping the rain from his soaked beard. "Of course."

Ed led the way to the library. He couldn't immediately see why Becca might find Randle creepy. He seemed affable enough: his manner was pleasant and his body language unguarded. But if Becca believed it, he wanted to dig a little.

They sat in the library, Randle warming by the radiator while one of the junior officers went to make them some coffee.

Ed smiled at Randle. "I'm really sorry to keep you from your lunch," he said.

Randle held up his hands to dismiss the apology, but Ed had already continued to speak. "You've heard what's happened?" asked Ed.

Randle nodded. "A couple of the kids have gone missing?"

"Right. A boy and a girl. This isn't a formal questioning. We're just asking a few questions. We're trying to make it fairly fast to begin with as we need to work around a lot of people. But I especially wanted to speak to you."

Ed held eye contact with Randle, measuring his reactions. Randle's reply was one of genuine surprise, without a trace of fear or hostility. "Oh? Why's that?"

Ed switched tack, hoping that sidestepping the question might wrong-foot Randle. "Do you know the missing children?" He held up two photographs, one of Becca and one of Matt.

"Not especially," said Randle, considering the pictures. "I know their faces, but there are hundreds of children in this school and I see them all every day."

The officer arrived with the coffee. Randle took a deep, grateful drink. "Thanks for that," he said. "I'm drenched and chilled to the bone."

"I'll try and be done quickly," said Ed. "I hope you don't mind me asking. I noticed your limp. Accident?"

"Sadly, no. I was in the army. Northern Ireland. On the wrong end of a car bomb."

That explains his build, thought Ed. *He clearly still keeps in shape, despite the leg.* "I am sorry," he said.

"No need," replied Randle. "I was lucky. Some of my mates didn't make it home."

Ed paused. "It may be that you were one of the last people to see the children. We don't know where they went after they left the school. Do you remember seeing them on Friday evening?"

It was an innocent enough question, but Randle's instincts told him that the policeman was testing him, as if he already knew the answer to the question. Randle took another look over the photographs to buy a little time. After a moment, he said, "Possibly. It really is hard to say. They're both familiar. I think so, maybe. I'm sorry, it's hard to be precise."

"Don't you know them by name?" asked Ed. *That,* thought Randle, *is definitely a trap.*

"I'm not sure. The boy is new – I think. The girl – I think she's called Rebecca?"

Ed nodded. "I thought you might have known her better, what with you having photographed her so many times."

Randle's heart skipped a beat. "I'm sorry?"

Ed fished out a handful of photographs from a file. "I think you took these – for the school website?" There was no indication of accusation in his voice. Randle wondered if he'd worried unnecessarily.

"Yes, those are mine," he said, with a touch of pride. "But I take so many photos for the school. I really don't remember everyone's name. But I remember her now – she's the swimmer."

Ed nodded. "They're good," he said, hoping the praise sounded genuine. "Better than mine. I've been into photography for a couple of years, but I'm never really that happy with the results. What sort of camera have you got?"

"A Canon. Not a great one, but good enough. You?"

"Nikon. It's only a basic model, but I don't know how to use half of the settings on it."

"I wouldn't have minded a Nikon," said Randle, "but I couldn't afford it."

"I probably couldn't buy a new one either," sighed Ed. "I got mine second-hand."

Like anyone asked about their hobby, Randle had visibly relaxed. Ed decided it was time to corner him. "I was speaking to one of the other teachers," he said, referring to his notes; more for effect than necessity. "Louise Sanderson. She says she was one of the last teachers to leave and you were still outside."

"Yes, that's right," he said. "I have to wait until all of the children are gone."

"One of the other children said that Rebecca and Matthew didn't leave right away, that they were hanging around. Are you sure you didn't see them?"

Randle felt the hairs on his neck rise. *I can't change my story now*, he thought. He shook his head. "Not especially. I'm sure I did see them, but I don't recall anything special or different about them that day."

It was a reasonable enough answer. Ed scratched his head. "I know what you mean. But sometimes people see things and forget them because they're not important. Right now, any little detail could be important."

Randle screwed up his forehead to give the impression of thinking hard. "No, I'm sorry, I really can't remember anything else."

"Fair enough," said Ed, gathering up the photographs and replacing them in the file. He deliberately left one on the table, a picture taken by Randle of Becca in her swimsuit, hair wet and slicked back, collecting a medal. "If you do think of anything, you will tell us?"

"Of course," said Randle, as earnestly as possible.

"Oh, one more question," said Ed. "Have you ever been to Rebecca's house, or met her family?"

Randle worked hard to keep his voice steady, but felt Ed's eyes burning into him. "I guess I may have seen them around, but I really don't remember. Like the kids, I see hundreds of parents every day. I've no idea where she lives."

Ed nodded. The answer wasn't unreasonable – it was possible that being on Lincoln Street was a coincidence, though Ed thought that unlikely. He decided to back off until he'd had a chance to find out a bit more about Randle. On top of that, he didn't want to push the questioning – that was a mistake he'd made once before and he didn't want to repeat it on such a high-profile case.

"We'll probably need to talk to you again, if that's OK? At the moment we only have the basic facts – if that, to be honest – so our interviews with other people may raise questions about other things we need to ask you about."

"That's fine," said Randle, "anything I can do to help. Am I OK to go?"

Ed nodded. "Thanks for your time."

Randle reached out his hand and Ed shook it. Randle's grasp was firm.

Ed picked up the lone photograph. "Pretty girl," he said, absently.

"I guess," said Randle, glancing at the picture.

"Thanks again," said Ed, closing off the conversation.

Randle gathered up his reflective jacket and left. He couldn't decide if he'd hit it off with the policeman, or whether that was just what he'd wanted Randle to think. He couldn't shake the feeling that the policeman knew more than he was saying.

In retrospect, Randle wished he'd been more honest. After all, he had nothing to hide. The girl's disappearance was nothing to do with him. *Still*, he thought, confidently, *a couple more conversations like that and they'll leave me alone.*

Ed went to the library door and watched Randle limp down the corridor. He had nothing concrete on which to base his conclusion, but he felt sure that Randle was hiding something.

10

Less than three hours after they'd started to drive around Becca and Matt's most likely routes home, Jenny and Sarah returned home. They'd exhausted each route, several times, but the search was mostly pointless. The pounding rain made it almost impossible to see anything.

Drenched and frustrated, Sarah threw her dripping coat into the sink and brushed her bedraggled hair out of her eyes. "Nothing," she said, in answer to Jim's questioning look. She didn't have to ask if Becca or Matt had called – if they had, Jim would have rung her straight away.

Sarah was exhausted, her body running on adrenalin. "I'm soaked," she said, "and I've only run from the car." She flopped onto the sofa and kicked off her shoes.

Ever practical (and increasingly uncertain how to handle Sarah's progressively angry mood) Jim busied himself making some tea. Jenny Greenwood was conferring in the hall with the policeman who had been left with Jim, Ashley Morgan. Jim thought that fresh-faced Morgan was improbably young to be working at all, let alone as a policeman.

Jenny put her head around the door. "Ashley's going now. If you don't mind, I'm going to call in for an update."

Jim sat down next to Sarah and handed her the tea. She cupped the warm mug in her hands and sipped from it, shivering.

"Do you want me to get a towel?" asked Jim.

Oh grow some balls and stop being so sensible, thought Sarah. She shook her head. "I'll change and dry off in a minute."

Jim put his hand on Sarah's knee. "Sarah? It's not my fault, you know."

Fury rose inside her and she pushed his hand away, hard. She slammed her mug down on the coffee table, hot tea slopping out. Jim put his hand back on her knee. "I know you're angry," he began.

She cut him short. "Angry? Angry? Of course I'm fucking angry!" The tension that had been building within her surfaced; the accusations already prepared in her mind. *His fault. His fault because it was Matt's fault. It had to be Matt's fault. We'd have come back sooner if it wasn't for you. You stopped me calling Becca.* The thoughts spun around in Sarah's tired, wired mind, ready to explode from her mouth.

But Sarah didn't explode. Without warning, she lost control and disintegrated emotionally: absolutely, completely crushed. Tears flowed down her face; she wailed, distraught. Jim pulled her close. She tried to push him away, hitting his chest. Jim just pulled her closer. She gave in and let herself be held while she cried uncontrollably.

"She's just a baby," she shrieked. "Just a baby."

She wasn't angry with Jim, she finally realised. Jim hadn't forced her not to come home right away. She'd been willing enough to go along with his suggestions to stay. She was angry with herself – and she was angry with the world: a warped world where innocent children go missing or are taken. Where sometimes they never come home.

Jim held her tight – silent but absolutely, totally there for her. He brushed her wet hair away from her eyes and stroked her head.

He held her until she cried herself dry. And, for each long tormented minute, Sarah was grateful to be in his arms.

11

In her dream, Becca was drowning. Alone in a vast dark place, she was trying desperately to tread water – and failing. Her head kept slipping under water while her arms and feet flailed around hopelessly. Somewhere, in a place she knew for certain would be light, warm and dry, a woman was laughing at her. "I thought you could swim," said the voice, its gently accented burr mocking her. It was one of those rare dreams where everything is so realistic you can touch and taste it – and yet still be certain you were dreaming. Becca spluttered and coughed, taking water into her lungs. There was a thunder-crack and Becca jolted upright, suddenly awake, spitting water.

Something was wrong, very wrong. For a moment, Becca couldn't place it, disorientated as she dragged herself reluctantly into the waking world.

She was in the well, with its familiar dark, cold and wet. The rain was deafening, the sky lead-grey. Lightning flashed. Then she realised what was wrong: the water was higher, far higher than it had been. She coughed hard, retching water and phlegm.

Becca hadn't meant to fall asleep, but her fever and exhaustion were now rooted in every cell in her body. While she'd slept – she had no idea for how long – the falling rain had swelled the water in the well and it was now up to her neck. Asleep, her head limp, she'd started to inhale the rising water.

Shit, she thought, dismayed. She'd initially welcomed the rain but hadn't realised the consequences of such a severe downpour. *This*, she thought, *is going to be a real problem.*

She wouldn't be able to sit down for much longer without being under water.

Standing would buy her time – but how much? And for how long could she stand upright? *I'll sit as long as I can*, she thought, but she knew that wouldn't be for very long. She coughed again, her throat raw. Her fever was getting worse, she instinctively knew. Everything around her seemed fuzzy and distant.

Becca felt massively weary. The last three days had been one terrible trial after another – and, although she'd not triumphed at any point, she'd managed to retain at least some determination. Now, for the first time, she felt like giving in. *Let it rain*, she thought, almost relieved to be resigned to her fate. *It's only a matter of time anyway.* She looked over at Matt, just a shape in the dark. *It would be something for them to find us both together, hand in hand*, she thought – but she couldn't bear the notion of holding hands with Matt's rotting corpse.

And then, just as in her dream, she heard a sound that cut easily through the pounding rain: a woman, laughing hard.

12

"Jim, I know this is difficult, but I could do with talking to both you and Sarah," said Jenny.

Sarah was sleeping. When she'd finally stopped crying, Jim had persuaded her to try to sleep for a while. After some protestation, she'd reluctantly agreed, but didn't think that she'd sleep – yet, both physically and emotionally exhausted, she'd fallen asleep within minutes. Jim had stayed with her until he was sure she was sound asleep, then made his way downstairs.

"Sarah's sleeping," said Jim. "But you can talk to me." Jim desperately wanted to sleep himself. He felt as if he was jet-lagged, but thought that he could grab a few hours' rest once Sarah had slept. *One of us needs to be awake*, he had thought.

He sat down opposite Jenny. "Fire away," he said.

It was hard not to like Jenny. She was young – in her late twenties, Jim thought – and very pretty. She kept her red, curly hair tied tightly back – presumably regulation. But it was her demeanour that won people over. She radiated calm. Jim imagined that the wrong person in a situation such as this could make it worse – someone too serious, or too emotional, could initially seem supportive but would actually heighten the mood of others. While Jenny didn't spend her time cracking jokes to alleviate the tension, her approach to every conversation turned things towards the positive; she was naturally good at herding the moods of others.

"We need to talk to the media," said Jenny, knowing that while being direct can feel initially like an unwelcome broadside, frankness can be the most effective way to acclimatise someone to a painful idea. As she'd expected, Jim looked uncomfortable.

"The media?"

"There are two sides to this," said Jenny. "The first, and most important, is that we could really use their help. Our top priority is to find Rebecca and Matthew – by any means. Today's search is not going well, to be honest, mainly because of the weather. We may well have to cover all of the same ground tomorrow, or when the weather clears. That's a lot of lost time."

Jim nodded. "OK," he said.

"Television and radio appeals can help us *a lot*," said Jenny. "Of course, the newspapers can too, although they're not anywhere near as instant. But it all counts. But – to make this work – we need to do this as soon as possible, which I know is going to be hard for you."

Jim reflected on the many television appeals he'd seen: parents pleading desperately for news of their children. He never thought that he'd be in the same position.

"No, it's OK. Well, it's not OK, but it needs to be done. We can do it."

Jenny smiled. "Good. We'll help you, give you a little coaching."

There was a pause.

"And the second thing?" asked Jim.

"This is a little more difficult," said Jenny. "Initially, the press will be on your side. But we need to work with them and keep them with us. In a situation like this, it's usually not long before there are some comments made about the parents."

"What?" said Jim. "We've done nothing wrong."

"Of course not," said Jenny. "But when reporters are not in full possession of the facts, they could write things as *they* see them – which may not be how *you* see them. They may ask you some difficult and upsetting questions. Questions that are not easy to answer."

"Such as?" Jim was working hard to control his anger.

Jenny looked at him directly in the eye until he'd calmed a little.

"That's exactly what I mean," said Jenny, gently. "I can tell that you're not a man to lose it easily. But in a situation such as this, it can be difficult to keep control – *but you need to.* We have to keep the press on-side, so they're one hundred per cent focused on finding Rebecca and Matt."

"But this is not our fault," said Jim.

"No. I know that. You know that. But what about outsiders? If the press handle it in the wrong way, Rebecca and Matthew become latchkey kids with uncaring parents."

Jenny paused, so that Jim could let the thought sink in. He breathed in through gritted teeth.

"Jim. Believe me when I say we have only one agenda. We have to find your children, end of story. I'm telling you these things to prepare you. If I don't say them, someone from the press will. And when they do, which they will, you need to – well, not react like that. You need to be more controlled."

Jim knew she was right. He nodded. "OK."

"It will help us and you," said Jenny, "if Sarah does most of the talking. An appeal has more impact from the mother. But Sarah's quite – well, wound up."

"She's not normally like that," said Jim.

"I know," said Jenny, "but this is not a normal situation."

"You're telling me."

"Sarah's not handling it well – but that's not unexpected. I think it is harder for a mother – no offence."

Jim raised his hand. "None taken. You're probably right."

"But we need to run through some of these more difficult questions, just in case, so she's not caught off guard. Do you think she will be OK with that?"

"I'm sure she will. With some help from you. She's not finding it too easy to lean on me right now."

"She's looking for someone to blame. She knows it's not your fault."

Jim shrugged. "Maybe."

"She *does*. You just have to stick with her. She needs you."

Jim rubbed his face, his eyes tired. "OK. When do we get in touch with the press?"

"They've already been in touch with us – we have reporters working within the police all of the time. And a story like this – well, you can't keep a lid on it for long. I'm afraid it will get pretty scary. But if we work with them, we can agree that they only have contact with you at arranged press conferences, so you shouldn't be bothered too much – although it's not going to be long before they're camping out in the street. Don't worry, they won't hound you so hard that it's unreasonable or upsetting. And we will be assigning more police to the house; that will help keep them at bay."

"We just want the kids back," said Jim. "I don't care what it takes, and I'm sure that Sarah won't either. What do we need to do?"

Jenny folded her hands into a steeple on which she rested her chin.

"We want to be on national television tonight," she said, "on the evening news."

13

Helen had decided to drive home via the lane up to the quarry. Although it took her in the opposite direction to Abby's shop in the centre of town, she wanted to see whether the police had begun looking nearby.

Her car bounced down the muddy, potholed lane – the pounding rain proving too much for her windscreen wipers; despite being switched on full, they were unable to keep the torrent of water off the window.

This is stupid, thought Helen, struggling to see more than a few feet in front of her. She eased her foot off the accelerator and peered ahead, through the curtains of rain. It was only just after four-thirty, but the sky was almost as dark as night.

As she reached the sharp left-hand turn just before the path to the quarry, Helen slowed as much as she could. She paused where the road took a sharp left. As she pulled away and accelerated, a blurred figure rushed in front of the car. Helen hit the brakes, hard, but too late – she felt the car jolt as it hit something solid. Helen brought the car skidding to a stop, her heart pounding.

Oh God, she thought, *I've hit someone.* She felt momentarily sick and breathed in deep to push the nausea away.

Helen pushed the car door open and ran to the front of the car, the rain soaking her instantly.

In the glare of the headlights, a young woman lay in the mud, motionless, long curly hair obscuring her face. She was barefoot and her untidy full-length dress had ridden up to expose her calves.

Helen knelt beside her. *I wasn't going that fast,* she thought, but shouted above the rain, "Are you OK? Are you hurt?" She didn't want to move the woman in case she was hurt, but she shook her shoulder, gently.

The woman's hand shot out and grabbed Helen's wrist. Her grip was tight and painful; her skin icy cold. Helen screamed. In one swift movement, the woman pulled Helen to the ground and rolled on top of her, pinning Helen down firmly.

Helen screamed again and then shouted, "Get off me!" She wriggled and struggled hard, but the woman held her tightly. *Shit, she's strong,* thought Helen. Helen's torso bucked, but the woman didn't budge. She squeezed Helen's arms so tightly it hurt, and then said, "Shhhh. Lie still, negru căţea."

Helen tried to push the woman off her, but couldn't. She stopped struggling, spitting the pouring rain out of her face.

The woman leaned forwards, until her face was close to Helen's – so close she could feel her icy breath. *Oh dear God,* she thought, realising who the woman was.

"Keep still, woman-lover," she hissed. The woman's wet hair cascaded down around Helen's face.

"Let me go," demanded Helen.

The woman laughed, defiant. "I do not do as you say," she said. "You do as I say."

"There's nothing you can make me do," shouted Helen.

"You think so? Let's see." The woman's face inched closer. "I want you to be still." The words came out evenly, as a command. The woman relaxed her grip on Helen's hands and, to her horror, Helen found that she couldn't move.

"You see?" The woman reached around behind her and pulled out a long knife. She held it close to Helen's face.

"No, please," pleaded Helen, tears forming in her eyes.

The woman laughed again. "So fast, from defiant to begging. So easy." She teased Helen's face with the blade, stroking her cheek with it.

"Some things you need to understand, iubitor de femeie."

Helen was crying openly. "No, no, no," she sobbed.

The woman put the blade flat to Helen's lips. "Shhh."

"First thing to know is that you stay away. You come back, you die. Do you know this?"

Helen nodded, sniffling.

"Second thing is that there are worse things than to die. I show you this, so you know it." The woman put the knife away and smiled. She stroked Helen's cheek, gently, then brushed the wet hair from Helen's face. Her hand was like cold meat against Helen's skin. "You want me," she said.

Helen shook her head and sobbed. "No, I don't!" The woman leaned right over Helen and whispered into her ear. "You want me." Then she kissed Helen. Her lips were icy, but the cold touch against her own lips felt so good. The woman was right – Helen did want her, with a strength of animal desire that she'd never before felt. Helen kissed her back, hungrily. She was instantly and enormously aroused; her fear had left her totally. She wrapped her arms around the woman and pulled her closer, kissing her deeply. After a moment, the woman pulled back and slapped Helen hard across the face.

Helen's fear returned and she felt repulsed at what she'd done. Realising that her hands were free, she reached to grab the woman's throat, but was far too slow. The woman grabbed her wrists and pinned her to the ground again.

"You understand, negru curvă? I decide what you do. If you live or die. I don't want your body, but if I decide to take it you will *want* to give it to me. If you come back. You understand?"

Helen nodded. "I understand, you fucking bitch."

The woman smiled, calm and unthreatened. She forced Helen's arms together and then held them both easily with one hand. She pulled up the sleeve of Helen's jumper, exposing her right arm; it was bare apart from the bandage, white against Helen's dark skin.

The woman reached for the knife again and stroked Helen's bare arm with the blade. The knife touched the bandage. "My friend he bite you. It hurt, yes?"

Helen said nothing. The woman slid the knife under the bandage and tugged the blade upwards, cutting it away. "Big bite for small bird," she said. "But not big enough to keep you away."

The woman brought the knife back to Helen's arm and she felt it dig into her. Helen struggled but couldn't move. She screamed as the woman pulled the blade downwards, making a clean five-inch cut along her forearm. "So this time you remember," said the woman. "You do remember?"

"Yes, I remember," Helen shouted back. The pain was agonising.

"Good. You stay out of things. Keep away."

The woman stood and put the knife away.

"Our secret," said the woman. She leant forwards and kissed Helen on the cheek – this time the kiss was chilling and awful.

Helen shook her head. "I have no secrets from Abby."

"This I think you will. You tell her how easily you gave yourself to me, how much you wanted me? I think not."

Helen was silent. The woman turned and walked away, disappearing into the falling rain.

Helen lay still for a few moments and then dragged herself up, supporting herself against the bonnet of the car. She was bedraggled, soaked to the skin. She looked at the blood running down her arm, being washed away by the rain.

Sobbing and shaking, she got back into the car, and locked the doors. Then she broke down completely, the windows of the car steaming up while she sat and cried, drenched and in agony.

But worse than the cut, worse than her bruised arms, Helen could still taste the woman on her lips and tongue.

14

It had been a hard day. Ed Davis took a long, grateful drink of his beer. "I needed that," he said.

"Steady, Eddie," said Stephen Carter. *That's nearly half a pint in one go*, he thought.

"I've only had a few hours off in the last few days and I'm not in until tomorrow. There's not going to be much downtime until this thing's sorted one way or another. I'm making the most of it."

Stephen sipped his drink. "Fair enough," he said. Ed was a bit too fond of his drink for Stephen's liking. They often shared an after-work pint, but whereas Stephen would have one or two at the most, Ed would have twice that, or more, before making his way home. Ed was a good cop, but not great; he had an impulsive nature that ran counter to good policing. If Ed had been a TV cop, he'd be the plucky maverick whose reckless nature delivered enough results to keep him in his job. The reality was that Ed wasn't bold enough to be a true maverick and only occasionally did his impetuous nature bring real results. In a bigger town with a larger police department, he probably wouldn't hold on to his job – but the Bankside force was a small team which looked after its own. They generally accepted each other's foibles and focused on getting the best from each other, although Stephen was pretty sure that Ed was stretching the station's camaraderie a bit too far – especially with his drinking.

"When are you back on?" asked Ed.

"In a couple of hours," said Stephen, "overlapping with Jenny at the family's house."

"Lucky you," said Ed. "I wouldn't mind pairing up with her."

"Who wouldn't?" agreed Stephen. "Best legs at the Bankside station. Possibly in town."

Ed drained his pint. "Great arse, too. Another?"

Stephen shook his head. "Not for me."

Ed bought himself another pint and sat down again. "How did the search go today?" he asked.

"We've only drawn blanks," said Stephen. "We've not really been able to do a proper physical search because of the rain and so far the CCTV's given us nothing, although we've only just got going on that. Spoke to the girl's real father; he's one hundred per cent clean. You?"

"Pretty much the same," replied Ed. "Nothing after they were seen outside school. I feel like we've interviewed half the school, but I guess we've only talked to a tenth – if that. We didn't really get much that we didn't already know."

Ed frowned. "I keep running one interview over in my mind, though. Something I can't put my finger on."

Ed explained what Hannah had said about Randle, then ran through his conversation with him earlier that day.

Stephen was dubious. "Doesn't sound like much to me. When you boil it down, all you've got is that Rebecca thought he was a bit creepy."

"Well, and he *was* seen near the house. But that could be a coincidence. No, it's not much. But right now it's all we have."

"Did he seem evasive?"

"Not at all. He was helpful if anything," said Ed.

"What about his record?"

"CRB checked out fine, has for years. He's well-liked. A war hero. A big part of the school," said Ed, finishing his beer. "Another?"

"No, I'm off after this one."

Ed sat down with his third pint. "It's just a feeling. There was nothing wrong with what he said, but it didn't quite tally."

Stephen shrugged. "That's not unusual. You don't often get exactly matching stories. People just don't remember things in the same way."

Ed couldn't shake the feeling that Randle was hiding something. "I want to talk to him again."

Stephen frowned. "Make sure you do it under caution, then – and have someone else there."

"What are you saying?"

"By the book, Ed, that's all. By the book. We've got outsiders running this one now. This is going to be a national news story by tonight. Everyone's going to be watching everyone else."

"I do know how to do my job, you know."

There was an uncomfortable silence. "I'm just saying," said Stephen, leaving the sentence unfinished.

"I know what you're saying. You're having a go about that Meadows kid."

Stephen didn't rise to the bait; Ed's temper was growing and any answer would probably make things worse – but he was right. The Meadows kid was exactly who Stephen had been thinking of.

Wayne Meadows had been informally questioned as a suspect. Another local boy, Sean something or other – Stephen couldn't remember – had been attacked with a knife. It was late at night and Sean hadn't seen his attacker. As these things go, it wasn't a serious injury, but in a small town that kind of crime is rare. Ed had handled the interview; convinced of the boy's guilt, he had handled it badly – very, very badly. He'd led the suspect in the questioning and, when he didn't get the answer he wanted, had lost his temper. He'd not hit Meadows, but he came close. He'd directly – and aggressively – accused Meadows. By the time Meadows was formally interviewed, he'd been assigned a lawyer who quite naturally used Ed's behaviour to demonstrate that Meadows had been bullied, led and told enough about the crime to compromise any real interview. Although Ed hadn't been formally cautioned, Sergeant Hutchinson had made his feelings clearly known. Ed wasn't in the least contrite. In his view, Meadows was just another young criminal who they'd struggle to convict anyway. Put him in front of a half-female jury, in a new high-street suit, and even if they found him guilty he'd probably get off with just a few months' community service.

Stephen brushed the matter aside as if it were unimportant. "That's in the past – and nothing came of it anyhow. But this is a much bigger deal. Come on Ed, I'm not having a go. I'm your mate."

Ed shrugged, disappointed that the argument had been defused. "OK, fair enough. It's just that we have so little to go on."

"It's early days. But if all we have is what your girl says about this bloke, then we need to follow it up right. You can't – you're her Dad."

Ed nodded. "I know. I'll call in and get someone else on it."

"Do you want me to call it in?" asked Stephen.

"No, it's fine – I'll do it."

Stephen drained his pint and stood up, patting Ed on the shoulder. "I've got to be off," he said. "Don't make it too late. Makes you think, girl the same age as yours goes missing. Family is important."

"Damn right," agreed Ed. "See you tomorrow."

Ed watched Stephen leave, drained his pint and then bought another and took it back to his table. Then he went outside, away from the noise of the pub. He pulled out his mobile phone and called Hannah's number. "Hi Han, it's Dad."

"Hi Dad," said Hannah. "Any news?"

"Sorry baby, no. We've been looking all day but we've not found anything. But that's a good thing. It means that they could still be alright."

"Do you think so?"

"I hope so," said Ed. "Listen, can I talk to you about the crossing attendant? Mr Randle?"

"Sure," said Hannah.

"I won't be mad, I promise. But I need to know. Did Becca say anything else about him? Anything at all?"

There was a pause. "I don't think so Dad, no. Have you talked to him?"

"I have, Han, but I can't really tell you about it, you know that. But he didn't say anything to help us. He said he didn't really remember seeing them."

"That's not true," blurted Hannah. "He kept looking at her, I said that."

"I know," said Ed, "but even though he made Becca feel uncomfortable, it probably didn't mean anything."

"I guess so," said Hannah, doubtfully.

"OK. Listen, we're going to have to talk to you properly – take a statement. Is that OK?"

Hannah paused. "Yeah. It sounds a bit scary, though."

"It won't be, Han, I promise."

"OK, Dad."

"And tell your Mum that I'm working late," he lied. "And I'll be stopping off for a quick pint later on my way home – it's been a long day."

"OK Dad, I will."

"And Hannah – I love you."

"I love you too Dad."

He rang off and went back to his pint, brooding.

Someone needs to talk to Randle pretty soon, he thought, and considered ringing the station to get someone onto it. He looked at his watch; it was approaching six.

Fuck it, he thought. He called into the station and Angela Jones answered. "Ange, can you go through today's notes and get me the address of Thomas Randle? The school crossing attendant. Can you text it through to me?"

"Sure," said Angela, at the other end of the line. "Give me ten minutes. Any reason?"

"No, not really," said Ed. "I'm just looking at where some of the staff live, if they might have walked home the same way as the kids."

"OK Ed, see you tomorrow."

"Night, Angela." He rang off, finished his pint and bought another.

A few minutes later, true to her word, Angela's text came through. *The benefits of working in a small station,* he thought, knowing that any properly run police department wouldn't put up with officers sidestepping protocol.

He went back to the bar and ordered another beer. *A couple more,* he thought, *and I'll go and have a chat with Mr Randle, when he's all relaxed, settling down to watch a night's television.*

15

"Mummy, Helen's hurt!"

Abby had closed the shop almost an hour ago, but had only just finished tidying and cashing up. She stopped what she was doing and looked at Sammy. Sammy had clearly been crying – and was still running a temperature, her hair sweaty and untidy.

"Did she phone, Sam?" asked Abby, knowing that she'd not heard the phone ring but asked anyway. Sammy shook her head, coughing.

"Do you know where she is?"

"Not really. She's in the car. It's dark and she's very upset so her thoughts are all muddled. She's been in the car for ages."

Abby reached for the phone. "You don't need to call her, Mummy. She's nearly home now. But she's very scared."

"Do you know what happened? What's she scared of?"

Sammy clung tightly to her mother. "The bad woman," she said. "She's scared of her. And –" Sammy's voice tailed away.

"Someone else?" prompted Abby.

Sammy wiped away a tear and nodded. "Yes." She seemed reluctant to say any more.

"Who?" pressed Abby, frustrated that she couldn't sense even slightly what Sammy saw so clearly. "Do you know?"

Sammy nodded. "Yes, Mummy. She's scared of you. Scared of what you're going to say. You have to be nice to her. She's very upset."

Dear God, thought Abby. She couldn't imagine what had happened and desperately wanted Helen to be home. She didn't have to wait long. Less than a minute later, she heard the back door to the flat open and close. She ran through to the sitting room behind the shop, Sammy following her.

Nothing could have prepared Abby for the sight in front of her.

Helen was wavering on her feet, steadying herself against the door – but Abby could only just tell that it was Helen. She was soaked, and covered in mud almost from head to foot. Her hair was a wild, dripping mess. The front of her jumper and skirt were covered in blood. Helen held her right arm protectively against her chest.

Abby couldn't see whether the blood was coming from Helen's arm or chest.

She rushed to Helen, who almost fell into her arms, sobbing. Abby led her to the sofa.

She turned to Sammy, who was crying again and had almost turned white. "Sammy, come here a second," said Abby, trying to sound calm. "I need you to be a big grown-up now. I need your help. Can you do that?"

Sammy nodded, brushing her tears away.

"Go and get me some towels from the airing cupboard. And a big bottle of water from the kitchen."

Sammy turned, then hesitated. "How many towels?"

"It doesn't matter. Four, get four," Abby replied. *And I thought she could read minds*, she thought. Sammy ran upstairs and Abby turned her attention to Helen, pulling her close.

Helen surrendered herself to Abby's embrace, shaking with both fear and cold –and sobbing uncontrollably. She tried to talk. "It – it was – her. It was her. God – it was awful."

Abby shushed her. "Don't talk. You can tell me about it in a bit. We need to get you cleaned up." She fought back her own tears. *Time for that later,* she thought.

Sammy returned with the towels. She handed them to Abby, and said, in a quiet voice, "I suppose you want me to go upstairs now?"

Truth be told, that was exactly what Abby wanted – not because she didn't want Sammy to see Helen in this state, but because she didn't feel she could cope with both of the girls in her life crying at the same time. "No, Sam, you don't have to. But I need you to be quiet for a moment, while I help Helen. I know this is scary stuff, but Helen's going to be OK, really. I promise. Can you sit and be quiet?"

Sammy nodded.

"Good girl."

Abby ignored the mud covering Helen and concentrated on her arm. She poured the water over Helen's arm. Then she soaked one of the towels with it before carefully wiping her arm. It was a long, clean cut. Although there was a lot of blood, it didn't look as though the artery had been cut – the blood was flowing, not pumping.

"Crap, Helen, this is a pretty bad cut." Abby realised too late that she'd sworn in front of Sammy. *As if she's not heard me say it – or think it – before*, she thought.

Helen nodded, sniffling. "Tell me about it."

"We need to get you cleaned up. Then see if I can stop the bleeding. If I can't, we'll have to take you to the hospital. You might need stitches."

Helen didn't protest, but Abby knew that taking her to hospital wouldn't necessarily be a smart thing to do. The cut was so straight that it was obviously intentional. Questions would be asked, such as *had someone done this, or had she done it herself?* They could come up with some kind of story, but if the doctor didn't believe them, the police could be called.

One thing at a time, thought Helen. She glanced over at Sammy, who was staring intently at them. "Is Helen OK, Mummy?"

"Yes, Sam, she is. We just need to get her cleaned up. She's a mess. Could you go and turn the shower on?"

Sammy nodded and ran upstairs again.

Abby stood and helped Helen to her feet. "Come on, you, let's get you clean. Just keep pressing this towel against your arm."

Abby led Helen upstairs and into the bathroom. She sat her on the toilet. "Helen, give me a minute to sort Sammy, OK?"

Helen nodded, sniffing back tears.

"Come on, Sam." She led Sammy into the sitting room.

"Look Sammy, I'm really sorry. But I need to clean Helen up and it's going to take a bit of time."

"I know, Mummy."

"Will you be OK on your own for a few minutes? Watching TV?"

Sammy nodded. "Will you have to take Helen to the hospital?"

"I don't know, baby. I hope not. I think it looks worse than it is." She squeezed Sammy's hand. "I'll be back in a few minutes."

"OK Mummy. Look after Helen." Abby turned to go, but Sammy held on to her hand. "Remember what I said, Mummy. Don't be mad. She's not saying, but she's scared of you." Puzzled, Abby squeezed Sammy's hand again and kissed her forehead. "OK, Sam. I promise."

She went back to the bathroom and closed the door gently. The hot shower was already steaming up the tiled walls. She knelt in front of Helen and took her hands. "You OK?"

Helen shook her head and started crying again.

"Come on," she said, "let's get you cleaned up and dried."

She undressed Helen, taking care when removing her jumper to not hurt her arm. She was a soaked, shivering, muddy mess. Abby led Helen to the shower. "Hang on," she said, realising that Helen couldn't manage on her own. She quickly undressed.

She washed Helen down, brushing the mud away with a flannel. The filth seemed almost endless, but eventually the water under their feet was running clear apart from the blood. She then washed Helen's hair, untangling it as much as she could. Then she reduced the temperature of the shower, took the showerhead and cleaned Helen's wound as much as she could, probing it with her fingers to push any mud or dirt out. Each time Abby pressed the wound, Helen winced – but her crying had almost stopped. Then she turned off the shower and led Helen out.

She wrapped a towel around Helen and sat her down. "Give me a minute," she said. "I just want to check on Sammy." Still wet, she put on her bathrobe and quickly looked into the living room. Sammy was curled up on the sofa; the television was on, but Abby was surprised to see that Sammy had fallen asleep. Abby checked her forehead: it was still fevered, but definitely slightly less hot than it had been. *She must be wiped out*, thought Abby. *I'll have to wake her in a bit, she's not had anything to eat yet.*

She went back to Helen who still seemed to be in shock, towel wrapped around herself, clutching her arm. There was blood on the towel, but less than Abby had expected to see.

"Come on," she said, rubbing Helen dry. "You can tell me about it now."

Their eyes met, Helen's full of torment. They began to fill with tears again, and Abby gently kissed her. "You're safe now. It's OK."

"Oh, Abby," said Helen. "It was terrible. It was – her."

"I know. Sammy told me."

"Sammy told you? Is she OK? What did she – see?"

"Not a lot, just that you were hurt and crying. She didn't know what happened. She's sleeping – her sleep pattern's all to cock and she's stressed out most of the time. Let's look at that arm again."

Helen extended her arm. The cut was clean; it hadn't stopped bleeding but the flow was definitely slowing.

"I'm going to have to clean it again," said Abby. "Hang on." She went to the kitchen and brought back a small plastic first-aid kit, then cleaned the wound carefully – and as gently as she could – with iodine. It started the bleeding off again, though not as bad as before. Helen gritted her teeth as Abby applied the iodine.

"We might get away with not taking you to hospital," she said. "Or at least we might buy enough time for you to settle down. You can't go like this."

Helen nodded. Abby dressed the wound with a bandage from the kit. "Not bad," she said. "That must hurt like hell."

"It does," said Helen, "but less now."

"Pain killers or alcohol?" asked Abby.

"Alcohol," replied Helen. "Definitely alcohol. No – screw it, I'll have both."

Abby led Helen into the bedroom. *At least she's moving of her own accord now,* thought Abby. *She was like a zombie before.* She helped Helen get into a t-shirt and some knickers. "I'll get you a drink."

When Abby returned with the half-full glass and tablets, Helen looked exhausted. "Whiskey," said Abby. "The good stuff." She passed the drink to Helen and sat crossed-legged on the bed, facing her. Helen took a long drink. Then she put the tablets in her mouth and washed them down with a little more.

"What happened?" asked Abby.

Helen told her.

If the woman hadn't said that she would need to lie, Helen wouldn't have even considered it – even so, she considered it only fleetingly. She told Abby everything. She'd never lied to Abby before and she wasn't going to start now. *My trust in Abby is as absolute as my love for her,* reflected Helen. *Well, perhaps not quite absolute, otherwise I wouldn't have even considered lying to Abby.*

Abby listened while Helen spoke, her hand resting on Helen's injured arm while she sipped whiskey with the other. As each minute passed, Abby grew increasingly angry.

Helen grew more tearful and hesitant when she reached the moment where she and the woman had kissed. "I'm so, so sorry," said Helen, breaking down again.

"Hush, now," said Abby. "It's not your fault."

"But it *is*," said Helen. "I wanted her. I – really wanted her. I *enjoyed* it." She lowered her voice. "I didn't even think about you."

Abby shook her head. "You wanted her because she told you to. Not because you really wanted her. Like hypnosis."

Tears poured from Helen's eyes. "No," she snapped. "I really did want her. She felt evil and cold – and I – I loved it. You can't possibly forgive me for that."

Abby shook Helen. "Listen to me. That's not you, and you know it." She lowered her voice. "Helen. You feel guilty. And because you feel guilty you want me to be annoyed. Well I am annoyed. I'm fucking livid. But not with you, not even in the slightest. I don't forgive you, because there's nothing to forgive. I love you."

Helen wiped away her tears and looked into Abby's blue eyes. They were unblinking, earnest.

"Sammy says that you're scared of me," said Abby, gently. "Is it because of this – the kiss?"

Helen nodded, her eyes lowered.

"Don't be so daft," said Abby.

"But I *wanted* her," said Helen.

I have to tell her, thought Helen. *Trust her, trust yourself and trust your relationship.* "Abby," she said, hesitantly. "I *really* wanted her. She – she turned me on. Maybe more than you ever have. It felt – good and awful at the same time."

There was the briefest of pauses. "Helen," said Abby, intently. "Nothing can come between us – and certainly not her. You don't have to be afraid of me. I trust you. Completely."

Helen met Abby's eyes, but said nothing.

"Is there something else?" asked Abby.

"Abby – I – yes, there is. I just don't agree with this. I try to. I try to see the alternative, but I can't. I can't get over the fact that an innocent girl is going to die – because we let her. Abby, *it's not right.* It makes us murderers as surely as if we kill her ourselves."

"Helen, we've talked about this."

"Yes, but – well, I guess I didn't say what I really thought."

"Which is?" said Abby, tersely.

Helen hesitated. "Well – I can't help feeling that you're letting things play out too easily. This is a girl. A real life. We're letting her die."

"And? What do you want me to do – go and save her so that ten other children can die? You know what's at stake here."

"Yes, but..."

"Ten, Helen. Ten." She held up both of her hands, with only one finger outstretched. "Which do you honestly prefer? One?" She extended all of her fingers. "Or ten?"

"Wrong is wrong, Abby. Have you forgotten that?"

"No I bloody well haven't," said Abby, annoyed.

Helen's eyes widened; she'd never seen Abby so cross.

"I damn well *do* know what's going on," said Abby, raising her voice. "And I really don't like it. But what do you really, honestly want me to do? Go and rescue her for five minutes of fame and a warm feeling that lasts about as long? By the next day, ten – *ten!* children will be gone." Abby extended her fingers one by one, her voice becoming more emphatic as she counted off each number, "One, two, three, four, five, six, seven, eight, nine and yes ten, *ten* other bloody children will be dead. I know it's crap, but I don't see what I can do. Do you?"

Abby was almost panting from her rant. Helen was stunned: never had they had such an exchange.

"Abby – I, I just don't know if I can deal with it."

Abby calmed herself and cupped Helen's head in her hands, kissing her forehead.

"Please, please trust me," said Abby. "All of my life, I thought that I would have to deal with this on my own. Now that you're here, with me, I don't want to be fighting you. If you really think there's something different I could be doing, I'm all ears. Otherwise, please – trust me. Crap though it is. I need you."

The two women faced each other, drawing breath. Helen clasped Abby's arms.

"I know you're right," said Helen. "Logically. It's one versus ten. But it feels so wrong."

"It does to me too," said Abby. "Really, it does."

Helen inhaled and closed her eyes. "I know," she said. "It's been brewing inside me since this whole thing began. But tonight – the power of that, woman, thing, whatever she is – made me feel so... I can't explain it. Against you. *For* her. I really wanted her. I didn't care about you. I wanted her."

"You've done nothing wrong," repeated Abby. "Nothing. Well, other than drive home via the lane – that was a bit stupid."

"I know," said Helen, feeling chastened.

"Anyhow," said Abby, "If anyone should be guilty, it's me."

"How so?"

"If you weren't with me, this wouldn't have happened."

"But –" Helen began, but Abby raised her hand.

"Don't worry. I won't be made to feel guilty for loving you," said Abby.

There was a long silence. Helen finished her whiskey and put down the glass. Abby got into the bed and hugged Helen. "This changes nothing," she said. "Not in the slightest."

"Thank you," said Helen. "I was worried –"

"I know."

"No. You don't. She said – that I'd need to lie to you. That – God, I don't know – me wanting her would be the end of us, I guess."

Abby smiled and kissed Helen. "Well," she said, "all that proves is that she isn't all-powerful. She doesn't know everything. She doesn't understand love, only hate. There's nothing she can do to drive you from me."

Abby spoke as if she believed it, but Helen wasn't convinced. "She's dead – gone. But she cut me. For real. How is that even possible?"

"I don't know," conceded Abby. "I'm not making up the rules here."

"What do we do now?"

"Same as we have been," replied Abby. "We wait. And hope. And look after each other." She kissed Helen on the nose. "Now, you need to rest a little. OK?"

Helen nodded. "I'll try. I don't think I can sleep though."

"Don't worry," said Abby. "I have some sleeping tablets. I got them after I was broken into. I had trouble relaxing at night after that. But I didn't use them all."

"Painkillers, whiskey *and* sleeping tablets," said Helen. "Bring it on."

Outside the bedroom door, Sammy decided that it was time to go back to the lounge and again pretend to be asleep. *If Mummy knew that I've been listening*, she thought, *she'd be upset.*

16

Day had turned to night an hour ago and still the rain was relentless.

The water within the well was so high that Becca had to stand; within the last few hours it had risen up to her chest and Matt's head had disappeared under the water. The image of Matt's lifeless body, below the water's surface, played on Becca's mind. It was perhaps the ultimate reminder of the miserably short distance she was away from sharing his fate.

Becca was drained. Even just standing on her feet took enormous effort. Every so often, she would wipe the water from her face, her eyes stinging from being wet for so long. She'd had to move some of her tiny store of items to gaps in the wall further up from the rising water – and all of the spare clothes and towels were now totally drenched.

Becca firmly believed that she wouldn't see the night through; more than once she'd seriously considered sitting down in the water to let herself drown. Whether it was the fear of drowning that stopped her, or a desperate need to cling on to life – no matter how futile that life might seem – she didn't know.

Either her fever had topped out, or she'd got used to it. She was still coughing hard, hawking thick phlegm, but nowhere near as frequently. And although she had as much water as she could drink, she was desperately hungry.

It's not fair, she thought to herself, deeply miserable. Becca had considered trying to climb out again – after all, she had nothing to lose – but she knew that the wet wall was now far too slick and, in any event, she just didn't have the strength.

Even the sound of the rain was a kind of torture; an unrelenting white noise that drowned out everything apart from the occasional peel of thunder.

It's not going to be long before the water's up to my mouth, she thought. *And then, I've got nowhere to go.*

17

Randle had arrived home drenched, the disquiet within him growing. He still felt confident that he could handle any conversation with the police, but he had realised that his home contained a glut of incriminating evidence. Against that, he had decided, his innocence would count for very little.

He made a hasty meal, his mind working hard, fretting about what to do. His tiny flat had few places in which to hide anything. He had no relatives and although he had a few acquaintances who might store a few 'bags of keepsakes' while he redecorated, he wasn't sure that he could trust anyone not to open them and take a peek.

I mustn't overreact, he thought. *I've not done anything. They've got no reason to search the flat. Still, better safe than sorry.*

The thought that he might destroy his trove of pictures and keepsakes didn't even occur to him. They were too precious, too much a part of him, for that.

His computer, he decided, was the first place that the police would look if they decided he was a suspect. So he carefully copied all of the photographs from his hard disc to a backup disc before deleting them from the computer. While he was working, he realised that he had access to the ideal place to store his collection: Arthur's flat. It wouldn't do as a long-term hiding place, but it was good enough for a couple of weeks at least. And, as far as he knew, no one at the school was aware of any connection between himself and Arthur – although they were known buddies at the gym. *It's not perfect,* thought Randle, *but it's better than here.*

So Randle gathered up all of his photographs, albums and keepsakes and put them into two large heavy-duty dustbin bags. *It'll take a couple of trips,* thought Randle, unsure of whether he could carry more than one bag at once.

He made himself a cup of tea and thought hard. Had he overlooked anything? He didn't think so. *The camera.* He realised that he had some photographs still on the memory card of his camera – including the ones he'd taken of the friend of the missing girl the other day. He pulled the camera out and placed it on the table next to his computer to remind himself to copy off the photographs and delete them from the memory card. *I'll sort that after I've moved the bags,* he thought.

Randle drained the tea from his mug and put on his raincoat. *At least no one will be out tonight,* he thought, recalling how he had heard at school that the rainstorm was hampering the search. He heaved one of the bags over his shoulder. It was heavier than he'd thought, but he could manage.

He opened the front door to the flat and stepped outside, awkwardly negotiating the narrow doorway with the bulky bag, not immediately noticing the man walking towards him.

"Hello, Mr Randle," said Ed. "I wonder if we could have a chat."

18

When she recorded the appeal, Sarah thought that it was the hardest thing that she had ever done – until the time came to watch it replayed on television.

She'd been grateful for the sleep she'd had and didn't know how Jim had managed to keep going, although he now seemed to be running out of energy. When it came to record the appeal, he had let Sarah do most of the talking.

"Becca. Matt," she'd said, unable to stop the tears rolling down her face. "We just want to hear from you. We don't care where you are or why you're not here. Just pick up the phone and give us a call." She had been holding tightly to Jim's hand and felt him squeeze hers.

Jim picked up the baton from her, and continued, his voice quivering although he was more composed than Sarah. "If you're with someone else, could that person please contact us or the police."

Sarah continued, more or less repeating what she'd already said. "We just want to hear from you, either of you. Please. We're so scared. We need to know that you're alright. Please call us."

The cameraman had wanted to try another take, but Jenny had stood firm. She knew that once was more than enough for Sarah and, to be honest, the more raw it was, the more effective it would be.

Although the reporters had wanted to ask questions, Jenny hadn't allowed it. Sarah and Jim had been flanked on screen by herself and George Wilkins, the Deputy Chief Constable for Lancashire. Part of her resented this – Wilkins had appeared towards the end of the day and, naturally, both she and Sergeant Hutchinson had stepped aside to let him speak on behalf of the Bankside police. But part of her was also relieved. Although liaison officers were supposed to remain detached, it was nigh-on impossible to not invest yourself emotionally in such an investigation. She wasn't entirely sure that she could have spoken in front of the cameras without breaking down.

"Rebecca Richards and Matthew Bradshaw were last seen on Friday afternoon, outside Bankside High School. Regional police have been drafted in to help the local police force and a thorough search is being made of the school and surrounding area. We appeal to members of the public to contact us if they have any information whatsoever." While he was talking, a freephone number flashed on screen.

There had been no mention of the gap between the children going missing and Sarah and Jim notifying the police. The press would probably find out soon enough, but right now it would be an unhelpful distraction.

The recording seemed to take ages, but now, on television, the whole thing was over in less than a couple of minutes. Sarah found it excruciating to watch. She'd seen many similar appeals, and couldn't recall many (or, in fact, *any*) occasions where the children had been subsequently found. She watched, crying, while Jim held her close, his arm tightly around her quivering shoulders. The video was occasionally overlaid with photographs of Becca and Matt. The news item finished with the presenter voicing over a video of Becca and Matt taken at Matt's sixteenth birthday party, not long after Jim and Matt had moved into Sarah's house.

"Do you think it will help?" Sarah asked Jenny.

Despite having been off duty for almost two hours, Jenny had hung on with Sarah and Jim until the night-time news broadcast – the interview hadn't been quite ready for the early evening news, although the children's disappearance had been covered.

Jenny nodded, but Stephen Carter answered for her. "It will get the news out faster than anything else. Right now, the more people who know the better. You don't know who could be watching."

In the centre of town, a couple of miles away, Sammy watched the broadcast intently. She noted down the telephone number on a scrap of paper and took it to Abby, who was making bacon sandwiches. "Mummy, look. The girl's on TV."

Sammy all but dragged Abby into the living room just in time to catch the last few seconds of the news story.

Abby stared, hand to mouth, at the photographs of Matt and Becca on the screen. Although a television presenter was talking, Abby didn't hear what he said: she felt queasy, seeing for the first time the *real* people who were caught up in what she had believed to be her own personal ordeal. Seeing the photographs made a knot in her stomach. *Keep it together,* thought Abby. *If you think this is bad, think what it would be like with ten pictures up there.*

Sammy handed the number to her mother. "They gave out a number to call. We have to tell them, Mummy. To help the girl. I think she's dying."

19

The water was now up to the top of Becca's neck.

Weary though she was, she felt that there must, somehow, be a way out of her predicament. The water had risen faster than she could have imagined and there was no sign of the rain slowing down.

She moved around the well, stones moving under her feet. *Perhaps if I build them up?* she thought, but she knew that not only weren't there enough loose stones, she couldn't build anything solid enough to stand on for long.

She reasoned that if she could hold on to the wall, she didn't need to keep her feet on the bottom – like being in the deep end of the swimming pool. But, tired as she was, she knew that she couldn't do that for long. She might buy herself another hour at the most.

Her cough had eased and was now only occasional and also far less savage, though her throat was still sore.

She bumped into a large solid shape, and backed away instinctively. *Matt.* Then the thought hit her: as repulsive and unthinkable as it was, she knew it was her only hope.

Dear God, she thought. *Am I really, really going to do this? You have to, have to,* she told herself.

Becca carefully climbed on top of Matt. His body was quite solid, more solid than she would have imagined. It yielded only slightly under her weight. *Rigor mortis,* she guessed.

With some effort, Becca managed to sit balanced on his lifeless shoulders almost as if he were carrying her, legs wrapped around his cold, rigid neck. She was, she realised, sitting on a carcass rather than a person. She sat, sobbing, her tears mingling with the rain. She leaned her weight against the wall, her head resting against a slightly protruding stone; her hand holding on to Matt's head. She wouldn't be able to sleep, but her legs were extremely grateful for the rest.

The rain continued to pour down and Becca began to wonder if the extra height gained by sitting on Matt would actually be enough to save her. She supposed that she could stand on him if she had to, but she doubted that she would be able to maintain her balance for long.

Rebecca Richards, aged fourteen (almost fifteen), had learned something that most people many times her age fortunately never have to: that to survive, you really will do almost anything.

20

"Taking out the rubbish?" asked Ed.

Randle nodded. "Having a bit of a clear-out," he said, raising his voice above the rain.

Randle's heart rate seemed to double and he hoped that he looked calm. "Come on in," he said, hefting the bag back into the flat and dropping it down gently onto the hall floor. "You look drenched."

Ed stepped into the flat, dripping water on the floor.

Randle could smell the beer on Ed's breath. He took off his raincoat and hung it up, then walked ahead of Ed into the flat, scanning around to see if he'd left anything incriminating in view. As far as he could see, he hadn't. "Cup of tea?" he shouted. *No point in trying to rush him out,* he thought.

"That would be great, thanks." Ed made his way into the small living room as Randle stepped into the kitchen. He noticed the other bin bag. "You really are having a clear-out," he said.

Randle put his head around the door. "Small place like this, it soon piles up. I have to throw stuff away every so often, otherwise there's no room to move. Sugar?"

"No thanks, just milk," replied Ed.

Randle went back into the kitchen. Ed took the opportunity to look briefly around the flat. It was small – tiny, really – only just big enough for the small collection of furniture within it. A battered two-seater sofa, a small corner table with a lamp on it, a sideboard and desk with a computer and camera on it. *A pretty decent camera for a man on a very low income,* thought Ed. He picked it up. It was, as Randle had said, a Canon, and a far better model than Ed's battered old Nikon. *More than just a hobby,* thought Ed. *A real passion.*

"Nice camera," said Ed, appreciatively, as Randle came into the room carrying two mugs of tea. Ed slurred his words slightly, Randle noticed.

Randle wasn't a fool. He could tell instantly what Ed was digging for. "You have no idea how many years it took me to save for that," he said.

"And these days, you don't just need a camera, you need a computer, too," said Ed.

"Tell me about it," said Randle. He didn't have to feign exasperation – he doubted that the policeman appreciated quite how hard it had been to save the money for both the camera and computer. He desperately wanted Ed to put the camera down but tried not to let his anxiety show.

Ed casually removed the lens cap from the camera and lifted it to his eye. "Nice lens. Do you mind?"

"Not at all," said Randle. He swallowed a large mouthful of tea.

Ed focused. "What is it, 28-135?" he asked.

"Oh no, it's 18-200."

Ed whistled. "Serious lens." *Serious cash*, he thought.

There was a long silence. Randle was uncomfortably aware that Ed was playing some kind of cat-and-mouse game. He guessed that Ed thought that he had something on him, but not enough to question him formally. *And if it isn't solid enough for that*, thought Randle, *it probably isn't much at all.*

Finally, Randle said, "I'm sure you didn't come here to talk cameras, er, Mr –?"

"Davis," said Ed. "Actually, I did."

Randle looked puzzled, but Ed was chasing his instincts. "It seems to me that you're a key part of the school," said Ed.

Randle shrugged. "Not really. I'm just the crossing guy. It's not like I'm a teacher."

Ed rested the camera on his lap. "Some say you're more a part of the school than a teacher. Everyone knows you, pretty much everyone likes you. Looking through the newspapers, trophy cabinets and noticeboards, it looks like you've taken nearly all of the school's pictures for years." Ed delivered his statements as if they were accusations; things of which to be guilty.

"Hardly," said Randle.

"You're too modest. I doubt that there's a child who's passed through those doors in – oh, fifteen years or more – who doesn't know who you are. Especially the top performers – the ones you've photographed the most."

"It's a lot of kids," said Randle. "Maybe they do know me, but I don't remember all of them."

"Yes. I can see that. Years pass – people change. You're not going to remember them all. But last week? The school's top swimmer?" Ed looked directly at Randle. His eyes were cold and sharp.

"You were, without doubt, the last person to see Rebecca Richards and Matthew Bradshaw. Rebecca Richards is the school's best swimmer in – oh, well, pretty much forever. I've seen at least two, maybe three-dozen pictures you've taken of her. And yet you don't remember seeing her on Friday."

The silence seemed to last an age.

"As I said, a lot of kids," said Randle. He felt he had the measure of Ed now. Clearly, Ed felt that he knew something – something he wasn't going to let go of. He'd probably keep pushing; overstepping the mark if he had to, until he got results. And the man was also drunk – it was doubtful that his superiors even knew he was here.

Randle knew that he was on his own and had no choice other than to tough it out. *It's not as if I've actually done anything*, he thought, well aware that Ed would certainly think otherwise if he opened one of the bin bags.

"And yet," said Ed, "everyone else has a clear recollection of that afternoon except you. The person who should remember the most."

Randle decided to fight back: anyone else would. "You seem to be accusing me of something."

"Just an observation," said Ed, innocently. He took a drink of tea. He was frustrated. *Shit, this could go on all night*, he thought. Randle was cool under pressure and Ed doubted that he would slip up. He decided to change tack. "Fair enough, I understand," he said, as if dismissing the whole conversation. He stood up. "Before I go, do you mind if I just use your toilet?"

Relieved, Randle shook his head. "No – it's in the hall, on the left."

Ed replaced the camera on the computer desk, walked through the hall, into the toilet and closed the door, loudly. Almost instantly, he opened it silently and crept back. Randle had already crossed the room and had picked up the camera – and was taking out the memory card.

Ed didn't hesitate, although he should have. Even having strayed so far from police protocol, he still should have verbally challenged Randle. *Waste of time*, he thought, dismissing the notion. He quickly crossed the room, grabbed the camera from Randle's hand and pushed him back onto the sofa, hard.

Randle didn't know how to react. "What the hell d'ya think you're doing?" he exclaimed, making his voice sound even more indignant than he felt.

Randle tried to get up, but Ed pushed him back again. "Something you don't want me to see?" Ed asked.

"No – it's just –" Randle flustered.

"Good. Shut up then and stay put." Ed hoped to God he was right. He could lose his job for this. He flipped the camera on and switched the dial to preview. Nothing could have prepared him for what he saw.

He flicked through the thumbnail photographs on the LCD display. There was Hannah: walking to Becca's house; up the drive; to the door; away again. It didn't make sense. "What the fuck –?"

Randle tried to rise again, but Ed pushed him down, harder this time – with more of a punch than a push.

"Who's the girl?" shouted Ed.

Randle shook his head. "I don't know."

"Too fucking right you don't know, shitface. That's my daughter. Why were you taking pictures of my daughter? And at Rebecca Richards' house?"

Randle's heart sank. *Holy shit*, he thought, desperately trying to work out how he could extricate himself from this mess. His mouth worked soundlessly.

Ed looked around, furious. "Makes me wonder what's in the bags? The bags you were just about to get rid of?" Ed picked the nearest one and tore it open. The contents spilled out onto Randle's threadbare carpet and Ed took a step back, aghast.

Dozens of photograph albums splayed out on the floor, many of them falling open to reveal their contents: pictures, mostly of teenage girls, though some were younger.

While Ed stared slack-jawed at the photographs, Randle tried to jump up and dash for the door, but Ed was too fast for him. He punched Randle in the face and pushed him back onto the sofa. "Don't even think about it," shouted Ed.

Randle clutched his nose, blood streaming down his face. *Not good*, thought Ed, knowing at this point the only thing that would rescue his career was an instant arrest and clear conviction. *Well, there's no going back*, he thought.

Ed tore open the second bag. More photo albums spilled out – along with some boxes. Ed sifted through the detritus with his foot, keeping one eye firmly on Randle.

One of the cardboard boxes – the flat-pack type you get from an office stationers – had Becca's name on it. **REBECCA RICHARDS**, it said, written carefully in black felt-tip marker. Ed picked it up and opened it. There were two photograph albums and a scrapbook. As he opened it, something fell on the floor: a girl's hair tie, or scrunchie, as everyone called them.

Randle made another try for the door, but Ed kicked him hard in the stomach. Randle doubled up on the floor, gasping for air. Ed kicked him again. "Fucker," he said, under his breath.

Ed opened the scrapbook. There was picture upon picture of Becca, stretching back several years. In many of them she was wearing her swimsuit, collecting awards. Each photograph was innocent enough on its own, but as a collection...

Ed lifted Randle up, roughly by the front of his shirt. "Where are they?" he demanded.

Randle shook his head. "I don't know –" Ed pushed him hard against the wall and shouted in his face, "Don't screw with me!" Randle struggled, but Ed held him firm.

"Do you know what I am?" said Ed. "I'm an angry father, with the protection of being a policeman. I could kick your insides out and make up any old story. Now – do you want to answer my questions?"

Randle shook his head and tried to speak but Ed hit him again. "Wrong fucking answer." He picked up the camera and thrust it into Randle's face, turning the preview back on. "This girl," he said. "Did you touch her?"

Randle shook his head, hard.

"You sure?" shouted Ed. "Because if you've touched her, I will kill you. And I'll take all night doing it."

"No," said Randle, spitting blood. "No."

"That better be the truth." Ed pushed Randle back down onto the sofa. "Stay, fuckface. One move and I will put you in the grave. Understand?"

Randle didn't need to respond. He might be in good condition, but the fact was he was old. Ed's punches, pushes and kicks hurt him more than he could have imagined. He held himself, groaning. For good measure, Ed kicked him again, in the shin. *Good fucking policing*, he thought. *Got the bastard.*

He pulled his mobile phone from his pocket and called Hannah's number. She answered after three rings. "Dad?"

Ed tried to sound calm, holding back his panting breath. "Hi Han," he said.

"You OK?" said Hannah. "You sound like you've been running."

"I'm fine," said Ed. "Working late." He struggled to calm his breath. "I just want to ask you a couple of questions."

"Sure," said Hannah.

Ed looked down at Randle, who was doubled up on the sofa. "That crossing guy. The one Becca mentioned. Did he ever talk to you?"

"I don't know, Dad, I guess. Maybe."

"Hannah, this is important." Hannah stiffened. Her father was curt, annoyed perhaps. She didn't like him when he was like that – which was usually after he'd been drinking. "Did he ever talk to you?"

"No, Dad, not other than to say hello."

"Hannah: are you sure? I won't be annoyed, whatever the answer, I promise."

Hannah was puzzled. Why should her Dad be annoyed if she spoke to the school crossing attendant? "I'm sure, Dad, honest."

Ed glanced at Randle. "That's good, Han, thanks. I've got to go now. Tell Mum I'll be even later than I thought."

"OK, Dad."

Ed rang off. "That's good news for you," he said to Randle. "Now, tell me about Rebecca."

Randle shook his head. Ed picked up the photograph album and thrust it into his face. "This girl!" he shouted. "The one who's gone missing. The one you just happen to have two albums of pictures of. Where is she?"

This was not, thought Randle, *an argument I'm going to win.* "I don't know," he croaked.

"You don't seem to understand," said Ed, pulling Randle back to his feet. "You *are* going to tell me. And I'm not going to piss around finding out."

"Fuck you," shouted Randle, kneeing Ed hard in the genitals. As Ed doubled up, Randle brought his knee up under his chin. Ed flew backwards. Randle reached for the nearest heavy object – the camera – and swiped Ed across the head with it. There was a *crack* as the camera connected with Ed's jaw. As Ed collapsed, a bloody tooth fell from his mouth and danced across the floor. Ed was clutching his groin, his whole world a symphony of agony. Randle kicked him in the face, glad he still had his shoes on.

"You're a big hard man now, aren't you?" Randle kicked him again, harder. *Ed had made the mistake of being caught off guard,* he thought – he wouldn't do the same. He kicked Ed again, in the face. The floor was covered with blood.

Randle went into his kitchen and came back with his recently acquired roll of duct tape. He hefted Ed onto his computer chair and pulled his arms tight around his back, then secured them with the tape. Ed was barely conscious. Randle put tape over his mouth, bound his legs together and then fastened him to the chair as securely as he could.

"Never, Mr Davis," he said, "underestimate an old fart. Especially an old army fart." Randle went to the kitchen and came back with a kitchen knife, with a four-inch blade. He slapped Ed. "Do you still have some questions?" he asked. Ed looked at him, but didn't respond.

"I think you do," said Randle. "I think your questions are, one: is he going to kill me? Two: did he touch my girl? And three: when will help come? Well? Am I right?"

Ed growled at him and struggled.

"So first, am I going to kill you? Well, Mr Davis, I am tempted. But on balance, no. I'm going to leave you here. Tied up. There are things worse than death. Which comes to the second question. Did I touch your daughter?" Randle paused. "No. *Not yet.*"

Ed wriggled hard and Randle leaned close to him and continued, softly. "I promise you this. I will find her. And I will have her. As many times as I can. Just before I kill her. Or maybe I'll let her live – which is worse, do you think? Losing her, or getting her back knowing what I've done? Either way, you need to know that while I'm enjoying your little girl, you'll be here. Tied up."

Ed struggled hard, but he was held tight.

"And that brings me to the third question," said Randle. "The answer to that is easy. No one comes here but me – pretty much ever. So I don't fancy your chances, to be honest. I'm sure if you could talk you'd be telling me about how you have to call in, or backup will come – but I'm not stupid. You've come here, drunk. I think that coming here was your idea. No one knows you're here. So I think that by the time they find you, I'll have done my business with your little girl and be long gone. I just wanted you to know that."

Then Randle punched Ed in the face, again and again, until he passed out.

21

Abby parked Helen's car in the dark lane and got out, closing the door behind her.

Although it was still raining, the force of the storm seemed to be spent. She was almost ten miles from Bankside and hoped that her memory wasn't playing tricks. If she was right, there was a public telephone box around half a mile away. She switched on her small pocket torch, covered it with a dark cloth until she was sure that it was giving enough light to see by, but not so much that she could be easily spotted. Then she started walking – keeping off the road and on the grass verge as much as possible. Then, she cut across a field to the next lane.

Abby had been as careful as she could, choosing a route that avoided main roads – and therefore not only other people, but also CCTV and traffic cameras.

She'd bought a pair of wellington boots and driving gloves from a local garage and had only handled them using a pair of her own gloves that she'd cleaned scrupulously. Inside every pocket she had something heavy: a bag of sugar, cans of beans, four small bottles of water and, for good measure, a house brick. (She'd considered filling her pockets with healing stones from the shop, but, if something went wrong and she dropped one, they could more easily be traced back to her.) She almost certainly weighed over a stone more than usual.

Of course, her knowledge of forensics was no better than any viewer of popular crime-scene dramas. She was sure that her efforts probably wouldn't stand up to deeper scrutiny. But she also knew that some things were very much in her favour. First, a detailed forensic investigation would take time. Second, the rain was going to wash away most of the evidence. Third, even if she did leave any DNA, she wasn't on the DNA database (as far as she knew). Fourth, no one had any reason to point the finger in her direction. Last, the police would be putting all of their resources into finding the children. In the scheme of things, one prank call – and possibly not the only one – wouldn't warrant a lot of police time. She hoped.

It wasn't easy-going underfoot. Abby stumbled several times but managed to remain upright. Going back would be harder, as she would have to be quicker. Much quicker.

She reached the telephone box. She had chosen this one not only because it could be reached from the back lanes, but also because that was the least obvious route to it. Even if the call were traced, it was unlikely that the police would approach it using the same route as she – it was just too indirect. Thankfully, the light inside wasn't working – and, for a terrible moment, she thought that the phone itself might be out of order, but when she lifted the receiver, she heard the familiar purr. She swallowed. It was one thing sitting back and waiting, but quite another to mislead the police.

Abby pulled out the piece of paper Sammy had handed her and dialled the number, breathing hard. She was more scared than she'd ever been, but galvanised too. As much as her heart ached for the trapped girl, when the chips were down, you protect your own: Sammy, and now Helen. When she'd left them half an hour ago, the exhausted Helen was in bed, sleeping next to Sammy. She'd probably not needed the sleeping tablets, but they had pushed Helen into a deeper sleep. If she'd told Helen what she was doing, her partner would never have slept – tablets or not. Abby would tell her everything when she got back.

"Hello, Bankside incident room, can I help you?" A man's voice.

Abby lowered her voice: enough, she hoped, to disguise it a little but not so much that it would sound false. "I have some information about the missing children." She hoped that she wouldn't be put on hold or transferred – every second on the line made it easier for the call to be traced.

"Could you tell me your name please?" asked the man.

Abby ignored him. "I think I saw them, tonight. Heading out of Hawksleigh, towards Manchester. With someone."

"Could you tell me your name please, madam?" the man repeated.

"Hawksleigh, towards Manchester. I have to go." She replaced the receiver. Then, she quickly picked it up and cleaned it before leaving it dangling.

She headed back the way she had come, as fast as she could without actually running – trying not to panic.

It seemed to take forever to reach the car. She started to panic: her sense of direction had never been especially good and the rain disorientated her. But, just when she felt sure that she'd taken the wrong route across the field, she came back onto the lane where she'd parked. She hurried back to the car.

She didn't see any other cars until she reached Bankside and then there was nothing unusual. She hoped that the police had heard what she'd said.

TUESDAY

1

At around daybreak, the rain finally stopped. It had slowed just after midnight – not that Becca had noticed. Exhausted beyond belief and, despite fighting the need to sleep with all of her remaining will, her body was so drained of energy that it could no longer hold on to consciousness. Balanced reasonably securely on the shoulders of Matt's corpse, she'd slipped into a sleep so deep that not even the occasional crack of thunder could disturb her.

Early in the morning, while she slept, her temperature dropped from its dangerous heights – and her slumber deepened further. Her body knew what she needed more than she did herself: without food or water, battered by fever, rest wasn't a luxury.

But, even in her sleep, her torment remained. A deserved release would have been a dreamless sleep; a healing coma. Instead, Becca found herself sitting, tantalisingly, at the top of the well. In her dream, the rain had stopped although the ground was still wet. The moon was high in the sky and the night was moderate – and, the luxury of it: she was dry and, if not entirely warm, at least comfortable.

She sat on the side of the well. On the opposite side sat the black bird, silent for once. At this close distance, it was far larger than it had seemed from down in the well. It regarded her with soulless eyes.

She was fixed to the ground in some way, unable to stand – and, although she was filled with fear, she now felt resigned. The end had been coming for days and now it seemed to be very close. She looked deep into the well. It was dark – too dark to see the bottom, at night as in the day – but somehow she felt that Matt was down there. Or what had once been Matt.

Then, from the ruined cottage, a dark figure walked. The silhouette was slim but curvaceous, approaching with an almost dance-like movement of the hips. As she got closer, her features became more defined. Dark, curly hair cascaded around her shoulders. Her lips were full, yet more hard than sensual. She had a strong, slightly hawk-like nose that gave her face a distinct character, and her eyes – her eyes were everything. Even in the dark, they almost glowed: large and deeply captivating, sad, insane and wise all at the same time.

She sat down close to Becca and smiled. Like the woman herself, the smile was beautiful and captivating. Part of Becca knew that she was dreaming – yet, even within the dream, she knew in her heart that what she was experiencing wasn't entirely an illusion.

When the woman spoke, her voice was soft and measured.

"Asleep or awake, I am with you, girl."

Becca wanted to talk but couldn't; her mouth felt dry, her throat constricted.

"You are ready to die, aren't you?"

Tears formed in Becca's eyes and rolled gently down her cheeks. She wanted to shake her head in defiance but she was so, so tired. Instead, she nodded, looking at the ground. The woman extended her arm and gently lifted Becca's chin upwards so that she looked her in the eye. Her hand was deeply cold and the dread within Becca's heart deepened.

The woman smiled again. "Is not so easy as that. You think you can take no more. I tell you that to die now would be too easy. You will die – and it will be soon. But your death will make your pain so far seem like – like nothing. As a summer's breeze before a winter storm."

"Why?" sobbed Becca.

"Why not?" replied the woman. "I tell you something. You think perhaps I am dream or vision of madness. I tell you that I am more real than you. The world passes and changes and I do not. I take you and what happens? You are gone. In one hundred years no one mourns you, but I remain."

Becca started to speak, but the woman silenced her. "Look at those around you. A selfish boy who wanted your body but not your heart. Friends you abandoned for excitement of the flesh. A father who didn't care enough for you to hold to his vows. A mother who always thinks of you as a child. At every step, you are nothing. You will die weeping, in despair, with a heart that is empty of hope. But worse, you will be with me, tormented in ways you can't imagine, forever. For you, there is no end to this." She pointed towards the cottage.

In the dark, Becca could make out the shadowy outlines of perhaps a dozen people; mostly small – children like her, she realised. "Those who came to me before you," she said, "and stay with me still."

At the back of the group of children, Becca saw Matt. "Matt!" she shouted. His face remained impassive; expressionless. "Matt!"

"He can't hear you," said the woman. "He's mine now."

Becca wept. "No, please. He doesn't deserve this. I don't deserve this. No one deserves this," she said softly.

The woman stood and gestured into the well. "Deserve or not deserve, you are where you are. A place of your own making."

Becca stood, defiant. "No! I'm not here for a reason! It's not my fault."

The woman laughed. Next to her tall, curvy figure, Becca felt herself once more to be the scrawny girl from which she desperately wanted to be liberated. A head shorter than the woman, possibly only just over half her weight, Becca was more conscious than ever of her immaturity.

The woman slapped her and Becca fell backwards. "You are where I want you to be." With that, the woman dragged Becca by her hair to the open mouth of the well. Becca screamed, the pain agonising. The black bird, silent until now, cawed as if in appreciation.

The woman pushed her, hard. Becca fell headfirst, into the darkness.

2

When Julia Davis awoke she was alone and, to a certain extent, relieved. Last night, when Hannah had related the conversation with her father, Julia had decided that there was a good chance that Ed was drunk – or at least well on his way to being so. He may or may not have been working late, but he'd almost certainly decided to down a few cold ones between shifts.

When he came home drunk (which wasn't so frequent that it happened every week, but nor was it rare), it usually went one of three ways. Most of the time, Ed would stumble into bed, fall asleep and snore the night away. Sometimes, there could be an argument, which might even escalate into a physical fight. The worst outcome was that Julia would find herself the rag-doll participant of what might charitably be called loveless sex, but could actually be almost as violent as a fight. Of the latter two options, she honestly didn't know which was worse, but in either case her strategy was the same: she'd learned that he calmed down faster if she remained detached and non-participatory. And of course, Ed wasn't dim: he seldom actually hit Julia and never where any bruises would show. The thought that he might have sobered up before he came home was something she welcomed.

While Hannah showered, Julia prepared her daughter's lunchbox. Julia knew that Hannah was finding it tough and hoped that she was getting enough support from her friends – she knew that children opened up to their peers far better than they did to their parents. Julia made herself some coffee and waited for her daughter to appear.

When the phone rang, she expected it to be Ed – but it wasn't.

"Julia, it's Steve. Steve Carter. Is Ed there?"

It was a full couple of seconds before Julia answered – two seconds within which her mind involuntarily jumped to the most obvious conclusions. He was sobering up in a friend's house, waking with another woman or perhaps still on a bender. Julia hadn't reached the point where she hated her husband, but she was close. The only thing that kept them together was that he was a genuinely great father to Hannah, behaving in almost the opposite way to Hannah that he did to her: caring, gentle and thoughtful almost all of the time. Almost – Julia knew that although Hannah loved her father, she was wary of him too.

"Isn't he with you?" asked Julia. "He called last night to say that he was working late and I've not seen him since. He's not been home all night – I thought it was all hands on deck searching for Becca and Matt."

At the other end of the line, in the Bankside police station, Stephen Carter clenched his fist. *The stupid fuck*, he thought.

"Julia," he said, "it's OK – I think I know where he is." He wondered what Bankside police were going to have to cover up this time, or whether Ed would have finally outstayed his welcome.

I need to jump on this fast, Stephen thought. He knew that he should really take another officer with him, but he had no idea what kind of mess he was going to find.

He checked the files for the address of Thomas Randle's flat and then radioed the officers who had the first shift at the school.

"John? It's Stephen. Has the crossing warden turned up yet?"

"Nope," said John Coombs, who had been Bankside's youngest police officer until Ashley had started with them. "I don't think he's due in yet. Any reason?"

None that you need to know, thought Stephen. "Not really. Could you do me a favour? When he comes in, could you call me? On my mobile, though, not on the radio?"

John hesitated. "Erm – OK. Are you sure there's no reason?"

"I'll tell you later. And John – keep this to yourself, eh?"

Stephen Carter picked up the nearest set of car keys and signed himself out – hoping against hope that he was wrong, and that when he got to Randle's flat all he'd see would be the old codger setting off for work.

3

Ed was a hardened enough drinker to seldom get hangovers, but when he woke that's what he first thought the pain was.

Then it all came back to him.

He was on his side, still bound to the chair, his mouth covered by duct tape. He lay in a disturbingly large pool of his own dark, drying blood. Almost all of his body hurt, some places more than others. His mouth hurt the worst, followed pretty closely by his shoulder, chest and abdomen. When he breathed in, the pain was excruciating. Running his tongue around the inside of his mouth, he found a tooth missing. It didn't seem to be in his mouth – he assumed that he'd swallowed it.

Shit, he thought. He tried to look around the room but found it very hard to focus on anything. He closed one eye, then the other. The vision in his left eye was fine, but in his right was horribly blurred – although he didn't know it yet, it was because his retina was detached.

From where he lay, he could see the front door, a blurry oblong outside the room. He struggled to move from the chair, but was held tight. Pain flared in his left shoulder and he (rightly) suspected that it had been dislocated.

Ed had no recollection of Randle leaving, but the silence in the flat told him that he had. What he clearly remembered was Randle's promise to him – and he strained even harder to free himself. *Old bastard,* he thought. The sure knowledge of his intent towards Hannah galvanised him. With tremendous effort and despite the awful pain, Ed tried to bounce his chair towards the front door but found that it was impossible. Each movement only slightly shifted him, barely disturbing the piles of photographs that lay beneath him, spilt from the night before. Even the smallest exertion sent bolts of pain up and down his body. After five minutes, Ed gave up, sweating and weeping.

He tugged and pulled against the tape, trying to wriggle himself free – but nothing he did seemed to loosen his bonds.

He realised that what Randle had said was true: he could be here for some time.

4

Around the breakfast table in Abby's flat the mood was sombre.

Helen was nursing her arm, sipping coffee. Abby found it shocking to see Helen, normally the most upbeat of people, so quiet and withdrawn.

Abby was fretting, reflecting on her phone call to the police. Rather than dispose of her clothes last night, which she'd decided would be far too risky, she'd brought them home and packed them into a thick plastic rubbish bag, which she'd stashed into one of the cupboards at the back of the shop. The fear of discovery loomed over her. What had seemed like an acceptable risk – to perhaps add a day or two's delay to the search, by sending the police in the wrong direction – now seemed, in the daylight, to have been nothing short of reckless.

Sammy slowly ate her cereal, occasionally looking at either her mother or Helen. Eventually, she said tentatively, "Mummy, can I go to school today?"

Abby shook her head. "No Sams, not today. Maybe tomorrow."

"You don't mean that," said Sammy, knowing it to be the truth.

Silence descended again. Normally, Abby would have comforted Helen, or Helen her, but both were lost in their own despair.

After a few minutes, Abby noticed that Sammy was crying, tears falling into the bowl in front of her. Feeling guilty, she moved and sat next to her daughter, brushing the tears away and kissing her forehead.

"Oh, Sammy," she said. "Is it the girl?"

Sammy shook her head. "No, she's asleep. It's you and Helen."

Helen looked over. "How, baby? Because we're upset?"

Sammy nodded and sniffled. "You're both saying nothing, but it's like you're shouting inside – and I can't get away from it. In my head."

Abby pulled Sammy close and kissed her. "I'm sorry, Sammy," she said. "You know we love you. It's just that things are – well, bad right now."

"I know," said Sammy. "But why aren't we helping the girl? That's bad of us."

"It's not that simple," said Abby.

"That's just a grown-up's way of getting me to shut up," said Sammy. "It's not a proper answer."

Abby and Helen exchanged looks.

"Mummy," said Sammy. "You know that I *just know* some of it. But it doesn't make sense. I don't understand it all. It frightens me. And I know you want to tell me, but you don't want to tell me *now*. You want to wait. But it's *happening now* – when you think I'm old enough to be told will be too late."

Too late for what? Abby wondered.

Abby looked at Helen for support, but she was silent.

"Helen thinks you should tell me," said Sammy. "Isn't that right?"

Helen nodded. "Yes, Sam, it is."

Abby inhaled deeply. *God help me,* she thought, *here goes.*

As she started to speak, Sammy interrupted her. "It's OK, Mummy. Telling me is OK. I already know bits. It's like a painting-by-numbers picture, where you add the colours, or –" Sammy thought for a moment, "– or a join-the-dots."

Not for the first time, Abby was humbled by her daughter's honesty and wisdom. Helen smiled for the first time that morning.

And so, using language that Sammy would understand, but never being condescending, Abby retold the story she had only previously shared with Helen. Sammy listened, taking it all in – and never once did she seem surprised.

5

For the third time, Stephen Carter banged on the door to Randle's flat. There was no response. He looked at his watch. *I could have missed him,* he thought. He pulled his mobile phone out of his pocket and called John. "Any news?" he asked. "Nothing," said John. "The kids are all going in now, and there's no sign of him."

Shit, thought Carter. *This doesn't feel right.*

"Give me ten minutes," he said to John. "I'll call you back."

He banged on the door again, harder.

One of the neighbours opened her door and peered outside. "He'll be at work, now," she said. Stephen nodded.

"Mind you," she said, "there was a right row last night. He's normally very quiet."

Stephen tried to look in through the window, but it was the bathroom – with frosted glass with net curtains behind.

He banged again and opened the letterbox, and shouted into it, "Mr Randle?"

Ed's probably half-killed him, he thought. He looked through the letterbox. At the other end of the hall, lying in the entrance to the living room, was Ed – gagged and bound to a chair.

Oh fuck.

Without hesitation, Stephen called into the police station on his radio, giving Randle's address. "I repeat," he said, "we have an injured officer. I need backup and an ambulance now."

He didn't wait for confirmation. Standing back, he kicked the door in. It took four attempts, but once it yielded, it flew open, crashing against the wall behind.

He ran to Ed, resisting the temptation to bring his chair upright, not knowing how badly he'd been hurt. As he moved forwards, he quickly took in the view in front of him. The flat was a mess, blood, papers and photographs everywhere. The photographs –

He paused and looked more closely. Picture after picture of young girls. Smiling portraits, girls with awards, girls running races, girls playing netball. *Holy fucking shit,* he thought, *Ed was right.*

He carefully pulled the tape from Ed's mouth and started to ask, "Randle?" Before the word had left his mouth, Ed gasped, "Hannah. He's after Hannah. Call into the school. Call home."

Stephen felt his blood chill. He'd never, ever, seen Ed Davis weep, but now he was begging like a child.

"Find him," he sobbed. "Get the bastard."

6

All things considered, Randle hadn't had a bad night. Once he'd got himself settled, calmed down and cleaned up in Arthur's flat he'd been able to sleep pretty soundly.

He'd not hung around at home other than to quickly wash the blood from his face, pick up the keys to Arthur's flat, his seldom-used contact lenses and the knife with which he'd threatened Ed. He'd also taken a moment to fish Ed's wallet out from his trouser pocket – which gave him exactly what he needed to know the most: Ed's (and more importantly Hannah's) home address, neatly printed on his driver's licence. Randle knew that being found anywhere near Ed's home would be a risk. *So what? Everything is a risk now*, he thought.

Arthur's flat wasn't too far from his own, just at the other end of the estate. In one respect it was dangerously close to his home – if the police made door-to-door enquiries, they would come here. Yet, it would be unlikely that they'd search for him here – they'd look further afield. He could wait here all day, as quietly as he could and then leave at night. If the police came knocking, he'd just not answer – and if they asked the neighbours, they'd confirm that Arthur was away.

Although his threat had been in haste, he knew now that it was what he was going to do. Ultimately, his chances of escape were nil. Once the police went through his flat (and if they weren't found first) he'd take the blame for those missing kids. Even if he didn't, the police wouldn't take lightly the beating of one of their own, even if he had arrived drunk and spoiling for a fight.

Then there were all of his pictures. Individually, none were actually pornographic – they weren't even erotic – but together they would be impossible to explain away. *There was no doubt about it*, he thought. *I'll be going down. And when – if – I get out, there'll be nothing for me. No work, money or home.*

With nothing to lose, Randle was determined to take the one thing he'd wanted but managed to hold back from for so many years – the warm, smooth, firm body of a young girl. *The policeman's girl.*

But he knew the odds were heavily against him. He'd have to act fast, before the policeman was found. Randle also knew that he would be easy to identify – so that was something he needed to fix. The police would be everywhere and he needed to move about unchallenged.

His boast to the policeman about him not being found was, he knew, an idle one – and unless the policeman was stupid, he'd have realised it too. Randle would be missed as soon as school started this morning, and the policeman as soon as he skipped his first shift. The policeman would almost certainly be found today – and the rest of them wouldn't waste any time looking for him. To get what he wanted, he'd have to act quickly.

Having slept late, Randle started the day by washing – from the sink, slowly, using cold water – aware that even the noise of too much water leaving the tank might alert Arthur's neighbours that the flat was no longer empty.

Then he carefully shaved off his beard. It took a while, but it was worth it. Without it, he looked almost ten years younger.

Is it enough? he wondered. He decided that it wasn't and set about shaving his head, too. Although he'd kept his hair fairly close, this was a whole new look – and one he didn't entirely care for – but it did make an astounding difference. Staring back from the mirror was an entirely alien face: a younger, harder man – the real Randle, the predator stripped bare. He smiled, satisfied.

He removed his glasses. That helped, but unfortunately he couldn't see too well without them. He carefully inserted the contact lenses. He'd decided to try them a couple of months ago, when they were available at half price. At the time he'd hated them – finding them too uncomfortable – but he was now pleased that he'd kept them.

Against his eyes they felt huge and rough, but once his eyes had stopped watering, he could see well enough with them. *I'm not sure I could wear them for long*, he thought, but resolved to wear them as long as he could today, to try to get used to them.

He dried his streaming eyes and limped his way into Arthur's kitchen. *Kicking that nosy copper had been very satisfying*, he thought, *but it really had hurt*. His limp was the one thing that Randle couldn't hide for long.

Randle made coffee – thankfully Arthur had some powdered milk, so he didn't have to take it black, although it was still pretty awful. He rifled quietly through the cupboards and retrieved a can of beans. He wondered if he'd have to eat them cold, to avoid the smell of cooking, but decided that he'd probably get away with it. It wasn't a great breakfast, but Randle had had worse.

Once he'd eaten, Randle looked through the drawers and wardrobes in Arthur's bedroom, looking for replacements for his own clothes. There was a decent dress suit that was quite unlike anything Randle owned, but he ruled it out as being far too conspicuous. In the end he settled for trousers, shirt and jumper – it probably wasn't anywhere near good enough to constitute a disguise, but it would have to do.

He hunted through the flat to find anything that might be of use. He couldn't find a replacement for his own rope. Nor was there any duct tape, but there was a part-roll of brown parcel tape – and a large flask that would definitely come in handy when the time came to stake out the girl.

The thought turned him on enormously. OK, he thought, *she'll fight and scream, but she'll get screwed all the same.*

Best of all, he was delighted to find that Arthur owned a computer and that he had a broadband Internet connection. After silencing its speakers, he turned the computer on and fired up the Web browser. *Time*, he thought, *to catch up with the news.*

7

Becca awoke with a scream, falling sideways into the water. She thrashed around and spluttered, panicking. Then she realised that even though she was sitting on the bottom of the well, her head was easily above the water. She calmed herself and looked around, astonished to find that the water level had dropped.

It was again low enough to sit in.

Aching and stiff, she chose to stand, stretching herself as much as she could.

The rain had gone and the day above seemed bright and warm – not that this much affected the temperature deep inside the well.

After her dream, Becca had almost woken, moaning and twisting in her sleep. But her exhausted body wouldn't let her wake and she'd slept almost until midday.

As she'd fallen, she'd dragged Matt's body sideways into the water. She heaved him back into a sitting position for no good reason other than it had just seemed wrong to leave him there.

She paused, noting something she'd overlooked when she woke. The smell inside the well was worse. There was a new smell, faint, but definitely there. Unpleasant. She'd almost got used to the background smell of the water and moss. This was different, like rotting –

As the thought hit her, she began to retch. *Matt?* she thought, hoping it was her imagination. *Dear God.* With some difficulty, she stopped herself vomiting and tried to breathe deeply. Faster than she would have thought possible, she began to regain control. *Holy crap*, she thought. *I'm getting used to this shit.*

Although her stomach kept cramping, Becca felt much better than she had the previous day and hoped that the fever had almost passed. She forced herself to cough phlegm into the water, trying to clear her chest, grateful that her throat was easing.

She tried to flip the lighter on, but it was too wet to work. She fumbled for a place to put it and left it with some of the other things, resting on an inset in the wall.

Realising that she needed to pee, she pulled down the football shorts and squatted in the water. She reflected on how quickly such abnormal behaviour had become normal. As she urinated, her stomach cramped badly and she involuntarily emptied her bowels – loose, watery waste that stank. *Oh great,* she thought, *that really is all I need.* But the moment quickly passed, leaving her feeling aching and empty. With Matt's decomposing body, the stench in the well was rancid enough already and this cranked things up to another level.

She took the water bottle down and drank from it, grateful that she now at least had enough water – *well*, she considered, *perhaps enough until the end.*

Above her, a noisy pounding of wings heralded the return of the bird. She looked up. It sat there, cawing. Becca did her best to ignore it.

As well as she could, she wrung the water out of her soaked clothes and arranged them to dry, as she had before. *Not that it makes much difference,* she reflected.

Then, she set about exercising as much as she could – hampered by the confined space and her weary body. She couldn't do much, but it did make her feel a little better.

After a while she reluctantly sat back down in the rancid water.

She felt drained – drained of energy, of emotion and of will. Although the thought crossed her mind to listen to some more music, she dismissed it, wallowing in the inevitability of her fate.

The speed with which the rain had fallen was preying on her mind. *What if it rains again?* she thought, doubting that she had the strength to live through another twenty-four hours like the last.

Something was wrong. Her mind was trying to make a connection, but she couldn't complete the thought. She backtracked, thinking again about the rain. She thought about how long it had taken to fill her lunchbox, even with the rain hammering down hard. It wasn't quick. Yet, by comparison, the well had filled up very quickly. *Just how much rain would it take for the water to rise above my head?* she thought. And the water had emptied from the well quickly – far faster than it had filled up. Her tired mind struggled to make sense of what she remembered.

It's coming in from somewhere else, she realised. *There's way too much water.* And then, another leap: *And it's going out somewhere, too. Somewhere fast.*

Although Becca had explored pretty much all of the well above the waterline, she'd not really considered anything below it. All she had been aware of under the water had been the deep mud and scattering of rocks – hurting her feet when she stood and her bottom when she sat.

She felt around carefully.

The bottom of the well was indeed muddy – a thick silt that she could dig deeply into. It was hard to tell how much there was of it. Maybe six or eight inches; more perhaps. Near the edge of the wall, her hands touched a large, smooth rock. She lifted it – no, it was too light for a rock. She held it up out of the water, and then dropped it in horror, screaming. It was a small human skull, that of a child. *Smaller than a child,* she thought. *A baby.*

Above her, the bird cawed in response to her scream.

Any thought, any hope that the woman had just been a dream or the product of her imagination disappeared. *Oh my God,* she thought. *Just how long has that been there?*

"You fucking bitch!" she screamed. The only reply came from the bird.

She pulled herself together. *You just spent the night sat on a corpse,* she thought. *You can handle a few old bones.* She began to feel around again.

She found the skull again, and moved it over near Matt – so she would know where it was. Then she continued hunting. Within a few minutes, she'd found dozens more bones and another skull. She grouped them all together with the first skull.

Her hands also began to find other items. There were several coins; she couldn't see well enough to identify them but some didn't feel like modern currency – they were too rough and thick. There were also, literally, dozens upon dozens of pins and needles. These were all old, badly made and large; even to Becca, who had almost no knowledge of archaeology, it was obvious that they were very old. The coins made some kind of sense – *after all*, she thought, *don't we throw coins in a well to wish?* She had no idea about the pins and needles, though. She placed all of these with the bones.

It took her over an hour, but she cleared the bottom of the well of everything except the silt. Where she could, she dug into the silt to retrieve objects lying there. There were more bones, pins, needles and lots of stones.

Tired and exhausted, she sat back – frustrated. *How is the water getting in and out?* she thought. After resting a while, she tried again, this time feeling around the side of the well itself.

Almost at once she found what she was looking for: a hole, perhaps a foot across, and three or four inches deep. She pushed away the mud which had collected around the entrance. Then, tentatively, she put her hand inside – gently probing around. There was mud, some more stones and a couple of bones within reach on the bottom, but above those, her hand wafted around in water.

It's got to be coming from somewhere and going out somewhere, she reasoned.

Of course! The thought hit her like a slap. *The culvert: high above the quarry pool. Most of the time it's nothing more than a trickle, but when it rains –*

She tried to gauge the place in the wall that was opposite the opening and then moved to it, feeling around. Sure enough, there was another hole, though this one was much, much smaller. *One in, one out*, she thought. *The well had been dug down to an underground stream, that had probably existed way before the quarry had been dug.*

Becca sat back, thinking hard.

She was pretty sure that from the well to the quarry pool wasn't *that* far. She wasn't good with distances, but she thought it might perhaps be between fifty or a hundred yards. *Closer to a hundred*, she decided.

If the weather was good, people often came to the pool. She wondered if there was any way she could get a message out. She had paper, pens and pencils, she realised. *Would the paper make it all the way to the pool?* There was no way of knowing, although common sense said that it would. *What if the paper got stuck at the grating? Even if it fell through, what if there's no one there? If there is someone, would they take any notice?*

Becca's initial excitement evaporated. *It might work*, she thought, *but it might not. More likely not.* But, since it was the only hope she had, she decided to give it a try anyway, once she'd rested.

Another thought was gnawing at her. She kept splashing her hand gently in the water until the *eureka* moment arrived. *Why doesn't the water all go away?*

Now that, she thought, *is interesting.*

There can't be water all of the way down the tunnel – or whatever it is – otherwise, the well would be dry. The water would all just run away. There has to be at least one air pocket.

It was, she realised, like the U-shaped drain from a toilet. An air pocket inside ensures that the water returns to the same height after a toilet has been flushed.

She went back to the larger hole, crouched in front of it, put her hand inside and felt around. It was hard to reach too far inside the hole without getting so low that her head was under water, but she stretched as far as she could. The tunnel was much bigger on the inside, but Becca found it difficult to determine its size.

How large? she wondered.

An idea surfaced in her mind: an idea so deeply frightening that considering it even for a fleeting second seemed utterly insane.

If I could just make the entrance big enough, she thought, trying to decide whether the hole beyond the entrance was big enough for her to squeeze into. Terrified, she dismissed the idea – there were just too many reasons why it would be foolish to even try. *Fifty yards,* she thought, *perhaps one hundred, under water, with possibly no air pocket, in a space that could be way too tiny for most of the distance.*

She sat back down in the water, her mind racing. Now that the thought had surfaced – and even though it was madness – it refused to go away.

She ran through the scenario in her mind, exploring its flaws. Tired and hungry, Becca found it hard to think clearly, but she mentally listed the problems as best she could. First, she had no real idea how far the tunnel ran – it could be twice what she had estimated. Next, there was no way of knowing if she could fit down its entire length – it could be little more than a crack in some places. Then, there was her strength – normally she had a great deal of stamina, but now she was desperately weak. Holding her breath while swimming under water in a public pool was something she'd been able to do for years, but that was totally unlike crawling through a tight tunnel. Also, since there would be no light – a dreadful thought – there would be no way of gauging progress. And, worst of all, she realised, she could crawl in entirely the wrong direction.

Two holes, thought Becca. *I've no way of knowing which one, if any, leads to the quarry. And what if I have a coughing fit partway down the tunnel? I'd end up trapped, breathing in water. And, if I did make it, I'd be stuck halfway up the quarry wall, behind a metal grille. So, if I can't move the grille, I'm just as stuck – although someone might come. If I can move the grille, it's got to be a ten or fifteen-foot drop into the water – followed by a swim that I probably won't have the strength for by then.*

It wasn't hard to come up with reasons why she would fail. There were plenty – and probably as many more that she hadn't even considered.

Any elation she'd felt at her discovery had been beaten down by Becca's own logical objections. She felt tears trickle down her cheeks and instinctively brushed them away, her wet hands only making her face wetter still.

Becca felt utterly defeated by the sheer volume of factors conspiring to keep her in the well. The most depressing thing of all was that if she did die halfway along the tunnel, she'd probably never be found. Even if they found Matt, she doubted it would occur to anyone to hunt for her *below* the water. It would be the bravest thing she'd done – and, if she died, no one would ever know.

There were so many reasons why she couldn't do it and only one reason why she must: if she didn't, she'd almost certainly die. The chances of someone finding her within the next few days were almost none, she knew.

What's worse, she knew that if she was going to take this insane route out, it would have to be very soon. She had plenty of water, but no food. She couldn't remember how long someone could last on water alone, but it was certainly only several days. But that would be several days of getting continually weaker. In a couple of days, any real exertion would be totally beyond her. *It might be bad now*, she thought, *but I'm in far better shape now than I will be in a few days. But maybe all I would be doing would be choosing how I die, fighting for at least a chance of life rather than sitting here waiting for the end.*

Becca's low morale was a depression that seemed deeper than the well itself, something she felt equally unable to climb out of. Her mood annoyed her because it ran counter to her usual determination to succeed. She decided that rather than focus on why she would fail, she'd think about how she could succeed.

Although she had never thought so until now, she was blessed with a petite build and light frame. *Bony Becca* was probably the only one of her group of friends who could even consider squeezing into such a tight place. And if anyone could hold their breath for so long, it would be her. And Becca was convinced that at some point along the way, there would be at least one air pocket – only that could explain the way the well's water level had dropped so quickly, but then stopped. Plus, if she needed a little extra air, she could carry the empty water bottle – it wouldn't be much, but it could be the mouthful that made the difference.

Even with all of those things in its favour, Becca knew it was still a harebrained plan. But harebrained was better than nothing. Better than sitting in the dark and wet, waiting to die.

Becca decided that she had nothing to lose by at least identifying which of the two holes led towards the quarry – and then perhaps trying to enlarge the hole until it was big enough for her.

She knelt in front of one of the holes and placed her hand inside, hoping to be able to feel the flow of the water. After a couple of minutes, she gave up. If the water was moving, it was impossible to tell. Disheartened, she moved to the smaller of the two holes and tried again. Again, she could feel nothing. *It probably barely moves when the water's at its natural level*, she thought. One hole was as good a choice as another, but even at 50/50, the odds did not seem good enough to Becca to justify her life on a guess.

Becca tried to think through the problem – to remember where she and Matt had been standing when they fell into the well; how they fell and where they had fallen. She was pretty sure that they had been standing on the side of the well facing away from the ruined cottage. That would mean that the quarry would have been to her left before she stood on the wall to kiss Matt and to her right when she was on the wall and fell backwards. So, it would be to Matt's left, unless he had twisted as he fell. That reasoning made it the smaller of the two holes. She held her hand there again, but still couldn't feel anything.

Becca sat back and pondered, coughing. *Even if it was flowing slowly, it still had to be moving,* she reasoned. *It trickles out of the culvert – but it does trickle, even in the middle of summer.*

Picturing the culvert in her mind gave her hope – it hadn't occurred to her before now, but the hole was easily big enough for someone to climb into, so perhaps the same was true of much of the tunnel. That was encouraging, but it didn't solve her immediate problem: which of the two holes led to the quarry?

A possible solution occurred to her. She stood and located one of Matt's exercise books and tore out a page. She knelt in front of the smaller of the two holes and waited until the water she had disturbed became perfectly calm. Then she held her hand under water, vertically, at the entrance to the hole – and placed the paper against her palm. After a few moments, it floated away, but for a brief moment she was positive that she'd felt it pressing against her skin. She went to the other hole and tried again, but this time with her palm and paper facing the hole, to confirm if the water was flowing out rather than in. Briefly, but without any doubt, she felt the pressure of the water against the paper before it floated away.

Above her, the bird cawed, making her jump. Although she'd not heard the first bird land, she did hear the flapping of wings as several others joined it, squawking and flapping their wings.

"Yes," said Becca, loud enough for them to hear. "You're worried now, aren't you? Well screw you. I'm leaving."

She knelt in front of the small hole and began to pull at the stones around it.

8

"He works for the school?" Sarah's exclamation was somewhere between incredulity and outright rage.

"Sarah, please," said Jim, placing his hand over Sarah's.

Sarah yanked her hand away. "I think I have a right to be annoyed," she snapped. "That's my daughter he had pictures of."

"I know," responded Jim, sharply. "But you're not the only one whose child is missing, Sarah."

The hurt look in Jim's eyes checked her anger. Ashamed, she settled back in her chair and put her hand back on the kitchen table. "I'm sorry," she said, quietly.

Jim shot her a cold glance but took her hand again. *It was bad enough having to cope with the loss of the children,* he thought, *without having to manage Sarah's bloody mood swings.* After a couple of days' veiled friction, Jim thought that they'd finally managed to pull together. Not that he especially blamed Sarah – he felt the same way. But in Jim's book there was nothing productive in losing your temper – it was a pointless drain of energy. He knew that Sarah was having a tough time coping – but so was he. And who did *he* have to lean on – and why didn't Sarah understand that this was as tough for him as it was for her?

Jim looked Sarah firmly in the eye. "I'm honestly as annoyed as you, Sarah," he said. "But this is progress. It doesn't help if you take it out on me."

There was an uncomfortable silence. Sarah wasn't used to Jim taking a hard line with her and it didn't help that he was right. She nodded, and for what felt like the millionth time in the last two days, wiped the tears from her cheek.

Jim squeezed her hand and put his other arm around her shoulder.

Jenny waited until the moment passed. She'd never been liaison officer in a crime as serious as this, but she had dealt with stressed families enough times to know that the best thing was usually to simply wait and let the tension dissipate. The family's anger had to go somewhere – sadly, as now, it was often directed at each other. Jenny felt sorry for Jim, who seemed to her to be a pretty decent guy. From what she'd seen, he'd been nothing but supportive to Sarah, who hadn't seemed to notice how he was putting aside his own feelings to give her the help she badly needed.

If she's annoyed now, Jenny thought, *just wait until I tell them the rest.* She exchanged glances with Stephen Carter. Although Stephen was older and more experienced, they'd both agreed that the news would be better coming from Jenny, who had developed a stronger rapport with both Sarah and Jim.

"If I can tell you as much as I can," said Jenny. "Some of what I tell you will be disturbing, but I have to stress that – at this moment – we have absolutely no reason to believe that any harm has come to either Rebecca or Matthew." Jenny saw Sarah pale and bite her finger.

"There are a few things I can't tell you," she continued. "But only because we're still investigating and we're not sure of all the facts ourselves."

"We understand," said Jim. "Please. Tell us what you know, or at least what you can. This is killing us."

"The person – the man – in question does work for the school. We believe that he's been watching Rebecca – and quite a few other girls – for some time."

"How long?" asked Sarah, the anger rising in her voice again.

Stephen interjected. "Sarah. We do know how hard this is. If you let Jenny tell you what we know, then we can answer any questions that you have."

Sarah nodded, on the verge of breaking down again.

"One of our officers went to interview the man in question. The officer found clear evidence that the man had been observing Rebecca over a long period – along with a number of other girls. Unfortunately, the man became violent and attacked the officer – who is now in hospital, seriously injured – before escaping." As she spoke, Jenny was painfully aware that her summary had provided a soulless, uncaring account of events.

"What sort of evidence?" asked Jim.

"Mainly photographs," replied Stephen.

Sarah was openly crying. "What kind of photographs?"

"Actually, nothing obscene," reassured Jenny. "They were taken mostly at school. In fact, in isolation, each photograph isn't really incriminating. It's just that there are a lot of them. Many of them have been catalogued."

"He's photographed lots of girls from the school," said Stephen. "But he seems to have singled out Rebecca."

"Just girls?" asked Jim. "What about boys – photos of Matt?"

Stephen shook his head. "So far, we've found nothing to connect this man with Matt." He paused. "We've also found a few personal possessions, at least one of which we believe could have belonged to Rebecca."

"Oh God," moaned Sarah. She felt as though she was going to be physically sick, but managed to contain the nausea.

"We're moving as fast as we can," said Jenny. "We're going to get as much of the evidence together for you to look at as we can. Hopefully tonight, although it might be late. I know this will be very tough on you both, but we really could do with your help."

Sarah and Jim nodded in unison. "Of course," said Jim. "Your officer, will he be OK?"

"He's not good," conceded Stephen. "He took a sustained beating. He's in intensive care." He glanced at Jenny. "You know him: he's Hannah's father, Ed Davis."

"Shit," said Jim. "I'm so sorry."

"Do you think –" said Sarah. "The children? Would he hurt the children like that?"

"We don't know for sure," admitted Jenny. "But Officer Davis took the man by surprise and he was desperate to get away. There's every reason to think that Rebecca and Matthew are still alright."

Sarah shook her head. "You don't know that."

"No, we don't," said Jenny. "But his motive for hurting Ed was clear. It would be wrong to jump to conclusions about the children."

Sarah snorted, clearly not convinced, but didn't pursue it.

"And you can't tell us who this man is?" asked Jim. "Is he a teacher?" Jim saw Jenny and Stephen's eyes meet and wrongly assumed that this was an accidental affirmation.

"We can't say right now," said Stephen. "I'm sorry."

"As soon as we can tell you, we will," added Jenny. "And we have had some positive results from the appeal. We didn't get many calls, but a couple of them have given us some leads. There was one call in particular. The caller placed Rebecca and Matthew – with someone else – between Hawksleigh and Manchester. We've already moved some of our search teams to the area to follow it up."

"God, could it really be them?" Sarah's eyes were beyond hopeful; they were almost pleading.

"We honestly don't know," said Jenny. "But it could be."

Stephen Carter very seriously doubted it. From what he'd heard, the call had all the earmarks of being a time-waster. And as for the children being found unharmed, he doubted that too – Ed Davis' face had been pounded out of shape. *Whoever did that isn't just capable of hurting someone,* he thought, *he's capable of killing them. And enjoying it. He's on the run and knows he's being hunted. God only knows what else he's capable of.*

9

Sammy had been withdrawn for most of the day and Abby was fretting anxiously, finding it impossible to read her daughter's mood.

It had been a massive risk telling Sammy at such a young age, but Abby was confident that she would keep this to herself. Sammy didn't have many close friends and – as far as Abby knew – she'd never exposed her gift for perception to any of them. *In any event,* thought Abby, *I had no choice. She had to know – and she had to know now.* But Abby's main worry was Sammy herself: her ability to understand the thoughts of others made her old-headed, but at the end of the day she was only eight. *Can she handle what she's been told? What does it do to her view of the world? Her trust in others?*

Sammy had been accepting enough of what she'd been told. She'd listened, asked some surprisingly perceptive questions and ultimately understood all of what she'd been told. But there was one thing she couldn't grasp.

"Why," she had asked, "don't we help the girl?"

So, Abby had explained everything again. "If the girl escapes," Abby had said, avoiding using the word *lives*, "ten other children will die instead."

"I get that, Mummy," Sammy had said, impatiently. "You already said. But it's not her fault. We *should* help her."

"It wouldn't be the other ten children's faults either. And we couldn't help them, either."

Sammy hadn't replied to that – but she clearly hadn't been happy about it.

Abby watched her daughter, snuggled up against Helen on the sofa, drinking milk and watching television. Helen, much calmer now, stroked Sammy's hair absently. Abby wondered what was going on in Sammy's mind and wished – as she often did – she could read people as easily as her daughter could.

Every so often Sammy would cough, but her fever was clearly passing.

Sammy wasn't concentrating on the television. She'd closed her mind to her mother, something she didn't think her mother knew she could do. She was letting her mind wander – making connections from one person to another. The girl in the well was tired, a kind of tired that was beyond anything Sammy had experienced. Sammy felt the same exhaustion. That was the way it worked, at least for Sammy. The girl was digging in the dark, her mind filled with a deep hope that was somehow wrapped in fear. From the girl, it was easy to find her mother, whose mind was broadcasting like a distress beacon. She was so, so deeply upset that it physically hurt Sammy – as if she'd been cut inside. Her mind was a mess; difficult to look into. It was like peering into a swirling bowl of brightly coloured paints, where each of the colours hurt your eyes to look at – and they had mixed together so much that it was hard to work out the actual colours any more.

Even at eight, Sammy had learned the dangers of looking into other people's minds – the experience could be overwhelming. Especially adults, who so often thought things that were the opposite of what they said. Adults also thought about *doing it/making love/sex* an awful lot – and sometimes not in a nice way. Her friends knew very little about what seemed to be a massive and often contradictory part of an adult's life and her view of physical intimacy was more confused, not better informed, by the thoughts of those around her. When they were *together* her mother and Helen's only thoughts were of love for each other, yet she knew that others felt that only men and women should *do it* and that two women *doing it* was *bad*. Sammy couldn't figure out why something that was so right to one person was wrong to another – so she preferred not to look.

From the mother, she went to the boy's father. His mind was different, with a calmer layer on top that covered what he was really feeling. Like the mother, he was deeply scared, but in a different way. He had less faith that they'd see their children again: he'd almost resigned himself to the loss and was brooding on the death of his wife, a pain that he normally hid deep within himself. From him, she couldn't get back to the boy. It was as if he didn't exist any more. She went back to the girl and then from her jumped through to several of her friends, most of whom were scared for both her and themselves, some of them even fearing the people around them.

One girl was especially missing her friend; a girl called Hannah. It was something of a relief to look into a younger mind; children's thoughts – even older children – were a lot less dark than those of adults. But her loss was still desperate, the bond of friendship between them was far deeper than her parents suspected. The girl was upset about someone else too: her father, who was very badly hurt somewhere. She could tell from Hannah's mind that her father was not a nice man, although he worked hard to pretend to be, at least to her. She tried to jump from Hannah's mind to her father's, but couldn't – his thoughts were there, but Sammy had never felt anything like them. They were woolly and vague, filled with pain, drifting in and out of view as if he was physically moving closer and then further away. But she did feel, stronger than anything, a different common link between the father and daughter: another man. The *bad man* she had felt before. But now he was worse, grown angry like a cornered animal. She gasped at the sheer lust, hate and desire to inflict pain that radiated from the man.

"You OK, Sams?" asked Helen.

Sammy nodded and snuggled further into Helen. "Yes," she replied.

The *bad man* was a strong link between the girls. He wasn't just bad in the way that lots of people are – little lies, thinking bad things without meaning to do them – he was deeply bad, bad enough that it hurt to look into him. His thoughts were so dark: he was a man with no real friends, whose father had beaten him and whose mother had never expressed love for him. A man whose uncle had hurt him and done *bad things* to him for years until, when he was older, he'd turned on his uncle and – the memory was almost too horrific to look at. It wasn't just the violence: it was the enjoyment that had come from it. The *bad man* believed that all of these thoughts were hidden and irrelevant, but in reality they were always, *always* with him.

Sammy felt suddenly cold and instinctively backed away; she returned to the girl, looking more deeply within her to find the boy.

Sammy didn't like digging in people's minds – if they were thinking something, it was easy for her to read the thoughts, but if she had to dig, she knew instinctively that she could hurt them. Sammy went into Becca's mind, as gently as she could – and then recoiled in horror. (At that moment, deep in the well, Becca winced as a sharp flash of pain cut into her, just behind her eyes.) The boy wasn't a boy any more; his mind was a gap that didn't exist and his body was just rotting flesh, stinking so badly that the girl who had once almost loved him now couldn't bear to think about him.

Sammy jolted, shocked, spilling her milk on her skirt. "Sorry, Mummy," she said, hoping that her mother hadn't caught any of her briefly unguarded thoughts.

Abby took the cup from her daughter. "That's OK – you go and get changed, I'll clean the sofa. You might as well put your nightie or pyjamas on now, anyhow, even if it is a bit early for bed."

Sammy disappeared towards her bedroom, glad to have a few moments alone both to cry and to collect her thoughts. And just time enough also to take some tablets from the bathroom cabinet back to her bedroom, crush them and hide the powder in Lady Mango's little plastic handbag. The bottle said: TAKE TWO TABLETS BEFORE BEDTIME, so Sammy had crushed four. Then she thought again and added another two. And then another two.

Sammy knew from her mother's mind what the tablets did. They'd been on the highest shelf of the bathroom cabinet, so Sammy had used the chair in the bathroom to reach them.

Back in the living room, Helen asked, "Worried?"

Abby nodded. "Damn right. It's like she's closed down."

"It's a hell of a lot for her to take in. Give her time."

"I guess," said Abby, reluctantly. "It would be easier if she'd talk, though."

"Ah," said Helen. "So that's it? You feel she's got the advantage. She can read you, but you can't read her?"

Abby nodded.

"I think that's something you just have to get used to. Look at it from my perspective – I don't know anything that my eyes and ears don't tell me."

Sammy returned, carrying Lady Mango.

"Sammy?" asked Abby.

"Do you want to talk? About what I said today?"

Sammy shook her head, and coughed.

"You scared to talk?"

"No. Well, a little. Yes – quite a bit."

Abby patted her knee. "Come on," she said. "Give me a hug."

Sammy sat on her mother's knee and wrapped her arms around her neck.

"Better?" asked Abby.

Sammy nodded.

"You don't have to tell me anything," said Abby. "It's your choice. But sometimes keeping things to yourself makes them harder to deal with."

Sammy was quiet. Then she said, "It's just that there's so much hurt. I have to shut it out. The girl and her Mummy. They're both very upset."

Abby pulled her daughter close. "I know, baby."

"No, Mummy, you don't. When they feel it, I feel it. It hurts me like it hurts them. I have to keep it out."

"Can you do that?" asked Helen.

Sammy nodded. "Mostly, if I try hard. Or if I think about other things."

"Then that's what you should do," said Abby. "If I could stop this happening, I would. It's harder for you than anyone – and I don't want you hurt. But it will be over, soon."

Sammy said nothing. *Over when the girl dies,* she thought.

"Do you want to sleep with me and Helen tonight?" asked Abby.

"Can I?" asked Sammy.

"Sure," said Abby. "I know when a little girl needs extra cuddles."

Sammy hugged her mother. She loved her very much, but it upset her that she didn't understand.

What Mummy and Helen are doing is wrong, she thought, not understanding their motives despite knowing what they were.

They think they don't have a choice, thought Sammy, sadly. *But they do. It's up to us. No one else will help. Anyhow, it's kind of our family's fault. They won't listen to me, I'm just a kid. But the girl needs help – soon. If Mummy won't do it, I will.*

10

Randle spent most of the day laying low, surfing the Internet. The story of the missing girl had made the national news websites, although it had not yet been covered in any real depth. The children's parents had made an appeal for information; this was now on quite a few of the news websites and Randle watched it a couple of times. He'd seen the girl's mother on a few occasions; she'd even asked him to produce a few extra prints of one of his photographs for her. He didn't know the boy's father – although he had seen him drop the two children off at school once or twice.

Randle was equally scared and excited, as if he were the lead player in a dangerous game; a one-shot game. He knew that he'd have to be careful. Depending on when the nosy policeman was found, it might not be long before his picture was on those same news websites. He'd have to move fast.

Randle had also decided that social networking was definitely a wonderfully useful thing. Armed with both Becca and Hannah's full names, it wasn't difficult to find their on-line profiles. Neither girl had their security settings especially high, so Randle was able to access not only their photographs but also many of their conversations with friends. *As a policeman's daughter,* he thought, *she really should know better.*

Browsing through the pictures, he decided that he definitely preferred Becca: she looked young for her age, which was more to his taste. She was neither plain nor beautiful, yet had slightly quirky features that made her striking. Hannah was, if anything, much prettier – although where Becca looked young for her age, Hannah looked a little older: she could easily pass for sixteen. The photographs gave him an exciting insight into Hannah's life. Especially rewarding were the parties and holidays with friends and family; Randle had lingered over those: *very nice*, he had thought, looking at pictures of her in a bikini.

Randle's more sensible, measured side nagged at him – telling him that Hannah was too dangerous a choice of target. It would be far, far easier to pick any other girl at random – and someone who was younger than Hannah, too.

But the animal side of him had taken over. She was in his sights and, unlike Becca, he didn't want her to slip away. And of course, there was the extra pleasure in knowing that whatever pain he caused her would be felt sooner or later by the nosy parker cop.

He had got the girl's home address from her father's wallet. He knew where she went to school. He could even guess her most likely route. If he were quick and forceful, if she were alone, even if only for a few minutes, he could take her. Take her, then bring her back here – where no one knew he was. Then he could do what he wanted. Time and again: for days, with a little luck.

11

"Would you mind waiting in here, just a minute?" asked Jenny Greenwood. She showed Sarah and Jim into the smaller of the police station's two tiny interview rooms. *Neither comfortable nor comforting,* she thought, *but it's only for a moment.*

She walked down to the main office and stood at the door, waiting to catch Stephen Carter's eye. Stephen was on the phone, engrossed in conversation, but once he spotted Jenny, he quickly hung up and walked over to her.

"They here?" he asked.

Jenny nodded. "In interview room one. How's Ed? Any improvement?"

Stephen frowned. "No. He's very badly hurt. Several ribs are broken, some more than once. His skull's fractured in two places. Jaw's broken in two. Bleeding inside the left eye and a detached retina. To be honest, he's a mess. I'm surprised he was able to talk when I found him."

"You OK?" Jenny touched his arm.

"Yeah, I'm fine," said Stephen. "I've never seen anyone in such a mess, at least not anyone I know." He lowered his voice. "To be honest, I'm fucking angry. OK, Ed probably made it worse, steaming in there drunk – but at least he smoked the bastard out. If I get to Tom Randle first, I'm not sure I'll be reading him his rights."

Jenny looked around. "Steve –"

"Don't worry, Jen, I'm just sounding off." He took a deep breath. "At least I think I am."

"What about his wife?" asked Jenny.

"Julia? Very upset. She's at the hospital now, with their daughter. We've assigned Lucy to them, round the clock. Well, to the girl, really."

"No luck with the hunt?"

"Nothing. This guy's a fucking ghost. Plus, we're still waiting on more people to come in. We need to move faster on this and we don't really have enough bodies on it yet. We've moved most of the team to Randle's flat, places he goes, his routes to and from school and so on. No results. We really need to widen the net. We got a few calls following the appeal, but all of them sound like cranks. One, a woman, we're taking more seriously, but even that one's weird."

"How so?"

"The call came from a really remote phone box. It's neither on the way to or from anywhere of note. Like it was deliberately chosen; not just someone nipping out. We're following it up, though, but that waters down our manpower even more. We're looking all the way between Hawksleigh and Manchester for God's sake. And all the bloody way between Hawksleigh and here." He took a breath. "Come on, let's get it done then."

They walked together to the interview room, where Jim was sitting and Sarah had been pacing until they entered. They greeted each other and Jenny led them to the second interview room. Before they entered, she said, "I need to tell you that this will be upsetting. You need to prepare yourself a little." She opened the door.

On the table were two cardboard storage boxes, without lids. Stephen asked them all to sit down.

"This is some of the stuff we've found at the suspect's residence," he said.

"Some?" said Sarah, incredulous.

Stephen nodded. "This is, as far as we can tell, everything that's related to Rebecca. We're still searching the flat."

Sarah began to reach inside one of the boxes, but Stephen stopped her. "We can look at some of these in a moment," he said. "But first, I want you to take a look at this."

He reached into one of the boxes and pulled out a plastic bag, within which was Becca's scrunchie. He passed it to Sarah.

"Do you recognise this?" he asked.

The plastic bag was far too large for the small item within it. Stuck on the front of the bag was a form, headed **EVIDENCE**, in bold. The form had dozens of fields, of which only a few had been filled in. Within the bag, she could see the scrunchie.

Sarah looked over it, tears flowing from her eyes. She remembered what it had been like emptying her mother's house after she had died; boxing up keepsakes, throwing out what had once been treasured possessions, like so much rubbish. This felt exactly the same. *If something belongs to Becca*, she thought, *is it still hers when she's gone?*

"I don't know," she said. "I think so. It could be hers. But it's like any other – you can get them from dozens of shops. But possibly."

"There were a few hairs on it," said Jenny, softly. "We've sent them for analysis. I'd like to see if I can find any in Rebecca's room – on a hairbrush, perhaps, for matching."

Sarah felt the room close in around her. The more time that passed, the more desperate she became – and the more she felt, deep in her soul, that she'd never see Becca again.

"Can I take it out of the bag?" she asked.

"I'm sorry, no," replied Jenny.

Sarah hesitated. "Can I open it?"

Jenny and Stephen glanced at each other. He shrugged. Jenny said, "Please don't touch it."

Sarah opened the bag, lifted it to her nose and inhaled. There was a faint smell, but Sarah couldn't be sure it was Becca. She inhaled again. "I don't know," she said.

"It's OK," said Jenny. "It's doubtful you can smell anything on something so small."

"I'm her mother," said Sarah, distraught. "I've known her for fourteen years. I should know. *I should.*"

Jenny and Stephen sat for a minute, while Sarah felt the scrunchie through the bag, sniffing it every so often. Jim looked on, his hand on Sarah's arm.

Jenny didn't want to show Sarah the photographs, but knew that they couldn't withhold them. She put on a pair of latex evidence-handling gloves, took out one of the photograph albums and passed it over, along with a second set of gloves.

"If you don't mind wearing these?" she asked.

Sarah shook her head, donned the gloves and picked up the book.

Sarah looked at it. On the cover was written **REBECCA RICHARDS**. She felt nauseous, but opened the cover and flicked through its pages. They were all of Becca – indeed, she'd already seen many of the photographs. Some, she was even familiar with – and at least two she had copies of. Then she remembered where she'd got them.

"The crossing man," she said. "It's him, isn't it?"

12

Sammy pretended to be asleep until both her mother and Helen had nodded off. Their sleep was natural: the crushed sleeping tablets remained unused in Lady Mango's handbag.

This would have been much easier, she thought, *if I'd not agreed to sleep with my Mum and Helen.* But Sammy had sensed that her mother would have been worried if she'd insisted on sleeping on her own. Sammy knew she had to behave as normally as possible: if her mother realised what she was thinking, she'd be horrified.

Not that Sammy wasn't scared. She was – deeply. She was about to do something that she knew might be brave, but was also dangerous. In truth, she didn't feel as if she had a choice: *someone* had to do *something*.

When she was sure that both grown-ups were soundly asleep, she slowly eased her way out of the bed. It would have been impossible if she'd been between Abby and Helen, but she'd chosen to sleep on the edge, at the side of her mother. As she put her feet on the floor, she worked to stifle a cough.

What she was about to do, she could almost certainly do without moving, if she were confident that she could contain her emotions – but she doubted that would be the case. She crept into the dark living room and sat on the sofa, her legs curled beneath her. Then she relaxed and let her mind explore, tentatively moving towards something so black and deeply evil that Sammy felt the room around her grow cold.

The easiest way to find what she was looking for was through the girl. Sammy hunted, with her mind, and found her: she was still digging hard, desperately tired, clinging on to one last hope for life. What she was doing scared Sammy: it felt as though the girl was literally digging her own grave. Somewhere nearby, yet not there at all, she could feel the woman; the same woman she'd felt before, hovering somewhere in the girl's mind. It was like looking for nothing, looking for a black gap, the space between people. Finally, she saw the woman, watching the girl. The woman was grimly satisfied, feeling – as Sammy did – that the girl was shaping her own death. Her mind was unlike any other Sammy had ever seen – black and deep, dark and terrible, bitter and ancient, knowing and arrogant. It shifted, twisted and changed – not the mind of a person as Sammy understood it. In its presence Sammy felt tiny – insignificant and deeply vulnerable.

The woman sensed Sammy hunting around and immediately turned her thoughts to the little girl. Gripped by an awful fear, it gave Sammy some slight satisfaction to register that the woman was briefly shocked, scared even, to see her. Sammy now felt chilled to the bone and noticed that, when she exhaled, she could see her own breath like smoke in the air. The temperature in the living room was now biting cold, like a clear December night.

With a feeling of certainty and dread, she turned and looked at the seat beside her. The woman was there, sitting casually with her legs beneath her – as if mimicking Sammy's pose. Terrified, Sammy fought hard to not back away – but this was not something she had expected, to see the woman so close.

She's just in my head, thought Sammy, *she just looks like she's here.*

She looked just as Sammy had imagined, tall and beautiful. An illusion, Sammy knew. This thing – whatever it was – had no shape. It had once been a woman, but no longer.

"Little, little girl." Such innocent words, but they came from the woman's mouth as if they were the foulest profanities. Sammy's fear intensified and, for one heart-stopping moment, she knew for sure that she'd committed herself to something from which there was no going back.

Sammy remembered, when she'd been two or three years younger, how her mother had tried to help her overcome her shyness around strangers. In small groups, Sammy wasn't shy at all – in fact she could be positively gregarious. In rooms full of people she didn't know, she would cling to her mother and refuse to mingle. Her mother had told her to behave as if she were a princess – because little princesses would be scared too, but needed to show that they weren't. They'd hold up their heads and appear calm. No one in the room would know what they felt inside – they'd just see the confident princess. Sammy lifted her head and held the woman's gaze. "Old woman," she said, evenly, though quaking inside.

The woman smiled. "I like that," she said. "Brave little girl. Few are those who come looking for me. You are strong. I know your family. You know this. Strong family."

The two regarded each other; there was a long silence, though the woman gave no indication of being impatient. Sammy kept quiet, feeling instinctively that to speak first was to surrender some kind of advantage. More than anything, she was conscious of her hands, empty, with nothing to hold for comfort. She wished she had Lady Mango – but part of her knew how ridiculous that would seem. Right now, and for longer, she had to be more than eight, much more.

Finally, the woman asked, "Why did you come looking for me, little girl?"

Without hesitation, Sammy replied, quietly, not wanting her mother or Helen to hear, "I want you to let the girl go. Let her live."

The woman waved her hand, absently. "If she goes, she goes. I cannot keep her."

"You know that's not true."

The woman hissed. "Do you say I lie?"

Sammy hesitated. "I say you know that's not true."

There was another long silence. The woman reached out and took some of Sammy's hair in her hand, gently. Sammy could feel cold radiating from the hand. More than anything else she wanted to run and hide, but she stayed still.

It's not real, she kept telling herself, over and over.

"How old are you?" asked the woman.

"Eight," said Sammy simply.

The woman tapped Sammy's forehead with her finger, leaving an icy spot where she had touched her. "Not in here, I think."

Sammy wasn't quite sure what she meant: she was, after all, eight all over – both inside and out.

"You pretend to be little girl," said the woman, "because it suits you. But you think like big girl."

The woman then tapped Sammy's chest, indicating, Sammy supposed, her heart. "But still the baby here, I think. You are old because you see much. But you don't understand all. You are not as wise as you think. Many things you do not see, mici fata."

"Let her go," said Sammy, quietly.

The woman laughed. "Fata de copil. She *can* go, this I tell you."

Sammy shook her head. She didn't understand all of the words the woman spoke with her mouth, but thought the meaning in her mind was clear: she considered Sammy to be a baby. "You won't let her go," said Sammy, coughing. "I see that *inside you.*"

The woman grabbed Sammy's blonde hair and yanked the girl towards her. Sammy yelped, unable to contain her fear.

She's not real, she's not real, she's not real, repeated Sammy to herself.

"What I want, I take," said the woman simply.

Sammy strained against the woman's grip. "You know what I think? I think you can hurt me, but you can't take me. That's right isn't it? You can hurt, but people have to come to you, don't they?"

The woman pushed Sammy away, angrily. Sammy knew she'd found the truth.

"Doesn't matter," said the woman. "I can hurt you. You, your mother. Your mother's woman-whore. I hurt them so much that you beg for me to take you."

The woman's mind, enraged, lay open for Sammy to see. It was terrible: burning like a cold furnace that wanted only to stay alive, to avenge and to kill. And in the woman's mind, she saw the truth – the truth that no one had questioned, thought about, considered. Why would the woman kill the children? Why did she take them? *Not without reason, but because that kept her alive,* Sammy could see. *More children meant more life.* They didn't even have to be children, but the more unspent life they had ahead, the more life the woman gained. *Like computer-game credits,* thought Sammy. The more lives she took, the more it made her – real. Sammy backed away, unable to contain her fear. The woman grabbed her pyjama top and pulled her towards her.

"Now you know I am real."

Sammy struggled, as quietly but as hard as she could, but couldn't break free. All of her instincts told her to get away, shout for her mother, cry, cry, cry – *no,* she thought. *I have to see this through on my own.* She felt warmth between her legs and knew that she'd wet herself. She held back a sob, feeling shame and fear.

"It's not the girl's fault," said Sammy, sounding petulant. "*Let her go.*"

"What do you know of fault? You do not see all. If I want, I take. What I take, I keep."

"What about a swap?" asked Sammy, breathlessly.

The woman was still. "An exchange. You would do this?"

Sammy nodded, feeling deeply sick. "One person for another."

The woman considered. "You try to trick?"

Sammy shook her head. "A life for a life. No trick."

"Why?"

"It's not her fault."

"Why do you care for this girl?"

"It's not her fault," Sammy repeated. There was a long pause. Sammy could feel her heart racing.

"To this I agree." The woman's smile was malevolent, her eyes dark and unfathomable – but Sammy glimpsed lusty satisfaction in her mind. "But I think you have to be fast. You know this. This girl has not much time."

Sammy nodded. "I know," she said softly.

Then the woman was gone; dissolved into the air like cigarette smoke in the breeze. Sammy slumped backwards, sobbing, trying desperately to be quiet so she didn't wake anyone.

Without warning, the door opened and Sammy screamed, backing away.

Abby rushed to her daughter and wrapped her arms around her, feeling the wet pyjamas against her as she pulled Sammy close. "Sams, it's OK, it's me. What's happened?"

"Another bad dream, Mummy," Sammy lied.

13

Getting across town had been nerve-racking, but easier than Randle had expected. The hardest part had been trying to walk without a limp – it was something that, with effort, he could just about manage, but which hurt intensely.

Wearing a decent coat, courtesy of Arthur's wardrobe, and sporting his newly shaven head, Randle knew that he presented a different enough silhouette to pass a casual glance – but probably nothing more.

Every time he'd seen a police car, his stomach had turned over – but he'd kept on walking, keeping his body as upright as possible.

He had distributed the knife and parcel tape across his coat pockets; the flask (filled with hot coffee) and some biscuits (which had gone soft in Arthur's cupboards, but were still edible) he carried in a plastic supermarket bag.

Dangerous though it was, he'd walked the most direct route between the school and Hannah's house, looking for places where he might hide. He reasoned that the closer he was to the school, the better the chance of snatching someone else if Hannah had walked by a different route; the closer to her house, the better the chance of snatching her. As much as he searched for the ideal lair, where he hid would depend mostly on chance – of finding a convenient location. He wanted somewhere from where he could easily get away across one of the many fields surrounding the town.

When he'd reached Hannah's house, his heart stopped and he felt sick: outside, a police car was parked. He'd walked on by, sweating, convinced for the first time that he was going to be seen. He risked a glance at the house; the curtains were drawn. *The details*, he thought. *Did the car mean that the nosy bastard had been found?* He now regretted his angry boasts, knowing that his carelessness could keep him from his goal. *How many police in the house? One? Two? More?* Randle doubted that there would be more than two.

Unknown to Randle, Hannah was asleep, upstairs. Julia was at her husband's bedside, at the hospital, wrestling between her waning love and increasing loathing for someone who had once been a good man. Inside the house, a lone woman police officer was watching television with the sound turned down low.

Randle had waited a while before walking back, knowing now where best to go. About a quarter of the way towards school, there was a disused garage and petrol station. It was boarded up, but Randle had known that it would be easy enough to break into; from the inside, he could watch the road. Behind the petrol station lay some scrubland and beyond that fields and a little woodland. The road at that point had few houses – a smattering of bungalows with ample land around most of them. At one side of the petrol station, a path ran from the road to the field behind, with a high fence between it and the garage and a tall hedge between it and the next house.

It was an excellent spot, he had decided. It had a good view of the road and was a place to temporarily drag the girl until he calmed her down – or, if she didn't calm down, perhaps he wouldn't take her any further. Better still, there was more than one escape route – leading mostly to woodland.

He'd carefully, quietly, enlarged a hole in the wooden fence behind the petrol station. Then, once he'd been sure he could get through it in a hurry (even dragging a protesting, wriggling girl) he'd broken into the petrol station.

It was dark, old, dirty and smelled of oil. Randle cursed himself for not having the foresight to bring a torch. He waited until his eyes adjusted, then worked his way to the front of the building, finding a gap in the wooden boards that covered the glass. It gave him an excellent view of the road, a wide sweep where he could see someone coming early enough to make his way back outside. He could then easily go down the path, grab the girl and pull her back in here. If she were alone, he'd only be visible for a second or two. If she were with one friend, he would (assuming it was a girl) scare her off or hurt her and still grab the girl. Of course, if that happened he'd have far less time with her, but still enough.

Randle hunkered down for the night, keeping the coffee and biscuits for first light. He didn't sleep much – he was far too excited.

14

"Can I help make the hot chocolate, Mummy?" asked Sammy.

"If you're very careful."

"Mummy! I'm nearly nine," said Sammy, offended. "You put it in the microwave and I'll put the chocolate in when the milk's hot. Like always."

"Do you want any more cough medicine, Sams?"

"No thanks, Mummy. I think it's nearly better."

"Just the same, Sammy, I think you should have a spoonful."

"Mum!"

"And then we can make the chocolate."

Only recently Sammy had, after some considerable pestering, convinced Abby to let her help make the bedtime drinks. She'd been initially excited by this (albeit supervised) elevation to adult status, but had grown bored with it after a week or so. Initially Abby had been apprehensive, despite Sammy's capable nature. Tonight, she was relieved and felt that her daughter was starting to engage with her again. She could never have guessed what her daughter intended to do.

Abby had spent half an hour or so calming Sammy, who hadn't needed to pretend to be either upset or scared. Abby had undressed her, washed her and given her warm, clean pyjamas. The noise had also woken Helen, who sat bleary-eyed, watching Abby gradually and lovingly coax Sammy back down to a more comfortable normality.

Once settled, Sammy had wanted hot chocolate. And, as she often did, she wanted everyone to have one.

Doing the rest wasn't hard, though Sammy was almost certain that her mother would see what she was up to. Lady Mango was on the worktop, *helping to make the hot chocolate*, Sammy had said. Her mother brought her the first cup of hot milk and Sammy slowly started to put in the chocolate powder. As her mother turned to put the second cup in the microwave, Sammy dropped into the cup roughly half of the powdered sleeping tablets. Then she added the rest of the chocolate and stirred it in. She then did the same with the second cup, while her mother took the third – the Hannah Montana cup that Sammy insisted on having – to the microwave. *That way*, thought Sammy, *I won't mix up the cups*.

Once all three drinks were made, Abby carried them on a tray into the lounge. "Right," she said. "Once we've had these, it's off to bed – again. OK?"

The question was directed at Sammy.

Sammy smiled, hoping that her mother couldn't sense any of her inner turmoil.

"OK, Mummy," she said.

15

"Jim? You awake?"

"Yeah." Jim rolled over. In the darkness he couldn't quite make out Sarah's features.

"I can't stop thinking about them," she said.

"I know. Me neither."

"I know I need to sleep, but I can't."

Jim pulled her close. "Do you want to talk?"

"I do," she said. "But I feel talked out. Cried out. I feel drained and empty. And just when I think I'm numb to it all, it comes rushing back to hit me again."

"I know what you mean. Do you want a drink?"

"Tea? Chocolate?"

"If you want. I was thinking more like a whiskey."

"I don't want to be asleep if – if anyone calls. And I don't want to be over the limit if we have to drive somewhere."

"You'll be fine with one," said Jim. He disentangled himself from Sarah, pulled on his robe and went downstairs. He returned with two glasses, each containing what looked to Sarah to be more than a double shot. She took the glass and drank. The whiskey burned as it went down.

"I keep asking myself – and wanting to ask – useless questions. Questions that only get me more upset. You know, like *where are they?* and *what are they doing?*"

Jim sipped his drink and let her talk.

"Do you think the police are doing enough?" she asked.

"I think that they're doing as much as they can. But to be honest, they could throw every policeman in the north of England at this and we still wouldn't know if it would be enough."

"I can't bear it," sobbed Sarah, tears beginning to flow again. "I keep seeing his face. *That man.* I can't cope with thinking about what he might be doing. What he might have done. Jim, I'm so scared."

"I know," said Jim. "Me too."

"I don't want – I couldn't cope – with losing Becca."

"Hey," said Jim, "don't think like that."

"It's hard not to. You must be thinking the same things?"

Jim nodded. "Sometimes."

"Can I ask you – when you lost Chris – how did you cope?"

Jim sighed. "Mostly, I didn't. It was very hard – but I had to keep it together for Matt. I thought that I'd lost everything; it was *so* awful. Even with lots of warning, with Chris being ill for so long, I still felt unprepared. But I had to keep going, for Matt. It took a long time."

Jim put his arm around her shoulders, his own face growing wet. "It's at times like this I wish I believed in God," she said. "So I could pray." Jim scowled. "I've never believed less," he said. "I hope they catch the bastard." "I don't care if they do," said Sarah. "I just want the kids back. I just wish – wish – that they're OK."

She took another drink and prayed anyway. *Please God*, she thought, *please let Becca and Matt be OK*.

She wondered again where Becca was and what she might be doing – but of all the awful things that Sarah might imagine, she could never have guessed the terrible reality that Becca was shaping for herself.

16

When she could work no more, Becca slumped backwards, dizzy with exhaustion. She couldn't imagine feeling more tired or hungry, but was satisfied with her progress.

Her whole day had been spent digging away the dirt of ages and pulling reluctant stones from the well wall. Considering that she only had to make a hole big enough for herself to fit into, it surprised Becca that it had taken her most of the day and nearly all of the night.

The work had been hard. The stones had been very difficult to shift, compacted as they were for hundreds of years. With no tools with which to work, she had to do everything with her hands. She had carefully worked her fingers along the cracks between the stones to shift whatever had been used in place of mortar; then pulled hard at the stones when there was little to grip; waggled them patiently for what seemed like hours, trying to loosen them. The progress was slow, glacial even – but it *was* there.

She'd stopped several times to rest or drink water – and had twice fallen asleep. Her stomach still ached, but whether it was solely from hunger or also from some kind of infection, she couldn't tell – she'd had two more bouts of diarrhoea, which had been very painful. Despite having enough to drink, she felt terribly dehydrated. When she stood, she felt dizzy. Much of her body was numb, especially her hands. They seemed bloated to her, pudgy and unfeeling.

The well was a hell-hole with a stench that she never got used to: rotting flesh, urine and excrement. Now that the water had reached its level, it wasn't moving enough to replenish that within the well. And, she guessed, Matt would be pretty ripe by now. She was relieved that she couldn't see him.

When night fell she continued to labour, almost like an automaton.

Down in the well, the darkness didn't make that much of a difference, especially as she was working under water where her hands were her only eyes.

Every so often, one or more crows would shout from above with their unnatural cry. Becca ignored them. At one point, she'd driven herself on by thinking of home – a warm bed, shower, food and hot drinks. She had no mirror, but knew that she must look like some kind of animal-child, filthy, cut, bedraggled. She pushed away thoughts of home and filled her mind with the most immediate task to hand – whether it was moving a stone or digging mud.

So now, her labours almost complete, she settled back to rest and think about the remaining work. She felt that there were just a few more stones to move: perhaps two or three. It would be best if she could move them tonight, but the effort was well beyond her. And she would need to rest – not only tonight, but probably again in the morning after she'd moved the last of the stones. It would be, she knew, difficult to judge how much to rest. If she rested too much, she'd probably pass the point of being able to even attempt to escape. If she didn't rest enough, she'd probably pass out partway, or not have the strength to pull herself along fast enough.

Time was, she knew, not on her side. One more full day in the well and she felt sure that she'd be too sick to even move.

All of her muscles ached. She coughed again and closed her eyes. Her body was trying to run on reserves that it no longer had – and when, within seconds, sleep claimed her, it was an absolute sleep with little room for dreams.

Every so often her mouth moved, murmuring fearfully, but even if there had been anyone to hear her they wouldn't have been able to make out the words.

17

The discomfort of lying on the hard floor didn't trouble Thomas Randle too much, but his leg hurt badly from walking with it outstretched. He'd slept fitfully: every so often he'd doze off, but then wake ten or twenty minutes later, his thoughts already on the girl. He couldn't wait for sunrise.

• • •

Entwined, Abby and Helen were out to the world, in a sleep so deep that they would have struggled to rise even if the house were on fire. For the second time that night, they'd not noticed Sammy carefully slip from between the sheets. She'd crept back into her own room; there she'd set the alarm on her clock radio for three hours ahead – to wake her well before dawn – and turned its volume down low. When she'd first got into her own bed, Sammy had thought that she wouldn't sleep, but she soon nodded off; it helped that the girl in the well was alreadyin a sleep so deep that Sammy could barely sense her.

Sarah and Jim lay awake, talking and crying in a perpetual emotional agony that only those who have suffered the same thing could in any way understand.

• • •

In the hospital Julia Davis sat by her husband's bed, drinking coffee. Ed was either sleeping or unconscious – probably the latter, since he wasn't snoring. After enough alcohol to fell almost any man, a beating that had taken him to the edge of his life and a dose of morphine to numb his pain, he probably wasn't waking up any time soon. Julia hated sitting alone and missed Hannah. A part of her even questioned why she was here. Despite everything, she still just about loved Ed – what she didn't know was *why* she loved him.

• • •

Stephen Carter and Jenny Greenwood were still very much awake, making love for the second time that night. They'd gone for a drink when their late shift had finished, both equally despondent at the day's events. One drink had turned to three, after which Jenny had thought *fuck it, life's too short*. After a couple more drinks back at the house Jenny shared with Trudy, her Border Collie, Jenny and Stephen had lost themselves in each other, but not before she had made it clear to Stephen – very clear – what would happen if anyone at the small police station ever found out. Trudy, who normally slept at the bottom of Jenny's bed, spent the night outside her room, mostly awake and occasionally whining softly for her mistress.

• • •

Hannah turned in her sleep and briefly awoke. For just a moment, everything seemed normal, but then the events of the last few days resurfaced in her mind. Becca. Her father. She sat upright, scared, imagining that she was alone in the house. Then she remembered the policewoman, sitting downstairs – and relaxed. She crept to the top of the stairs and looked down into the living room. The policewoman was sitting on the sofa, the television turned down so low that Hannah could barely hear it. She turned and went back to bed, closing her eyes to sleep. Just before she slipped away, she saw for a curious moment the face of a young girl, who was perhaps eight or nine, smiling at her. Hannah felt that she somehow knew her, but couldn't place from where. When sleep came back to her, it was shallow and restless.

• • •

At the top of the well, a large black bird hopped from stone to stone.

WEDNESDAY

1

When Becca awoke, she felt far worse than before she had slept. In addition to her familiar hunger, cough, stomach cramps and fatigue she now ached comprehensively from her prolonged exertion the day before.

She looked up to the sky. She couldn't tell what time it was: it was still dark. She groaned inwardly, wishing she'd slept longer. She considered trying to sleep again but decided to press on.

She stood, unsteady on her feet, and took a drink of water from the bottle. She realised that she'd drunk more than she thought the day before. *It doesn't matter,* she decided. *I only need enough for today. And not even for all of that.*

Last night, when faced with moving the few remaining stones, she had felt unable to continue and had fallen asleep exhausted. Today, she really wished she had kept on and finished the job.

She slowly stretched herself, as she would before swimming, feeling her body protest but knowing that she had to not only get her circulation moving but also loosen her tightened muscles. As she moved, her stomach groaned, loud enough to hear in the well.

Christ I'm hungry, she thought.

As she stretched, she briefly lost her balance. *Whoa,* she thought, the well swimming around her. Disorientated and dizzy, she steadied herself against the wall until she felt able to stand.

It would have been all too easy to sit back down and rest, perhaps sleep, but Becca pushed herself on. *I'll rest later,* she thought, *when I've finished digging. At least my cough has settled down.*

She knelt back down, put her hands into the grimy water and felt her way around the hole, seeking the remaining stones with her fingers. There were just three, as she'd thought. She ran her hands behind these; beyond them, as with the rest of the stones she'd moved, there was compacted mud and smaller stones. She would have to clear most of that, too.

Unbidden, her mind kept dwelling on her biggest fear, that once beyond where she could currently feel with her hands, the tunnel narrowed to the point where it couldn't be traversed. If it happened within the first few feet, perhaps within ten feet or a little more, she might be able to back out. Becca really didn't like to think what would happen if the tunnel narrowed when she was much further out than that.

She began to tug at the first stone, reflecting on how hardened she'd become over the last few days – not physically (although she now suspected she had the hands and knees of a labourer) but emotionally. *Emotionally hardened,* she wondered, *or just numb; uncaring?* She reflected on how little she now objected to sharing a confined space with a corpse. She felt that she'd fallen into the well as a girl; if she emerged alive it wouldn't be either as a girl or a woman. She'd be something else. Something stronger, perhaps. Or something less caring, less connected. Something harder.

The stone felt like a large, troublesome tooth. As she pulled, there was only the smallest amount of give. Not enough to loosen it, but enough to work with. She pushed her fingers around the edges of stone, gradually rubbing the cement-like dirt away. She worked for around twenty minutes and then tried the stone again. It was a little looser but not enough. She returned to scraping away the dirt.

They must know that I'm missing by now, she thought, wondering where they were looking for her. *And for Matt,* she corrected herself. *They'll look here in the end,* she guessed, shuddering at the thought of what they might find.

Becca worked for another fifteen minutes or so and then tried again. The stone was noticeably slacker, moving a few millimetres when she pulled it. She shifted her weight to get into a better position, got a firm hold and then began to pull the stone steadily to-and-fro. As she worked it, the stone gradually became loose enough to start pulling away from the wall. Within a few minutes, it was free.

She stood, her legs aching and stiff. She tossed the stone to the other side of the well. *One more down,* she thought, *just two more to go.* She took another drink of water – being a little more prudent this time.

Becca wanted desperately to stop but knew that could be a fatal mistake. *I have to keep at it,* she thought, kneeling down to start again.

The second stone took longer than the first, not because it was held more firmly in place but because Becca's stamina was evaporating. When the third stone came away on its own, as she pulled out the second, Becca was as close to being elated as her physical and mental weariness would allow.

She tossed the stones away and took another drink, wiping the grit and sweat from both her forehead and around her eyes. *I must look like total shit,* she thought, realising she was still dressed in Matt's football kit. It wasn't that she couldn't be bothered to change – the thought hadn't even occurred to her. Becca wondered, absently, if she should be bothered about her appearance. Nothing seemed important any more – nothing apart from staying alive and getting out.

Becca knelt again and began scraping away at the remaining dirt. *I'm nearly there,* she thought, both amazed at the feat she'd accomplished – and frightened by what she intended to do next.

When she'd finally finished, she stopped, resting on all fours, breathing hard. *Shit,* she thought. *Am I really going to do this? I must be mad.* She glanced over at Matt, realising she really didn't have any choice. *Otherwise,* she thought, *there'll be two bodies down here.*

Fuck, she thought, standing up. She felt truly terrified. Gripped with fear, her body close to total collapse, she took another drink.

Looking up, Becca could see that dawn was just about breaking.

Time to rest one last time, she thought, hoping that she wasn't being prophetic.

She sat down, trying to settle, struggling to find somewhere her body didn't feel sore. *How much of me will be left,* Becca wondered, *if I get out?*

Becca felt alone and desperate for comfort. Although she knew it was a useless gesture, she lifted her protesting body upright and then moved next to Matt. She sat down gingerly. She didn't think that she could either embrace or hold him, but she wanted to be close to him. Finding that she couldn't even bear the thought of leaning her body against his, she sat a few inches away, drawing no comfort from the closeness.

"Wish me luck," she said, emptily. Within minutes she was fast asleep.

2

When Sammy woke, she realised instantly that she'd slept too late. Daylight was already glowing through gaps in the curtains. She panicked and almost slipped as she jumped out of bed. Her alarm clock was flashing, silently. She pushed the off button, relieved. She'd only slept an extra hour; it could only have just started to get light.

She dressed quickly and quietly. Not naturally deceptive, she nonetheless realised that if she didn't wear a school uniform, she could look out of place on the street during a school day – but if she did, then it would look odd once school hours began and she wasn't actually in school. She didn't reflect on it for long: she'd fit in best in uniform, she decided, even if it meant that she looked a bit odd walking the streets at around five in the morning.

Sammy also considered leaving a note, but knew that there was no need. When she finally woke, her mother would soon realise where she had gone. As she always did, Sammy straightened the quilt on her bed and sat Lady Mango on the pillow. She leaned over and gave her doll a little kiss.

Sammy crept down the landing and peeked through the gap where Abby's bedroom door was ajar. Both Abby and Helen were still sound asleep.

She slowly made her way to the kitchen. Not wanting to make any noise, she took a banana. *I'll eat it on the way,* she thought, grabbing a carton of juice from the fridge.

Sammy went softly down the stairs and routinely pressed the four keys of the alarm code (it was the day and month of her birthday, chosen partly so she could remember it), each keystroke punctuated by what seemed to be an almost deafening beep. She almost dropped her banana in shock as the sound echoed around her. The light on the control panel went from red to green. She listened hard, holding her breath, but couldn't hear any movement upstairs. She exhaled, relieved. *You need to be smarter than that,* she thought.

Sammy went through to the sitting room at the back of the shop, unlocked and then opened the door. She went through it and carefully closed it behind her. Outside, she coughed gently in the cool air. *I'm glad the girl's getting better,* she thought.

She didn't take a key.

3

It had been a long night. By the time the first rays of sunlight cast a warm, yellow glow across the bedroom walls, Jim at least was nodding off.

There had been tears, conversation, silences and then more tears. Topics that had been discussed to exhaustion were dragged out and picked over again. There was nothing else to do except wait, talk and cry.

Jenny Greenwood had arranged a larger press conference for later that day; another appeal along with questions and answers from the press – a parental ordeal which both Jim and Sarah were dreading.

Jim kissed Sarah's forehead. "It's after five," he said. "We're supposed to be doing that press thing at one. We need to get a few hours' kip. And Jenny's probably going to be here between nine and ten."

"I know," Sarah huffed. She genuinely, desperately wanted to sleep but it was an escape that had eluded her all night. No matter how heavy her eyes, how dulled her senses, her mind just wouldn't stop working. Like Jim, she was so fatigued that she couldn't honestly recall what it felt like to be alert and fresh.

At least the phone hadn't rung since last night. Each time it did, without fail, Sarah rushed to it, adrenalin pumping. She was weary of repeating the same sentences again and again, to friends, Rachel, family and well-wishers – speaking hurriedly, always conscious that she was rushing the call to free up the line, just in case.

"Jim?" Sarah asked, pensively.

"What?"

"What do you think – really think? Do you think they'll be found? I mean really think."

Jim paused. "I don't know. Honestly. You know, you see stuff like this on the TV. How many times do you remember – remember the kids being found? Alive and OK?"

"Oh, Jim –"

"Well, you asked. Shit, of course I hope they're alive and fine. But the more days that go past –" He didn't have to finish the sentence.

"That man," said Sarah. "I met him. *I shook his hand.* I bought photos off him." She gritted her teeth. "The same – the same fucking photos we looked at yesterday."

Jim put his arm around her.

"She's fourteen," said Sarah. "Fourteen. What in Christ's name is he doing with her?"

"Becca's not the only one that's missing," Jim reminded her.

"But Matt's not the one he wanted, is he?" snapped Sarah.

"No," said Jim, raising his voice. "And that's probably worse for him. It might be sick and perverse, but at least he has a reason for keeping Becca alive. Matt's just – just – he'd just be in the way."

Sarah went quiet. That thought, though obvious, hadn't occurred to her. "I'm sorry, Jim," she said. "I – I hadn't realised."

"No," said Jim. "You keep thinking that this only affects you."

"That's not fair!"

"No, you're damned right, it's not fair," snapped Jim. "But that's the way it is."

"No it's not," she retorted. "We have two children. I think of them the same."

Jim snorted. "No you don't. At least you don't until you actually *stop to think.* When you talk to other people about it, you usually just mention Becca. When you talk to me, your biggest concern is still Becca."

"Well of course it is," shouted Sarah. "I'm her mother! But that doesn't mean I don't care about Matt."

Jim stood up. "But you don't, do you? I know you love me – at least I think you do – but he's just hassle."

Sarah sat up in bed, furious, tears running down her face. "Well, he is hassle. How much trouble has he been in? Eh? How much?"

"Compared to your do-nothing-wrong goody-two-shoes daughter? Some. But he's not a bad lad. He just had bad friends."

"He's been screwing my daughter," screamed Sarah. "She's fourteen. He's sixteen. That's pretty bad to me."

"*Your* daughter, *your* daughter. Not *our* daughter is it?"

Sarah gritted her teeth, but before she could say anything, Jim continued. "What they're up to took two people, Sarah. Two of them. Whatever their ages. She wasn't being forced."

"We don't know that," said Sarah under her breath, instantly regretting it.

"What are you saying?" demanded Jim. "Are you saying he – he's like that animal out there?"

"Well," said Sarah, raising her voice, "he's not exactly well-behaved, is he?"

"Matt *would not* hurt Becca," shouted Jim.

"No, but he'll happily screw her," retorted Sarah. "She's fourteen. That's bloody rape, isn't it?"

"Like I said, Sarah, it takes two. Becca's a strong-willed child who gets what she wants. If she didn't want it, Matt wouldn't get it – end of story."

"He'd keep pestering her, wouldn't he? Until he got what he wanted. Because *you* don't control him. He does what he bloody well likes."

"Matt is not a bad boy," shouted Jim. "Don't make out that he is."

"No one's controlled him since Christine died. *You damn well don't.*"

There was a brief moment's silence. Sarah could see Jim gritting his teeth, holding back his temper. Finally, he slammed his fist against the wall and shouted at the top of his voice, "You fucking cow! How can you say that? That is so fucking low at a time like this."

Sarah went quiet, ashamed of what she'd said and shocked at Jim's rage. Always so calm, it was all the worse to see him almost out of control.

"Well?" screamed Jim.

"Jim, I'm sorry, I – I didn't mean it."

"Yes you did," said Jim coldly. "You might wish you hadn't said it, but you bloody well meant it."

"No, I didn't. I'm really sorry." She stood up and took both of his hands.

Jim pushed her away. "You bitch," he said. "Don't touch me."

The word *bitch* was like a slap. Sarah forced down her rage, her natural reaction to retaliate. She took his hands again. "Jim. I've been selfish. I know. But you have to understand why. Just because I've been – putting Becca first, and yes, I know I have been. Just because – I'm me – it doesn't mean I don't love you, *and Matt.*"

The foremost thought at the top of Jim's mind was to push Sarah or even slap her. He forced himself to keep his arms by his sides, trembling. He realised that his face was now wet with tears. With some effort, he reined his temper back in.

Sarah pulled him close. "The kids need us. We need each other."

He nodded, crying openly. Sarah kissed his streaming eyes, first one and then the other. "I am sorry. We're strung out and tired. Are we really going to do this now?"

Jim shook his head. "No," he said, through gritted teeth.

"Come on," she said. "Let's get back into bed for a couple of hours."

"I don't think I'll sleep," said Jim.

"We can just hold each other. We need to not fall apart, Jim. I'm sorry."

They got back into bed. Sarah held Jim as he sobbed and trembled, stroking his head. After twenty long minutes, he quietened and his breathing slowed.

She looked at him, sleeping, deeply regretting their argument, knowing that it was the kind of exchange from which there was no return.

"I just want things back the way they were," she whispered, knowing for certain – whatever happened – that wasn't possible.

A few minutes later, Sarah was also sleeping.

4

Hannah stirred, disturbed from her fitful sleep. She tried to bring her alarm clock into focus; it was just before six. She rubbed her eyes and turned over, intending to go back to sleep. *If I'm being kept off school*, she thought, *I might as well*. She wondered if her mother was back from the hospital and how her father was. Julia had promised to wake her when she got back, so Hannah assumed she was still at the hospital. She closed her eyes again.

Although Julia had been open with Hannah about what had been found at Randle's flat (much of which Stephen had told Julia in confidence and some of which Hannah found deeply disturbing) she'd played down quite how badly Ed was hurt, not wanting to worry Hannah further. Hannah had gone with her to see Ed when he was first admitted and Julia immediately regretted taking her – he was just too shocking to look at. Julia resolved to only take Hannah again if Ed's condition either deteriorated or improved – right now, another visit wouldn't benefit either of them.

Hannah has enough pain to deal with at the moment, Julia had thought, knowing also that her daughter, like her, had very mixed feelings about her father. Sure, she loved him – but she was scared of him too. Although Ed had never (to the best of her knowledge) hit Hannah, Julia suspected that Hannah knew at least some of the things that went on between herself and Ed. It was a jumble of emotions that Julia struggled with; she wanted to spare Hannah the same torment.

There was a sharp *crack!* against her window. Not loud, but clearly audible in the quiet morning. In a moment of déjà vu, Hannah realised that this was the same sound that had woken her moments before. Instantly awake, she swung her legs out of bed, then paused.

What if – what if it's *him*? Her heart skipped a beat and it felt as though her stomach had turned over. *I'll scream*, she decided. *There's a policewoman downstairs. If he's outside, I'm safe.*

Hannah padded slowly to the window. Carefully, she peeked through a crack in the curtains.

Standing on the lawn was a vaguely familiar young girl with blonde hair, dressed ready for school. She had a finger to her lips in a mime gesture: *shush*.

Hannah looked again at the clock, thinking she had misread it – and then her eyes went back to the girl, trying to place from where she knew her. School, maybe – or someone's sister, although Hannah didn't think she knew anyone from the primary school – and then another thought bubbled to the surface. *It's the girl I saw just before falling asleep*, she thought. Bizarrely, as Hannah realised this, the girl put two thumbs up, as though she knew what Hannah was thinking.

Hannah held up one hand: wait. She walked slowly to her bedroom door and then across the landing. She looked down into the living room. The policewoman was fast asleep, slumped on the sofa. The television was still on. *Fat lot of good you are*, thought Hannah. She walked back into her bedroom and gently cracked open her window.

The girl pointed to her. "I need your help," she said, in a stage whisper, her mouth opening and closing in exaggerated movements.

Hannah furrowed her eyebrows and held up her hands. "Why?" she asked.

The girl looked exasperated. She placed her finger to her lips again. Then she mouthed one word that was unmistakable: *Becca*.

Hannah felt a chill inside her. She looked around. She was still alone.

The girl beckoned her to come closer to the window. Hannah opened it a little wider and put her head outside; the morning air was cool.

"Please," she said. "Trust me. Becca needs you. We have to help her."

Hannah didn't know how to react. She held her hands up again and said, "What?"

The girl looked around. "I know where she is. We have to help her."

Hannah whispered back, "There is a policewoman here. She can help." The girl shook her head vigorously and pointed to Hannah. "*You*, me, not them," she said. "No grown-ups."

"Why?"

The girl looked frustrated. She didn't answer the question, but instead pleaded, "*Please.*"

Hannah held both hands up, wide: *what do you want?*

The girl looked relieved. "Come down. I'll tell you then. But no grown-ups – promise?"

Hannah nodded.

"School uniform," said the girl, pointing to Hannah. Hannah looked puzzled. The girl frowned. "School uniform," she insisted, mouthing the words as well as whispering them: *school-uni-form.*

Hannah rapidly brushed her hair and then quickly dressed, struggling to make sense of the last few minutes. She thought that the girl was too young to be a friend of Becca's, but maybe she was. Somehow, despite having never met her, she trusted the girl – at least enough to want to talk to her.

Once she'd dressed she realised that, with the policewoman downstairs, getting out of the house was not going to be easy – whether she was asleep or not.

Hannah crept downstairs, very slowly, the feet within her black school tights tentatively seeking each stair. When she was about a third of the way down, the policewoman stirred and Hannah froze, panic rising within her. The television murmured away in the background. Hannah remained motionless while the policewoman settled again. Then, she slowly carried on down.

In the hall, she decided against wearing her usual school shoes and instead put on her ballet-style flats – mostly because they were quiet. She crept to the back of the house, moving slowly, directly behind the sofa where the policewoman slept, to the kitchen.

Very carefully, she took a set of keys down from the hook. She located the back door key and slipped it quietly into the lock, turning it slowly. The clicks as she turned the key seemed loud in the quiet morning. Once she'd turned the key all of the way, she looked behind her and listened for movement – there was none. She relaxed and gently opened the door just wide enough to slip through it.

The girl was waiting in the garden, the grass still wet from the recent storms. "Hi, Hannah," said the girl. "I'm Sammy." She was younger than she'd looked from upstairs, decided Hannah, but her manner was somehow older. She had the confidence of someone perhaps Hannah's own age.

"Do I know you?" asked Hannah.

"We have to hurry," said Sammy, turning to go. "We can talk on the way."

"Hold on a minute," said Hannah, grabbing Sammy's arm. "On the way to where?"

Sammy shushed Hannah. "Quiet – you'll wake the policewoman."

Hannah was taken aback. "How do you know about the policewoman?"

Sammy rolled her eyes. "Well, *dur*. There's a police car parked at the front."

Hannah stood her ground. "And where on the car does it say how many people came in it, and if they were men or women?"

Sammy started to protest, but Hannah cut her short. "I'm not going anywhere until you tell me everything. And if you don't, I'll shout – loud – and that policewoman will be outside in a second."

"I doubt it," said Sammy. "She's asleep."

"OK – how do you know that?"

Sammy exhaled, irritated, then coughed. "There isn't time. I can tell you on the way. Becca's in a bad way. We have to get to her very soon. *Very soon.* Please?"

"Tell me how you know Becca."

"I'm her friend. Like you."

"She never mentioned you."

"We're wasting time," said Sammy, pulling at Hannah. "Please."

"Look, this is weird. I'm not going anywhere."

Sammy didn't quite know what to do. Any lie to explain how she knew Becca's location would probably have to be more preposterous than the truth – and she'd never told the truth about herself to anyone. Even her mother only knew part of what she could do.

Sammy sighed and took Hannah's hands, and looked up, into her eyes. Hannah looked uncomfortable, but didn't pull away. "This is a secret. No one knows. You understand?"

Hannah nodded, uncertainly. "I guess."

"Promise you won't laugh. You won't believe me."

"Try me."

"I can see what people – some people, not all people – are thinking."

Hannah groaned. *What a fucking waste of time.* "You're right, I don't believe you."

"I can prove it," said Sammy. "Right now. But you won't like it."

"Go on then, prove it," said Hannah, defiantly.

"Come away from the house a bit," said Sammy, leading her into the garden. "You're going to be upset. And we have to be fast."

They walked across the wet lawn and sat on two of the four wooden garden chairs. The chairs were damp but not too uncomfortable.

"You have to promise me," said Sammy. "Once I tell you, we have to go. There's no time."

"Prove it first," said Hannah.

"Promise me."

Hannah sighed. "I promise."

Sammy looked into her eyes. "Your father is in hospital, hurt badly."

Hannah shrugged. "That's no secret," she said. But as she met Sammy's stare, she felt slightly unnerved: she might have the face of a child, but her eyes looked mature and knowing.

"Part of you is glad," said Sammy.

"That's not true," retorted Hannah.

"It is true. Because he hurts your Mummy when he drinks beer. And he scares you."

Hannah felt instantly hot. She was certain she was blushing.

"That –" she began.

"He drinks *a lot*," interrupted Sammy. "He usually calls you Han, not Hannah." Sammy pressed on. "You've only kissed one boy and it scared you because he touched your – your boobs." Sammy blushed. "It scared you but you liked it. But you fancy a boy called Simon and don't want to tell anyone because he's not popular at school."

"Enough," whispered Hannah, pulling her hands away from Sammy. "How do you know all this? Who told you?"

"No one. Did you tell anyone? Did you tell anyone about any of this? You only told Becca about the boy who touched you, didn't you?"

Hannah nodded.

"I *can see* where Becca is. She's trapped. She's really hurt. She's hungry. And very scared."

"Right now?" said Hannah. "I don't believe you. It's not possible."

Sammy shook her head. "Right now she's asleep. She's very tired. But she's going to do something very dangerous. We have to stop her."

Hannah was still struggling. "No one can see things with their mind. Not for real."

"I can. My Mummy can – a little bit. How else could I know all those things?"

"Someone could have told you."

Sammy frowned. "We have to go. No – hang on." She took Hannah's hands again and closed her eyes for a moment. Hannah winced as a small pain flashed briefly in her forehead.

"I'm sorry," said Sammy, "I don't like to do that."

"Do what?"

"Pry – deep inside. It can hurt you."

"Yeah right, so what did you find?"

Sammy smiled. "How many people know where your birthmark is?"

Hannah blushed. "Just Mum and Dad, I think."

"On your bum, but low down, near your – well, you know," said Sammy. "It's small and shaped like a kind of potato. It can't be seen even when you're in your underwear. You'd have to know where to look even if you had nothing on. Anyone other than your Mummy or Daddy seen it?"

Hannah shook her head, stunned.

Sammy stood up. "We have to go now. *Now.* You promised. There isn't much time. I'll tell you the rest on the way."

"So – so you can read minds and stuff? For real?"

"Some. Usually only the stuff that's at the top. Or random stuff. And not everyone. And not all the time."

"And Becca?"

"Not until she got stuck. But now a lot. I think because she's so upset."

"Where is she?" asked Hannah.

"I don't know the place, because I've never been, I've only seen it through Becca. But I know where it is."

"And why the school uniform?" asked Hannah.

"It's a school day, stupid. Where we're going is not far from school. In normal clothes we'd stand out."

"OK, then," said Hannah. "Let's go."

"One more thing," said Sammy. "Have you got any rope, or washing line?"

Hannah nodded. "In the garage."

"We'll need it," said Sammy.

5

Randle sipped his coffee without taking his eyes off the gap between the wooden boards. He glanced at his watch. It was still too early for the girl to be on her way to school, but several other people had already walked past. He didn't mind waiting. He had nothing better to do – and didn't want to miss the girl.

When it became light enough to see, Randle had found an old chair in one of the back offices of the garage. He ached from sleeping on the floor and his leg was complaining terribly. Worse, his eyes were smarting from wearing the contact lenses for too long and it had become harder to see. He had his glasses in his pocket, so he could take the lenses out, but he thought it best to wait until he had the girl.

Randle had spent most of the night playing out fantasies in his mind: what he would do with the girl; how she would react; what she looked like naked; what she would feel like; how long he could get away with it before he was caught. He'd become a being with one goal; one focus.

On balance, Randle had decided that – if he could – he'd let the girl live, that this was far worse for her father than if she were dead. Every time he'd look at her, he'd be reminded of Randle. The thought made him smile. He sipped his coffee again.

Movement at the edge of his vision caught his eye. It looked like the girl, but his sore, watering eyes couldn't quite focus. He stood, wiping his eyes. He moved to press his face against the gap. It was her, but she wasn't alone.

Shit, thought Randle, almost furious. He could probably still grab the girl, but he wouldn't get far without the other one raising hell.

The more rational part of his mind kicked in.

Where are they going at this time? he thought. *It's way too early for school. Paper round? And the second girl –*

The second girl was too young to be a friend. A sister?

They were now almost halfway past the garage. Randle felt his opportunity fading. *I'll have to follow them*, he thought, *and hope they separate.* They were so tantalisingly close that he almost went ahead with his plan anyway, feeling sure that he could still have the girl before the police arrived, if only once.

Then the older girl did something which made him pause. She was pointing to the path at the side of the garage. The two girls hesitated briefly, appearing to compare routes. It was a brief discussion; after a few seconds, the two girls set off again.

To Randle's delight, they took the path at the side of the garage. As a route to school, it didn't really make sense. Yes, they would reach the school, but it was far longer and for most of the way there was no path. Indeed, they would largely be in open country, passing near the old quarry as they worked their way around the outskirts of town before turning back towards the school.

Still puzzled, Randle set out to follow them.

In many ways, he didn't really care where they were going. This was his opportunity. Far enough away from town, he could easily cope with both of the girls – if he was fast enough, brutal enough or threatened them in the right way.

6

"Sammy!"

Abby's shout roused Helen from a deep sleep. She felt awful, sluggish and dehydrated – as if she'd been drinking the night before. She rolled over in the bed, onto her arm. A sharp, sudden pain flashed along it. She yelped involuntarily and sat up, cradling it. "Ow!"

Abby ran into the bedroom. "Sammy's gone," she said, her voice full of panic.

Helen threw back the quilt, adrenalin pushing her drowsiness to one side. "Where's she gone?"

"Where do you think? There's only one place I think she'd go without telling us."

"The well?"

Abby nodded. "I should have spotted it. The way she kept saying that we had to help the girl. That's what she's gone to do."

"Get her out?"

"I think so."

"Shit," said Helen. She thought for a moment. "How will she do that? She's not big enough to lift her out on her own."

"Well, I don't know," said Abby. "Maybe she thinks if she can throw some rope down, the girl can climb out."

"Maybe," said Helen, "Although –"

Abby interrupted her. "There isn't time to debate this. I have to go and get her."

"What do you mean, *you* have to go?" demanded Helen. "*We* have to go."

"You can't," responded Abby, sharply. "Look at your arm. Look at what happened yesterday. I won't let you."

"You can't stop me."

"Helen –"

"Abby, we're a team. A couple. A family. I don't care what could happen, there is no way on Earth you're going on your own."

Abby started to protest, but Helen silenced her. "*None.* And we're wasting time. Let's get dressed. You'll have to drive."

By the time Abby had dressed, Helen was only just in her underwear, struggling to put her jeans on. "My arm," she said apologetically. "Will you help me?"

Abby helped her dress. Before they left, they checked all of the rooms again – more to see if Sammy had left a note, rather than with any expectation of finding her.

At the back door, Abby paused. "Sammy's keys," she said.

"So?" asked Helen.

"She's not taken a key. Like she's not coming back." Abby closed her eyes and tried as hard as she could to feel for Sammy. Somewhere distant, she had no idea where, she could just about feel Sammy's determined, resolved mood; nothing more. A thought struck her. "Oh my God," she said. *Shit, shit, shit. The stupid, stupid girl.*

"What?" asked Helen.

"I'm not sure she's gone just to help the girl out. I think she's going to offer herself – do a swap. She kept saying that it's not the girl's fault."

"Oh, fuck," said Helen softly, her hand covering her mouth. "Why would she do that? Doesn't she realise –"

"I don't know," snapped Abby, exasperated. "Maybe she thinks she'll be a hero. Her generation's been brought up on Harry Potter and Twilight for fuck's sake. Like witches and demons are just misunderstood and not actually evil. She's no idea what she's getting herself into."

Abby's eyes were filling up. She grabbed her keys and mobile phone. "Come on," she said.

7

When Becca finally woke, she felt as rested as she could ever be. To say she was anxious would be a dramatic understatement: when she considered what she was about to do, she was filled with a fear so deep that it made her feel physically sick. Becca knew her chances of success were remote and had to work continually to keep her tears at bay.

While she had been busy digging, her mind had run over the logistics of what she intended. Now, awake, she set about her preparations as methodically as she could. All the while, she tried to breathe slowly and deeply – partly to keep her panic under control and partly to prepare her lungs, as she would before swimming. Every so often, she would cough, not as uncontrollably as before, but still painfully and usually followed by her hawking phlegm into the water. She desperately hoped that her chest would settle down – if she had a coughing fit once she had started, it would almost certainly be fatal.

The first thing she did was to change. Initially she thought that it wouldn't matter what she wore, but she then realised that was foolish. *Nothing should be left to chance*, she decided. *Every decision counts.* There was no telling how cramped the tunnel was, so the less she could wear, the better. Her desire for some kind of normality tempted her to change back into her school clothes, but Becca reasoned that her swimming costume was the garment best suited to the task ahead. She considered it fortuitous that she had it in her bag. Of course, this did present another problem, should she be lucky enough to emerge from the other end: walking into town, filthy, in her swimming costume, would be embarrassing. But after the continual degradation of the last few days, Becca found it easy to dismiss this concern as trivial. Alive and embarrassed was preferable to dead and well-dressed. She'd walk home naked if she had to.

Less fortunate was that Becca hadn't packed all of her swimming kit. She had her goggles, but not her nose clips or swim cap. She hadn't expected her Friday swimming lesson to be especially demanding, so she'd left them at home – something she now regretted. For most swimming lessons, the nose clips just gave her an additional edge. Today, they could have meant the difference between life and death.

Becca undressed and tried to wash as much mud from herself as she could. It wasn't easy – partly because she just couldn't see well enough to know when her efforts had made a difference and partly because she was washing in dirty water. She smiled to herself; even when she was about to embark on an almost certainly suicidal attempt to escape, she was taking a minute to make herself a little more presentable. She felt sure that it wasn't worth the effort.

Then she put on not only her swimming costume but also her shoes, which she felt would provide a little better traction against the mud and stone inside the tunnel.

When she came to tie back her hair, she looked through her bag and pockets for her scrunchie, missing it for the first time. Unable to find it, she used one of her socks as a tie, after first dipping it in water and wringing it out so she could tie it as tightly as possible.

Next, she emptied the water bottle, after first drinking as much of the water as she could. She shook it dry and replaced the cap. The bottle held far, far less than a lungful of air, but would perhaps be enough if she was desperate. She even considered trying to fill a condom or two with air, but knew that they would be cumbersome to carry and she could only fill them with the useless air she had exhaled. The bottle wasn't much, but it would have to do.

Her next preparation was, she decided, a stroke of genius. Inspired by how her iPod had lit the inside of the well when it was playing, she realised that it would make a just-about-adequate light. Deep inside the dark tunnel, it should be enough. Of course, it wouldn't work long under water. She could either put it inside her sandwich box, which was transparent but bulky, or within a carrier bag. Coloured white, a carrier bag would block some of the light from the iPod, but perhaps not all of it. Carrying the sandwich box in addition to the bottle seemed too difficult, so Becca opted to use the carrier bag. Then she realised that the bag had holes in it, by design, and wasn't watertight at all. For a moment she felt frustrated and then realised that a condom would make the perfect container for the iPod. A bonus of doing this was that, since the condom was so thin, she could still turn the iPod on and off without taking it out.

Finally, Becca sat down to concentrate on her breathing. She was already fatigued from merely changing and preparing herself; dragging her tired body down the length of the tunnel would be by far the hardest thing she had ever done.

Despite growing familiar with the idea of crawling out, her fear at the prospect had never diminished. *This*, she thought, *was not an idea you could ever, ever get used to.*

Becca felt a tear in her eye and brushed it away with a sob. *I don't want to die*, she thought, certain for one moment that this was not only the most likely outcome, but also the only possible outcome. *No*, she thought. *Staying here is the only sure way to die: at least this gives me some kind of chance, however small.*

She paused. *They could be searching here, today. They could still find me. If I stay...* The thought was tempting, but Becca dismissed it. *If they've not looked here so far, it could be days more before they do. Oh God. There really is no choice. Am I really going to do this?*

She allowed herself a few minutes of weeping, then forced herself to start breathing deeply again, realising that she had begun to consider abandoning her escape. *You have to do this*, she thought, *you just have to. You **can** do this.*

Becca kept breathing, thinking in time with her breaths, *you can do this, you can do this.*

8

At the edge of the quarry pool, Sammy stopped. Hannah watched her – she seemed to be listening for something. A look of despair crossed Sammy's face.

"What's the matter?" asked Hannah.

"We're too late. By the time we get to the top, she'll probably have started."

"Oh, shit."

They had walked briskly through the fields, frequently breaking into a run. The grass was still wet from the rain and the ground often muddy. Hannah's tights and shoes quickly had become both soaked and filthy. During the walk over, Sammy had told Hannah as much as she could – but was smart enough to leave out the less believable bits, such as the gypsy woman and her curse. "I don't know it all," Sammy had said. "It's not as if I see what Becca sees. But I can feel a lot of what she feels. What she's going to do is loud and strong in her mind. But it's stupid. Her mind is –"

Sammy struggled for words, "– jumbled and messy. Because she's tired and sick, I think. She doesn't think straight."

The more Sammy had told her, the more worried and upset Hannah had become. It wasn't a full story, as Sammy only saw things in random patches, but it was enough to piece together Becca's misery. When Sammy had told Hannah that she thought Matt was dead, she'd had to stop walking. Despite not liking him, it was impossible not to feel intense grief – not only for him, but for his Dad and for poor Becca, alone with his body. For Hannah, the reality of the situation had transformed the morning from being an adventure into a deadly race.

"What do we do?" asked Hannah.

"Give me the rope," said Sammy. "You wait here. If she does make it, she'll come out there." Sammy pointed to the culvert. "She won't be able to get down other than by jumping – and we can't get up. If she can jump, she'll need you to get her out of the water." Sammy squeezed her hand. "And it will help her to see you."

Jesus, thought Hannah. *How old is this kid?*

Sammy started to run up the hill, and turned around. "If I get there in time, I'll come back and get you," she shouted. "If she's already gone in, I'll wait up there in case she can't do it and comes back out."

Hannah watched as Sammy scrambled up the steep side of the quarry, the rope slung over her shoulder. When she got to the top, she disappeared into the trees without looking back.

After the rush of getting to the pool, the near silence that surrounded Hannah was now almost overwhelming. The only sounds were the breeze in the trees and the birds singing. Hannah knew she was too far from town to be able to hear anything else, even traffic.

Hannah paced up and down, glancing from the culvert to the trees, hoping to see either Becca or Sammy appear. Neither did. She sat down on a large stone, watching and waiting.

Without warning, a huge, sweaty paw of a hand clamped itself tightly around her mouth and pulled her backwards onto the floor. She hit the ground hard, mud squelching beneath her. A face loomed over her: a bald man, mean and hard-looking and somehow familiar. She struggled, but he pressed his hand hard into her face while his other hand pushed against her stomach, holding her firmly on the ground while her legs kicked around.

"Don't move," said the man, quietly, squatting at her side. "Don't scream. Don't struggle. Understand?"

Once he had spoken, Hannah recognised him; panic and fear filled her mind. *Oh God, no, no, no, no, please no*, she thought, writhing as hard as she could, but the tightness of the man's grip gave little scope to move.

"I said don't struggle." He pressed his hand harder against her mouth; so hard it hurt. Hannah slowed her struggles, hoping that Randle would relax his grip when she did so. When he didn't, she tried again with all of her energy. Keeping one hand firmly on her mouth, Randle raised his other hand and punched her in the stomach, hard. The pain was excruciating and, with Randle's hand pressed against her mouth, she struggled to breathe.

"The more you struggle, the more I'll hurt you," warned Randle.

She shook her head as vigorously as she could, her eyes, full of tears, pleading with him. Randle took his hand off Hannah's stomach and reached into his coat. When he pulled it out, he was holding a kitchen knife. He brought it slowly up to Hannah's face.

"I don't want to kill you," he said, "but I will if I have to. Do you understand?"

Hannah nodded, eyes wide with fear.

"Do you want to live?"

Hannah nodded again.

"Good girl. Now, I'm going to ask you a question. When I move my hand, you answer it. If you scream, it will be the last sound you make, I promise. Understand?"

Hannah nodded. *Oh God, please, please*, she thought.

"Where's the other girl gone?" Randle asked. He slowly lifted his hand away. Hannah drew breath, gratefully. "Answer," Randle demanded, softly.

"Up to the well," said Hannah, spitting the words out between gasps.

"Is anyone else here? Anyone coming? Don't lie to me."

Hannah shook her head. "Just us," she said.

"What are you doing out here? What's she doing up there?"

Hannah thought quickly. "We're bunking off school," she said. "She wanted to – you know – have a pee. I'm going to follow her up in a bit."

"Good," said Randle. Hannah seized the brief opportunity: Randle was holding the knife with one hand while the other hovered over her face. Hannah was pretty certain what was about to happen and was willing to risk getting hurt by trying to escape. She rolled to one side and sprang to her feet. She was fast, but Randle was faster. In one move, he dropped the knife and grabbed both of her ankles. He yanked them hard, pulling Hannah's feet from under her. She landed with a thud on the floor, face down, her chest and face taking the full force of the impact. Hannah yelped.

Randle rolled her over onto her back and slapped her hard across the face, a powerful blow that hurt like fire and set her ears ringing.

"No, please," she started to say – but once again the hand was on her mouth. Randle picked up the knife.

"I told you," he said.

She shook her head and tried to plead with him, but the only sound that came through the wall of flesh was a desperate murmur.

"You're bleeding," said Randle. He wiped the back of his hand against her forehead and showed it to her. "Such a pretty girl. We don't want to spoil your looks."

Hannah stopped struggling.

"Good girl," said Randle. "Now, you try that again and I'll use the knife. I used to be a soldier. I know how to use it. I can make sure that you're dying slowly, while I screw you. Understand?"

Hannah nodded. Deep in her stomach, she felt hideously sick.

"Now, you know what's going to happen. What's up to you is how much it hurts when I do it – and whether you get to wake up tomorrow."

Oh, please, please no, she thought.

"Now, you do as I say. Roll over onto your stomach and put your hands behind your back."

Randle relaxed his grip. Hannah rolled over, sobbing, and put her hands behind her. She heard the sound of tape being taken off a roll and felt him bind her wrists, tightly.

"Now roll onto your side," he said. As she did so, he pulled the last of the tape from the roll and stuck it across her mouth. *Not enough for two girls,* he thought. *Well, I'll just have to be all the more firm with the other one.*

Randle stood. As he did, Hannah saw him wince and rub his leg. She remembered that he walked with a limp and wondered, if she got the chance, if she could outrun him. He pulled her to her feet.

"Right," he said. "Let's go and meet your friend."

9

Kneeling on all fours in front of the hole, Becca took one long, final deep breath. *You can do this,* she told herself.

Her fear was so tangible that she could almost taste it, like bile rising from her empty stomach.

She held her breath and submerged, flattening herself against the bottom of the well. In her left hand she held the empty water bottle, in her right the iPod in the condom. Although grateful for her goggles, there was little to see. The dim light from the iPod illuminated only a foot or so around it.

She stretched her arms in front of herself and pushed forwards into the hole, terrified. Before she had entered it, the hole had seemed easily big enough. Once she had squeezed her shoulders inside, she found that the confined tunnel seemed to press against her on all sides. She tried to move forwards, but her fear instantly smothered her ability to think clearly and she backed out, panicking.

She surfaced, panting. "I can't," she sobbed to herself with angry frustration, defeated and exhausted. "I can't."

Becca sat down in the water, pulled off her goggles and wept. *I don't want to die,* she thought, over and over again.

Above her, a loud caw signalled the return of the bird.

"Oh, you're back are you?" she shouted. The bird cawed again.

I'll die if I stay here, she thought. *I have to do this. I have to. There's no choice. No other way. And I have to do it now. By tomorrow I'll be too tired, too hungry and probably too sick.*

The bird cawed again.

Angry, Becca returned to the front of the hole and positioned herself on all fours. "Fuck you!" she shouted at the bird.

She brought her breathing under control, taking long slow breaths. "Fuck you," she murmured each time she exhaled, her determination growing with each breath.

She put on her goggles, grabbed the empty bottle which had been floating on the water and fished around for the iPod.

Her breaths were getting slower and deeper. *You can do this,* she told herself. *You have to do this. You're good at this. You're good in the water. The best in school.*

Above her, the bird cawed again. Becca looked up and raised her right hand, middle finger protruding from her clenched fist.

Then she took one long breath, submerged and pushed herself into the hole.

10

Exhausted, Julia dropped her handbag on the living room floor and hung her car keys on the hook by the door.

"Hannah not up yet?" she asked.

PC Lucy Keelan shook her head. "I didn't want to disturb her. I was going to wake her just before my replacement came, so it wouldn't be a shock when I was gone."

Julia looked at her watch. Hannah wasn't usually one for sleeping in. *Perhaps she just doesn't want to face the day,* she thought. *I know how she feels.*

It had been a long, purposeless night – Ed had regained consciousness for only a few moments. She wasn't sure that he had even been aware of her presence. She'd tried to sleep at around three, her eyes red and sore from being awake so long. But she couldn't. Too much coffee and too much tension kept her mind from relaxing.

She poured herself an orange juice and one for Hannah. "Do you want one?" she asked Lucy.

"No thanks. I could do with a coffee, though – but I can make it."

Julia took the drinks upstairs, thinking about grabbing a hot shower and a couple of hours' sleep before going back to the hospital.

She knocked on Hannah's door. There was no answer. She knocked again and pushed open the door. "Hannah?" The room was empty, the bed unmade – and the window open. Julia scanned around the room, as if she had somehow failed to see her daughter. The t-shirt and shorts she normally slept in were on the chair at the side of her desk as if she'd dressed, but her mobile phone was still on the shelf above her bed.

She put down the two glasses of juice and walked to the bathroom, calling out, "Hannah?"

The bathroom door was open – the room was empty. Julia felt her initial apprehension shift into panic. She ran from room to room, shouting Hannah's name. Each room was empty. Running downstairs, she almost collided with Lucy who, hearing Julia's increasingly anguished shouts, had come running.

"She's not here," shouted Julia, distraught.

Julia scouted around downstairs. A pair of Hannah's shoes were missing and the back door was unlocked.

"I've been here all the time!" protested Lucy, her voice full of shock, her eyes wide with fear.

"What, asleep?" screamed Julia. She could only think of three possibilities: for some reason, Hannah had decided to go to school. Or she had gone out – somewhere. *But where?* wondered Julia. *And without telling anyone?* The final possibility chilled her: *could that man have crept in and taken her?*

"You just pray that she's at school," said Julia, picking up the phone. "You work with my husband. You know what he's like. You know that if any harm comes to Hannah when you were supposed to be watching her, he'll –" Julia shook her right hand in front of her, in a tight fist.

Lucy knew exactly what Ed would do. And that would probably be after she lost her job. Feeling sick, she went into the kitchen to radio back to the station.

The irony of using the threat of violence by her husband, against another woman, didn't occur to Julia until much later.

11

As Sammy ran to the well, a large black bird that had been perched on the wall flapped its wings and flew into the trees, startling her.

Breathless from the climb, she peered inside. It was too dark to see the bottom clearly, though she thought she could just about make out a vague shape below.

Her foot kicked something. She looked down: it was a mobile phone; beside it lay the battery. She dropped the rope on the ground and knelt at the edge of the well.

"Hello?" she shouted. Her voice echoed around the well; no reply came. Despite knowing it to be useless, she shouted again.

She closed her eyes and tried to find the girl, but couldn't. That was the problem with trying to see others' thoughts: you couldn't rely on it. Sometimes it was easy, sometimes very hard – and sometimes it didn't work at all. Sometimes, Sammy could tune people in and out as if they were radio stations, yet other times everyone's thoughts were a jumbled riot of noise that couldn't be shut out. *Still*, she thought, *I normally feel **something**.* It was a feeling of isolation with which Sammy wasn't familiar.

It's this place, Sammy realised. *It's a bad place.*

It was almost as if the place itself had thoughts; dark thoughts, far worse than Sammy had ever seen, even from *that man*. It felt like a black light, radiating evil, blocking everything out. It was not a good place to be. Sammy looked around. The well was bad, but the ruined cottage was worse. She stood and walked towards it slowly, both drawn to it and repulsed by it at the same time.

Inside, the remains of the rooms were completely overgrown – except, bizarrely, one room where nothing grew at all. Sammy stood at the threshold to that room, unable to put a foot inside it. She shuddered. It made her feel just like when she'd had flu – hot and cold, nauseous and dizzy. She backed away, steadying herself against the wall.

She could feel the house talking, murmuring, but it wasn't using words – more of a low tone, like a group of men humming and whispering at the same time. It was deeply unsettling. She turned and ran from the house.

It wasn't that far from the house to the well, but when she reached it she was panting hard and trembling with fear. Until now she'd felt brave and almost grown-up. But in this terrible place she felt very much like the child she was: small, helpless and woefully out of her depth.

Still feeling sick, Sammy knelt at the side of the well and shouted into it once more – and was again met with silence. She was annoyed with herself for sleeping in and setting off late – and equally cross with Hannah for refusing to set off straight away. Just being a few minutes earlier could have been enough.

The minutes dragged by. Every so often Sammy would shout into the well, but always without hearing a response. The only sound was a bird's occasional caw, which, for some reason, Sammy found incredibly unnerving.

After five more minutes, despondent, she decided to go back to the top of the quarry, to see if Becca had emerged. She stood and ran back to the gap in the wall. Just as she reached it, Hannah came stumbling through, falling face down on the muddy ground as if she had been pushed.

"Hannah!" Sammy rushed forwards and squatted down beside her. "Are you OK?"

Too late, Sammy noticed that Hannah's hands were bound. Hannah rolled over; her mouth was covered with brown tape and the side of her face was dashed with blood.

A big, stocky man jumped down from the gap in the wall, pushing Sammy to the ground. Before she could move, one of his hands covered her mouth; the other was holding a knife. *It's him*, she thought, *it's the bad man.*

Sammy struggled, but the man was strong – brutishly strong. The hand on her face was easily enough to keep her pinned to the ground. She kicked around with her feet, pointlessly. She had instantly known that he was the *bad man* but it was only now that she recognised him as someone she had seen often. The thought that the *bad man* lived inside someone she knew, someone who everyone trusted, made her even more terrified.

"Calm down," said the man, insistently. "Don't struggle."

Sammy bit into the man's hand. He yanked it back, swearing. Sammy shrieked and scrambled away. She got to her feet, but the man was already up. Before she could run, he kicked her feet from under her. As she hit the ground, he rolled her onto her back and then sat astride her, on her chest, pinning her arms down with his knees. She struggled as hard as she could but the man was very heavy – so heavy that he hurt her chest. She tried to scream again but the man covered her mouth with his hand; it was wet with blood.

"Scream once more and I'll fucking kill you," said the man, enraged. He pulled back his arm and slapped her hard with the back of his hand, across the side of her face. Sammy felt as though she'd been hit with a hammer.

The man covered her mouth again, stifling the sound of her weeping. He was talking, but she couldn't quite hear what he was saying. He had gone blurry and the ground beneath her seemed to be spinning.

He shook her. "Did you hear me?"

Sammy shook her head; when she did, it made her feel sick.

"If you scream, or run, I will catch you. But first –" he gestured towards Hannah, "– I'll kill her. And when they find out, people will blame you. Because you ran away. It will be your fault. Understand? I'll kill her – but they will blame you."

Sammy nodded.

"Do you want to live?"

Sammy nodded, terrified.

Randle gestured to Hannah. "Do you want me to kill her?"

Sammy shook her head.

"Then you're going to be quiet? And do everything I say?"

Sammy nodded, shakily. Tears covered her face. She sniffed up, hard, her nose running as freely as her eyes. She didn't know what doing *everything I say* would entail, but she was pretty sure it wasn't going to be good. *A dirty-bad-sex thing*, she assumed, shuddering. *Like bad people think: hurting not loving.*

"Right," said Randle. "I'm going to let you up. When I do, you keep quiet and don't run. If you do, she'll be dead before you've gone fifty feet. Understand?"

Sammy nodded. She knew that the man was absolutely telling the truth.

Then he spoke to Hannah, who still lay on the ground. "The same goes for you. You run, she gets it."

Randle pulled both of the girls to their feet and looked them over. One was a touch young for him, one a touch too old – but when all was said and done, he'd done far better than he could ever have hoped. *Two for the price of one*, he thought.

He gestured over towards the ruined cottage. "Walk," he said. "Get in there."

12

Inside the tunnel, almost everything was black. The iPod cast an eerie glow for about a foot in front of Becca; beyond that was nothing but dark. Her movements kicked up silt from the tunnel floor, reducing her visibility further.

Not that she *needed* to see: the light was something that helped her maintain her sanity and narrowly kept her fear in check. It provided just enough light to see if the space immediately in front of her was large enough to move into.

Becca wriggled forwards, as fast as she could without either panicking or wasting energy. Arms outstretched in front of her, she frequently had to twist and turn to negotiate the changing shape of the tunnel. If anything, the tunnel was a little larger than she had thought. It was tight, but not impossibly so.

She kept moving: rest meant death. This was not under water as Becca knew it. The familiar environment where she excelled was one of warmth and freedom, where arms and legs propelled you at speed. This was cold and harsh. As she moved, she felt herself continually scraping against sharp rock. Her shoulders, knees and elbows seemed to catch something with each movement. Sometimes the pain was almost enough to take the air from her lungs but she always managed to keep moving.

Every so often she would slow, holding the iPod high in the tunnel to check for air pockets. Always finding none, she nevertheless remained confident that they existed – although knowing that they existed and living long enough to find one were two different matters.

As best she could, she counted in her head, to try to keep track of time. Yet, once she had counted up to one minute – a duration that Becca could normally easily remain under water – she already felt as though she couldn't hold her breath any longer and that somehow she had drastically miscounted.

Then the tunnel narrowed. She held up the iPod, pausing. It narrowed only briefly, but it looked too tight for even her slender body. She didn't have time to think: going back would be far harder, she decided. It would take her twice the amount of time to go back that it took to get here. She pushed forwards, wriggling herself into the tight space. *Shoulders and hips*, she thought. *If I can get my shoulders through, I should be OK – although it will be tight on my hips too.*

She moved her head into the gap and then tried to wriggle her shoulders through, but it was just too tight. Determined, she twisted her body around until she found the best position, and then tried to push just one shoulder into the tight space, bracing her feet against the tunnel wall. She inched forwards – and then pushed again. Her shoulder scraped along the sharp rock, sending a screaming pain up her arm and down her spine. She dropped the iPod, but just managed to hang on to the water bottle. She didn't waste her time even trying to pick the iPod up. She pushed again and inched forwards, tighter into the gap. For four or five seconds, it seemed that she was firmly stuck; no manner of pushing and squeezing would move her in any direction. Then, with one hard push and a twist at the same time, her right shoulder almost literally popped through into the wider space beyond.

Getting her left shoulder through was easier, though still tough, but once that was through she retrieved the iPod and pulled her chest and abdomen clear. Getting her hips through was tricky, but she managed it, just, by wriggling and twisting continually. As she squeezed through, she felt her pelvis scrape along the rock agonisingly. She felt sure that she'd cut a gash where the hip bone was closest to the top of the skin, but had no way of seeing if she had.

Keep moving, she thought. *You have to keep moving.*

Once clear, she increased her speed. She'd initially wanted to move at a steady pace, to conserve air, but she had forfeited a lot of time. Worse, she'd now lost count completely – she didn't know if she'd spent fifteen seconds, thirty seconds, a minute, or more trying to squeeze through the gap.

For a terrible moment, Becca thought that she was going to have a coughing fit. She halted, trying desperately to stop herself from coughing, knowing for certain that it would kill her. Of all the things that had happened in the last few days, that one moment was for Becca the most terrifying. Once she was sure that the need to cough had passed, she moved on.

Her right shoulder screamed at her with every movement. Becca didn't think that she had dislocated it, since she could move it (albeit with a great deal of pain) but she suspected that she had either cut or sprained it badly. *It doesn't matter*, she told herself. *You can live with the pain for a few minutes. By then, I'm either out of here or it makes no odds.*

Becca could feel that both her confidence and strength were waning. There seemed to be no end to the tunnel. Her chest was beginning to seriously hurt and she wondered how long she had been under water. *Two minutes? Three? Four?* One thing was sure, she was well beyond the point of being able to go back.

For a few feet, the tunnel widened out and Becca had the luxury of being able to move a little more freely. She paused, checking for an air pocket; finding none, she moved on.

It's much further than I guessed, she thought, starting to feel real panic. Just as she'd lost track of time, she had no idea how great a distance she had covered. She could be halfway there, or a quarter.

With each passing second, the pain in her chest increased. Often, when swimming under water, she would slow and rest – the brief pause would usually be enough to buy her a little extra time under water. Right now, Becca didn't feel that she could waste even a second.

Then she felt it.

It was unbelievable, but unmistakable: a cold hand slowly wrapped long fingers around her ankle and held her fast. She kicked, but the hand remained firm. Then it started to pull her back.

She gritted her teeth and kicked vigorously with both feet, only to find that she was kicking against empty water.

You don't like this, bitch, do you? she thought, knowing that this meant one thing: she had a chance of success. But Becca also realised something else. If the woman had really wanted to hold on, she would have. She was being teased, to the last. *Does she want to kill me*, Becca wondered, *or frighten me?*

Her determination doubled, she pushed forwards even harder – trying her best to disregard the agony in her chest.

13

Abby and Helen left the car at the bend in the lane. Abby had to help Helen (who held her injured arm tight to her chest) over the stile; then they ran up the hill towards the quarry.

It was deserted.

Abby closed her eyes and searched for Sammy with her mind, but couldn't feel anything.

I hope that doesn't mean anything, she thought.

They climbed the grassy hill at the side of the quarry pool as quickly as they could, Abby holding Helen's good hand to help her balance. Where the hill was steepest, they struggled – Helen unable to scramble on all fours.

"You go ahead," said Helen, panting hard. "I'll catch up."

"No chance," replied Abby. "You'll slip. Come on, there's no time to argue."

Despite their panic, when they reached the top they both stood for a moment, doubled over, gasping for breath.

A woman's voice ahead of them brought them sharply upright.

"Te-am avertizat. Negru cățea."

Helen unconsciously took a step back, sick with fear. Long curly hair blowing in the wind, feet outstretched in a confident stance, the woman blocked their path.

Abby stood her ground. "I want my daughter," she shouted.

The woman laughed, hawked and spat on the ground. "As do I," she said.

Abby advanced on the woman. "You can't stop me," she said, defiant.

"Perhaps. Perhaps not. You try. You see." The woman drew a long knife from behind her. "Ask your lover-woman. She tell you how real I am."

"Abby, don't," said Helen, touching Abby's arm.

Abby ignored her and rushed forwards. The woman sidestepped Abby's lunge neatly and pushed her to the ground. As Abby fell, the woman kicked her hard in the stomach. Abby doubled up on the wet ground, screaming. The woman knelt beside Abby; she grabbed her hair and pulled her head back. Abby screamed again. The woman drew back the knife, ready to plunge.

Helen rushed forwards and grabbed the woman's forearm, holding it back. The woman's flesh was icy cold, almost burning Helen's fingers. The woman spat at her. "Mâinile de pe mine, cățea!"

She stood, dropping the knife, and pushed Helen back towards the edge of the quarry.

"Helen!" shouted Abby.

The woman ran forwards and kicked Helen in the stomach. Helen doubled up and dropped to her knees, gasping for breath. "I warn you," said the woman. She grabbed Helen by the hair, dragged her to the quarry's edge and pulled her to her feet.

"I warn you," she said again. She took a step back and kicked Helen hard. Helen fell backwards, screaming, against the rotten fence. The fence offered no resistance to Helen's fast-moving body; it fell apart readily – and Helen went through it as if it wasn't there. She disappeared over the edge. Her scream only ended when she splashed into the water below.

Abby grabbed the knife and almost dropped it – it was cold to the touch, burning like ice. She rushed forwards, bringing the knife down hard towards the woman's chest but striking only empty air. The woman was gone.

Abby peered over the edge of the cliff into the quarry pool. Ripples were expanding across the water, but Helen was nowhere to be seen.

"Shit," said Abby under her breath, torn between going back for Helen and pushing on to find Sammy. "Shit," she said again. But when you have to choose between the life of your child and that of your life's love, there's little contest. "Oh, Helen, I'm so sorry."

She gratefully dropped the icy knife into the grass, turned and ran towards the estate wall rubbing her chilled hand against her leg.

And then, in her head, something unexpected: Sammy's voice. "Helen," it said. "You have to save Helen. She's dying."

Disorientated, Abby spun around, half expecting to see Sammy nearby.

"Sammy?"

"Trust me, Mummy," said Sammy's voice. "You have to get Helen." The voice in her head was more than mere words: it was more like a command; a *touch* inside her head.

Time seemed to telescope. Abby took only moments to decide, but it seemed that entire minutes passed. She'd felt Sammy's voice – and she knew her daughter well. She could tell that she was scared – way beyond scared. Abby sensed for certain that she was in terrible danger. But she also knew that Sammy saw and felt many things that she didn't. If she said that Helen was dying, and dying now, it was the truth.

"I'll be back, baby," whispered Abby, hoping that somehow her daughter could hear her. She turned, fighting her every instinct as a mother – and scrambled down the rough edge of the quarry pool as fast as she could.

14

Although she didn't know it, Becca had been under water for approaching five minutes, well over her personal best time. The pain in her chest was excruciating and she knew she couldn't avoid exhaling for many more seconds. Her head was spinning and she was starting to feel lightheaded – but still she kept pushing herself forwards, forwards.

Keep moving, keep moving, she told herself.

And then, the moment came, when she knew she could not hold on any longer. Almost bursting, she slowed herself, trying to relax. Then she gently exhaled – just part of her lungs, not all of the way. She'd hoped that doing so would alleviate the pain, but it hurt even more.

Shit, she thought, *I'm not going to make it.*

Then she realised what she had been desperately clutching all of the way. She held the bottle upside down and slowly unscrewed the cap. Then she positioned herself underneath it, exhaled and brought the bottle to her lips. She inhaled as deeply as she could, but the bottle didn't even hold a quarter of a lungful of air.

It just was enough to restart her oxygen-starved mind. She rolled back onto her front and wriggled forwards as fast as she could, wondering how much additional time the bottle of air had bought her. Desperate, she let go of the bottle and moved forwards almost recklessly, continually scraping herself against the rough stone as she went.

Then, something strange happened. The light from the iPod no longer reflected from all around the tunnel; she could only see it glow beneath her and to her left. The change happened in an instant and was so unexpected that she stopped dead, looking to see what was different. It was too dark – she couldn't understand what had happened. She moved the iPod around and the light shifted. Puzzled, she lifted it up and the light changed completely in an instant. On the bottom of the tunnel the light now twisted and shifted like smoke. It took a moment for her to recognise what she was looking at. Her hand and the iPod were above the surface of the water – she was seeing the reflection of the top of the water, cast onto the rocks below.

She raised her head upwards into cold air and exhaled, coughing. The air was stale – but it was air. She breathed it in, deeply, coughing and spitting for a few minutes before regaining control of her ragged lungs.

She pulled off her goggles and held up the iPod. She was in a tiny cavern, perhaps about the size of the inside of a small car. The light from the iPod wasn't strong enough to tell her exactly how large it was, but she could easily sit up. She held the iPod as high as she could and could just about make out the natural ceiling above her. Large enough to sit, but not to stand, she guessed.

Becca realised that she was having to work much harder to breathe than she normally would. *Not much oxygen here,* she thought. *I'll soon use this up.* But the cavern had given her one thing she'd never expected – not only air, but also a much-needed opportunity to rest. She took it, gratefully, though wondering if what she'd found was not a resting place, but her tomb.

Not wanting to waste the light from the iPod, she flipped it off – and absolute black descended. It took all of her willpower to keep the iPod turned off.

She sat with her back against the rock and tried to relax, taking slow breaths.

"You are strong," said a woman's voice. Becca screamed, recognising the voice instantly. She splashed around in the water, backing away from the source of the voice. She flipped on the iPod and there she was – smiling, confident and beautiful in the half-light.

"So strong. So clever. So resourceful. But you not make it. You die down here."

"No," shouted Becca. "No I won't!"

"You die." The woman's voice was flat; factual.

Something wasn't right, but Becca couldn't place it. "Just try and stop me," retorted Becca with a fearlessness she didn't feel.

"Little girl. Strong voice but inside you scared."

Becca looked at her. The woman's face was as resolute as ever, but an insecurity or doubt flickered in her eyes.

"I'm not the only one who's scared, am I?" challenged Becca. The woman said nothing.

"You know I can do this," said Becca. "And you can't stop me, can you?"

The woman shrieked and leapt forwards, her hands on Becca's throat. Becca dropped the iPod and the light was gone, except for a small glow beneath the water.

"Remember this?" said the woman, squeezing Becca's neck.

"Go on then," coughed Becca, not caring any more. "If you want to kill me, just fucking kill me."

The woman released her grip.

"No need," she said. "You will do that."

Silence fell.

"I'm not going to die," said Becca. "And you know it." The words sounded brave but Becca knew that her defiance was empty.

There was no response. Becca reached for the glowing iPod and pulled it out of the water. She moved it around, shining the dim light on the stone. The woman was gone.

Maybe she's right, thought Becca. *I've no way of knowing how far I've gone or if I'll get out at all.* She sat back again, crying softly.

After a minute, still sobbing, she held the iPod over her body. Her arms and legs were lacerated all over – no wonder she hurt so much. A few of the cuts were deep and seemed to be bleeding freely. Her swimming costume was torn in several places, exposing the battered skin beneath. *Dear God,* she thought, despondent.

All this way, she thought, *all of this pain. For what?*

She flipped off the iPod and let the darkness embrace her, finally, totally and utterly broken. She cried for several minutes, occasionally cursing.

15

Randle pushed the two girls into the overgrown, ruined room. Hannah stumbled and fell forwards onto the floor; Randle heaved her to her feet and pushed her into a sitting position against one of the walls. He grabbed Sammy and pushed her down beside Hannah.

"Don't move," Randle growled. He took off his coat and sat against the opposite wall, stretching and rubbing his leg. Then he carefully took out his contact lenses and replaced them with his glasses. Even with his glasses, the loss of his hair and beard made him difficult to recognise.

"That's better," he said, standing. *I want to be able to see properly.*

As he stood, there was a flutter of wings from above. A huge black bird landed on the top of the ruined wall, cawing into the roofless house. Randle picked up a large stone and threw it clumsily at the bird, missing by a foot. The bird fluttered its wings angrily. "Piss off," said Randle, throwing another stone. The bird took off, but the stone clipped its wing. The bird came down in the room, stunned, flapping around on the ground. Randle stepped forwards and stood on it, hard. He slowly pressed down and twisted his foot; the bird crunched and squawked under his heel. Flapping, the bird tried to escape but Randle brought his heel down again. Then the bird lay quiet, twitching. He kicked it out of the room, leaving a smear of blood and entrails on the stone floor.

Hannah and Sammy watched, terrified at his brutality.

After years of simmering, watching and waiting, the real Randle was unleashed. Today was the first day in his entire life when Randle felt he was behaving like himself. It was liberating.

He looked at the two girls. *Which one first?* he asked himself. *The young one,* he decided. *The other one's tied up and can't run as easily. And I want to save the best until last.*

Randle moved forward, pulled Sammy to her feet and pointed the knife at her. "You," he said, "undress."

Sammy burst into tears and backed away. "No," she pleaded, "please, no."

"I said *undress.*" Randle's voice was commanding and clear.

Sammy shook her head. Randle raised his hand to slap her, but Hannah had stood and placed herself between the girl and the man. She stood, shaking her head frantically, trying to say something through the parcel tape.

Randle slapped Hannah hard across the face; she fell backwards into Sammy and both collapsed on the floor. "Get out of the way, girl. Your turn will come soon enough."

Still on her bottom, Hannah scrabbled around with her feet in the mud, keeping herself between Sammy and Randle, murmuring loudly through the tape, desperately trying to make herself heard. Randle leaned forwards and pulled the tape away sharply.

Hannah shrieked in pain and then said, "Me – not her, me."

Randle laughed. "There's no choice," he said. "I'm doing you both. And she's first."

Hannah shook her head. "No, just me."

"Why would I do that when I can have you both anyway?"

Hannah tried to hold back her tears. "Because – she's just a little kid. You can't."

"I can and I will. Now move, or I'll kick you out of the way." He waved the knife in her face. "Or worse."

"If you leave her alone," said Hannah, "I'll do whatever you want."

"You'll do that anyway. Now move."

"Not willingly. Neither of us will. But if you leave her, I'll do whatever you want. Willingly. No fighting or screaming."

Randle paused, his imagination racing.

"And just why would you do that?"

"She's just a kid," said Hannah. "If you leave her alone and let us go free – I'll do what you want. *Anything.*" She'd wanted the words to sound brave, defiant, but she'd sobbed them out as a desperate plea.

"Anything?"

Hannah nodded. "Anything. All day if you want. But you let us go. And you don't touch Sammy. You have to promise."

Randle considered it. While part of him wanted the mixture of sex and violence, the thought that the girl would surrender herself to him, as she would to a boyfriend, was intoxicating. It was something that had been beyond his hopes. He trembled as he pictured it in his mind.

"OK," he said. As he uttered his agreement, he knew it to be a lie. He could – and would – take the older girl all day long. When he'd had enough, he would beat her – and screw the other girl anyway. He could have it all; her compliance and her terror. Randle cut the tape from Hannah's wrists, freeing her.

"Get undressed," he said, waving the knife, indicating that Hannah should move away from Sammy. Sammy backed into the corner, a wide-eyed unwilling observer. "And you," he snapped at Sammy, "if you run, I'll kill her – understand?"

Sammy nodded.

Hannah undressed slowly, trembling as she did. She stood in her underwear, facing Randle, goosebumps forming on her skin. Randle didn't think he'd seen anything as beautiful in his life. It was as if the world around him had ceased to exist: he was totally captivated by her slim, pale young body.

"The rest," said Randle, his voice quivering.

"You don't have to do this," said Sammy, quietly. "Please mister."

Randle turned and snarled at her, infuriated that his mood had been broken. "Quiet, you." *You'll pay later, bitch*, he thought.

Hannah took off her bra and knickers and dropped them on the wet ground beside her other clothes. She stood there naked, shaking with fear, trying desperately to hold back her tears. She felt incredibly vulnerable.

"Lie down," he commanded.

She lay down on her back with her arms folded in front of her, covering her breasts. The ground was cold and slimy against her back. Randle put the knife into his trouser pocket and knelt beside her. He winced and wobbled slightly as his bad knee made contact with the rough stone floor. His hand reached out and his fingertips stroked the perfect, flat, smooth skin of her stomach. It twitched beneath his touch. He was so aroused that he felt almost dizzy.

Hannah looked up at him. He was a huge man, old, nasty. *It's not supposed to be like this*, she thought, loathing him, trying desperately to stop herself from shaking with disgust. When his fingers ran over her skin she felt as though she were already violated. She shuddered and wondered what she had committed herself to. Randle pulled her arms to her sides, exposing her fully. He leaned forwards.

Randle's face filled Hannah's field of vision, smiling, the light reflecting off his glasses. She supposed he was trying to be nice, but to her it was the face of a beast as it pounced. *Oh God, no*, she thought.

Suddenly, there was a sickly crunch. Randle jolted and fell forwards, on top of Hannah, his face frozen in shock. His sudden weight pushed the breath from Hannah's lungs. Over his massive shoulder, Hannah could see Sammy, standing, holding a large, bloodied stone.

"I said you didn't have to do this," she repeated, softly, to Randle.

Hannah squirmed, trying to get from underneath Randle, but his weight pinned her firmly down. As she tried to move, Randle groaned and tried to get up, his hands seeking the ground around him.

Sammy swung the stone and hit him once more, hard, on the side of the head. He went limp, his twisted glasses falling from his face onto Hannah. Sammy dropped the stone; it landed on the ground with a thud. Then she squatted down next to Hannah. "I'm sorry," she said, tearfully. "I – I didn't know he'd be here."

"Help me get him off," groaned Hannah.

Sammy pulled Randle's body as hard as she could – while Hannah pushed against his dead weight. Even with the two of them heaving, Randle was hard to shift. When they finally rolled him off and onto his back, Randle groaned again.

Sammy helped Hannah to her feet. Hannah stood shakily, winded, holding her arm to her chest. "I thought you could read minds," she said, reaching down for her underwear.

"I said not always," protested Sammy. "And not everyone. You can get dressed in a minute – you have to help me first. We have to be quick."

"What?" said Hannah, putting on her knickers.

"Help me," insisted Sammy. "Before he wakes up. We have to drag him to the well. I can't do it on my own. You can dress in a minute."

Randle groaned again.

Hannah quickly put on her bra. "Why don't we just hit the bastard with that rock again?" she asked, the words spat out with hatred. "You know what he was going to do."

Sammy shook her head. "Please. He has to be alive. When he goes in."

"What? Why can't we just leave him here?" demanded Hannah.

"I can't explain," implored Sammy. "Trust me. Becca's almost out. She might make it – we need to get there before she does. We have to go. We can't leave *him*. We have to be very quick. *Trust me.*"

"Come on then," said Hannah.

Together, they dragged Randle's massive carcass-like body out of the house. As they crossed the threshold into the light, Sammy felt relief wash over her to be out of *that bad place*. Hannah felt exposed, the breeze blowing against her semi-naked body. She pulled Randle as hard as she could, desperate to be done and get dressed. "Come on," she huffed.

It was very tough going; not only was Randle a dead weight, but he was also extremely awkward to grip. Every so often, as they dragged him, bumping his body along the uneven ground, Randle would moan softly. It took them almost five minutes of hard work to get him to the well.

"Here," said Sammy, "where the wall is lowest."

They propped him against the wall.

"Thank God he didn't see that," said Hannah, pointing to the rope on the ground. "If he'd have tied you up..."

"I can do this now," said Sammy, coughing. "Go and get dressed."

"No," replied Hannah. "I'll help."

Sammy looked at her and shook her head. "This – isn't something you want to do."

"Of course it isn't. But I'll still help."

"Just onto the stones. Then you go." The two girls looked at each other for a long moment. "Please," said Sammy.

"OK," replied Hannah. Together they pushed him until he was half-rested on the lowest part of the well wall. *Just one push and he'll be in*, thought Sammy.

Randle groaned again and started to move. His lips moved. In his mind, he said *little bitch*, but it came out as "rikkle witch".

"Go," said Sammy.

Hannah shook her head. "No way. Let's do this."

"This isn't your business," snapped Sammy. "Now go. Fast." Hannah was taken aback; her face looked hurt as if Sammy had slapped her. "Please," said Sammy, softly, her normal little-girl voice returning.

Hannah nodded. "OK. I'll be back in a sec. Be careful." She ran back to the ruined cottage.

Sammy turned to the well and spoke into it, clearly.

"Here he is," she said. "I promised. A swap."

From the well there came a rush of wind, swirling like a tornado up from the inside and out into the open air. The sky above darkened.

From deep inside the well came a voice; a woman's voice. "You. The deal was you."

"No, it wasn't. A life for a life. That was the deal. I'm holding you to it."

The air in the well spun and growled. "Him no good. Old and bad. Give me the other girl."

Sammy shook her head. "A deal's a deal."

"The girl. And I lift the curse. Your children will be free."

Sammy hesitated. She'd thought a lot about the story her mother had told her, but she had no way of appreciating a woman's agony of delivering a child who was also cursed to deliver cursed children. At eight, babies were something other people had, or something you had when you were old. Sammy didn't even think she wanted babies. *But still –*

The temptation of a normal life hung in front of her for a second.

"My Mummy?" asked Sammy.

"She would be free as you," said the voice.

It would be easy, she thought. She only had to call Hannah over and then – just one push. She could blame Randle. No one would know.

"No," she shouted, shaking herself free from the spell. In her mind, she saw Hannah, selflessly putting herself forward to Randle, to save *her* – someone she hardly knew.

Sammy put all of her weight against Randle's body and pushed. He wobbled backwards but didn't fall. *Harder,* she thought, bracing herself against him. His head wobbled on his shoulders, blood flowing from his two wounds.

Without warning, Sammy felt a punch in her stomach. A weak punch, but a punch. She drew back and looked down. Protruding from the side of her lower abdomen was Randle's knife. Surrounding it was a growing bloodstain.

"Bitch," choked Randle, smiling and drooling at the same time. He slumped back against the broken well wall.

Behind him, the woman laughed.

No, thought Sammy, tears rolling down her face. *He stabbed me.* The blood seemed to be everywhere. She felt sick. Her hands reached for her stomach, feeling the knife buried within her. She looked at her hands; they were full of blood.

Randle reached forwards to grab Sammy, almost drunkenly. With great effort, driven on by anger, Sammy put her shoulder against him and pushed. He rolled backwards into the well and, with a groan, tumbled over the side. His body paused briefly as he hit what was left of the metal grating and then he vanished from view. After a second's silence, there was a dull crunch followed by a splash. Somewhere, a woman screamed – an angry, terrible scream.

Sammy fell backwards onto the ground, clutching herself. She looked up; the sky was clear, but seemed to be spinning. The howling vortex of wind had vanished. "Mummy," she said. She closed her eyes but the world kept spinning.

Then Hannah was kneeling over her, crying. "Sammy, Sammy! Oh God. Are you OK?"

Sammy opened her eyes and shook her head. Her mouth was dry. *He stabbed me,* she thought again. "You can kill him now, if you want," she said, softly.

Hannah didn't hesitate. She removed the largest stone she could lift from the well wall. Aiming it at the dark she threw it down with all of her strength, shouting "You bastard!" There was a sickening sound: a mixture of a thud, crack and squelch. Although it was impossible to see, the stone had hit Randle on the head, cracking his skull.

Hannah went back to Sammy and knelt beside her. She looked awfully pale to

Hannah, a shade of white that she'd never seen before in a person. Hannah held Sammy's hand.

"Mummy," whispered Sammy. "Get Mummy. She's in the quarry." She closed her eyes.

16

Abby scrambled down the steep side of the quarry pool as quickly as she could. Twice she lost her footing and almost went head over heels, but both times she just about managed to retain her balance as she skidded downhill in the mud.

At the bottom of the hill, she stopped to scan the water. The ripples had almost vanished and there was no sign of Helen.

"Shit," said Abby, discarding her shoes and jacket. She wasn't a strong swimmer and was only average under water. The quarry pool was large and probably deep – if she didn't look in the right place first time, it could take hours to find Helen.

She waded into the water, as quickly as she could. Although the morning was warm, the sun hadn't yet warmed the water and its cold temperature took Abby's breath away. The bottom of the pool quickly fell away, at which point Abby took a deep breath and struck out towards where she thought Helen had fallen.

Swimming in her clothes was like moving through treacle and Abby regretted not stripping off to her underwear before getting in – but it was now too late.

Abby reached her goal: width-wise, almost dead centre of the pool but close to the roughly cut vertical wall of the quarry. She trod water for a moment, orientating herself and then, taking a deep breath, she closed her eyes and forced herself under water. Once under, she kicked downwards and opened her eyes. The water stung her eyes and she blinked furiously, rubbing them. She'd never really mastered being able to see under water, always hating the sensation of water against her eyes. Between blinks, she looked around.

Everywhere was dark, misty and ethereal – a dirty, gloomy half-world of uncertain shapes. Abby started to panic. She was poor at holding her breath and already at the limits of her lung capacity. Cursing to herself, she surfaced, coughing and drawing water. "Helen!" she screamed pointlessly.

Calming herself as much as she could, she took another deep breath and submerged. This time she kicked down as hard as she could; she opened her eyes and scanned around. There was nothing solid to see, just vague, motionless shapes – but further down, to her right, something was moving, swaying. She kicked towards the shape, hoping desperately.

As Abby swam closer, the phantom shape resolved into that of a person, limbs flailing around. A silhouette, but recognisably Helen. She was on her back, four limbs waving around, her arms trying to reach behind her to free herself. Having fallen backwards into the water, she had caught herself on something submerged in the pool; it was impossible to see what. Abby kicked hard and found herself next to Helen, who hadn't yet noticed her. Abby took Helen's hand and gave it a squeeze; Helen turned to look at Abby, her face full of panic.

Lungs straining, Abby felt behind Helen. Her jumper was caught on some twisted metal cabling. Despite wriggling around and tearing her jumper, Helen had been unable to work herself free. Without being able to see what was holding her down, she probably felt more tethered than she actually was.

Abby got hold of each sleeve of Helen's jumper and pulled her arms out; then she hurriedly pulled the jumper over Helen's head – fighting against her panicking, flapping arms.

Once Helen was free, Abby grabbed her roughly by the arm and pulled her upwards. The return journey to the surface seemed to take minutes, Abby struggling to swim for both of them while taking random blows from Helen's flailing arms and legs.

They broke the surface together, both fighting for air, Helen still thrashing wildly. Abby grabbed Helen around the middle and shook her, shouting, "Helen! Helen! It's OK!"

Helen's limbs slowed, but her breath remained frantic, punctuated by watery coughs. "Abby, Abby, I thought –" she spluttered.

"Don't talk," shouted Abby. "Don't talk."

Abby had never learned basic rescue training, but instinctively swam around behind Helen and held her from the back. "Lie on your back," said Abby. "Kick with your legs." Abby kicked as hard as she could and paddled with her free arm. Helen's kicks were almost non-productive and getting back to the shore was a slow, tiring process. After the first few kicks, Helen had begun to sob and Abby didn't have enough spare energy to calm her – so just kept on kicking.

Eventually, Abby felt her feet touch the bottom of the pool. She grabbed Helen firmly and dragged her out of the water.

Abby dropped Helen, exhausted, onto the muddy ground and collapsed at her side. They both lay there, gasping for air, Helen's gasps and coughs mixed with sobs.

After a moment, Abby pushed her fingers through her hair, squeezing out the excess water. She knelt beside Helen. "Helen, are you OK?" Abby was desperate to run after Sammy, but needed to make sure that Helen was alright first.

"I think so – I – my back hurts like holy hell."

Abby rolled her over. The metal cable had cut her back in half a dozen places; a couple of the cuts were deep and angry-looking. Helen's arms sported a few less severe cuts – she'd lost the bandage from her arm and the knife wound was again open and bleeding. Mud, dirt and tiny stones stuck to her wet body and filled the bloody cuts on her back.

"Helen, I need you to get back into the water," said Abby, "to clean the cuts."

Abby led Helen back to the water and quickly washed her back and arms. The water was almost certainly far from clean, but it was better than leaving dirt in the wound.

She led Helen back out of the water and sat her down.

"Helen," she said, "I have to go."

Panic flashed across Helen's face.

"Sammy needs help. I have to go. I'll be back."

Helen nodded. "Go. I'll be OK. Abby –"

"What?"

"Thanks. I'd be – I'd be dead now."

"Later. If you have to lie down, lie on your side not your back." Abby took her jacket from the ground and put it around Helen's bare shoulders. "Try not to move."

Abby stepped back into her shoes and set off at a run. After just a few paces she paused and returned to Helen, fumbling around in the pockets of the jacket covering Helen's shoulders. Abby pulled out her mobile phone. "I think we may be passing the point of keeping this to ourselves," she said.

"You can't," said Helen.

"You need an ambulance," said Abby. "End of story."

She kissed Helen, quickly. "Love you," she said – and was gone, clambering frantically up the steep path on all fours.

17

Eyes closed, sitting in the darkness, Becca had managed to calm herself. Her breathing was now slow and steady. The cavern was a place of unimaginable silence. If she kept perfectly still, the only sounds were her own breathing and heartbeat. Even in the well there had always been the distant sound of the wind, blowing the trees in the distance – *and that bastard bird*, Becca thought. She was almost completely relaxed and wondered if she had fallen asleep, if even for a moment. *Very likely*, she thought, dog-tired. Each time she had pushed her exhausted body through one more challenge, she had thought it would be the last. Yet still she had demanded more of it. But now, her muscles were a pump that had run dry.

If I stay here, she thought, *I'll die. I can't go back, I'm too tired. If I go on, the chances are I'll die panicking, afraid, clawing at the walls for air. Here, I slowly run out of air and fall asleep.* Of the two options, the latter seemed to Becca to be the best.

She took a deep breath and opened her eyes. The blackness surrounded her. She held her hand in front of her face but could see nothing. The only light came from the faint glow of the iPod, distant in the water.

Becca did a double take. The iPod was still in her hand, turned off.

She knelt in the water and peered carefully towards the light, straining her eyes. It was dim; barely there – but it was there.

The way out, thought Becca, heart racing once more. *It has to be.* For a moment she thought that she might have lost her bearings and be looking the wrong way, but quickly decided otherwise. *The well is too far back to shine light in here.*

She put on her goggles and submerged, staring ahead. The light was clearly there, a soft, distant yellow glow. But there was no way of telling how far away it was. She surfaced, elated.

You can do this, she told herself, as she always did before and during races – time and time again. *You can do this.*

She'd been foolish, she reflected, to abandon the empty water bottle. Once it had saved her, despite holding a trifling amount of air. Now, she had to move forward with only what she could carry in her lungs. *It will have to be enough,* she thought, determined. *It will be enough.*

One more thing gave her hope. Where the water came out of the culvert into the quarry pool, it flowed with little more than a trickle. That meant that although the tunnel probably inclined upwards from where she was now to the outside, some of it – perhaps most of it – was out of water. It had to be. *That explains why the glow is so faint,* she thought. *The hole isn't directly ahead, it's slightly up.*

Becca found that she was crying – and not, for the first time in days, from fear, anger, remorse, hate or pain. She was overjoyed.

When she'd first set off (which seemed like days ago, not minutes) she'd prepared herself: rested; slept; slowed her breathing. Now, she knew she didn't have the time or the energy. She had to go – and quickly.

Becca allowed herself a scant few minutes' deep-breathing exercises, which weren't easy in the thinning air. By the time she decided that she was ready to go, she still felt drained and lightheaded.

She donned her goggles and took as large a lungful of air as she could. Then she submerged and crawled out of the cavern, into the tunnel.

Exhausted almost to the point of collapse, her stomach screaming with hunger, her flesh torn and battered, Becca pushed herself on with a determination that was beyond anything she had ever mustered before.

18

When Abby reached the top of the hill, she almost ran headlong into a girl running away from the estate.

"Are you Sammy's Mum?" asked the girl, breathless.

"Yes," she said. "Where's Sammy? Who are you?"

Hannah pointed to the gap in the wall. "This way," she said, "quick – she's hurt."

"Show me," said Abby, desperately.

She followed Hannah, towards the wall of the estate. "Who are you?" she repeated.

"I'm Hannah. Becca's friend. Rebecca Richards. The girl in the well."

OK, I know who she is, but I don't know why the hell you're here, she thought, but said nothing, realising that everything had spun hopelessly out of control.

They clambered over the wall, Abby slipping on the loose stones. Sammy was just a few yards away, at the side of the old well. She was lying on her back, holding her stomach. Between her fingers a knife protruded from her body. Her eyes were closed and her skin was the colour of paper. Around her hands, her shirt and skirt were covered with blood; the ground around her was soaked in it.

Abby dropped to her knees. "Oh Sammy, baby," she said, stroking Sammy's hair, tears falling from her eyes. She grasped Sammy's hand; her arm was limp. "Oh dear God no," sobbed Abby. *What the hell*, she thought, *was I thinking chasing after Helen?*

Sammy half opened her eyes. "Mummy," she whispered.

"Oh Sammy!" Abby leaned forwards and kissed Sammy's forehead, then held her cheek to hers.

"I've done something naughty," said Sammy.

"Hush," said Abby.

Abby turned to Hannah. "Who did this?" she demanded.

Hannah paled.

"Old Tom," said Hannah. "The – the school crossing man."

Abby looked around. "Where is he? Did he run away?"

Hannah looked very uncomfortable. "He's in the well," she said. "I think he's –" Her voice trailed away.

Abby tapped 999 into her phone and held it to her ear, her mind racing. She looked around, but there were no clues as to what had happened. The call connected on the first ring.

"Emergency services. Fire, police or ambulance?"

Keep it simple, she thought. *Keep yourself calm, don't lose it.* She sniffed and wiped the tears from her cheeks and face.

"Ambulance. Police. No, ambulance."

"What address are you calling from?"

Shit.

"I'm not at an address," said Abby. "I'm at the top of the old quarry, just outside Bankside. Near the old lane – er – Harper's Lane."

"Can you tell me what's happened?"

Abby took a deep breath. "I'm with my daughter." Abby held back a sob. "She's eight. She's been stabbed. She's lost a lot of blood." Her voice quivered. "There's so much blood. Oh God." She paused, pulling herself together. "And there's a woman. At the bottom of the quarry, not far from here, she's badly hurt."

"Could you tell me in what way she's hurt?"

"Her back," said Abby. "She fell into the quarry from high up. Her back's badly cut."

"You also said you wanted the police?"

"There's a man here," said Abby. "The one who – who stabbed my daughter. I think he's dead."

"Can you stay on the line, please?"

"What?"

"Can you stay on the line to give us some more details?"

"No. I can't," said Abby, only just holding back her temper. "My daughter is beside me, dying. She needs me way more than you do. Do you have enough information to get here?"

"Yes, but –"

"Then hurry, I think she's dying," snapped Abby. "I can answer your questions later." She lost control, sobbing. "I think she's nearly dead. If you can just hurry –"

Abby hung up. Sammy had drifted off again.

"Sammy?"

Sammy didn't move. Abby gasped and shook her. "Sammy?"

Sammy stirred. "Mummy?"

"Stay with me, baby. Don't go to sleep."

This is your time, Abby thought to herself. *Your problem. You messed up and your little girl stepped in to sort it for you, because you weren't up to the job. And look what happened.*

Hannah touched her shoulder. "I have to go."

Abby turned to her, astonished. "What? Go where?"

"Becca. She's – it's hard to explain. She's – I have to go. Sammy told me I have to."

"Go where?" Abby struggled to comprehend.

"Down to the quarry. Becca's crawling out of the well, through a tunnel."

Oh my –

"Two minutes," said Abby. "Just wait two minutes. Tell me everything. I need to know *everything*."

"I don't know –"

"*Please,*" said Abby. "It's important." Abby turned and squeezed Sammy's hand and kissed her again. *If Sammy dies,* she thought, *then none of this matters. But if she lives* – "Hang on, baby," she said. *Why did I not come to her first?* she thought, chastising herself bitterly.

She turned back to Hannah. "Tell me."

Hannah recounted the events of the morning, as quickly as she could.

Oh my God, thought Abby. *Fuck.*

Hannah turned to go; Abby grabbed her arm. "No wait."

"But you said –"

"Listen," said Abby. "This is the most important thing ever. When the police get here, they'll want to know what happened. If you tell them – about Sammy. What Sammy can do – she won't be safe. Someone who can do what she can do – she won't be safe." Abby grasped both of Hannah's hands. "Please."

"I don't know –" stammered Hannah.

"You don't want to tell them that you killed that man, do you? There's no need. We can protect you. And Sammy. Please."

"OK," said Hannah. "What do you want me to say?"

"Not just you," said Abby. "Rebecca too. And down by the water, there's a woman, Helen. She's – my friend. You have to tell her, too."

"What about telling Sammy?" asked Hannah.

"She'll know what to say," said Abby, turning back to her daughter. *If she makes it,* thought Abby. *If she makes it, she'll know what to say.*

Abby explained quickly to Hannah what she wanted her to say.

19

Once out of the cavern, the tunnel was as cramped as before. Becca dragged herself forwards in the dark. The iPod, still switched off, was held tight in her hand. She pushed herself towards the dim glow as if it were a beacon, but the light wasn't enough to see by. For the first few feet, Becca banged and scraped herself more badly than before, so she turned the iPod back on. Its light, though hardly bright, was strong enough to banish the glow from the tunnel's exit. *It's enough to know it's there,* thought Becca.

As Becca had expected, the tunnel started to shift slightly upwards. This change in angle was marked by a definite kink in the rock: a point where the tunnel's ceiling became briefly much lower, although it seemed to maintain most of its width. The change in angle was enough to make it difficult – if not impossible – for Becca to continue on her stomach. She rolled herself onto her back, aware that it would slow her progress – but at least her spine now bent in the same direction as the tunnel. It was a tight squeeze. She had to turn her head on its side to get it through the gap. Her shoulders were next, but her breasts – small though they were – scraped painfully against the rock above as she forced herself through. *Thank God I'm only a 32A*, she thought, gritting her teeth. She wriggled her stomach through fairly easily, but her hips were a different matter. Though slender, they were still tight against the rock. For a few moments, Becca thought that there was no way to squeeze them through; whichever way she twisted and pulled, she just couldn't move any further.

Fearfully, Becca bent her legs as much as the tight space would allow, braced her feet against the rock and pushed hard. Her right foot slipped. She tried to push again and found that her foot had become lodged firmly in a crack in the stone. Unable to reach down to free it, she pulled as hard as she could without success. Desperate, she wriggled her foot around and just about managed to extricate it from her shoe, scraping it along the rock as she pulled it free.

Becca cranked her head backwards to look behind her; although she still couldn't see the exit, the light was definitely much brighter. The thought of failure, after all she had been through, and so close to the outside world, was not something that Becca could endure. She gritted her teeth, twisting her hips from side to side and pulled as hard as she could. Her pelvis grated along the rock, sending a searing pain shooting around her hips. The iPod slipped from her fingers. She had to stifle a cry – but then she was through.

She fumbled around briefly with her hand for the iPod but her fingers only found rock and silt. *I don't need it now*, she thought.

She pulled herself to where the tunnel's angle evened out a little and then twisted herself back around onto her stomach, her hips protesting in agony whenever they made contact with the rock.

Shaking with pain, chest straining, she pressed forward as fast as she could.

Then it happened: at first without Becca realising it. As she pulled herself forwards, the top of her head was out of the water. After a few yards' further frantic crawling, she realised that she was hearing a familiar yet unexpected sound: water splashing against rock.

She twisted her head on its side and could just about make out the surface of the water above her. It was a moment of unbridled elation. Becca rolled herself onto her back, but the surface was still just too high for her mouth to fully break water. She arched her back and pushed her body as high as she could. Her face broke the surface of the water and she took long, deep grateful breaths of the clean, fresh air.

She was too weary to hold her body up for long. After a few moments, she took a deep breath and submerged. Then, staying on her back, she pushed herself on. She guessed that she was now moving gradually upwards as, with each push, the water level got a little lower. At the same time, the tunnel got progressively lighter.

Before long, her face was entirely out of the water and she allowed herself to lie there, panting between violent coughs, revelling in a satisfaction beyond comparison.

I did it, she thought, her mind almost singing the words. *I bloody well did it.*

Becca pulled the goggles from her face, squinting in the unbearably bright daylight, and gave herself a few minutes to rest. Then she rolled back over onto her stomach, raised her head and looked forward, her eyes struggling to adjust to daylight. Ahead was another upward kink in the tunnel, but much shallower than the last. Beyond it, Becca could see the last few yards of the tunnel. Her eyes hurt to look towards the bright sunshine but she forced herself. There it was: the entrance to the tunnel, capped with a metal grating. Beyond that, she could see sky and trees.

I did it, she thought again, still not quite believing it. She crawled forwards.

20

Helen kept watching the spot where Abby had disappeared from view, expecting – hoping – for her to return with Sammy. Long minutes passed; the deep, throbbing pain from her back and arms causing her to wince or yelp each time she moved even slightly.

Then, unexpectedly, two things happened at almost the same time.

First, a blonde girl, who Helen at first thought must have been the girl who was trapped in the well, came scrambling down the hill. Helen looked closer, puzzled. From what she recollected from school, she was sure that the missing girl – Rebecca – was dark-haired.

While Helen watched the girl pick her way down the final part of the hill, there was a movement in the corner of her eye. She looked across to the other side of the quarry, but at first couldn't see anything unusual.

The girl ran up to Helen and squatted at her side, gathering her breath.

"Helen?"

"That's me," said Helen, mystified. "Who are you? Where's Abby and Sammy?"

"I'm Hannah – I'm Becca's friend. Sammy's – Sammy's hurt bad. A man stabbed her. He tried to –"

"Stabbed?! Is she OK? *Is Sammy OK?*" interrupted Helen, desperately. *Oh Christ*, she thought.

"Sammy's Mum called an ambulance. She –"

At the edge of her vision, Helen caught the movement again: inside the culvert, partway up the quarry face, something – *someone* – was moving. She glanced over. *Not moving*, she thought, *waving*. Waving through the metal bars of the culvert.

Helen pointed; Hannah looked around then jumped to her feet. "Becca!" she shouted. "Jesus, it's Becca!" Her voice was filled with astonishment and relief. "Becca!

Becca!" Hannah was jumping up and down, delighted.

What the hell is going on? thought Helen, standing as carefully as she could, gasping with the pain of simply pulling herself upright.

The girl shouted, though her voice seemed far away. "Hannah!"

Hannah turned back to Helen. "The other woman – Sammy's Mum – says you're to stay here," said Hannah.

"Like hell," said Helen.

"Yeah, she said you'd say that too. But you have to. The ambulance and the police are coming. She told me some things I have to tell you. They're important."

"But –"

"For Sammy, her Mum said. To keep her safe."

"Tell me," said Helen.

There was a splash behind them. Hannah and Helen looked over to the pool. The metal grating that had covered the hole was gone, and vast ripples were spreading across the surface of the water.

"Stay there," shouted Helen. *Dear God,* she thought, *she's going to drop into the water, where she just pushed that grating.*

"No," said Hannah to Helen. "We have to tell her too. We have to get her before the police come. We have to be really fast."

Hannah took off her pumps and waded into the water, gesturing to Becca to stay put. Becca shook her head.

"Wait," shouted Hannah. "Wait for me."

Hannah swam over, as quickly as she could, until she was just beneath the hole – leaving enough room for Becca to drop into the water beside her.

When the moment came for Becca to leave the tunnel, she had no choice. The hole wasn't that much bigger than her, so it was impossible for her to turn herself around to exit the hole backwards – which would have allowed her to climb out and hang down with her hands, reducing the distance she would have to fall. Instead, Becca came out headfirst. Although exhausted, she did her best to push herself as far away from the quarry wall as she could and curl herself into a ball as she fell. In reality, she tumbled head over heels, only just managing to tuck her legs partway to her body. She landed next to Hannah with a large, ungainly splash.

The instant that Becca disappeared under the water, Hannah submerged and hunted for her, her eyes trying to make sense of the gloom below. Not seeing anything in the murk, she waved her arms around hoping to grab hold of Becca – but they grasped nothing but empty water.

Hannah surfaced, only to find that Becca was already there, treading water. *I should have known*, she thought. The two girls embraced in the water, Becca sobbing with sheer relief.

A reddish cloud was growing in the water round the two girls. Hannah looked at Becca's scarred face and shoulders and realised that it was blood. *Shit*, she thought. *That's a lot of blood.*

"Oh, God," said Becca, gasping for breath. She burst into tears. "I thought I was dead. Oh Hannah!"

"We have to get out," said Hannah.

Becca barely had enough strength to stay afloat; she wrapped her arms around Hannah's shoulders. "I can't make it," she said.

Hannah, a competent enough swimmer but nowhere near in Becca's league, took them back to the bank – not by the shortest route, across the centre of the pool, but by the safest, around the edge, holding on to the side of the quarry as she went. She moved as quickly as she could, grimly aware of each passing second.

When Hannah could feel the bottom of the pool with her feet, she grabbed Becca and pulled her upright. Becca's feet went through the motions – but she was unable to stand, let alone walk. Hannah dragged Becca out of the water and put her arm over her own shoulder. Then she half-carried Becca up to where Helen was standing, dropping her onto the ground as gently as she could.

Hannah knelt next to Becca, panting. Becca lay on her back, coughing.

Helen looked down at Becca. Her swimming costume was ripped in several places. She was wearing only one shoe and her bare foot – her left – was scratched deeply on both sides. Becca's skin was cut, scratched, ripped and torn. One of the gashes – on her hip – looked so bad that Helen could swear she saw bone in the middle of the blood and pulp. Becca's feet were puffy, swollen and covered with sores. The gaps between her toes and fingers were filled with deeply embedded filth. Her hair was a tangled mess. She looked like something wild.

With enormous effort, Becca lifted herself up and hugged Hannah. "Oh, Han," she said. Both of the girls were crying.

In the distance, Helen could hear sirens. She knelt down next to the girls, her back protesting – and touched Hannah on the shoulder.

"The police and ambulance are coming," she said. "What do you need to tell us?"

21

Sarah and Jim were both still sleeping when Jenny arrived. Jim answered the door in his dressing gown, his eyes red and tired. "I'm sorry," he said. "We didn't get to sleep until – I have no idea when. Not long ago. We've not slept for days. Mind you, you look a bit tired yourself."

"Yes, I am a bit," said Jenny, as casually as she could, trying not to blush.

Jim made coffee while Sarah showered. Even the hot water, shampoo and soap didn't banish the tiredness from Sarah's body; she went through the motions of washing her hair and body wearily, dreading the day ahead. *Is this it?* she thought. *Is every day from now on pointless? Just another tedious twenty-four hours on the treadmill, missing Becca a little more every day, and remembering her just a little less?*

Fighting back the tears, Sarah was towelling herself dry when Jim tried to burst into the bathroom. He hammered on the door, frantically. "Sarah!"

Sarah's heart skipped a beat; she unlocked the door and pulled it open.

"Jenny's on the radio. The police have been called out to some old quarry."

They both ran downstairs, Sarah almost tripping as she struggled to wrap a bath towel around herself as she went. Outside, in the garden, Jenny was talking into her radio. When she saw Jim and Sarah, she held up her hand to indicate that she needed to listen to her caller. Sarah and Jim remained at the door, catching only snatches of the conversation.

Jenny came running back to the house. "We've had a call-out," she said. "To the quarry near Harper's Lane, at the other side of the school. I haven't got a clear picture – in fact, it's a very confusing picture – but it looks like Becca's been found."

"Oh my God," said Sarah, her hand covering her mouth. "Is she –?"

Jenny shook her head. "She's alive, but she's hurt and on her way to hospital."

"Hurt? How badly? How?"

"I don't know," said Jenny, "I'm sorry. The ambulance and police have only just got there – it seems there's more than one person hurt. I don't know any details."

Sarah fell backwards onto a kitchen chair, sobbing. Jim put his arm around her wet, bare shoulders.

"If you get dressed," said Jenny, "I'll drive you there."

"Matt," said Jim. "What about Matt?"

22

Stephen Carter took off his cap and wiped the sweat from his forehead. The quarry was alive with activity – dozens of police (both uniformed and non-uniformed) and paramedics swarmed around him. It was not an easy place to mobilise emergency services to. Harper's Lane was backed up with police cars and ambulances, but at least they'd managed to close the lane off at both entrances to keep the press at bay for a while. The old well was even harder to get to – the air ambulance had flown over a few minutes ago, seeking a clearing deeper into the abandoned estate.

The paramedics had split into two teams, one group running up the hill to the old well while the other tended to Becca, Helen and Hannah. Becca had been the first to be taken away – not because she was most in need of help, but because Sammy's injury meant that there was no way the paramedics could safely get her down the hill. Not that Becca looked good. Carter couldn't get over just how much of her body was bruised and cut. He thought that she looked like she'd been in a fight with a lion and lost.

While the paramedics carried Helen down the field, Carter pulled his mobile phone from his pocket and dialled. At the other end, the phone was picked up on the first ring.

"Hello?" said Julia, fearful and anxious.

"Julia, it's Steve." He replaced his cap and looked over at Hannah who was sitting on the ground, wrapped in a blanket, waiting to be taken to hospital. "I've got someone here you might want to speak to." He passed the phone to Hannah.

"Mum!"

Stephen paced around, close to Hannah, listening to one side of the conversation.

"No, I'm fine. Really." There was a pause. "No, I'm out by the old quarry. Mum! No, it's a long story. No, I'm fine." Another pause, during which Hannah frowned. "I'll tell you later Mum. But we found Becca, Mum! Me and this other girl, Sammy – Mum!"

Stephen gestured for Hannah to pass the phone back to him.

"Mum," said Hannah, "I have to go, Mister Carter wants to speak to you. Mum! No, I'm not hurt – I love you too, Mum."

She handed the phone to Stephen.

"Hi, Julia," he said.

"Steve, what the hell is going on?"

"There's too much to go into right now, and we don't yet have a full picture of what's happened. But Hannah is fine – she's totally unharmed, I promise. She's something of a hero: she helped to rescue Becca."

"Can I come and get Hannah?"

"Not here. We're just about to take her to hospital –"

"Hospital? I thought you said she was fine?" Julia's voice was almost a shriek.

"Julia – she is fine. She just needs checking over. She swam out and rescued Becca from the quarry pool – and the water's not too clean."

"She did what? Becca can swim way better than Hannah."

Not when she's not eaten for a week and just crawled through a one-hundred-yard tunnel, thought Stephen.

"As I said, it's a long story and we don't know it all yet. I'll fill you in later. Get Lucy to run you to the hospital. You can meet Hannah there."

"Lucy? If it wasn't for her –"

"I know, Julia, I know. She's very upset about it. She knows what she did –"

"Too damned right she knows. I'll –"

Stephen interrupted. "Julia, can we talk about this later? Lucy screwed up, OK, but I'm up to my neck in it here. It may well be that Hannah sneaking out saved Becca's life. If Lucy *had* stopped her, Becca might be dead now."

Stephen finished the call as quickly as he could, then went back over to Hannah. "I think you're going to get some earache from your Mum," he said.

Hannah nodded, frowning. "I know. She's going to be as mad as hell." She paused, clearly worried. "Not as mad as Dad, though." She put her hand to her mouth, shocked. "Oh God, Dad," she said, flushing, realising that for most of the morning she'd not thought about her injured father at all.

"I wouldn't worry about your Dad. He's going to be too busy getting better to have much of a go at you. And he is going to be fine, Hannah."

"Is he? Really?"

"I think so. He's badly hurt, but he's a strong bloke. Now, before you go, any chance of you running through what happened again – one more time?"

23

Abby kissed Sammy's pale face on the forehead and watched her being wheeled into the operating suite. It had taken just under an hour from Abby's call for them to arrive at the hospital. Abby supposed that, all things considered, this was good – although every second had been agony for her. The paramedics had arrived first, and immediately called for the air ambulance. Then they set about doing what they could – which wasn't much. At least when the helicopter had landed at the hospital, the doctors and nurses had been waiting – Abby guessed that from wheels down to the theatre hadn't been much more than five minutes. The paramedics had been able to give Sammy some blood in the air ambulance, which Abby hoped would buy a little more time for the surgeons to do their work – if anything could be done.

Abby sat down heavily on the uncomfortable plastic seat in the corridor, feeling sick and alone. Helen, she guessed, would be somewhere in the same hospital. She was quite possibly in another operating theatre close by – Abby had no idea whether Helen's wounds would require surgery or just a lot of suturing. The latter seemed unlikely – some of the gashes had looked very deep.

It occurred to Abby that she wasn't annoyed with Sammy – and that perhaps she should be. A man was dead, Helen was badly hurt – and Sammy herself might not see the next day. On top of that, Sammy could have signed the death warrant for another ten children in the town. But actually, Abby understood – and, to a certain extent, admired her daughter. Sammy had seen things clearly and simply: right and wrong. The girl in the well was innocent; she didn't deserve to die. It was our family's responsibility. Sammy knew – although almost certainly didn't understand – the possible consequences of her actions. Yet she chose to do what was right, not what was easy. Abby wished she hadn't been so weak.

The doctor had said that they'd be in surgery for several hours; Abby guessed that she had easily enough time to find Helen or at least check up on her progress – but she didn't want to move. Although Helen would be lonely and perhaps afraid, Abby knew she would understand. *I left Sammy for Helen before,* she thought, *but not this time.*

24

"You can see Rebecca now," said the nurse. "I have to tell you that she's sedated, so she may not react very much to you. And I'm sorry, but we can only let you have a few minutes, because we really need to tend to her injuries – and that's going to take some time."

The nurse led Sarah and Jim into the room. At the sight of Becca, Sarah gasped, but it was Jim who broke down – as he had earlier, when told about Matt. Jim, who was normally an anchor of reason and calm, had lost all of his usual composure and cried – wailed – openly when the news was broken. But still he'd opted to stay with Sarah so that they could see Becca together.

Although the nurses had begun to clean up Becca, she was still an horrific mess. Dirty, bruised, cut and swollen – she looked nothing like the girl who had set off to school on Friday morning, less than a week before. Sarah sat beside Becca and clasped her hand, avoiding pulling one of the two drips feeding into her arm.

"Re – Becca," she corrected herself. "It's Mum."

As the nurse had said, Becca didn't respond.

"I don't know if you can hear me," said Sarah, "but if you can, I want you to know that we're here for you. Me and Jim. We love you."

Sarah lifted Becca's hand to her face and kissed it, then inhaled through her nose, expecting the familiar smell of her daughter. Perhaps it was there, but if it was it was masked by the stench of dirt and filth. She couldn't imagine what Becca had lived through over the last few days.

The nurse came back into the room. "I'm sorry," she said. "We really need to get working on Rebecca."

"Can we stay?" asked Sarah.

"For most of it," the nurse replied, "of course. But some of the treatment will have to be done in surgery."

Sarah nodded, sniffing back her tears. "I understand. How bad is she?"

"The good news," said the nurse reassuringly, "is that – as far as we can tell – there are no bones broken. We'll be running a full set of X-rays later, though, to be sure.

It could be that there are bones broken in her feet and even she doesn't know – as you can see, her feet are very swollen. It's the early stages of trench foot, which can be very serious, but we're pumping her full of antibiotics. It's the cuts that are the worst – some are days old and still open; quite a few of those are infected. The worst cut is more recent, on her hip, which we have dressed but will need surgery – she's scraped her skin off to the bone."

Sarah felt physically sick and swayed slightly in the chair; Jim squeezed her hand.

"And we're testing for things like Hepatitis A," said the nurse. "We'll be very surprised if she hasn't got some kind of blood-borne infection."

Sarah brushed away a tear. "None of that sounds very – very hopeful."

"I'm sorry," said the nurse, smiling. "It doesn't help when I reel it off like that. All of these can be serious, but we're on top of things. I think she's going to take a while to recover, probably several weeks, maybe more, but she'll get there."

Sarah nodded, numb.

"We have a lot to do," said the nurse, as the room filled with doctors and nurses.

Dear God, thought Sarah, as half a dozen people all began to work on Becca at the same time.

"You know," said Sarah, "we're just going to be in the way. We'll sit back here." She and Jim withdrew to the side of the room and watched from there, holding each other.

25

Helen lay on her side while a nurse and doctor worked to clean and suture her wounds. They'd been busy for nearly an hour – and had warned her at the start that some of the wounds might need to be closed in theatre. It was shallow of her, she knew, but she couldn't stop thinking about how her back would look when it had healed. She had a good body and loved the way Abby watched her dress, sometimes pulling her back into bed immediately afterwards. Helen suspected that the days of her having a lean, smooth back had gone.

Helen winced and sucked in her breath as the nurse fed the needle back into her skin. Despite the local anaesthetic, it felt like she was digging into her with a knife.

"I'm sorry," said the nurse, automatically.

"It's OK," Helen replied, absently.

"I know it feels bad," said the nurse, "but I'm going a bit slower to try to get it as neat as I can – to try to reduce the scarring."

Helen nodded, but didn't reply.

More than anything, Helen felt alone. She'd asked about Sammy and been told that she was in surgery, but no more. She knew that Abby would be with her, or waiting outside and wished that she could be with her, holding her hand.

26

It was just like in the television hospital dramas. The surgeon came out of the theatre first, accompanied by a nurse, and asked to talk to Abby. He led her to a small, informal meeting room. Abby was shaking with fear, desperate for answers but scared to ask. She sat down, anxious for the surgeon to speak.

"It's not all good news, I'm afraid," he said.

Abby stifled a sob, fearing the worst.

"The main thing is that Samantha is doing well, very well really. We can't say for certain at this stage, but it's looking very hopeful."

"What does that mean?" asked Abby. "She could still die?"

"It was touch and go for a bit," admitted the surgeon. "And while there is still that chance, I'm pretty confident that she'll pull through."

Abby felt sick with relief. "Oh, thank you," she said, meaning it sincerely.

The surgeon waited while Abby composed herself and then pressed on. "As I said, it's not all good news. The knife went in here –" he indicated to the side of his lower abdomen, "– just about missing her bladder. Well, actually, he did nick it, but only just. The knife went in just above it, chipping the pubic bone. If she'd had a full bladder, he might well have hit it. That can be very serious – not just the wound itself, but also the damage caused by releasing waste into the body."

He paused and Abby saw the nurse briefly glance at him.

"I'm really sorry to tell you that the knife penetrated the uterus – and pretty deeply," said the surgeon. "That's where a lot of the blood was coming from."

"Oh God," said Abby.

The surgeon held up his hand and continued. "We have been able to repair the wound – just about. The last thing we wanted to do was perform an emergency hysterectomy on an eight-year-old girl. But the uterus isn't an easy organ to repair. Overall, we do think she will be fine, but the next few days will be critical."

Abby's mind was racing, but the surgeon got there first.

"The really bad news is that we'd probably advise against Samantha having children. Despite our best efforts, I'd say that her womb is permanently compromised. I don't really think that she could carry a baby to term."

Abby slumped back in the chair and screwed up her tear-filled eyes tight, pressing her hands over them. Outside, in the corridor, people walking by couldn't help but hear her inconsolable wailing.

THURSDAY

1

"Can I just read this back to you?" Stephen asked Hannah. She sat herself a little further up in the hospital bed and nodded. "Yep."

Julia sat beside her, holding her hand; she'd spent the night wandering between Hannah's hospital room and Ed's. By the doctors' own admission, Hannah was fine – they were just keeping her in the hospital while they ran some blood tests; she'd probably be discharged that morning.

Stephen Carter and Jenny Greenwood sat on the other side of the bed. Stephen had questioned Hannah, Abby and Helen and got the same story – he intended to talk to Becca when she came around and was strong enough to be interviewed.

"You said that both you and Samantha were suspicious of Mister Randle, because Rebecca was scared of him?"

Hannah nodded.

"You told Samantha's Mum, and you all followed him to the well."

Hannah nodded again.

"Why didn't you tell the police?" he asked.

"I don't know," replied Hannah. "Right now it seems stupid that we didn't, but at the time – we thought we might be wrong and look daft."

Stephen continued. "At the quarry, the grown-ups challenged him and he threw Helen Goodwin over into the quarry?"

"Yes," said Hannah, carefully.

"Then while Abby tried to save Helen, he attacked and tried to assault you?"

"Yes," said Hannah uneasily, feeling ill at the memory.

"You hit him and knocked him out, but he came after you again and stabbed Samantha. You ran at him and pushed him into the well?"

"Yes," said Hannah.

"But you were too late to rescue Becca," he said.

Hannah nodded. "We didn't know, but she was already crawling out."

"OK," said Stephen, snapping his notebook closed. "That's enough for now." He smiled at Hannah. "You did well, Hannah. I know it's not easy to keep telling the same story, especially when it's so upsetting, but we have to get it straight."

"I know," said Hannah. "It's OK. It all happened so fast – it's hard to remember."

"You remembered fine," he said, standing. "We'll leave you to it," he said, leading Jenny out of the room.

"What do you think?" asked Jenny.

"Well," he replied, "we've had the same story from three of them. It's quite a story, but it adds up."

"Not for me," said Jenny. "Not quite."

They stopped walking. "How so?" he asked.

Jenny shrugged. "At the top of the quarry, Abby chose to leave her daughter with someone they suspected of abducting a child."

"It was a snap decision," he said. "She went after her partner, who probably would have otherwise died. Come on, it's a result. How often do we get a happy ending in a case like this?"

"All the same," said Jenny. "It's not what I would have done."

2

"Hi, Sammy," said Abby.

Sammy pulled her heavy eyes open, reluctantly. She felt dreadfully tired and a bit sick.

"Mummy," she said.

Abby pressed the buzzer for the nurse, who came quickly and checked Sammy over. "Samantha's going to feel rough from the anaesthetic," said the nurse. "But she'll soon perk up." She gave her a little water, sat her up slightly and then left.

"Mummy, I feel very poorly," said Sammy. "I feel sick and I hurt."

Abby held her hand, tightly. "You're fine," she said. "You'll get better."

There was a long silence.

"Where's Helen?" asked Sammy.

"Somewhere in the hospital, in another room," replied Abby. "She's fine too."

Sammy frowned. "She's lonely, Mummy."

Abby smiled. "I know. I'll go and see her soon. I had to stay with you, though."

"Thanks," said Sammy. "Mummy –" She paused.

"What, baby?"

"Mummy, I'm sorry. This is all my fault. Helen's hurt. All the trouble. It was me. I shouldn't have done it." Tears were forming around Sammy's eyes.

"Hey," said Abby. "It's OK. You don't have to say sorry. What you did was very brave. And very right. You did something you believed in. I'm proud of you."

"You are?"

"You know I am, don't you?"

Sammy nodded. "I didn't just do it because it was right," she said. "I did a deal. With – with *her.*"

"You *talked* to her?"

"Yes. I was going to trade me, for the girl in the well. I took Hannah so she could get her out – after. But I was too late, and then the bad man came."

"She said she would do a trade?"

Sammy nodded. "A life for a life. She had to take the bad man instead of me. I made her. *She was very scary.*"

"Oh Sammy," said Abby.

Sammy's eyes closed and she drifted off for a few minutes. Abby kept quiet and let her sleep. After a while, her eyes opened again.

"The policeman is coming," said Sammy. "He wants to talk to me."

"Sams –"

"It's OK, Mum," she said. "I know what to say."

"I thought you might," said Abby. She paused and then asked, quietly, "Sams, you can do a bit more than just *read* minds, can't you?"

Sammy looked a little shocked. "Mummy?"

"When Helen was hurt, I was going to come to you, not Helen. You – you spoke. In my mind. Do you remember?"

Sammy nodded. "I could see what you were thinking. And Helen. I knew she was –"

"It's OK, baby," said Abby. "You did the right thing. How long have you been able to do that?"

Sammy shrugged. "Always, I think. I just don't like to. It's hard and – I can hurt the person when I do it."

Abby thought for a second and decided to change the subject. "Sammy – do you know what happened to you? To your tummy?"

"I think so," said Sammy. "But it's all a bit confusing. I can't have babies, can I? The man cut me where I have babies – and now I can't?"

Abby couldn't hold back her tears. "That's right, baby. I'm sorry. I'm so sorry."

Sammy shrugged. "It's OK."

"Oh, Sammy, it's not OK, you say that now, but –"

"No, Mummy, it *is* OK."

"Why do you say that? How can you know?"

"The woman. It's only us keeping her alive. Us and whoever she takes. When we're gone, she's gone. She's not gone now – but she's dying. I can feel it: it's like she's – suffocating, slowly. When I die, she dies. If I have a baby, she'll carry on. It's fine Mummy – like with the girl. It's the right thing."

Christ, that's deep, thought Abby.

"Well, there's always girls. Like me and Helen."

"Ew, Mum! Please. No offence, but I don't fancy girls."

3

Stephen passed Jenny a cup of coffee from the hospital vending machine. She took a sip. "Ugh," she said. "It tastes worse than it looks."

"That's some going," replied Stephen. "It looks like crap."

They walked slowly down the corridor. "Jen?"

"Um?"

"About the other night –"

"It's OK, Steve, just let it go. I don't mind."

"What if I do?" he asked, stopping.

"I don't know. I wasn't looking for anything. Not sure I am now. And I don't want a – you know, a fuck-buddy."

"I wasn't saying that," replied Stephen. "I was thinking of – well, do you fancy going out?"

"I don't know," said Jenny. "Is that horrible of me? You know, I like you, but – well, I don't know."

"Fair enough," said Stephen, hiding his disappointment badly. "If you change your mind –"

Jenny slapped Stephen's shoulder, playfully.

"Of course I fancy going out," she said, laughing. "I'm just messing with you."

4

Abby gave Helen a long, loving kiss, not caring about the nurse in the room.

"God, I missed you," said Helen. "How's Sammy?"

After the nurse left, Abby told Helen everything that had happened; it wasn't a tale that improved in the telling. For the most part, Helen remained quiet, but several times she broke down – especially when Abby told her about the outcome of Sammy's injuries.

"And how do you feel about that?" asked Helen, softly.

"Crap," said Abby, wiping away a tear. "Really crap. It's not what any mother wants to hear: that her daughter can't have children."

"Is there no chance?" asked Helen. "Surely it's only as if she'd had a caesarean? Don't doctors cut wombs open all the time?"

"I asked that," said Abby. "Apparently a wound is different in lots of ways. It was a rough cut, rather than a clean incision. Plus they had to remove a small part of the womb in order to repair it properly. And the wound was open for a good while –

with a knife inside it, moving and twisting around – with a c-section they try to get in and out quickly. They're not saying she definitely can't have a child – but there's only a tiny, tiny chance that she and the baby would survive more than a couple of months into pregnancy. Once the baby grows, the uterus could tear open."

Helen squeezed Abby's arm. "Oh, Abby," she said.

Abby laid her hand on Helen's. "I know. I thought it was bad enough when I knew that Sammy could only have one child. But now –"

"At least she's OK, Abby."

Abby nodded. "Yep. I really thought we'd lost her."

The two women paused, neither knowing what to say next.

Helen broke the silence. She kissed Abby's hand and paused briefly. "Ab, I've been thinking," she said. "While I've been lying here. This might not be the right time, but –"

"Yes?"

"Do you want – how do you feel about having another baby?"

"Helen – you know I can't. I can only have one. A girl. That's it."

"I'm not so sure. I think there's a loophole," said Helen.

"A loophole?" asked Abby, puzzled.

Helen nodded. "Your egg. My womb. Our baby."

Abby looked doubtful. "I don't know," she said. "It's still my baby."

Helen smiled, slightly smug. "Recite the rhyme to me," she said. "Your family curse."

"The baby you carry will never be male –," Abby began, before stopping, stunned into silence. "Oh my God –" she said.

"That's right," said Helen, enthusiastically. "It's your baby, but you don't carry it, I do!"

Abby was lost for words.

"What do you think?" asked Helen.

"I think it's mad," said Abby, astonished to find that she was beaming in the middle of so much misery. "And brilliant. I'd love to."

5

"Hannah, would you give me and your Dad a moment, please?"

"Sure," said Hannah. "I'll go back to my room and get dressed."

"No, it's OK – I won't be long. Just wait outside?"

Hannah left the room and sat outside, waiting. Her Dad didn't look good, but at least he was now awake and talking.

Julia gently closed the door and sat down next to Ed, gathering as much courage as she could.

"Hannah was stupid," said Ed.

"No," replied Julia, firmly. "She did a stupid thing. There's a difference. She did it for the best of reasons. She's very brave."

"I suppose," conceded Ed, reluctantly.

"Ed. I've got something to say. I don't want you to interrupt or say anything."

Ed looked at Julia. "What?"

"I don't want you to come home."

Ed started to protest but Julia silenced him. "This isn't a discussion," she said. "This is an ultimatum. You don't come home until you get help. You stay somewhere else. And you get proper help with your drinking."

"Now hang on –"

"No, you hang on. I mean it Ed. You get help with your drinking and – your temper. Or, you don't come home. Ever. And if you come home before I agree to it, I'll leave – with Hannah. And I'll press charges for domestic violence."

"Julia, I never –"

"Ed. You're a policeman. You know what you've done to me, even if you're trying to tell yourself that you didn't. I've had enough. You've got one chance to put things right – and after that, no chances to slip up again. And, if you do come home – there's no drinking. At all. That's my offer. Take it or leave it."

Ed said nothing, boiling inside.

"Look Ed, right now, you're a hero – even if Steve and everyone else at the station know that you blundered in there drunk. Well, you can stay a hero – or you can be the hero who turned out to be a drunk who beat his wife. It's your choice."

"I want you to go," said Ed, through gritted teeth.

"You're mad right now, I know," said Julia. "But you'll calm down. When you do, I hope you're grateful that I'm at least giving you a chance. Because to be honest, I don't think you deserve it."

Without saying anything else, she stood and left the room. Outside, she rested her back against the closed door, shaking.

"Are you OK, Mum?" asked Hannah, putting her hand on her mother's arm. *Go, Mum!* she thought, having heard most of the conversation clearly.

"I'm fine," said Julia. And, for the first time in many years, she believed that she was.

6

"How do you feel?" asked Sarah.

"Pretty rubbish," replied Becca, understating just how terrible she felt. The physical pain was bad enough, but the guilt was eating away at her. The fact that no one had even mentioned Matt to her – probably out of consideration for her feelings – didn't help.

They were alone; Jim was busy organising Matt's funeral. *I want the funeral to be near Matt's home*, Jim had said; the allusion that Bankside was no longer Matt's home wasn't lost on Sarah.

The doctors' best guess at the moment was that Becca would be in hospital for a week or two – perhaps a few weeks more if the results of her blood tests weren't good. Most of her scars would probably heal, they'd said, though a few could be lifelong trophies – especially the one on her hip.

Becca had remained pensive and unforthcoming since waking, something the doctors said was normal but would have to be addressed – probably with long-term counselling. Even the police had questioned her only briefly – after all, when most of the action had taken place, she had been below ground.

"Do you want to talk about it?" asked Sarah.

Becca shook her head. "Not really. It's – it's too horrible. Like a horror film. Except it was me in it."

Sarah hesitated. "It doesn't help to keep it to yourself, you know."

Becca shook her head, tearfully.

"You feel a bit guilty, don't you?" asked Sarah. "Like – why am I alive? And Matt's not?"

Becca nodded.

Sarah hesitated. "Did you – did you love him?" she asked.

"I don't know," replied Becca, crying openly. "Nearly. I nearly did."

Sarah wiped her daughter's eyes and kissed her forehead.

"Mum?" said Becca.

"Yes?"

Becca paused. "Have you – have you told Dad?"

"I have. I had to, really. Didn't you want me to?"

"No, it's fine. I think – I think I want to see him."

"Well, he wants to see you. In fact I had to insist that he stay away. I guess if he'd really wanted to, I couldn't have stopped him. He was pretty upset. But I've kept him up-to-date with what's been happening. He does want to see you, but I told him it would be up to you, like always. Are you sure you want to see him?"

Becca nodded. "I think so. It's not like I forgive him or anything. But, well, he's my Dad. You know."

Sarah nodded. "I understand."

"Thanks, Mum." She paused. "How's Jim?"

Sarah sighed. "Really bad, to be honest. I think he doesn't know what to do. He's busying himself organising things – but then he just sits in the chair and stares into space, or cries."

"Oh God," said Becca.

"Well, if I lost you I'd probably do the same. He's devastated."

Becca nodded in understanding.

"If you want to talk, I'm here," she said. "I don't care what happened, or what might have happened. I still love you."

"I'm not worried about you being cross – well maybe a bit. But there's stuff – horrible stuff – I had to do. All the detail. I can't stop thinking about it. It's stuff I don't want you – anyone – to know."

"I think," said Sarah, "that you *do* want to talk about it. You're just worried about me hearing it. Is that right?"

Becca nodded.

"I can take it, Becks, I promise. If you can live through it, I can at least handle listening to it. I'm *always* here for you. The doctors will want you to talk to people, the police will want to talk to you – you'll have to tell the same story over and over. Or at least some of it, maybe not all the detail. But I'll always be here for you, to listen properly, and understand. If ever, whenever you want – I'm your Mum."

Becca hesitated. Sarah passed Becca a tissue and she blew her nose.

"OK, Mum, I'll tell you," said Becca. "All of it. But only once. Don't make me tell you again. Not all of it."

Sarah listened – horrified inside, attentive and caring outside – while Becca hesitantly retold the events of the last few days. Becca told her everything – except the parts Hannah had asked her to leave out.

7

Murderer, thought Hannah, considering her reflection in the mirror. It was the same face that she'd always seen when sat at her dressing table: slightly rounded and cupped by short, neat blonde hair that was still damp from her shower. For a moment she imagined that her eyes were somehow wiser or even tormented, but they weren't. They were pretty, striking even, blessed with long, curved eyelashes.

She looked at her shoulders, still dotted with water – and pulled the towel closer around her. From the outside, she still looked like a normal teenage girl. But on the inside, there was a different truth, a truth that only she could see. A truth that had started to eat at her. *Killer*, she thought.

I ended a life. It didn't matter that the man had wanted to rape and kill her. The man was no more – because of her. She'd done it in anger. At the bottom of the well, Randle had no longer been a threat to anyone – they could have left him to the police. But she'd killed him anyway. *You can kill him now, if you want,* Sammy had said. She *had* wanted to. When she had flung the stone, it was with *satisfaction.*

The eyes in the mirror filled with tears. *I killed him,* thought Hannah, *and I fucking loved it.* Throwing the stone was exciting, like a death in the movies. But this wasn't like a death in the movies. No one said, "cut". The antagonist didn't get up, dust himself off and go for a coffee in his expensive trailer. *He stayed down. Forever. Because of me. Worse,* she thought, *I'd do it again.* Hannah didn't know what made her feel the most sick: the memory of Randle's finger stroking her naked stomach or the awful sound she'd heard when the rock had ended his life. *The rock I threw.*

Why don't we just hit the bastard with that rock again? The words echoed in her mind.

Both when the police had come and when she'd been reunited with her mother she'd felt like a hero. Her name and photograph were going to be in the newspapers and on the television – one of the girls who'd rescued the girl in the well and helped to catch a paedophile. But the fact was that Becca had rescued herself and the paedophile hadn't been caught, he'd been killed. *Killed by me.* Whether he deserved to die wasn't the issue: Hannah hadn't stepped on a bug, she'd stopped another human being from breathing. *In the future,* she wondered, *who could trust me? Is this something I could do again? Easily? What if I get married to someone like Dad? Would I give him another chance, like Mum? Or –? People who know me – friends – will they trust me, knowing I'm a killer? Will anyone, ever?*

In one angry sweep, Hannah brushed everything off the top of her dressing table and onto the floor – brushes, make-up, lipstick, perfume, glitter, phone, everything. *Shit,* she thought, wiping her tear-soaked face. *I woke up one morning a teenager and went to bed a killer.* A little voice nagged in her head: *no, you woke up a killer, you just didn't know it yet.*

Hannah kicked a bottle of perfume across the floor and threw herself on her bed, sobbing. Downstairs, Julia was making bacon and eggs. The smell wafted upstairs and Hannah's stomach groaned. *I killed someone,* she thought. *How can I think about eating?*

Hannah felt utterly alone. She rolled off the bed and turned on her computer. While it was starting up, she dressed and rubbed her hair dry.

She thought about Randle's eyes on her body; his hand touching her – and realised that while she may have escaped the physical act of rape, she was nonetheless violated. Yesterday, the thought of a boy kissing her, touching her, had been exciting.

Today, it made her feel ill. *When will I forget? When I'm twenty? Thirty? Fifty? Never? Will a man ever, ever touch me without me seeing those glasses, that tongue licking those lips, that big hand reaching out, that awful bulge in his trousers?* She realised with absolute certainty that not only was she a killer, she'd do the same thing again in a heartbeat. *I've been robbed,* she thought. *That bastard's spoiled sex for me forever.* Hannah took her towel and wiped the tears from her face.

Hannah had scoffed to herself when she'd overheard Mister Carter talking to her mother about counselling and social workers. Now she couldn't for the life of her see how any number of conversations could cleanse her of this feeling. Hannah thought about how her mother had allowed her father to take the joy from their marriage. *That bastard Tom Randle isn't going to screw my life up,* she thought, determined but not convinced.

Hannah dropped the towel on her bed, sat at her computer and logged on to Simon's on-line profile, hoping she could find his mobile phone number. She was a friend of his on-line, if not especially off it. His number was there – she tapped it into her phone and paused, her heart racing. *God this is hard,* she thought. In her mind, she saw herself holding Simon's hand or perhaps letting him put his arm around her. She wanted to feel thrilled or turned on, but she didn't. She felt repulsed.

Hannah stood up and screamed, throwing her mobile phone against the wall. The battery cover cracked open, releasing the battery. In three pieces, the phone fell to the floor with the rest of her scattered possessions.

EPILOGUE

1

After the funeral, everyone went back to the upstairs room of the Three Crowns, a pub not far from Jim's house.

No funeral is easy, but the funeral of a child is something so deeply wrong that even the most positive person would struggle to make sense of it.

The service had been well-attended. Sarah had been worried that Becca wasn't strong enough to come, but she'd insisted – although her doctor had required her to go in a wheelchair; she was still weeks away from being discharged.

Becca was grey and gaunt, unusually wearing make-up to help disguise her worst scars. Her distant eyes were inset within dark rings that the make-up hadn't been able to hide; she was still unable to sleep for more than a few hours at a time and even then usually required sedatives. To make matters worse, she could no longer bear to be alone in a room with the lights off. Like Hannah, she was finding her newly started therapy sessions little more than useless and was desperate for a time when she, Hannah and Sammy could speak openly and unsupervised. Her hair was cut into an untidy layered bob. Sarah had been horrified when her daughter had decided to rid herself of her long dark hair, but once Becca had taken some surgical scissors to it she had no choice but to help her daughter to make the best of it.

Sarah had pushed Becca to the front of the church so that she could lay a rose on the coffin. Sarah then let Becca spend a few moments alone before wheeling her to the first pew. Although they weren't family, Sarah had asked both Hannah and Julia to sit alongside them.

Sammy, still in hospital, couldn't come – but both Abby and Helen were there.

Stephen and Jenny had sat on the last pew, in uniform, with three higher ranking police officers from the regional force. Conscious of their superiors, they'd avoided holding hands during the service – but when Stephen had sensed Jenny gently shaking next to him, he'd clasped her hand and squeezed it tightly.

The church was full of children and teachers from both schools – Matt's old one and the one in Bankside.

Jim, ashen-faced, sleepwalked through the whole day. He nodded and shook hands, greeted people and even occasionally just about managed a smile – but that was his body executing a series of automatic gestures. Inside, he was numb.

Jim picked up both his beer and Sarah's wine from the bar and went to sit next to her. Hannah and Becca were sitting at the next table, deep in conversation.

There was a long silence between Jim and Sarah; then he said, simply, "Sarah, I'm not coming back."

"What?"

"I've been thinking. I'm not coming back. I don't think I could."

Sarah was shocked; she leaned towards Jim and whispered, "Can this wait? It doesn't seem like the right time."

Jim shook his head, sadly. "You'll want me to come back, tonight – and I, well, I just can't."

"Is this because of me?" asked Sarah, softly, looking around.

"A bit. Well, it's what got me thinking. When things are tough, people should pull together. I think I was there for you – but I don't think you were there for me."

It hurt, but Sarah knew it was true. "I know," she said.

One of Matt's teachers interrupted, offering clumsy commiserations. When she'd left, Sarah said, "I don't want you to go. I love you."

"This isn't all about love," replied Jim. "It's about respect. I still love you, but I don't know if I respect you."

"You sound like you've made up your mind."

"I have. I feel hollow. Like I have nothing. *Like I am nothing.* I just want to be alone. I know Matt wasn't perfect, but – well, I don't have to explain it. It's like part of me is gone. The most important part. I lost Chris. Now Matt. It's like all of those years were for nothing. I just want to be on my own."

"Jim," said Sarah, holding his hand tightly. *Never,* she thought, *never has a single sentence been so important in all my life.* "I could beg," she said. "And I'm prepared to. I could move in with you, at your house. I'd be prepared to do that too – happy to do that – or move somewhere else completely. Look – I got it wrong. I was a cow. I was preoccupied and selfish. And I know that I'd probably do the same again. But I do love you. If you want to go, then at least let's not fight or fall out. But how about this – how about we at least try? Start again?"

Jim shook his head. "I don't know."

"It will be hard. Very hard. But I think we need each other. Will you at least give me a chance?"

Jim glanced over at Becca, who was chatting to Hannah. For a moment, Becca caught Jim's eye before lowering her head. "It's not just you. Becca's never really taken to me. And – I know this is wrong – but I find it very, very hard to be with her right now."

Sarah took both of his hands in hers. "I can understand that."

Jim was lost in thought and Sarah struggled to think of anything to console him.

"Jim," she said. "No one can make this less crap than it is. But we don't have to make it worse."

"This couldn't be any worse," said Jim.

Hannah hadn't missed how her friend avoided eye contact with Jim.

"Something wrong with you and Jim?" asked Hannah.

Becca swallowed and glanced towards Jim. "I just – I just don't know what to say to him," she said.

"You feel you're to blame?" offered Hannah.

Becca nodded and wiped away a tear. "I know I am. And I know Jim knows it too. He's been to see me, most times that Mum's come. But he doesn't say a lot. I can see he's, I don't know, uncomfortable around me. Like he wants to say something but can't."

"Becca," said Hannah, taking her hand. "He probably does. And I bet you want to talk to him too."

"I do – but I don't know what to say," Becca replied. "When he and Mum first got together I didn't give him a chance," she admitted. "I resented him. He made Mum happy, but that annoyed me. I didn't trust him. I didn't *want* to like him, in case he – he hurt Mum."

"Like with your Dad?"

Becca nodded. She wiped her face. "Are all men shits?"

"You know they're not," said Hannah, thinking about what her mother had now told her about her own father. "But plenty are. I don't think Jim's one of them, though."

Becca reflected on this and nodded again. "Yep."

Hannah tried to change the subject. "What about your cuts and stuff?"

"That's the pits," said Becca. "I've always been – you know – really bony. But at least I was proper toned. But my body's a mess. I hate it. I can't look at it. Scars everywhere – and not all of them are going to go away."

"Oh, Becks." Hannah was stuck for words. She wanted to tell her how *she* felt: how she couldn't stand naked without thinking of Tom Randle leering at her. She decided that now wasn't the time.

Becca took a deep breath. "Do me a favour, Hannah? Wheel me over to Mum and Jim, while I've got the nerve up to speak to them?"

"You sure?"

"Yes. No – but I have to."

Hannah stood and took the brake off Becca's wheelchair. Becca reached her hand out to Hannah's. "Han?"

"Yeah?"

"I never really said – thanks. Proper thanks."

"You did, several times."

"I love you, Han." She reached up and hugged her friend.

Hannah hugged her back. "You big girl," she said.

"I mean it," said Becca. "What you did –"

"Enough," said Hannah, wiping away a tear. "Right now I don't want to talk about it."

She started to push Becca's wheelchair, but again she stopped her.

"Hang on," said Becca. "Let's just talk to Sammy's Mum first." Hannah wheeled Becca over to Abby and Helen, who were sitting alone, holding hands. There'd been a few rumours around the school that Miss Goodwin was gay, but Becca had always disregarded them. She didn't see why some people thought it was such a big deal, but she admitted to herself that she did feel a touch uncomfortable seeing them hand in hand – but there was something sweet about it too. *Get over it*, thought Becca.

"Miss Goodwin? Mrs – Henshall?"

"It's Miss," said Abby. "But call me Abby. You'll make me feel older than I am."

"And it's Helen," said Helen. "At least out of school."

Becca had seen them both around the hospital, but hadn't spoken to either of them – although she knew that her mother had, several times. Becca had asked her mother to take her to see Sammy, but when they went, Sammy had been asleep. Hannah had now told Becca everything she knew about Sammy – the unedited version of events. Nothing about it seemed unbelievable; it fit in perfectly with her own experiences. And, after having had several conversations with a long-dead witch, it wasn't really a big leap to accept that a little girl could read minds.

"I just wanted to ask," said Becca, "if it's OK to come and see Sammy."

"Of course it is," said Abby. "Your Mum told me you went to see her, but she was sleeping."

Becca nodded. "I didn't just mean at the hospital, though. I meant after. When she comes home. Can I –" she indicated to Hannah, "I mean, *we* – come and see her?"

"I'd love you to. And I'm sure Sammy would too."

There was a pause. Abby leaned forwards to Hannah. "Hannah?"

"Yes?"

"I haven't said. I haven't – thanked you. Sammy told me. What you – what you were going to do. To save her."

Hannah blushed, lost for words. "I didn't think," she said. "I just – Sammy's only a baby. I couldn't –"

Abby put her hand on Hannah's. "I can't thank you enough. Ever. What you did – I don't think I've ever heard of anything so – so brave. So selfless."

Hannah rubbed a tear away. "Anyone would have –"

Abby interrupted her. "No, Hannah. I don't think anyone would. You're very special."

Hannah was lost for words.

"Look, Hannah," said Abby. "Do you know my shop? *No Stone Unturned*?"

Hannah nodded. "I've been past it lots," she said.

"Well," said Abby. "Next time, don't walk past, come in. I'm not well off, but the shop has some pretty nice crystals and fossils. You come in and take your pick."

"Thanks," flustered Hannah.

"Really," said Abby. "Whatever you want."

They chatted for a little while before Becca made her excuses and asked to be taken over to see Sarah and Jim.

"Are you sure you're up to this?" asked Hannah.

"I'm pooped, to be honest. I've not been out of bed this long since – well, you know. But I need to do this."

Becca felt her stomach somersault as Hannah pushed her to the table. Hannah put the brake on the chair and sat down beside them.

"Han," Becca asked. "Do me a favour?"

"Oh, sure," said Hannah, "I'll go catch up with Simon."

Becca took a deep breath. *Shit this is hard*, she thought. After everything that had happened, this seemed to be the biggest challenge of all.

"Jim" she said tentatively, holding back her tears. "Can I – can I – talk to you a minute?"

Sarah stood. "I'll give you two some time," she said.

Becca nodded, and then thought better of it. "No, Mum. Please stay." Sarah sat down.

"This is really hard for me," said Becca. There was a long pause and Sarah reached out for her daughter's hand, squeezing it. Becca squeezed it back and then reached for Jim with her other hand. Time seemed to drag. *I can't say it*, thought Becca. *I'll screw it up.*

"It's OK," Jim offered.

"No, Jim," said Becca. "It's not OK. Nothing about this is OK. It's all – horrible."

"Honey," began Sarah.

"No, Mum. Please. Let me try to – let me try?"

Sarah nodded.

"I told Mum everything. And said I didn't want to ever, ever tell anyone." A tear ran down Becca's face and Sarah brushed it away for her. "But I will," said Becca. "If you want. I don't want to – but I will."

Jim didn't know what to say. He nodded, slowly.

"But I want you to know one thing," said Becca. "Well, two actually. First, I've been – well – I didn't give you a chance. I know that."

"I think you're being hard on yourself, Becca," said Jim, softly.

"No I'm not. I'm being easy on myself. I was a little shit. Sorry Mum. But I was. You didn't deserve it. Mum's not been so happy for – well, pretty much as long as I can remember. She loves you but Dad screwed up her head, so sometimes – well, you know what I mean."

Jim looked uncomfortable, but said nothing. *This is so hard*, thought Becca.

"Jim – I want to have a proper chance at having a real Dad. I really want that – my Dad – to be you."

It was Jim's turn to cry. "Oh, Becca," he said. Sarah let go of Becca and put her arm around Jim, pulling him close.

"And –" said Becca, not wanting to lose her momentum. "I have to tell you something else. About Matt."

Jim looked at her, rubbing his eyes.

"The last thing –" Try as she might, Becca couldn't stifle a sob. "The last thing he did was to try to save me. He fell in because he was trying to save me. It was – it was the bravest thing ever. *Ever.*"

Jim nodded. "I appreciate that, Becca. I really do."

With some effort, Becca rose from her chair and sat beside Jim. Still raw, her body hurt all over. She hugged him and gave him a kiss. "*Ever –,*" she repeated.

They talked and cried for a while. Once the mood shifted back to something a little more approaching normality, albeit a sombre one, Becca said, "Jim, I've got something I really want to ask you."

"Sure," said Jim.

"Matt's stuff – his schoolbag. Have you got it back yet?"

"Yes," said Jim. "But I've not done anything with it. It – well, it's been too hard. I put it in his room. It stinks, though."

Becca felt relieved. "There's something I'd really, really like. If you don't mind and if you don't want it?"

"What's that?" asked Jim.

"A drawing he did of me," replied Becca. "It's in his art book. I didn't know he'd drawn it until – until I saw it in the well – but I'd really like to keep it, if I can."

"Of course you can have it," said Jim. "Of course. We'll keep it for you. Until you come home."

It was several weeks before Becca came home and, of course, the drawing was waiting – dried, cleaned, framed and hung on her bedroom wall. But, by then, Jim had moved out.

2

Jenny held down the blue and white crime-scene tape and stepped over it. **POLICE – DO NOT CROSS**, it said. She let Trudy off her leash and the collie ran into the field, glad to be free. Jenny had half-expected at least one officer to still be patrolling the area (and had brought her warrant card just in case) but there was no one there but her. She guessed that the tape would be removed in the next few days, once someone got around to it.

She crossed the field, whistling for Trudy to follow, and made her way to the quarry pool.

The wind blew her red hair around her face and she brushed it away from her eyes with her hand. When it wasn't tied back, it could be unruly – even annoying – but right now she wanted to feel the breeze blowing her mood away. The funeral and reception had been harder than she'd expected and she was glad of Stephen's support – but afterwards she felt that she needed to be alone. Or, at least, alone with Trudy – whose unconditional and unspoken love for Jenny was a great source of strength. She seldom came here to walk Trudy, since she lived on the other side of town, but something had been bugging her for the week and a half since the girls were found.

Jenny climbed the steep side of the quarry, taking care to keep away from its edge. Trudy followed her, but needed a little help where the hill was steepest – Jenny tugged at her collar to keep her moving. Once at the top, she sat and admired the view, breathless for a minute. Trudy sat beside her and Jenny rubbed under her chin.

Jenny could see most of Bankside. Although the day was warm, high on the hill, the wind was blustery though not uncomfortable. She stood up and walked as close as she could to the top of the quarry. Police tape was strung along the broken fence, offering no more protection than the rotten wood. The mayor and other councillors were already debating what to do about the quarry – whether to put up a new fence (the cheapest option) or to drain and fill the quarry pool (an idea that had already raised many objections). The well, of course, was going to be capped again – and concerted effort put into finding the legitimate owners of the estate. The old stories about the estate, the cottage and the well had come alive again as local people tried to connect the events of the last few days with the long-dead witch. *They'll die down again*, thought Jenny, who regarded the stories as nonsense. *Give it a few weeks or months.*

Jenny walked along the length of the fence, Trudy following her. She looked down into the quarry pool. *It's one hell of a drop*, she thought, reflecting that Helen Goodwin had been extraordinarily lucky. She'd spoken to both Helen and Abby, apart and together, and the two women's deep love for each other was obvious – indeed, it was a depth of feeling and mutual commitment that Jenny felt envious of. Despite that, she still struggled with the idea that Abby would abandon her daughter to rescue her partner. But the case was currently being wrapped up and it seemed that only she harboured this lingering doubt.

Looking down at the quarry pool, she thought she could almost understand Abby's motives in leaving her daughter – the sheer terror at seeing your life's love vanishing into the water could be enough to force an irrational decision.

A sparkle in the long, untidy grass caught her eye: a flash of light, reflecting off something bright. She took a few steps towards it; beside her, Trudy halted and growled. Jenny looked down at her. "Hey, Trude," she said. "What's up?"

Eyes full of fear, the dog looked at her owner through untidy black hair and growled again.

Jenny walked forwards and moved the grass with her foot. On the floor was a knife. Trudy barked – a warning bark, as she would if she sensed someone outside the house.

"It's OK, girl," soothed Jenny. She reached into her pocket, grateful that she had brought a couple of extra dog poop bags. She turned one inside out and covered her hand with it and squatted down to reach for the knife. It was abnormally cold to the touch – so cold that it almost burned. Jenny dropped it back to the ground and rubbed her fingers, surprised. She studied it where it lay; Trudy continued to growl and wouldn't come any closer.

The blade was around five inches in length and seemed to be roughly made – not mass-produced or machined. The edges of the blade were sharp, but uneven. The hilt was dull metal, a shallow S shape. The handle was almost as long as the blade and was wooden, battered and old. There was nothing ornamental about it, but nor was it mere cutlery or kitchenware. It was a fighting knife, Jenny was sure – and an old one, too. She picked it up again, ignoring Trudy's insistent growls.

This time, the knife felt less cold – though still somehow deeply unnatural. One edge of the blade was stained dark. Somehow, the knife itself had a presence – in the way that some people project an untrustworthy or violent demeanour, only worse. Much worse. The knife felt *evil*; no other word came close. Holding it, Jenny felt physically sick and more terrified than she could ever recall being. Yet, there was something about the knife that was both hypnotic and compelling. It was almost as if it wanted to be kept, ready to do dark deeds. Fascinated, she turned it over in her hands. She could almost feel its ancient history replaying in her mind and winced as she imagined it cutting flesh, time and time again. In her mind, she saw it carve into the black skin of someone she'd only recently met.

Without warning, Trudy ran at her and jumped against her stomach, pushing her to the ground. Jenny dropped the knife and the moment was gone. She lay on the ground, panting and then pulled herself to her knees. Trudy nuzzled against Jenny, whimpering. Jenny leaned forward on all fours and then vomited on the ground. She felt awful, shaking as if in traumatic shock.

After a few moments, she stood, unsteady on her feet, regarding the fallen knife with fear and disgust.

Jenny knew what she should do with the knife: collect it as potential evidence and check it in at the police station. But the mere thought of handling it again made her want to retch. She felt hot, as though she were infected and ill. There was an unnatural humming in her ears. *Screw it*, she thought. *There's no way I'm taking that in.* Gingerly, she kicked the knife three times, each time moving it closer to the quarry face. With each kick, her foot sparked as if the knife were electric. Then, when she was right at the edge, she kicked it hard and watched it arch downwards, disappearing into the water with a small – almost disappointing – splash.

Jenny backed away from the edge of the quarry, Trudy milling around her feet. She couldn't comprehend what had just happened, but there was no disbelief in her mind. Whatever she had touched was ancient, terrible and connected in some way that she couldn't comprehend to Abby and Helen. Counter to all of her training and instincts as a policewoman and her scepticism of the supernatural, whatever the knife was, whoever it had belonged to, whatever it had done (or been used to do), Jenny really didn't want to know. Ever.

She pulled her mobile phone from her pocket and called Stephen.

"Jen?"

Jenny paused. She didn't want to tell Stephen about what had happened: not because it would sound insane, or because he might not believe her – but because she honestly wanted to forget all about it.

"Steve, I've changed my mind. I really don't want to be alone. Can you meet me at mine, in half an hour? And bring wine. Or maybe something stronger."

Jenny trudged down the hill with an unusually sombre Trudy at her side.

Later that night, she lay awake as Stephen dozed next to her, her mind unable to banish the horrific feeling of holding the knife. Yet, despite her fear and disgust, something deep inside her wished that she hadn't thrown it away: that she could hold it again. It was a feeling from which she would never be completely free.

3

Sammy felt the hospital bed shift and creak under someone's weight and assumed that her mother, Helen or both of them had come to see her. She opened her eyes and was immediately wide awake.

There was no light in the small room, but the light from the corridor outside provided enough illumination for her to see who it was.

The woman raised a finger to her lips. "Shhhh," she said, softly.

She was older. Her hair was turning silvery grey and her face was lined. Sammy would have guessed that she was between fifty and sixty, though she wasn't good at judging the age of grown-ups. Her increased age hadn't diminished her beauty in the slightest. Sammy struggled to back away but could do no more than sit herself up in the bed, the stitches in her abdomen protesting against the sudden movement.

"Be calm," said the woman. "I don't come to hurt."

Sammy looked around for the call button, but couldn't see it. She started to shout but the woman leaned over and placed her hand firmly on her mouth. Her flesh was wrinkled and cold and smelt of – Sammy couldn't place the smell. Something awful and dirty, like old meat. Sammy felt the whole room chill.

"Shhh," repeated the woman. "I no hurt you tonight."

Tears stung Sammy's eyes. "What – what do you – want?" she stammered.

"Fear. Good. I like fear. Not so clever now?"

The woman didn't wait for Sammy to answer.

"Your mother tell you story? Yes? Story of me?"

Sammy nodded.

"Is story only. I show you *truth*."

Sammy shook her head. "You're lying. You always lie. Mummy told me the truth."

The woman shook her head, smiling. "She thinks is truth. Is not. Her mother's mother lie. I show you. I show you so you know it is truth. You can see into me, I know."

The woman placed her hand on Sammy's forehead, closed her eyes and took a deep breath.

"Be brave," said the woman.

It was dark. There was a cottage, in a wood. Sammy recognised it, though she had only previously seen it in ruins. Now, it was intact. There was a light inside. Sammy knew instinctively that she was seeing the past: a long time into the past. **The cottage in the old estate**, *she thought. She looked around. There was the well, its wall intact. Constructed above the well was a rough wooden frame, from which hung a rope and bucket – all long gone now, Sammy realised.*

The sounds around her swirled as though she had a seashell to her ears and her vision was slightly blurry. She felt so, so scared, standing alone in the woods, in her nightie, her feet bare on the cold dry earth.

A woman approached, dragging a child alongside. The woman was dressed in old-fashioned, ragged clothes. The child was a girl of perhaps six or seven; she was battered and bleeding. She sobbed as she was manhandled to the door.

Sammy moved a little closer. The woman seemed somehow familiar. It was as though she were looking at someone she knew well. Sammy looked into the woman and felt this to be true. She knew that somehow she was related to the woman. It was as if she was her grandmother (although Sammy had never known her), but older still. Not even a great-great-great-grandmother – much further back in time than that. She looked vaguely like her mother, thought Sammy, about the same age, in her thirties, though less pretty; more worn. Sammy realised who she was: the apothecary's wife (although when Abby had said the word apothecary, Sammy hadn't been able to pronounce it). **That's right**, *said a voice in her head.* **She your family; from long back**.

The woman banged on the door and another woman answered – Sammy recognised her at once. **It's her**, *she thought.* **The witch-woman.** *She was young, beautiful and pregnant – not yet a demon of nightmares, she was just a woman. A woman with a name. Sammy could sense it; she knew what the woman was called: Emiliana.* **Is me**, confirmed the voice inside her. **It's Emiliana**, thought Sammy, **not Awful Anna or Evil Anna**. *The two women spoke, though Sammy could only hear muffled underwater noises. Emiliana looked around, suspicious, and pulled the child into the house. She passed something to the apothecary's wife – Sammy couldn't see what – and she left in the same direction from which she had come.*

Time passed. Sammy wasn't sure how long. It could have been minutes, hours or days. She looked around.

Then, the same scene repeated itself – no, it wasn't quite the same. This time the child was a boy; younger too. He was four at the most. **Oh God**, *Sammy thought. She tried to shout but although her mouth moved, no sound came out. She felt sick. The boy was taken inside the house and again the woman left.*

Part of Sammy wanted to walk to the cottage and peek in through the gaps in the shuttered windows to see what was happening. A bigger part of her was too scared to move and she kept her feet rooted to the spot.

Then, a group of both men and women arrived – creeping up to the house. They didn't knock: the men beat down the door; several of them disappeared inside. **No**, *Sammy tried to shout.* **I don't want to see this**.

A voice in her head said: **sshhhh**.

The men dragged the young woman – Emiliana – outside. She was desperately clutching a tiny baby. She pointed to the apothecary's wife, who shook her head, shouting savage accusations and pointing back towards Emiliana.

Sammy could see flames coming from within the house. Emiliana was screaming, trying to get back to the house. From inside the house, Sammy could just make out someone else, screaming, terrified.

The apothecary's wife wrenched the baby away from Emiliana and held it high. Emiliana tried to get the baby back but one of the men punched her hard in the face and then kicked her to the ground.

No, no, *thought Sammy,* **please, no, oh Mummy, please** –

Then Sammy felt the baby in her own hands; she had become – or was in the mind of – the apothecary's wife, feeling and seeing events from her perspective. She felt the woman's awful glee as she carried the baby to the well and threw it down inside, hard. The crowd around her cheered. Sammy felt both triumphant and sick at what she had just done.

Sammy was herself again, watching from the sidelines in her nightie. The men were tearing the clothes from Emiliana's body. She was begging them to stop. She tried hard to look away, but she felt a cold hand firmly holding her head in place.

"Please no," Sammy begged, "make it stop, I don't want to see it."

The hand held her head tight. **This is me**, *said the voice,* **see me suffer**. *The men – they were just like* him. *Like the* bad man. *All of them. She counted them: there were eleven men and five women. The women were cheering the men on. The apothecary's* *wife looked on in satisfaction, arms folded. Emiliana was now naked, pinned to the ground. The first man unfastened his trousers and approached Emiliana.*

Please, I've seen enough – please –

Sammy felt herself falling, nauseous, towards the ground.

The hospital room came back into focus. Sammy knew she was going to be sick. She leaned over the side of the bed and vomited on the floor. When she sat up, she wasn't surprised to find that she'd also wet the bed.

Emiliana was still there, but the hard look in her eyes was gone; they were filled with sadness. "Is truth," she said, pointing to her heart. "You see truth, here."

Sammy nodded. "I don't understand," she began.

Emiliana pointed to Sammy, her finger touching her chest. "You is witch. Not just me."

Sammy shook her head. "No –"

"Is true," snapped Emiliana. Then, more softly, she said, "My first baby I lose. Your family is witch family. You help. Bring us children, to kill, to take the life from. You show us what to do, to – teach us. We also family witch but not so strong as you, not so bad as you. You make us witch like you. Do dark things. To feed me. To give me baby that lives. My boy."

"You want me to feel sorry for you?" said Sammy, petulant. "You're still a killer. You didn't *have* to do it. I don't feel sorry for you. I don't."

There was a long pause. Sammy couldn't stop shaking.

"You family lie," said Emiliana. "You trick. Tell lies. Woman –" She was frustrated and seemed to be struggling for words. "I show you one more thing. And then you know. Then you – certain."

She again placed her hand on Sammy's head. She felt herself falling.

*Sammy was inside the cottage. There was warmth from a fire. Across the room, an old, kindly woman looked at Sammy, proud. Sammy was grown: a young woman. She realised that she was now Emiliana; she was seeing this through Emiliana's eyes. No, she thought, **not just seeing it, but feeling it just as if I am her**. It was a powerful rush of sensations, far more than when she had been inside the mind of the apothecary's wife. She felt so much love. In her arms Sammy held a baby, not long since born. It was feeding from Sammy's breast; tugging at her nipple. Sammy looked down, fascinated by both the sight and the sensation. It was pleasure beyond anything she could have imagined. Sammy could feel her eyes fill up, but not from fear, from love. Her boy. He was – he was beautiful. His name, Sammy knew, was Emil. Named after the woman, Emiliana, but with the boy name. Sammy watched the child, captivated. He opened his eyes and Sammy couldn't help but love him.*

And then Sammy was back, panting as if she'd been running.

"You thought you not missing having no baby? I show you loss. Show you what you cannot have. I think maybe your curse now worse than mine."

Sammy began to cry. "Please," she said. "I don't want to see any more. I'm sorry."

"One more thing," said Emiliana.

Sammy backed away. "No, please –"

Emiliana held her hands up. "I no hurt. Just want to show you. So you see. So you know. Father of Emil."

Emiliana touched her one last time.

*A man. He was dressing. He threw something at the young woman, a coin perhaps – Emiliana – lying naked on the straw-covered floor. **It's her**, thought Sammy – **so young**. Sammy realised that she was seeing a time before the baby had been born. **No**, said Emiliana's voice in her mind. **Is when baby was made**. Most of Sammy's friends didn't have a clear idea of how babies were conceived, but Sammy had the advantage of taking the knowledge from the mind of adults. It wasn't something she'd shared with her friends, knowing that it was the kind of thing that would set her apart – but it still wasn't something she fully understood.*

Time passed. Sammy could literally see the baby grow within Emiliana. She had slept with many men, Sammy could see that, but this man was the father. Sammy realised that she already knew his face: when Emiliana had been raped, he had been the first in line.

***No**, she thought, **please, you promised**.*

***Not yet finished**, came the reply.*

*Emiliana, more heavily pregnant, stood at the door of what looked like a shop. In the window were lots of bottles, of all shapes and sizes. Emiliana was arguing with the man – the man who had just – made the baby inside of her. The man was shouting. A woman came to the door: it was her, the apothecary's wife. Sammy saw some of herself in the woman's eyes. The apothecary's wife shouted something and slammed the door. **It's him**, thought Sammy, looking at the bottles in the shop window. **The apothecary**.*

Sammy felt faint and grasped the side of the bed to stop herself from falling out.

"Now you understand," said Emiliana.

Sammy thought she did, but wasn't sure. She felt dizzy and confused.

"You and Emil. Same people. Same family. Share same fathers."

Sammy shook her head, but knew in her heart it was true.

"I not only witch," said the woman. "You witch too. You family bad. Bad as me. Now you understand."

"So you – cursed us? Forever?"

Emiliana stood. "I think forever end with you." She pointed to Sammy's stomach. "You pay price."

"The children," said Sammy. "What happens to the children?"

"With me until I gone. Then, who knows?" She wafted her arm in the air. "Gone, perhaps. At rest, maybe. Who cares?"

"Me. Can you let them go?"

"If I choose. I choose not."

"Let the boy go. Matt. Please."

"Why should I?"

"I think I can give you something," said Sammy, shaking but determined to appear in control. "Something small. Tiny. But special. Something you would want."

"I no bargain with you. You cheat. You have nothing I want."

"I did not cheat! I gave you what I promised."

Emiliana scowled. "And now, what can you give me?"

Sammy told her.

"This you can make happen?" asked the woman.

"I think so. It will take time."

"*Think so* not good enough."

"I can't promise. That's the best I can do. Please."

Emiliana nodded and then snapped her fingers. "Is done. What does it matter? You can't have him back. Is no better. He still gone. Still dead."

"Yes – but – proper dead. Like in heaven and everything?"

Emiliana laughed. "Child. There is no heaven. I let him go into nothingness."

The air started to blur around the woman, but Sammy shouted, "No wait – please? Please?"

"Enough," said Emiliana, stepping forwards again and touching Sammy's chest, her finger outstretched. "You keep your word – give me what you say. You witch. Bad family. Know this." Then she was gone.

Sammy raised her hand to her mouth and inhaled, shakily, tears flowing down her face. Her nightdress was covered in sweat. After a moment, she composed herself as best she could and then found the call button. She pressed it, the icon of the nurse lighting up red.

It was only a few seconds before the nurse came into the room. "Are you alright, Sammy?" she asked, snapping the light on.

Sammy blinked in the glare. "I had a bad dream," said Sammy. "And I was sick. And I wet the bed. Sorry."

"Don't worry," reassured the nurse. "I'll clean it up. Do you want a drink?"

Sammy nodded. "Some water please."

The nurse turned to go, but Sammy stopped her. "Can you call my Mummy?"

The nurse looked at her watch. "It's two in the morning, Sammy."

"Please," said Sammy. "She'll want to know. I want to see her. I need to." Sammy burst into tears. "Please. I need her."

"OK," said the nurse. "I'll call her."

Sammy heard the nurse's footsteps disappear down the hallway.

Try as she might, she couldn't get the woman's last words – *Emiliana's last words* – out of her head.

"*You witch,*" she had said – and Sammy knew she was telling the truth.

"No," said Sammy under her breath, wiping her wet face, "*I'll* be what *I* want to be."

4

"Come in Sammy – meet your new brother."

Abby showed Sammy into the little hospital room. In the bed, Helen held a newborn baby, loosely wrapped in a hospital blanket, his skin pink and still a little bloody.

"He's so tiny," said Sammy, sitting next to Helen. "He's beautiful."

Helen nodded. "Just like his mother," she said, glancing at Abby. Helen looked totally exhausted – her eyes tired and her hair matted. Her nightshirt was covered with sweat and, where the baby had been placed, a little blood.

Abby looked at her two children. Sammy, just turned fourteen, was well on the way to becoming a woman. The tiny boy – so perfect – was making little crying noises, his eyes closed and arms moving around aimlessly.

Sammy looked at her mother. "Can I touch him?"

Abby nodded. Sammy extended her arm and touched the baby's hand. His fingers wrapped themselves around Sammy's outstretched finger. She gasped with pleasure.

His fingers are so small, thought Sammy.

Tiny, aren't they? thought Abby back, grateful again that Sammy's patient coaching was paying off.

"Do you want to hold him?" asked Helen.

"Can I?"

"Of course you can," said Helen, smiling.

Abby lifted the baby from Helen and passed him to Sammy, showing her how best to hold him.

Sammy held him close, instinctively rocking him gently. Her eyes filled with tears. She pushed away the unwanted memory from when she was eight: a strong vision of holding a baby that felt totally like hers but yet was not. For a moment, the memory was clear in her mind but then the reality that replaced it was all the more painful. A warm, live, beautiful baby. *Something I can never have.* She tried to hide the thought from her mother, but was unable to stifle a sob.

Abby put her arm around Sammy. "You OK, Sams?" she asked, softly.

Sammy shook her head and a tear rolled down her cheek. *I can never do this,* she thought.

Abby wiped Sammy's tear away and kissed her forehead. *I know, baby.*

"Come on guys," said Helen. "Out loud, please."

"Oh you know," said Sammy. "Baby stuff. And me. You know."

"The way I see it," said Helen. "He's got three mums. One of them just happens to be his sister, too."

Sammy nodded. "Sure. I know. I can't believe it. He's so lovely."

It had taken Abby and Helen almost two years of hard work and saving before they had been able to afford the gestational surrogacy. In the end, Helen's parents had paid over half of the money required. After another year of waiting, doctors had taken eight oocytes from Abby and fertilised them with a donor's sperm. Then the successfully fertilised egg had been placed inside Helen.

"Have you changed your mind, Sammy?" asked Abby.

Sammy shook her head. "No, Mum," she said, firmly. "Is it still OK?" She looked to both her mother and Helen for confirmation.

Abby nodded. Helen smiled and said, "That was what we said. Your Mum gave up the eggs. I carried him. You get to name him."

Sammy smiled down at the tiny baby. She lifted his forehead to her lips and kissed him. Sammy had expected him to smell of blood – but he smelled wonderful.

A deal's a deal, she thought, ready to fulfil a six-year-old bargain.

"Hello, Emil Matthew," said Sammy. "Welcome to the family."

5

"Well, that must seem weird," said Hannah.

"It does," replied Becca, "No doubt about it."

The two girls gazed into the glass cabinet. It was filled with coins and rough-hewn pins and needles.

The label beneath the artefacts read: *Just as we offer coins into wishing wells, it used to be customary for people to throw items of value into holy wells. In a common household, pins and needles were very hard to come by and were typically handed down from mother to daughter for many generations. To throw one into a water source, as an offering, was a great sacrifice – practically as well as spiritually.*

Above the cabinet, framed on the wall, was a newspaper cutting alongside a picture of Becca. **MISSING GIRL ESCAPES FROM ORDEAL IN WELL**, the headline read. She didn't bother to read the descriptive text under her photograph.

"You'll be signing autographs next," said Hannah, but the joke didn't pierce Becca's reflective mood.

It's always about me, she thought. *The girl who got out. They always overlook Matt.*

Somewhere, around the corner, Becca knew there was a cabinet containing the bones she had found. *I'll give that one a miss*, she thought.

Hannah's mobile phone chimed as a text message arrived. **JUST GOT HOME, COMING ROUND TO MEET EMIL? EXCITED!**

"It's Sammy," said Hannah, enthusiastically.

"They're home. Shall we?"

"OK," said Becca, pulling herself away.

"Thinking about Matt again?" asked Hannah.

Becca nodded.

The two girls left Bankside library and walked down the street towards *No Stone Unturned*. Hannah linked Becca's arm and pulled her close, without saying anything. She had learned – and understood – that when Becca was missing Matt, nothing she said could help. *Seeing the baby will cheer her up*, she thought.

THE END

About Peter Labrow

Peter Labrow has worked as a copywriter, writing non-fiction, for around twenty years. His output includes copy for websites and brochures; for around a decade he wrote a regular column for IT Training magazine. He has published one non-fiction book about learning within the corporate environment. The Well is Peter's first novel.

Peter lives in Stockport, in the United Kingdom, and runs his own marketing business. He is married, with two children. He loves curry but hates both sprouts and custard.

Keep updated: www.peterlabrow.com

Peter Labrow

2008113R00138

Printed in Great Britain
by Amazon.co.uk, Ltd.,
Marston Gate.